PROXIMITY

PROXIMITY

A Novel of the Navy's Elite Bomb Squad

Stephen Phillips

To order additional copies of this book, contact:
Xlibris Corporation
1-888-795-4274
www.Xlibris.com
Orders@Xlibris.com
25836

For Christina

Thanks

I would like to express sincere appreciation in developing this story to my family; my wife—Christina, my sons—Stephen and Zachary, my parents—Steve and Maureen, and my brother—Tim. I would also like to thank Adam Bentley, Dick Couch, Kathryn Dunfee, James Dunfee, Mike Huete, Will Lagasse, Chuck Pfarrar, Chris Ruediger, Tom Tyler, Steve Waterman, and Jim Wightman.

Cover Photo

U.S. Navy photo by Photographer's Mate Airman Ryan O'Connor.

AUTHORS NOTES

The methods, procedures, and tactics used by military Explosive Ordnance Disposal Technicians are often classified. This is to prevent the architects of military ordnance or improvised explosive devices from incorporating countermeasures into their design. This book only reveals procedures that are intuitively obvious or so widely publicized that mentioning them here could not be considered irresponsible. Where required, the methods described are fictitious while maintaining the flavor of explosive ordnance disposal work.

While this is a novel, the story is based on actual events. The characters are all fictional.

EOD Memorial Foundation

A portion of the proceeds from this novel will go to the EOD Memorial Scholarship Fund. Donations to this cause can be made through the Combined Federal Campaign number 0858, at the website: http://www.eodmemorial.org, or by mail to:

EOD Memorial Committee
PO Box 594
Niceville, FL 32588

PREFACE

SAN DIEGO

Getting on base was easy. The four men drove through the gate onto Naval Amphibious Base, San Diego, without incident as they had several times before. The Marine guard observed the base sticker affixed to the bumper of their van and waved them through.

It took them a mere week to find a vehicle with a Department of Defense vehicle sticker and a "For Sale" sign in the windshield. The owner was a sailor who was transferring to Japan and did not want to ship it overseas. Gabriel pretended that he was in the Navy again, and asked the seller to leave the sticker on.

The building they were interested in was on a part of the base with little traffic outside of normal working hours. Because the Navy did not consider its contents vital to national security there would be no guards or alarms. Their initial plan was a simple break-in; it was Nasih's training that led them to the more surgical entry.

"The gates of western society are well protected," he had said, *"but both figuratively and literally, there is always another way to infiltrate your target. There is always a back door that can be opened."*

Gabriel now fully understood what Nasih meant. This was the second time he applied Nasih's pessimistic notion of human nature.

"In the intelligence gathering phase, befriend drug dealers and prostitutes. Find out who is in debt and who is a sexual deviant. These people can be compromised, utilized, and euthanized."

Again, Gabriel's past proved invaluable. He knew by reputation the bars in Tijuana that were frequented by drug users. Gabriel sent one of his cohorts to El Perro Negro in search of someone who worked in the Personnel Department, a Personnelman or a Yeoman. Miraculously, one was found during the first weekend, Personnelman Third Class Ronald Diebert. After studying Diebert closely for a month, they approached him. Gabriel explained that they were dealers of marijuana, ecstasy, and sometimes coke, who were trying to move their business on base. He and his partners solicited Diebert for a one-time deal; identity cards for drugs. Diebert accepted. Gabriel was sure that their good fortune was due to divine intervention.

Ask and you shall receive.

After driving past the Marine at the gate the intruders went unnoticed. They parked the van in the lot next to the Personnel Support Detachment building. At 5:07 the lot was empty, just as the previous four Friday evenings. At 5:10 the men got out, so they did not have to stop or slow their stride as Diebert opened the door at precisely 5:11.

Gabriel smiled and shook his head in amazement watching Diebert go about his work like a kid playing a video game. The whole operation was proceeding much more smoothly than he expected. It only took Diebert fifteen minutes to enter bogus identities into the computer and snap a digital picture of each man.

After Gabriel and his compatriots each had a laminated military ID card cooling in his hand, they gave Diebert what he craved. They were in New Mexico driving east when Diebert's body was found in the office, the victim of an overdose.

As the sun rose over the highway in front of them, Gabriel smiled.

Now we can go anywhere

He knew Nasih would be pleased.

ONE

UNDERWATER

Increasing pressure was the only sign of progress for Lieutenant James J. Jascinski Jr. as he lumbered through the water like a manatee. He kicked hard pulling the cumbersome lift balloon with him as he headed for the bottom. Jascinski's diving rig, a Mark-16 re-breather, was like a small refrigerator on his back. The only sound he heard was the whisper of his breath each time he exhaled through his mouthpiece. Three electronic sensors monitored the oxygen level and added more if it was needed.

Jascinski felt his fins hitting the bottom. He kneeled and instinctively looked to the light affixed above his right eye. It would flash red if the oxygen content of his Mark-16 dropped dangerously low or green if it increased to toxic levels. Unfortunately, he could not see the light.

Jascinski tried to re-orient himself. His task was simple; find a mine in the dark, attach a lift balloon to it, and return to the surface safely—alone.

With his left hand the lieutenant dragged the cumbersome lift balloon assembly. It was comprised of two scuba tanks with a canvas balloon fastened above them. Jascinski's other hand held onto the AN/PQS-2A sonar. Commonly called the two-alpha, the diver's sonar reminded him of a police radar gun or a large flashlight with a pistol grip. It was secured to his right hand with a bungee cord.

Jascinski set the lift balloon assembly gently next to his left leg. He trailed his hand from the manifold, to the scuba tanks, to the bag around the balloon. Searching for the towline with his hand was a lesson in blindness. If he lost contact with the balloon, he may never find it again. He could flail around on the bottom within inches of it for hours.

Finally, his hand bumped the line. He grabbed it and slid it into the crook of his left elbow. Now he had the use of his left hand.

Jascinski flipped the switch on the back of the sonar. It began to ping, sending sound waves through the water. If one of the waves hit an object it would bounce off, coming back toward Jascinski's position. The audible return of both outgoing and incoming waves traveled from the sonar's receiver, through the electronic cable on its rear face, up to the earpieces in Jascinski's skullcap. He interpreted the changes in pitch like a dolphin searching for fish.

Ping ping, ping.

He listened for the proper return.

Ping, ping, ping. Thud, thud. Ping, ping ping.

Jascinski swung back to the "thud," the change in pitch signifying a contact.

Ping, ping. Thud, thud, thud.

There it is, he thought.

Thud, thud, thud, thud.

Jascinski pulled his left arm back, sliding the towline from his elbow down the inside of his forearm to his left hand. Then he slid his left hand down the line until he made contact with one of the scuba bottles, and finally the manifold connecting the two together. He gripped the manifold again, pulling the balloon with him as he swam with his sonar pointed in the direction of the contact.

Thud, thud, thud, thud.

The audible return got louder as Jascinski closed the distance with the object.

THUD, THUD, THUD.

Jascinski stopped again and knelt still facing the direction of the contact. It was very close. He repeated the process of shifting his hold from the lift balloon so that he could turn the sonar off and clip it to his belt. His right hand was now free. Jascinski held his right hand in front of him hoping it would find the contact first. Almost imperceptibly, he felt something brush his right forearm. He had found it.

He knew that time was running out. Jascinski quickly ran his hand over the mine and based on its diameter, determined that it was a Mark-36 bottom mine. The mine's shape reminded Jascinski of a 55 gallon drum, or a water heater.

Jascinski wrestled the lift balloon over the mine so that it was on the side opposite from him. His movements around it were deliberate and silent. Any noise would "wake up" the listening device. The mine's electronics package would begin searching for an acoustic noise, or a magnetic field anomaly, or a seismic signature. Maybe the mine would be searching for all three or a combination of two of the three. He knew that the magnetic search coil would not detect his presence. All of his equipment was "Lo-mu," or low in magnetic signature. His wetsuit, watch, booties, fins, gloves, even his knife had been inspected with a magnetometer for any signature. So had the sonar components, the lift balloon assembly, and the Mark-16 itself. Jascinski was also acoustically silent. Because the—16 was a re-breather, no bubbles escaped to make noise in the water.

"No bubbles, no troubles," was the mantra of the Mark-16 diver.

If Jascinski made a mistake, if he burped gas from his Mark-16 and sent sound into the water, if he clunked the lift balloon onto the mine's metal skin, or if he touched the bottom with too much force, the mine would awaken and begin hunting for prey. Jascinski would never know if he made a second mistake, the mine would simply detonate.

Under the balloon assembly were two sections of thick line. These would be used to attach the lift balloon to the mine. Jascinski blindly secured each section in a "trucker's hitch," one on the nose and one towards the tail of the mine to evenly distribute the weight under the balloon. Otherwise, it would slip out from the harness and plunge back to the bottom.

He checked each line twice, pulling on it to ensure it would not slip. He unsnapped the bag encasing the balloon so that it would not be hindered as it inflated. Then he performed the most important step, he reached under the scuba jug's manifold and opened the explosive valve that would allow air to pass from steel to canvas.

Jascinski traced his hand along the balloon and again found the towline with his left hand. He knelt one more time and held up his right hand with four fingers.

"Four. I am ready to surface," in Navy Diver language.

Jascinski felt a hand grip his right wrist. It squeezed once.

One. Hold.

He felt the pull on his mask as the thick duct tape was removed from it. After almost forty minutes of darkness Jascinki's eyes were overwhelmed. He felt like a newborn as he tried to focus on the light blue color of the training pool's sides and bottom. Opposite him was Senior Chief Benson, also in a Mark-16. Benson was the senior instructor of the Underwater Division at Naval School Explosive Ordnance Disposal.

Benson held up his wristwatch so Jascinski could see it.

41:23

To pass his lift balloon test, Jascinski had to assemble the balloon, locate, and raise the mine, within forty-five minutes.

Benson inspected the lift balloon attachments. From where Jascinski was sitting they seemed okay. The senior chief looked up at him and flashed him a *Four.* Jascinski turned and swam to the surface following the towline. He heard the "beep" of Benson starting his stopwatch again.

Jascinski broke the surface at the edge of the pool and flashed the "OK" sign at Petty Officer Lynch standing on the pool deck above him. Lynch, another instructor like Benson, was the dive supervisor.

Lynch clicked two stopwatches hanging on a lanyard around his neck and called out, "Diver reached surface time one three two three! Time's ticking on this problem; let's get him up and over!"

Two other students came over to the edge of the pool to help. Jascinski took off his weight belt and handed it up to one of them.

Lynch stepped to the edge and looked down at Jascinski.

"Go off-gas, sir."

Jascinski cycled the barrel valve on his mouthpiece to the closed position and pulled his facemask/mouthpiece assembly off and over his head.

"Diver on surface, diver okay!" he shouted.

"Get moving."

Jascinski undid the waist strap and crotch strap of the rig, and slipped it off like a jacket. Tim Bullock, a fellow officer, lifted it up to the pool deck. Jascinski scrambled onto the deck and over to Lynch.

"Petty Officer Lynch, I am ready to initiate my lift balloon."

"Wait until Senior Chief gets to the surface. I'll give you the extra time if you need it."

A few seconds later, Lynch handed Jascinski the Mark-186 detonator transmitter. Jascinski pressed all of the requisite buttons to ensure it was working properly.

"FIRE IN THE HOLE! FIRE IN THE HOLE! FIRE IN THE HOLE!"

Jascinski pressed the fire button and a "Pop!" came from the pool. Fifteen seconds later the balloon popped to the surface, hissing and gurgling. Across the pool he saw Benson still in full dive gear, but with his mask off. The chief was holding on to the side but had his face in the water looking at the mine with a pair of swim goggles. He lifted his head.

"It's holding!" he called out.

Jascinski breathed a sigh of relief but anxiously wondered what the time was.

"What's the time?" Lynch asked.

"Forty-four twenty-five."

Jascinski had done it.

Lynch chuckled and shook his head. "You did it, sir. And believe it or not I've seen a lot of guys come closer."

Jascinski breathed a sigh of relief. He surveyed the rest of his class and their cadre of instructors. He noticed that the other officers in the class—Bullock, York, and Smitty—were no longer in UDT swim trunks; they had switched to camouflage utilities.

Lynch said, "Lieutenant Jascinski, you have to go see the executive officer with the other O's. Hit the showers. Lieutenant Smith will observe you until you are clean—no pun intended."

The onset of arterial gas embolism, or AGE for short, was foremost in the dive supervisor's mind. When gas bubbles expand in the body's pulmonary system blocking oxygen to the brain, the symptoms usually appear within the first ten minutes after a dive. Naval diving protocol held that all divers remain on station and under close scrutiny for the first ten minutes following a dive. If no telltale signs of AGE appeared, the diver was termed "clean."

Jascinski showered with Smith just outside the stall, watching him. Smith continued to observe Jascinski as he dried off and donned cammie trousers and boots. Jascinski tightened his rigger's belt and slipped a lock-knife in his right pocket, both accoutrements of the men in Special Operations or "Spec Ops" as it was commonly known.

Just as he finished dressing and blousing his trousers, Lynch came in.

"Sir, how do you feel?"

"Hooya, Petty Officer Lynch."

"You're clean."

Lieutenant Commander William Massie was the Executive Officer of Naval School Explosive Ordnance Disposal, also known as NAVSCOLEOD, or simply "EOD School."

The four lieutenants casually walked through his open office door without knocking. Massie was on the phone. He motioned for them to all sit down on his couch.

As Jascinski sat, he realized he could still smell the chlorine on himself. He looked over Massie's head and admired his "I love me" wall. Besides the normal plaques and degrees, Massie had photos of himself taken during Desert Storm. He spent a lot of time aboard a minesweeper, USS *Affray*, with his EOD detachment. There were photos of him placing explosive charges on various mines and a plethora of "Farewell Disposalier" certificates from different EOD commands.

Massie hung up the phone and leaned back in his chair.

"Welcome, gents. How are things?"

As the class leader, Jascinski always answered for the group.

"Fine, sir."

"Great. Well, I have news for all of you. Orders came in the message traffic today."

The four officers all started. As graduation drew closer, each student anxiously awaited news of their first assignment following EOD School.

Massie opened his desk drawer and pulled out four envelopes. He read the first one.

"Bullock."

"Sir."

Massie handed the envelope over the desk. "EOD Mobile Unit Two, Little Creek, Virginia. High speed, low drag."

"Hooya, sir," Bullock replied.

"Smith."

"Sir."

"EOD Mobile Unit Five, Guam. That is going to be fun times, hooya."

"Hooya, sir!" exclaimed Smitty.

"York."

"Sir."

"EOD Mobile Unit Eleven, Whidbey Island, Washington. You like hunting and fishing?"

"Yes, sir."

"Good, it's an outdoorsman's paradise out there. And finally, Jascinski."

"Sir."

"EOD Mobile Unit Six, Detachment Ingleside, Texas. Report no later than August 1998."

Jascinski's shoulders visibly slumped.

"C'mon, Jazz, Ingleside isn't so bad," the executive officer said. "It's 1140 world down there. You'll do a lot of diving and you'll be a time zone and hundreds of miles from your commanding officer."

"Do they jump there, sir?"

"Uh, nope."

TWO

THE ADMIRAL

Jazz pulled his 4Runner into the parking spot behind the townhouse that he and his wife Melanie rented. He paused knowing that Melanie would not be happy with their orders. They both expected an assignment to EOD Mobile Unit Two in Virginia Beach. While all Navy communities are tight, Melanie had a strong network of friends and family already established in the greater Norfolk area.

Entering the living room, Jascinski heard his wife and their two boys upstairs.

"Jazz?" she called out.

During his plebe year at the Naval Academy, despite having no musical talent, James Jascinski became "Jazz." Anyone who knew him from that time, including the woman who now shared his last name, called him "Jazz." Some of his classmates did not even know his first name.

"Yeah, hon. I've got something important to tell you," he yelled upstairs.

"Wait there, I'm coming down."

Melanie waddled down the stairs, carrying their third child in her belly. Her short stature accentuated her pregnancy, but Melanie still had svelte muscular legs. Jazz watched her long blonde ponytail sway back and forth as she concentrated on her foot placement and handhold, ambling across the landing and the last few stairs. She smiled at him as she reached the bottom. He hoped their third baby would have her blue eyes.

"Let me guess, you died ten times today?" she said giggling.

Normally Jazz would have laughed. Melanie knew that EOD students often made fatal mistakes on training ordnance. Instructors at EOD School were known to yell at their students.

"BOOM! YOU JUST DIED! YOU'RE DEAD!"

In fact, some of the problems in both the practice area and the test area were rigged to real explosives. A small demolition charge was placed in a four-foot pit filled with water nearby that detonated if the students made a mistake. It would harmlessly knock the wind out of them and shower them with muddy water—some lessons had to be learned the hard way.

The school was just as stressful for Melanie as it was for Jazz. Her husband often studied until ten o'clock at night. Most days they had no time together; he simply came home, ate a cold dinner, showered and went right to bed. So Melanie usually endured long lonely days battling her morning sickness while caring for two active boys.

Jazz held both of Melanie's hands in his.

"We're going to Ingleside."

"Texas!" Melanie tensed up and pulled her hands away. "You're kidding me."

"No, I'm not."

"What happened to Mobile Unit Two and Virginia Beach?"

"They need me in Ingleside."

"Damnit, Jazz!"

"Mel, I'm sorry. I'm so sorry. I don't want this either."

"Sorry isn't good enough! We've paid our dues, damnit! You're the top of the class! Where is Petty Officer Huang going? Virginia Beach, probably! And once again Jazz Jascinski gets screwed! You extended on *Anzio* and had to do another deployment, LEAVING ME FOR ANOTHER SIX MONTHS! It took three tries for you to get into EOD, for what! To get sent to Texas! When are you going to take control, Jazz!"

Jazz was silent.

Melanie crossed her arms over her chest. "You need to call the Admiral."

"I'm not going to do that," he said dejectedly. "I mean, I'm gonna tell him. But that's it."

Melanie spun on her heel and headed toward the kitchen.

"I should have married an accountant," she said acidly as she left.

Jazz knew that his wife would be upset, but the ferocity of her reaction surprised him. He thought she would at least have some sympathy for him; she knew that Ingleside would not be professionally rewarding for him or his career.

Jazz heard his wife coming back into the room.

"I have one more thing to say to you, James Jascinski," she said pointing an accusatory finger at him. "I know that you are brave or you have courage or whatever . . . but you need to grow some balls. The Admiral has fucked you up. You are too sheepish in the face of authority. You need to learn to put yourself and your family first. If I am going to continue to sacrifice, if our KIDS have to, then you damn well better learn to put us first sometimes."

Melanie turned and headed for the kitchen again. This time Jazz followed her.

"Hon, I'm sorry."

Melanie scooped up her purse and extracted her keys.

"All I wanted was Virginia Beach, Jazz. Feed the boys."

Jazz was even more stunned as his wife walked through the screen door, got in her car, and drove away.

The Admiral was Jazz's father. In contrast to his son's nickname, Jascinski's father was called "James" by his friends and "the Admiral" by his family.

Deep down Melanie knew Jazz would never ask his father to exert his influence over the Navy's Bureau of Personnel to have his orders changed. First, the Admiral would never aid his son in that manner. The senior James J. Jascinski would consider that as a prostitution of his position. Jazz would also never expose himself to the notion that he needed his father's help. It was not enough that Jazz never felt he lived up to his father's expectations. To approach him for help, for intervention on his behalf, would be viewed by the Admiral as a sign of weakness and would invite criticism and ridicule.

Jazz grabbed a beer from the refrigerator and walked through the back door to the yard. He removed the twist top and took a long drink.

Jazz knew that like his wife, the Admiral was going to give him hell. The Admiral never wanted his son to go into EOD in the first place. Now going to Ingleside would take him away from the Navy's hub of influence in Norfolk. It would be another straw of criticism on the haystack of Jazz's ruined career.

Jazz would never forget the Admiral's anger the day he told him he was applying for lateral transfer from Surface Warfare to Special Operations. He and Melanie were visiting his parents for the weekend. Jazz told them over Sunday dinner.

At the time, Jazz was fire control officer aboard USS *Anzio* in Norfolk, Virginia. For a Surface Warfare Officer on his second assignment there was no better job. Jazz worked for the ship's weapons officer and was responsible for the ship's surface to air missile systems, which included the SM-2 Standard Missiles and their fire control radar as well as the 30mm defensive gun called Close in Weapons System (CIWS). Additionally, Jazz was a qualified engagement control officer for planning and executing land attacks using the Tomahawk cruise missile.

As the only son in a definitively Navy family, Jazz never considered any path to adulthood other than the Naval Academy. There was no external influence in his youth to lure Jazz away from his father's legacy. All of the families that the Jascinskis' socialized with were Navy; most had a father who attended the "boat school." Jazz thought a Naval Academy ring on his finger would make him a made man in the eyes of his father. He thought that going to the Academy would do more than improve their relationship; he thought it would create it.

Growing up, Jazz felt he and his father never connected. The Admiral spent whole soccer seasons in the Persian Gulf. When he was in port or on shore duty the Navy still seemed to consume all of his time. Jazz's relationship with his mother was much better, but she was empathetic to her husband's career and its required sacrifices. Eleanor Jascinski seemed to derive personal satisfaction from her identity as an officer's wife.

Despite high marks at the Academy in academics and military performance, the Admiral remained lukewarm. So after graduation, like his father before him, James J. Jascinski Jr. worked on his naval career like an attorney trying to make partner. His effort was fruitful and his peers agreed that Jazz was on the fast track to command and admiral stars. He soon reached a point, however, where this fact brought him no pride or pleasure. Jazz abandoned all hope of establishing a rapport with his father once he became a dad himself. The moment he held his firstborn, Jazz's priorities changed. Jazz decided that his career should be for him, not his father. It was then that he applied for EOD. Jazz even requested an extension onboard *Anzio* and subsequently incurred another six month deployment from home in order to remain eligible for selection. On his third attempt his name was included as one of only six officers selected from the fleet for Special Operations.

Jazz's application process immediately changed the Admiral's demeanor toward him from disinterest to disdain. He winced recalling his father's reaction that Sunday evening.

"Admiral, I want to let you know that I am going to make a lateral transfer to Special Operations."

"What! You wanna be a SEAL!"

"No, sir, that's Special Warfare. I am interested in Special Operations—diving, salvage, and explosive ordnance disposal."

"What the hell are you talking about? That community with the stupid-looking SWO pin? The 1140 community?"

"Yes, sir."

"What the heck do you want to do a thing like that for? Damnit to hell! You'll never make admiral and you'll end up retiring as CO of a damn weapons station."

"Yes, sir."

Dinner was never served. The women left their men at the table. The ensuing lecture was like an intervention. The Admiral grew more and more angry through the evening, but Jazz's mind was made up. His father's rant only solidified Jazz's resolve to follow his own path.

Now Jazz had to tell the Admiral that he had orders to Ingleside, which would undoubtedly evoke another tirade from the Admiral. He decided that sooner was better than later.

*   *   *

Immersing himself in the Navy again brought back many memories for Gabriel. While the others were animated during the drive home, relishing their success, Gabriel was silent. He quietly reflected on his journey from disgruntled sailor to movement leader.

With over five thousand people aboard, an aircraft carrier is its own city, a microcosm of American society. While there were a disproportionate number of conservative Republicans aboard the USS *Carl Vinson*, the whole political spectrum was represented in the five thousand man crew. Gabriel found the extreme right in one Electronics Technician Third Class Owen Channing.

He met Owen in the aft weight room immediately below the area of the flight deck where aircraft slammed onto steel trying to hook onto one of *Vinson's* four arresting wires. Their first encounter was circumstantial—Owen asked him for a spot. Soon they began working out together which eventually led to a friendship and chumming around when off of the ship.

They had a common disdain for the Navy. Owen wanted to be a SEAL, but a few violations of the Uniform Code of Military Justice in his record prevented that from becoming a reality. Gabriel was simply disappointed. His single mother upbringing led him to yearn for an unforgiving, structured military world. He first thought of going into the Army, but decided on joining the Navy after seeing *The Sand Pebbles* on television one Sunday afternoon. Thereafter, he imagined that someday he would be like Steve McQueen, strolling the streets of Shanghai in cracker-jack whites with all of his possessions in a canvas seabag over his shoulder. In his mind, he lived a night of hard drinking with his shipmates at the local whorehouse, ending in a fight with the brothel's Marine Corps patrons.

"*Nothing personal, just skin on skin,*" he imagined himself saying to another sailor on the mess decks at breakfast the next morning.

Gabriel found out too late that none of the old Navy remained. Technology and political correctness wiped it out. In the new Navy everyone had sensitivity training where they were told that alcohol consumption and swearing were bad and homosexuality was okay as long as it was hidden. It made Gabriel sick. Like Owen, he was getting out as soon as he could, but his bitterness made each day pass slowly.

When Gabriel began hanging around Owen's apartment he noticed that Owen was very suspicious of the government. Owen's anger manifested itself largely in complaints about the FBI, ATF, and the notion that the federal government had far more control than people realized. Strewn about the apartment were books on anarchy and magazines for mercenaries. Gabriel read a few magazines at first, and then borrowed a couple of Owen's books.

At first, Gabriel was skeptical. But as he delved deeper into the literature, what at first seemed like propaganda began to have real plausibility. One of the writers purported that if his reader only believed ten percent of what he documented about government control and abuse, liberty in the United States was a myth. It was especially interesting considering what Gabriel read in the mainstream press about the FBI at Ruby Ridge and the ATF debacle in Waco, Texas.

Slowly Gabriel became a believer.

When Owen left the Navy he joined a survivalist reservation where the members called themselves, "The Mountain Men of Montana" or simply "Mountain Men." Gabriel finished his enlistment six months later and joined him.

As a Mountain Man, Gabriel had finally found the lifestyle that he sought from the military. He especially liked the real machismo that pervaded everything they did. He learned how to ride a horse, to shoot various weapons, to hunt, and to live off of the land. Gabriel even went to Bible study on Sunday afternoons. The discussions usually emphasized that the United States, a nation founded by Christian men, was now controlled by a corrupt government of non-believers and Jews.

For the first time in his life everything made sense to Gabriel; everything felt
right. It was as if he was given a codebook to the world around him. For the first time
in his life he felt like a real adult, like he finally *got it*. Before long he began leading
Bible study. He taught newcomers how to ride and shoot. He put all of his pent up
enthusiasm into the reservation. After about a year, however, Gabriel realized that
he was different from Owen and the other Mountain Men. Deep down they were
impotent; happy to live in the woods and bitch. For Gabriel that was not enough. He
wanted to fix the United States, to return to the notions of the country's forefathers.
Gabriel wanted to take action.

Politically, Gabriel moved further and further toward the right. He found extremists
like himself in roadhouses and at gun shows. He was finally fortunate enough to get
connected with a group in South Texas, now almost two years ago. Like the Mountain
Men they were heavy on rhetoric, but he sensed right away that the members intended to
take action. They hoped to start a revolution, to continue the work of Timothy McVeigh.
For a while they called themselves Freedom Catalyst. On Gabriel's recommendation
they agreed that it would be best to not have a name, no means to identify themselves
as an entity. So they erased all references to Freedom Catalyst. Thereafter, in speech
amongst themselves their body was referred to as the group, or sometimes just "it."

"It is going well."

"The group will meet tomorrow."

After a few botched attempts at creating local havoc the group realized that they
needed education in anarchy. Setting fires and vandalizing government buildings
was just not enough. So they saved and raised money to send a few of the members
to Libya for advanced training in insurgency and low intensity conflict. Gabriel was
chosen as one of the men to go.

Before he left, Gabriel told his mother and his neighbors that he was going to
tour North Africa. The highlights would be Casablanca and Marakesh, Morocco and
Tunisia where he would visit the Tattoine set from *Star Wars*. To develop an explanation
for a long absence, Gabriel suggested that he may even bum around Egypt searching
for work in archeology. Gabriel hoped his listeners would suspect that he was looking
for a drug connection in Marakesh, not that he would be preparing to overthrow the
central government.

In Libya he met Nasih.

THREE

MOBILE DETACHMENT

The workshop was as dark and still as solitary confinement. Only the hum of the air conditioning system and the occasional crackle on the radio reminded Boatswain's Mate Second Class Theodore Ball that he was on an aircraft carrier.

He lay on a cot contemplating whether or not he should get up and go to his rack—his assigned bunk in the berthing space where the ship's compliment of SEALs and EOD Technicians lived.

Ball was once jealous that EOD Techs were nearly unknown while their counterparts in the SEAL Teams enjoyed fame in fact and fiction. Now he considered their obscurity a badge of honor. Ball explained to anyone who asked that their roots were the same, yet both had a uniquely different mission. He liked to point out that while there were over three thousand SEALs in the U.S. Navy, there were fewer than seven hundred EOD Techs.

"You tell me then, who's elite?" he often asked young sailors who visited their shop inquiring about the EOD program.

BM2 Ball spent the night in the EOD workshop because he was responsible for the flight deck watch the previous night. In the early morning hours, the air boss told him he could retire to the shop, just two decks below the flight deck in the port aft corner of the USS *George Washington*, provided he monitored the radio for trouble.

Ball was standing by to render safe any explosive hazard on the deck of the aircraft carrier. *George Washington's* aircrews were flying in the North Arabian Gulf, some even flying over Iraq, in support of Operation Southern Watch. This hostile zone required all of them, even the Search and Rescue helicopters, to be fully armed and ready for action. This made the always important EOD presence, imperative.

This was not his first deployment; it was in fact Ball's second "float" away from his home and his young family. On his previous sojurn he fixed a 30 millimeter cannon that jammed, removed damaged fuzes from Mark 82 bombs, and even rendered safe a High Speed Anti-Radiation Missile (HARM) that careened across the deck just as the EA-6B Prowler it was connected to hit the four-wire. Ball was ready for any and all of these ordnance accidents to happen again. He was also ready in the event of a plane crash. As the EOD watch, he would be needed to render safe the explosive components of the ejection seats as well as any ordnance on the aircraft.

When any of the six-man EOD detachment on board *George Washington* stood the flight deck watch, he wore a red turtleneck and a red life vest identifying him as an ordnance handler. Each had a painted stencil of the EOD "crab," on the back; an inverted bomb on a shield superimposed over a wreath and two lightning bolts. All EOD Techs are required to learn its meaning upon beginning Phase I of their training.

> *The wreath is symbolic of the achievements and laurels gained by minimizing accident potentials, through the ingenuity and devotion to duty of its members. It is in memory of the EOD personnel who have given their lives while performing EOD duties. The bomb was copied from the design of the World War II Bomb Disposal Badge; the bomb represents the historic and major objective of the EOD attack, the unexploded bomb. The three fins represent the major areas of nuclear, conventional, and chemical/biological warfare. The lightning bolts symbolize the potential destructive power of the bomb and the courage and professionalism of EOD personnel in their endeavors to reduce hazards as well as to render explosive ordnance harmless. The shield represents the EOD mission which is to protect personnel and property in the immediate area from an inadvertent detonation of hazardous ordnance.*

The EOD students also learned that completing the course would not end their training. Each would continue to build upon their expertise, advancing from Basic to Senior, and finally Master EOD Technician.

Like all students, when Ball learned the meaning of the EOD crab it became more to him than military insignia, it was a source of pride; a symbol. Upon graduation from the EOD pipeline, Ball wore the Basic EOD crab, commonly called a 'slick bomb' because the bomb was naked. Now as a Senior EOD Technician his bomb had a star on it.

Ball pulled the poncho liner that served as his blanket up to his chin. He decided to go back to sleep, to find his wife Jeannie in a dream. Suddenly, the door opened throwing fluorescent light into the room. Then the overhead light of the shop was turned on.

"Get up, T-Ball!"

Ball grunted in response to hearing his moniker. An instructor gave him the nickname his first day at dive school in Panama City, Florida.

"Damn it, Johnny! It's Sunday! I'm trying to get some holiday routine here!"

"Right, shipwreck . . . holiday for some . . . routine for others. Come on, we just got a short fuse on an op."

"What?"

"Ship takedown with the frogs."

Aviation Ordnanceman First Class Jonathon Hooke was the detachment's leading petty officer, the senior enlisted man who was not yet a chief petty officer.

Additionally, Hooke was at the pinnacle of an EOD career as a Master EOD Technician. His EOD crab had a star on the bomb, with an additional star and wreath above the shield.

Ball threw off his poncho liner and got up.

"What happened?"

"Sanctions violator made a run for it last night. We're going to take it down."

"Who's going?"

"You and me. It's our turn in the barrel. Get suited up with the basic stuff. We brief in fifteen minutes. We'll come back here after the briefing if we need more shit."

"Okay."

T-Ball and Hooke began by donning flight suits and bulletproof vests. Each had a load-bearing vest fitted over the body armor that was designed to carry ammunition and a few select tools of the trade. It even had a bladder in the back for carrying water called a "Camelbak" to prevent dehydration in the hot Arabian sun.

Gunner's Mate Second Class Tommy Ving, another teammate, entered the shop carrying two large bags.

"I drew weapons from the armory—what do you guys want?"

"Shotgun," said Hooke.

"I'll go with the CAR," T-Ball replied referring to the M-16 variant used by "Spec Ops" forces.

"You sure? Shotgun might be better on the ship."

"Nah, I'm more comfortable with the 5.56."

Each Tech wore a nine millimeter Beretta on his hip as a last line of defense.

T-Ball, Hooke, and their officer in charge, Lieutenant Guterson, were the last to arrive for the briefing. Gear and weapons were stowed neatly in the back of the briefing room. T-Ball and Hooke removed their packs and set them down, stowed their weapons, then took their seat next to Guterson.

One of the ship's Intelligence Officers began the brief. If they were not on a military ship, T-Ball would have thought the man was hung over. He clearly had not slept in many days.

"Good morning, gentlemen. Yesterday afternoon USS *Elliot* encountered a suspected sanctions violator; motor vessel *Green Leon. Elliot* made several attempts to hail the ship with no response. She continued to track and report but could not pursue because she was involved in another boarding at the time. USS *San Jacinto* was directed to leave her station in plane guard in order to track and pursue the *Leon. San Jac* has remained beyond *Leon's* visual and radar range."

The officer clicked on a projector with a remote, displaying a photo of a container ship on the wall behind him.

"This is a file photo of the *Leon*. Note she has a large deckhouse aft and a small one forward. We believe that all living spaces are in the aft house; it is almost ten stories off the waterline. The forward one probably just houses storage for the ship, line lockers and the windlass machinery rooms."

He clicked the remote again. Now there was a naval architecture drawing of the *Leon* depicting a view of the ship from the right side.

"This is the general layout of the *Leon*. It is a composite from the shipyard that built her ten years ago and intelligence gathered after she came under suspicion nine months ago for smuggling military parts into Iraq. The debrief from a SCI classified source noted that she had modifications from her original configuration. One of the most notable changes was that she might have received an upgrade to her communications suite that will enable her to provide early warning to Iraqi national assets without any effort. Keep an eye out for this suite. As always the codeword for a sophisticated comm suite is 'Five Aces,' the word for contraband weapons is 'Thoroughbreds,' and for illegal fuel oil is 'Payback.'"

T-Ball only half paid attention to the intel brief. He was distracted thinking of Jeannie. He looked at his divewatch. She was probably sending the kids to bed right now, half a world away.

When he focused again, Ball realized that he was not the only one who was drifting off, almost half the SEALs returned to their Sunday slumber. Ball thought that at this point in the float, all the intel briefs sounded the same. After four months at sea, each of the Techs on the detachment had by now completed countless boardings with the SEALs.

Despite living and working together, Ball did not know any of the SEALs very well. The SEALs usually treated the Techs like they were the junior varsity. On most missions the EOD Techs stayed in the rear, only coming forward if a booby trap was located or if explosives or some ordnance were found. It was only then that the Techs were treated like royalty.

Lieutenant Holt was the SEAL officer in charge for this operation. He was one of two SEAL Squad Leaders on the *George Washington*. The other was Lieutenant Junior Grade Barnes. Holt gave his standard brief reviewing the team assignments, their movements on the ship, and everyone's call sign. T-Ball would be with the first SEAL squad and would use call sign "Echo One" on the radio. Hooke was "Echo Two."

Holt always ended his brief the same way. "Okay, I want everyone fully geared up when you walk out this door. Balaclava hoods and Protec helmets on. Body armor, assault vests and packs on. All radios on but secured for the rope-in. Hoods over faces, lock and load weapons and secure them for the fast rope when you get the word that we are five minutes out. Questions?"

There were none.

"Right, then let's go get 'em!"

The ship was still quiet as the team traversed the passageways to the flight deck. Because it was Sunday and a "no fly" day most of the crew was allowed to sleep in. T-Ball felt the stares of the few *Washington* crewmembers that did see the takedown team. It was not common to see sailors wearing black rappelling helmets, body armor, tactical vests, and carrying assault weapons, striding down the ship's passageway. In fact, most of the ship would never hear of their exploits.

A pair of SH-60 Seahawk helicopters was already turning on deck. Their blades pushed a high volume of air, causing them to jump slightly against the tie-down chains that secured them to the ship. T-Ball was the first to enter the aircraft. He sat down on the canvas seat, placed his weapon between his legs with the barrel pointed down, and watched the horizon move slowly up and down with the movement of the ship.

When both aircraft were full, a pair of blue-shirted flight deck crewmen slid under the rotors and removed the tie-down chains. T-Ball looked forward through the cockpit window and watched the yellow shirt signal the pilot to takeoff. In seconds they were flying.

The ocean sliding by at over a hundred knots mesmerized T-Ball and he lost track of time. He thought of home, daydreaming again about seeing Jeannie, Ted junior, and his daughter Kathryn. In a few days the ship would pull into Jebel Ali and he would be able to call them. He reminded himself to send Jeannie an email before the day was through.

One of the SEALs, the one they called Digger, tapped him. He looked over. Digger pointed outside. T-Ball looked out the open door to see *San Jacinto*. Ball always thought the silhouette of an Aegis cruiser, with its tall superstructure and five inch guns both fore and aft, emanated *Navy*.

Ball remembered that *San Jac* would be following the *Leon*, so the target ship would not be far away.

T-Ball felt someone tap him again. He looked away from *San Jac* toward the front left side of the cabin. Senior Chief Daranchak who was the Helo-Rope Suspension Team (HRST) Master held up both hands, fingers spread and mouthed, "Ten minutes."

T-Ball double-checked his gear. He collapsed the stock on his weapon so that he could move with it easier through the close quarters of the merchant ship. His vest carried five magazines of 5.56 ammunition for the M-16, and one magazine was loaded in the weapon. He had two magazines of nine millimeter rounds on his belt and one already in his sidearm. The front of his vest also had pouches carrying dikes, crimpers, electrical tape, leather gloves for the rope, and paracord—the basic tools of the trade. On his back was a specially tailored pack for EOD Technicians.

Several of the SEALs now pulled on leather gloves over their flight gloves, so T-Ball did the same. Then he double-checked that the strap from his M-16 was fed through the carabineer on his vest and that the carabineer was locked shut.

He looked up to see Daranchak with one hand up, fingers splayed, signaling, "Five minutes."

Now T-Ball pulled the hood up over his mouth so that only his eyes were visible under his flight goggles. Then he pulled back the charging handle on his M-16, chambering a round. He checked to ensure the safety was still on and wrapped a bungee cord around it, securing it close to his body for the descent. He heard the clicks of several SEALs doing the same. Out of the corner of his eye he saw the *Leon* through the open left door. Daranchak held up his index finger. "One minute."

His heart began to race now. Fast-roping was a simple evolution that could go badly when done incorrectly. Done right, he would simply slide to the deck like a fireman on a firehouse pole; done wrong, he would freefall until steel converted him from a sailor into a carcass for a trauma course.

The helo shuddered and its blades thwapped louder in the air as it came into a hover over the main deck in front of *Leon's* pilothouse. The aircrew kept the helicopter moving forward slightly, matching the speed of the ship, while maintaining a position seventy feet off the deck.

Daranchak kicked out the heavy line and tapped the first SEAL. T-Ball watched as one after another, each of the SEALs stepped over to the line, grabbed it and slid down toward the deck. They were so fast that four would be on the line at one time.

T-Ball was second to last. He jumped almost without thinking. He looked down at his feet wrapped tightly on the line, but focused more on the man on the line just below him. The EOD Tech squeezed his hands together slightly to break his fall before crunching his fellow sailor. Once he was off the line and clear, T-Ball reached the deck and stepped away, making room for Daranchak coming down behind him. He unclipped his weapon from his side and assumed a position in the tight circle that the SEALs formed for security. He felt like he was in a tornado with the downwash of the helo pushing him toward the deck.

In seconds another helo came into a hover over the deck and the rest of the team descended in perfect rhythm.

T-Ball scanned the ship in front of him for any movement. In his earpiece he heard Holt's voice.

"Rebel, this is Kermit. All hands on deck safe. Starting takedown."

FOUR

TAKEDOWN

T-Ball stayed right behind Digger as they entered the superstructure. Their objective was the bridge. The staircase seemed never-ending. T-Ball lost count at seven stories. As the last man in line, he kept swiveling his head, looking behind them to prevent ambush and listened for the sounds of alarm.

The group stopped just outside the door to the bridge. Lieutenant Holt was in front. He surveyed the team to ensure everyone was there and knew what he was about to do. No words passed. He pushed on the door to open it. It was locked.

Again, without commands, from just behind the lieutenant, the first class boatswain's mate SEAL called Pops sprang into action. He slung his MP-5 over his shoulder and opened Holt's pack. Pops pulled out a mini-battering ram and slammed it into the door. With the first impact, yelling began in the pilothouse. It was in Arabic. T-Ball had no idea what the crew was saying. He quietly hoped they were not armed. Pops' third try knocked the door open. Lieutenant Holt and the other SEALs burst into the room with their guns up. Each one quickly put his sights on one of the *Leon's* bridge crew.

T-Ball set up a position at the door with his weapon pointed down the stairwell, providing rear security. The screaming in Arabic continued. One by one the SEALs forced the seamen to lie face down on the deck.

"Echo!" Kermit called out.

T-Ball stepped in the door.

"Zip them."

The SEALs kept the crew covered while T-Ball began zip-tying their hands behind their backs.

"Who's the fucking Master?" Holt said out loud.

Just then one of the men called out. T-Ball looked to the starboard side of the bridge and saw a seaman in coveralls get up and run.

"We got a runner!" his guard yelled as he chased after him.

"Six, go with him!" commanded the lieutenant.

T-Ball heard the squelch of the radio and Holt's voice again. "All in Kilo, this is Kermit. We have a runner from the bridge, Kilo Two and Six in pursuit."

A calm answer came from one of the helicopters circling the *Leon*. *"Roger, Kermit this is Viper Nine. We got him, heading down an external ladder behind the wheelhouse. Looks like your element is following."*

"Fozzy, Kermit. Runner coming your way down pilothouse aft ladder."

"Roger, Kermit, we'll find 'em."

"DAMNIT!" Holt yelled to nobody in particular.

All of the men seemed to distance themselves from their leader for a second. This was probably a minor setback, but allowing a runner was shoddy. After a quick moment, the lieutenant regained his composure.

"Who is the Master?" Holt now said with ice in his voice. "Who is the Captain?" The Master knew it would not be long before he was identified. One of the men made a noise.

"You?"

He nodded.

"Get up. Get up motherfucker! I am pissed now! Where did that guy go?"

"He's scared, sir, we all scared."

"Yeah, you ought to be! I'm gonna cut you loose now, Captain. Don't run. Do you understand?"

"Yes, sir," the Master replied with steely arrogance.

T-Ball thought it strange that while the Master claimed to be frightened, his voice did not seem concerned.

Holt pulled out a knife and held it front of the Master for effect. He swiveled the man and cut the zip tie binding his hands.

"Take the helm."

The man walked over and took the ship's wheel. Holt looked in front of the ship. The sea was clear for miles in front of the *Leon*.

"Slow to just one knot."

The captain slowed the ship's speed.

"See, not so bad, huh? Now listen, I'm Lieutenant Kermit De Frog of the United States Navy. We are boarding your vessel to conduct an inspection . . ."

Just then a report interrupted Holt.

"Kermit, this is Fozzy. We got your runner. 'Seems scared. You want us to keep him here?"

"Fozzy, this is Kermit. Roger that."

When the SEALs were confident that they had control of the ship they moved all non-essential personnel to the deck in front of the ship's main superstructure and placed them under guard. The captain remained at the helm and a second crewmember was in engineering also under guard.

"Kilo Four, Five, Seven, Eight, search the house. Look for hidden Tangos or contraband," said Holt.

"Four," Foote acknowledged for his element.

"Kilo One and Three, Echo One, secure the bridge team and keep eyes on the main deck to help cover the security team there."

"One," Senior Chief Daranchak answered.

"Echo One," replied T-Ball.

Holt looked out the front windows of the bridge. "Fozzy, Kermit. Begin search of the main deck and all holds."

"Fozzy."

T-Ball stood in the starboard corner of the bridge. He faced his body toward the captain, now at the helm, steering the ship. T-Ball pointed his weapon at the deck just in front of his feet.

Holt was outside on the bridge wing now, talking to the *George Washington*, giving them a situation report. Senior Chief Daranchak walked around the bridge slowly opening doors and cabinets.

T-Ball looked at the ship's captain from behind the anonymity of his balaclava. The captain was short and thin with a very dark complexion. He appeared more African than Arab. The captain's hair and three days of beard growth were white and his eyes looked glassy. He held the helm steady and looked back and forth between the compass and the forward bridge window.

T-Ball caught the man stealing a glance toward him.

Again, he sensed something different about this captain. Most masters would talk really fast and act nervous, especially if they had contraband onboard. This one, despite his words to the contrary, seemed calm.

Though Holt was just a few feet away out on the bridge wing, Daranchak called to him over the radio.

"Kermit, Kilo One. Jackpot. I say again Jackpot."

"What ya got?"

"Five Aces, over."

"Be there in a second," said Holt.

T-Ball walked to the back port corner of the room where Daranchak had opened a set of accordion doors to what appeared to be a closet. He stepped past the senior chief through the door into the shack. It obviously did not fit for a common merchant ship. He counted four separate consoles and guessed there were four separate systems, at least one of which was encrypted.

Absent-mindedly, T-Ball swiveled the chair at the center console and saw an olive drab rectangular shaped canvas bag sitting on it. Though a flap on top hid most of its contents, through an opening in the corner he could see what appeared to be four large green blocks with bright orange cable running into them. The EOD Tech knew immediately what it was.

"Kermit, all in Kilo, this is Echo One. Clear the house. Now!"

"What!" exclaimed Holt and Daranchak together.

T-Ball turned on his heel toward them.

"No time, sir! Clear the house now!"

Holt keyed his mike. "Kilo, this is Kermit. Clear the house!"

Daranchak and Holt handcuffed the captain again and dragged him off the bridge. They knew the ship would not go far at such a slow speed.

From his belt, T-Ball removed his K-bar knife. He flipped open the top of the pouch. Inside were a total of sixteen blocks of plastic explosive. Each block was about twelve by three by three inches. The orange cable running into each was probably some form of detonating cord.

It was a military destruct charge. The crew did not place it precisely. That meant that the explosives had enough power to destroy the room easily, and it would probably take out the whole bridge.

T-Ball had to determine how the explosives were initiated. On destruct charges it was usually a timer. He pulled a penlight from his vest and shined it into the sack. On one side he saw a black box. Undoubtedly, it held an electronics package designed to initiate the charge.

Next he pulled a pair of cutters from his vest and cut the satchel from top to bottom on both sides, opening a flap on the face where the box was. He studied it quickly. It was a black metal rectangle, about the size of a hardback book.

T-Ball knew that he had to act fast; the timer on this device was probably initiated just as they got onboard. The crew knew that SEALs would be on the bridge quickly, therefore the timer probably had no more than ten minutes on it. In a microsecond he realized that the runner may have been afraid of them, but he was more afraid of this bomb.

T-Ball dropped his response pack to the deck and unzipped it fully. Inside was a collection of mesh compartments. He opened one and pulled out a small pouch. From the pouch he extracted a handle with a square fixture on the end and a circular saw blade slightly larger than a silver dollar. He attached the blade and pushed a button on the handle. It sung to life.

Next T-Ball selected a small suction cup with a handle from another compartment. He leaned over the metal box that contained the electronics package and placed the suction cup on it with his right hand. While still holding on to it, he pressed the button on the saw with his left hand.

With the saw, he traced a rectangle just inside the outer edge of the box. As he cut, T-Ball was careful not to go any deeper than the thickness of the metal. He winced as hot shards pierced into his gloved hand and forearm.

As he finished the trace, he pulled on the suction cup, removing the cutout. Now he could see the circuitry inside.

It was a smorgasbord of chips, diodes, resistors, and lots and lots of wires. In the bottom right hand corner was a digital timer. When he first looked at it, it read:

0:05:16:21

He had just over five minutes.

T-Ball studied the wires. He knew the answer was there. From his vest he pulled a pair of wire cutters. He cut the plastic sheathing of one of the wires, careful not to cut through. He stripped off the sheathing, pulling it back like the skin of a banana. Now the bare wire was exposed.

Then he pivoted back over to his response kit and grabbed a clear plastic bag. T-Ball pulled down his hood and brought the bag to his mouth opening it with his teeth.

The first number on the timer was now a "4."

Out of the bag popped a small one by two inch box. It had two wires protruding from it. Each had an alligator clip. T-Ball clamped each alligator clip to the wire he stripped. Then he snipped the wire between the clips.

He looked at the timer. It was now under four minutes.

T-Ball continued to study the circuitry to ensure his procedure was correct. Then he stepped out onto the bridge wing and keyed his radio.

"Kermit, Echo One. Procedure complete, standby."

"Kermit."

T-ball strode back onto the bridge and into the hidden communications shack. The time read:

00:00:00

The destruct charge did not detonate. Smiling, T-Ball clicked his mike again.

"Kermit, Echo One."

"Go, Echo One."

"Rendered safe."

FIVE

ANNAPOLIS

After going to mass, Jazz and Melanie loaded their kids in the car for a trip to Annapolis. The strained relationship with his father prevented Jazz from enjoying being near his parents these past few months. The one positive thing of living close to them was that his mother watched the kids from time to time to give Melanie a break.

As they turned from Maryland Route 301 to Route 50 Melanie said, "So, what are you going to tell the Admiral?"

"What can I say? I'm going to have to tell him. He's probably going to flip. I'm going to get yet another lecture on how I'm wasting my career wearing cammies, diving and blowing shit up, and how I need to be driving ships and subtly highlighting the flaws of my peers."

"And how are you going to respond?"

"I'll tell him that I'd rather be an ex-Navy Diver coaching little league than a retired war hero whose family refers to him by rank."

"Oh sure, fine," she said with a sarcastic tone. "Please do it after dinner this time so at least the boys are fed before I have to put them back in their car seats for the hour long ride home."

Jazz breathed heavily. She knew he wasn't going to respond to the Admiral with a rebuttal. Jazz grew tired of that long ago. It was easier now to just keep quiet and let the Admiral rant and rave at him like he was a derelict sailor standing before him at Captain's Mast or a negligent Officer of the Deck standing by to be fired after running his ship aground.

"Jazz, I'm sorry," Melanie said after a moment of silence. "He makes me tense too."

"I know."

"I was letting myself get excited again about getting back to our house. I mean, you are going to deploy and I'm going to be alone with three kids in Texas while all of our family and friends are here or in Virginia."

"I'm sorry. I didn't want it this way either."

"I know that," Melanie paused for a moment. "I disagree with the Admiral on something else though."

"What's that?"

"Unlike him, I'm glad you did this thing. I think it is crazy, the diving and blowing stuff up and all, but I can tell it makes you happy. I would have liked to see you put on admiral's stars, but it took courage to defy your father, to be your own man."

Melanie put her hand on his knee.

"I know what you're doing is difficult. I guess what I am trying to say is I think in many different ways you are very brave, and I think that's very sexy."

Jazz smiled. "Well, hooya, baby."

"Stop right there, sailor—I was not implying anything," Melanie giggled.

"Too bad."

The Jascinskis fell quiet again and remained so for the rest of the trip.

The Jascinski estate was on the Chesapeake Bay. The Admiral was a competent financial manager. He invested wisely and now owned most of the houses that the family lived in over the years. There were two in Norfolk, Virginia, one in San Diego, and one in Pearl Harbor, Hawaii, in addition to the one in Annapolis. Each one was rented only to fellow naval officers who the Admiral deemed reliable and likely to maintain the properties in good condition.

Jazz's mother came to the door as he pulled the 4Runner into the circular driveway. She smiled and waved enthusiastically. His mother knew that coming home, wherever that was, held mixed emotions for her son.

Eleanor Jascinski began her marriage as a Navy wife of the old school. She was a junior officer's wife in the days when you had to be ready to entertain the commanding officer and his wife at a moment's notice. If you wanted to help further your husband's career, upon joining a new wardroom you inquired as to what the CO and his wife liked to drink, and kept your bar stocked accordingly. It was not uncommon for a junior wife to receive a phone call from the CO's wife at two in the morning.

I need diapers. Do you have some? Or could you please go out and get some for me?

In the late sixties and early seventies a Navy wife rarely had a career unless it allowed her to move with her husband. Those women who worked were likely nurses or teachers. Eleanor chose not to work, but when her husband finally realized positions of command she also rejected the culture of their early Navy life. Still, she exuded a loyalty to the Admiral and his career that Jazz never understood. It was almost as if through her suffering and sacrifice it had become *their* career.

"Melanie, you are simply glowing!" Eleanor said as she hugged Melanie.

"Thanks Mom. Could you help me get Tyler out of the car? I'm having trouble bending over."

"Of course, dear."

Jazz was unbuckling Nicholas from the other side.

"Hey, Ma, how ya doing?"

"I'm fine, dear. The Admiral's down on the pier if you want to speak to him about something."

Jazz stopped at his mother's words. He shot a look past her to his wife standing behind her on the driveway. Melanie was flushed. Jazz realized that she already told Eleanor about the assignment in Ingleside. He frowned at both of them.

From the back of the house, Jazz could see the Admiral on the pier. He was polishing the teak on his 50-foot sailboat, *Grace*. Jazz walked down the stairs they built together that ran from the bluff that the house sat on to the deck at the foot of the pier. There was a fair amount of boat activity on the bay. He wished he could go out there today, but even if there were time, his father would never allow it.

The Admiral looked very Annapolitan dressed in an oxford shirt, khakis, and boat shoes. Jazz noticed that the skin on his head was starting to darken with the spring. He was thankful that male pattern baldness passed through the female side of the family.

He caught his father's eye as he walked down the pier.

"Junior, good to see you."

"Good to see you, sir."

"How is school going?"

"Fine, sir, I'm almost done."

"That's what I understand. Do you have orders yet?"

"I do . . . to Ingleside, Texas."

"The HELL you say!"

"Yes, sir. Officer in Charge, Explosive Ordnance Disposal Mobile Unit Six, Detachment Ingleside."

"What the heck is that?"

"Well, sir, Mobile Unit Six is in Charleston but they have two detachments in Ingleside, Texas to support of all the minesweepers and minehunters there."

"So your CO will be in Charleston?"

"Yes, sir."

"Hundreds of miles and a full time zone away."

"Yes, sir."

"Bad enough you guys never deploy with your CO's, now you won't even be in the same damn state."

A silence passed between them.

Finally the Admiral said, "Ingleside, near Corpus Christi right? Isn't that where *Inchon* is now?"

"Yes, sir. She has been reconfigured from an Amphibious Assault Ship to a Mine Warfare Command Ship."

The Admiral looked at Jazz a minute with a frown on his face. He looked as if he was going to say something important.

"Unfuckingbelievable," the Admiral cursed suddenly.

Jazz felt sick to his stomach as the Admiral stepped over the lifeline on *Grace* into her cockpit, and through the hatch into the cabin below.

Jazz was not invited on board so he turned and headed back toward the house. He looked up as he began ascending the stairs and saw his wife and mother looking down at him from the porch off the kitchen. They knew without being there what transpired between their husbands.

Their early supper was at least cordial. Nothing more was said of the future. Jazz and Melanie packed the boys in the car with the Admiral and Eleanor watching from the front porch. Jazz imagined that to an outsider, the scene could be on the cover of the Saturday Evening Post with "Rockwell" written in the corner. He knew better.

Eleanor continued to wave as the 4Runner headed down the street. She spoke through her smile to her husband.

"If you don't fix this soon he'll never come back."

"He's already gone. I suppose being a Navy brat did it to him. Junior has been rebelling against me all along. That boy is as different from me as they come."

"You're wrong, Admiral," she said. "He is exactly like you."

*   *   *

"Echo One, Echo Two, Bravo Zulu. Good job, hooya, and Merry Christmas."

"And don't forget Happy Anniversary."

There was a pause on the circuit.

"Are you shitting me?"

"Eight years and two kids to date."

T-Ball re-packed all the tools in his pack and vest with the exception of his crimpers. He thought of the crimpers as the most basic tool of the EOD Tech; like a scalpel for a surgeon or a pipe wrench for a plumber. T-Ball's crimpers looked like a pair of pliers but the jaws had two openings. The first had no edge to it and was slightly smaller than the M-7 non-electric blasting cap used to initiate military and many commercial high explosives. The second was a cutter with an edge designed for slicing detonating cord at an angle that would not crush the explosive crystals inside or create enough friction to set it off.

T-Ball used the cutter to snip the detonating cord that connected each of the blocks of explosive.

How did the signal get from the electronics to the det cord? he wondered.

He had to study the box closer.

From the backside of the box two wires emerged. They appeared to run into the closest block of explosives. There was undoubtedly an electrically initiated detonator inside.

Hooke was the first one back on *Leon's* pilothouse.

"You dumb motherfucker," he said. "I should shoot you right here. If you came from together on your damn anniversary Jeannie would have killed me! Then Rebecca would send me over your place shoveling snow, unclogging toilets, and changing oil for the rest of my natural life! I coulda brought Tommy, damnit! Why the fuck didn't you tell me!"

T-Ball gave him a smug look.

"It was my turn."

Holt, Daranchak, and Pops were right behind Hooke with the ship's Master. The Master now looked more like a whipped puppy. They replaced him at the helm.

"Slow the ship to bare steerageway. Understand?" asked Holt, ". . . very slow." Then the SEAL officer in charge called out.

"Echo One, come here, man!"

"Sure, LT, what do you need?" he said.

"Hooya on the bomb disposal. We need to send a full report back to *GW*. I'm sure Guterson wants to know what is happening."

"Roger that, sir."

T-Ball followed Holt out on the bridge wing and into the Arabian sun yet again. The SEAL called the *George Washington*.

"Rebel, this is Kermit. Romeo sierra on that Five Aces package . . . Say again? Roger here he is."

Holt handed T-Ball a hand-held radio.

"It's Guterson. You are secure so nobody outside *George Washington* can hear you, but I don't know who over there is listening."

"Oscar, this is Echo One, over."

"Roger One. Good job. What happened?"

"Oscar, this is Echo One. Unknown military destruct charge located with Five Aces. Net explosive weight precluded need for precise placement."

"Copy, Echo One. How did you romeo sierra, over?"

"Oscar, Echo One. Little black box."

"Copy, Echo One. We'll send over a CMC, a closed metal container, soonest so that you can safely store and transport. Standby for further instructions. Let Kermit know that prize crew from Lone Star and trees from Rebel are standing by."

"Echo One."

T-Ball saw *San Jacinto* now. She was less than a thousand yards off the *Leon's* port side. He could make out the ship's boarding team preparing to launch their boat. One of the helos that brought the takedown team from *George Washington* was on *San Jac's* deck, probably refueling. The other was circling around overhead.

"Echo One, Oscar. I almost forgot, your orders came in last night. You got Ingleside."

"Roger that, Oscar. Anything else?"

"Negative, Echo One. Keep up the good work."

He handed the radio back to Holt.

"Sir, Lieutenant Guterson said that a boarding team from *San Jacinto* and Marines from *GW* are standing by to secure the ship."

"Right. Well, they will have to wait. We need to complete our own initial search first. For now, I want you to remain on the bridge as I directed before."

"Aye, aye, sir."

T-Ball found Hooke and Pops inspecting his handiwork.

"Hooya, brother," Pops said.

"I always said you were a solid motherfucker," agreed Hooke.

"What'd you do, T-Ball?" asked Pops.

Now I'm 'T-Ball,' the Tech thought to himself, *Save the day and suddenly I'm one of the boys.* He pointed to the device he put into the circuit. "See that little black box connected with alligator clips?"

"Yeah."

"Well, I evaluated the circuit and determined where the signal was going out to the explosive train. The electrical impulse to the detonator will only work if there is sufficient current. I put that black box in, which is basically a large resistor, to increase the electrical resistance in the circuit so that the signal could not travel through to the detonator."

"Huh?" Pops looked confused.

"Basically, Pops, that thing puts a large load on the battery so that it doesn't work right."

"Fucking-A man. Now you gonna cut the blue wire, just like in the movies right?"

"Yeah sure."

"Tell you what, T-Ball, you must have a ten-inch dick. That there is some good shit. You guys are no joke."

Pops turned and strolled away shaking his head.

In a hushed tone Hooke asked, "How did you know which one to use?"

"Simple, I pulled out the biggest one I had."

"Go large or go home?"

"Exactly."

"All in Kilo, all in Lima, this is Kermit. Victor bravo sierra sierra. We've done visit, and board, we need to finish search and prepare for seizure by Lone Star."

"Kilo Five."

"Fozzy."

"Gotta go," Hooke said to T-Ball.

One of the helos went back to *George Washington* to re-fuel. Guterson gave the aircrew a CMC for T-Ball to store the explosive charge in. *George Washington's* EOD detachment would place it in a magazine in case the FBI, the EOD Technology Division, or some other government entity wanted it for evidence of intelligence. Otherwise, they would dispose of it at the next possible chance. T-Ball placed the charge in the CMC and set it on the bridge wing opposite of *George Washington*. He stretched some duct tape over the hatch so nobody would go near it.

"Kermit, I recommend informing *San Jacinto* that I have placed the charge on the bridge wing there, that they may want to back off some."

"Okay," said Holt. "Did you receive that last call from Echo Two?"

"Uh, no, sir."

Just then T-Ball heard Hooke's voice.

"*. . . this is Echo Two. Request assistance in main hold from Echo One. Meet Fozzy on main deck over.*"

T-Ball looked at Holt who nodded and answered Hooke's request.

"Roger, Two. This is Kermit, One is on his way down."

T-Ball met Lieutenant Junior Grade Barnes on the main deck. Then he followed the young officer three decks down into *Leon's* innards. They reached a long passageway that looked as if it ran about half of the ship's length. T-Ball saw Hooke and two of the SEALs from Lima forty feet ahead of him in the passageway. Just beyond them was a door. As T-Ball got closer he saw that it was a hatch constructed of heavy steel. Its hinges looked like they would hold a lot of weight.

Just as T-Ball got up to where the SEALs were, Hooke called out, "Stop."

"What?"

"Look closely."

"Unfuckingbelievable," one of the SEALs remarked.

"I'd have never seen it," said the other.

T-Ball studied the door. He started at the large knob on the right side and circled around the top, past the hinges. Then he saw it. On the bottom edge there were two small, gray boxes, each the size of an AA battery. One was on the door and one was below it on the bulkhead.

"A sensor."

"Bingo."

"Damn, Hooke, that was a good eye. I'm not sure I'd have seen it either."

"Well shipwreck, that's why I'm a Master Tech and you're a Senior Tech. So what is it?"

"Actually it's stupid whatever it is. I mean, we've seen it. If you wanna hide it, why not put it inside?"

"Good point, but what is it?"

"Could be a booby trap. Open the door, it sets something off. Boom."

"Or?"

"Or it could just be an alarm. Heck, it might just be a status sensor. If this is the main hold, maybe it lights a light somewhere telling someone the door is open."

"Good point. So what do we do next?"

"Bring one of those A-rabs down here and have them open it," quipped one of SEALs. T-Ball smiled. The frogs were getting bored now.

T-Ball took a drag from his Camelbak and thought.

"It's an alarm or an indicator, not a booby trap."

"How do you know?"

"If it was a booby trap, they wouldn't want us to see it."

"Maybe they want us to see it so we don't go in, a proverbial explosive fence."

"Nah, that ain't it. These guys have been boarded before. They put a destruct charge on the bridge that definitely would have zapped us. They want to take a couple of us out if they can."

"Okay, I'm sure you're right. So go ahead."

"What?"

Hooke smirked. "Open the door."

T-Ball reached for the door handle. One of the SEALs said, "Shiiit!" as they scrambled down the passageway.

They stopped when they heard Hooke and T-Ball laughing together.

"Fuck you guys," Barnes said with a smile on his face.

Hooke caught his breath first. "Listen, sir, we can 'what if' this thing all day. The long and short is . . . T-Ball is probably right, but we're gonna bypass this sensor anyway."

"How ya gonna do that?"

"With two very precise and highly calibrated EOD instruments, the K-bar knife and a roll of duct tape."

T-Ball slipped off his pack and dropped it to the deck again. He got some duct tape from the outer pouch on his response pack. Then he knelt down and taped the top sensor to the bottom one. Next he pulled his K-bar from its sheath. He stuck the point under the sensor on the door and started to pry it off. It snapped off easily.

Now he taped around the two sensors, cocooning them together. He folded the unit below the door so that it now could open freely. The sensors taped together would continue to act as if the door were shut.

T-Ball opened the door. The five men looked through the hatch into the hold. "Holy shit," said Barnes. The SEAL officer keyed his radio. "Kermit, this is Fozzy. Do not let the trees or Lone Star's crew onboard yet. We've got a hold full of Thoroughbreds."

SIX

SHORE DETACHMENT

The slightly bitter taste of cold beer always seemed better after an afternoon mowing the lawn and trimming the hedges. Johnny Ashland sat back on the chaise lounge by his backyard pool and relaxed his 210-pound frame. He took another swig and lathered some more sunscreen on. An even greater reward for completing the day's work emerged through the sliding glass door—his wife, Judy. The bombshell was wearing her fluorescent green bikini.

I'll be mowing that lawn later, he thought.

Judy came out with a beer in one hand and a portable phone in the other.

"Johnny, hon, your beeper was going off. It was Tony's cell number."

Ashland raised an eyebrow. He wondered if his Leading Chief Petty Officer, Senior Chief Antonio De Napoli, was reviewing his ammunition and explosive inventory logs prior to their Explosive Safety Inspection on Monday. De Napoli was a perfectionist. Ash had visions of drinking coffee in the shop until midnight with De Napoli, reviewing their books for correctness. Then he remembered that his boss was in the shop this weekend.

"Damn it. LT's got the duty today. Think he'd call us in?"

She shrugged and handed him the phone and stretched on the lounge next to him and closed her eyes. Still admiring his wife, Johnny hit the speed dial for De Napoli's cell phone. He picked up on the first ring.

"Senior Chief."

"It's Ash, what's up? Called to tell me you finally caught something?"

"Nope, this is a recall."

Johnny sat up and scratched his head.

"Really, what for?"

"Helo with a weapon onboard crashed into its mother ship at sea. I don't know the details."

"No shit? Okay, I'm on my way in."

"See you there."

Ashland hung up the phone and stood up.

"I've been recalled, hon."

Judy looked surprised. "It's not a drill is it?"

"No."

She was already used to this.

"Be careful."

He leaned down to kiss her. "I will."

Twenty minutes later Ash was driving through the delivery gate near the airfield at Norfolk Naval Air Station. It was just one small part of the world's largest naval base.

Ash zipped through the recreation area, turned his International Scout left and parked next to the old fire station that housed the base's EOD team. A sign in front, decorated with manila line read:

EXPLOSIVE ORDNANCE DISPOSAL MOBILE UNIT TWO
DETACHMENT NORFOLK

The Mobile Unit Two and EOD Group Two logos were displayed prominently on either side.

As Ash got out of his International Scout he noted by the cars already there that he was the last det member to arrive. He chuckled to himself as he mounted the stairs. Every single vehicle in the parking lot was a 4X4.

He recalled once hearing a diver groupie remark to her girlfriend, "Pilots drive sports cars, divers drive trucks."

Det Norfolk assembled in the conference room on the second deck of the station. The rooms that the firefighters used to bunk in transformed into offices. The high bay garage downstairs now housed the detachment's equipment, boats, and an ambulance-like response vehicle.

Ash donned a flight suit as the OIC, the officer in charge, began his brief. Tim January was just promoted from lieutenant to lieutenant commander. The shore detachment would probably be his last operational tour. He already received orders to join an Amphibious Squadron as the Staff Special Operations Officer.

"Okay fellas, here's what's up. About forty minutes ago I got a call that an SH-60 Seahawk helicopter crashed aboard the USS *Normandy*. The helo carried an experimental air to surface missile onboard. To make matters worse the helo did not make it to the flight deck. She squished into the aft vertical launch system right above sixty-some SM-2 and Tomahawk missiles."

January paused. Nobody was interrupting him, they knew by his demeanor that it this was not a drill.

"The *Normandy* is so far out to sea that she can not be reached by helo. Obviously, all ordnance has to be rendered safe before she can come back in. This means we are going to insert by parachute."

This statement led to catcalls of joy by the Techs.

"WHOOHOO!"

"Right on!"

"Water jumpin' baby!"

January raised his voice. "Okay, okay guys. Yes it will be fun. I've already got a C-2 lined up. Here is what I recommend . . . Chief Billings,"

"Sir?"

"I want you to be the jumpmaster. Make sure all of our gear is ready, prepare the aircrew, etcetera. You know the deal."

"Roger, sir."

"Willy, I need you to gather pubs. Check the classified fax and the computer for new info on this missile. The EOD Technical Division called and said they had some stuff to add to what they gave us in anticipation for the first firing next month."

"Got it."

"Senior Chief, assign the rest of the crew as you see fit to conduct the load-out. Any questions or suggestions?"

The Techs looked around at each other; they had trained so well together that there was no need for questions.

De Napoli assigned Ash the F470 inflatable boat. Ash opened the high bay door to let the sun in and prepped it for the jump. Secured inside would be much of the detachment's support gear including a hardened laptop and waterproof cases containing tool sets with everything from titanium pulleys to surgical clamps. He secured the MARS engine in the back and lashed everything in.

Torpedoman Second Class "Willy" Wosniak brought the det's portable hardened laptop computer into the high bay from the rear workshop. Zeke Donovan, a first class boatswain's mate like Ash, pulled the detachment's response "bread truck" out of the high bay and connected one of the det's pickups to the trailer for the F470. Bailey and Martin also emerged from the workshop bringing the toolsets they expected to use on this operation. Ash checked and re-checked the equipment to ensure it would remain secure in the inflatable after they kicked it out the back of the airplane and as it dropped through the atmosphere.

Forty minutes later Detachment Norfolk drove onto the flight line at Norfolk Naval Air Station. All other flights were re-routed to Oceana NAS in Virginia Beach to clear the way for the C-2 cargo plane that waited for the EOD team.

The C-2 was a small twin-engine prop plane that was used to ferry cargo aboard aircraft carriers. The standby flight crew was called in on Lieutenant Commander January's request. They spent the last hour configuring the aircraft for the para-drop. The pilot and co-pilot were in their seats, and the engines were already turning, drowning out all other sound. The two aircrewmen wordlessly helped the EOD Techs lift the raft from the trailer and walk it up the ramp to the rear of the aircraft. Ash recognized the tall one. They had trained with Det Norfolk and knew what to expect.

An officer drove out toward them in a staff car. January seemed to recognize him and walked over to greet him.

Probably the command duty officer from the DESRON, Ash surmised.

Chief Billings set about checking everything for the jump. In the aircraft, as the jumpmaster, he was God. He controlled this aspect of the mission and even had authority over the OIC.

January climbed up the ramp and sat in the canvas seat next to Ash. Willy was already leaning over to his left, sleeping on a flight bag. The tall aircrewman pushed a button to close the ramp as the C-2 taxied down the runway. Then, one by one, each of the members of Det Norfolk went to sleep.

Suddenly, Ash woke up. He was hot. He opened his eyes and was immediately blinded by the sun coming through the window of the C-2. It was setting lower in the sky but had not yet touched the horizon.

He shifted to the other side of the aircraft.

Judy was probably cooking dinner for one. By now she would know that he was not coming back tonight. He did not have time to call her before the Techs left NAS Norfolk.

Ash looked at the other det members, all sleeping. It was a way to deal with the stress, a few moments of meditation to relax the body and mind. That way they were more prepared to handle the physical and mental tasks ahead.

He closed his eyes and tried to sleep some more. As he dozed, Ash wondered how many times he had flown in military aircraft. He knew his takeoffs far outnumbered his landings.

Heck, he figured *I've probably jumped out of this very bird twenty times.*

All of the Explosive Ordnance Disposal recruiting media touted dive and jump pay as an incentive, though it was not necessary. Most Techs love to dive, hate to jump, and want to do both whenever possible. It's not about the pay, it's about the rush. Besides, diving and jumping are both easy, but they only get the Techs to the problem. That's when the real fun begins.

Ash recalled something that a crusty old EOD Tech said when Ash was still a Basic Tech at EOD Mobile Unit Three in San Diego. There was a massive beach party where SEALs, EOD Techs, Seabees, and all manner of unwanted sailors were present. A harem of beautiful, nearly naked women graced the frogs' presence as always. SEAL groupies. The senior chief on Ash's detachment was wooing one of them. He captivated her with his underwater exploits.

"So is it dangerous?" she asked, oozing awe.

"Sure babe, I mean being a Navy EOD Tech is a lot like being a brain surgeon except if you fuck up, the patient explodes . . . . oh, and we do it underwater."

The senior chief got laid that night

Ash woke again when Willy kicked him in the foot. He sat up and rubbed his eyes. He watched Willy going around waking the rest of the det up. For a moment he forgot what they were doing in the C2. He remembered when he looked forward and saw the lieutenant and Billings in the front of the aircraft talking; probably reviewing the plan for the jump.

Everything started to go like clockwork. Wordlessly, each man donned a wetsuit, his parachute, and any other gear they were jumping with. Each strapped flexible swim fins to his shins to be used after entering the water. Ash looked out the window beside his seat and noticed the ship on the horizon. Fortunately the seas appeared relatively calm.

Billings lined them all up on the port side of the aircraft. The tall aircrewman checked his safety harness and pressed the ramp button again. The ramp opened allowing some air circulation in the plane.

The first thing out of the aircraft was the boat. Billings and the aircrewman released all the cargo straps keeping it on the deck. Billings checked its parachute once more and gave the aircrewman the "thumbs up." The crewman talked into his mike for a second and pointed at the light to the right of the ramp.

When the light turned green, the two men pushed on the boat. It slid out the opening in the plane's tail.

The light turned red again and the C2 banked coming around for a second pass.

Billings was all business now, quickly giving them all commands via hand signals. Willy was first in line; behind him was De Napoli, followed by Ash, January, Martin, Bailey, and Zeke. Billings would jump last.

As the jumpmaster, Billings made one last final check on each man. He walked down the line tapping each piece of gear on each jumper top to bottom.

Protec helmet, goggles, chute, reserve, fins, knife, flare.

He inspected each chute closely without disturbing it, ensuring there were no outward telltale signs of it not being packed properly or that it was disturbed during their flight.

It was time. The light fixture on the left side of the plane changed from red to green again.

Willy stepped up to the ramp. Billings slapped him on the ass and shouted, "Go!"

As De Napoli shuffled forward, Ash followed right behind him.

Billings looked to see Willy's chute just starting to deploy. He then slapped the senior chief on the back.

"Go!"

Ash could feel his heart pumping in his chest. He reminded himself not to hold his breath. He kept his eyes forward, seeing Willy's chute fully open as De Napoli's began to bloom.

"Go!"

Ash kept his body upright as he made two steps down the ramp. The third step was air. He tucked his head into his chin, slammed his feet together and brought his hands to the reserve pack on his front. He focused on his wetsuit booties waiting for the pull of the harness as his chute opened. It came violently; Ash felt the straps digging into his crotch and thighs and around his shoulders. The chute opened in seconds and slowed his descent. Ash looked up now to check the risers, the lines supporting him under the canopy. Then he inspected the canopy itself, ensuring that it was filled completely with air and that he was not slipping.

When all seemed as expected, Ash looked around and enjoyed the ride. First he looked to the USS *Normandy*. He could make out the helo just aft of the flight deck. It was black and still smoking. The deck around it appeared scorched. From Ash's position, it looked like a bug that had been stepped on. He noticed that De Napoli already descended further than Willy due to his weight. He also noticed the wake from a small boat near the *Normandy*. The ship must have deployed a chase boat to ensure the jumpers' safety.

That was smart, Ash thought to himself.

The ocean seemed to rush up at him faster during the last hundred feet. Just before he hit the water Ash held his breath and closed his eyes. As he hit the water, he quickly he pulled the releases to free himself of the parachute. He did not want it to pull him under. Ash undid the bungee holding the fins to his lower legs and put them on his feet. As he bent over he felt cool water seeping down the back of his neck. In a few moments his body would raise the water temperature so that it would be comfortably warm.

Ash finned a few feet away from his chute. He decided that separating himself from the canopy and the lines slowly sinking in the water would be prudent. Then he kicked hard, treading and bringing himself out of the water to conduct a quick survey.

Zeke and Billings were still descending. *Normandy's* launch had picked up Willy. He and a *Normandy* sailor were pulling his chute into the boat.

As he continued a 360 sweep, Ash saw January, De Napoli, and Bailey in the water. He realized that he was closest to the F470 inflatable. Leaving his chute behind, Ash swam hard toward the boat.

The inflatable was not moving. Its parachute fell off to the boat's starboard side and was filling up with water. It was like a large sea anchor.

Ash searched the water around the boat to ensure he would not become fouled in its lines. The port side was clear. He swam over, kicked hard again, and pulled himself into the boat.

At initial look, all the gear appeared in good condition. Ash wondered if the weight of the water in the chute would pull the boat under or if the risers would part first. He pulled his knife from the sheath on his inside calf. Since there was tension in the lines, they cut easily. Each line popped with only three or four strokes.

The lines disappeared quickly into the gray water. Ash caught his breath a moment and surveyed the ocean surface once again to check the status of his teammates. Willy was still pulling his chute into the *Normandy's* boat. The ship was about a hundred yards beyond. De Napoli was between Willy and the F470, swimming toward Ash. In the opposite direction he saw January, Bailey, Zeke, and Billings all swimming toward him in the order they jumped.

Ash set up the MARS engine and started it. Then he drove down the line of swimmers, picking them up one by one.

SEVEN

NIGHTFALL ON NORMANDY

By nightfall, the whole detachment was recovered onboard *Normandy*. The Techs were able to save five of their chutes before they were lost to the sea.

From the boat deck, the executive officer, the *Normandy*'s second in command, escorted them to the quarterdeck. The ship was still at general quarters. All of the sailors were at their battle stations. Only the damage control teams had free access to move about the ship. Ash saw a pair of *Normandy* crewmembers dressed in firefighting gear walking down the ship's starboard side. They were surveying the damage. An entire hose team was staged just aft of the boat deck on the starboard side also, ready to respond if the helo caught fire again.

January agreed with the XO that the quarterdeck was a great place to establish their response command post, called a "CP." Located on the main deck just aft of the forward third of the ship, it provided a lot of open space to layout the detachment's gear. As on all ships, the quarterdeck already had hardwire communication circuits with the bridge, combat, and with damage control central.

The Techs began stripping off their wetsuits, drying off and drawing their flight suits again from waterproof packs. They donned the flight suits and steel-toed boots.

January talked with the XO as he dressed.

"I want the DCA up here, the senior pilot available, and the weapons officer."

The ship's damage control assistant, or DCA, was *Normandy*'s officer responsible for responding to any damage the ship incurred due to fire, flooding, even collision. He was in effect, *Normandy*'s fire chief. The weapons officer was the department head responsible for all the weapons onboard, from the .45 caliber pistols used for security to the missiles in the ship's vertical launch systems. After being summoned, all three officers arrived at the quarterdeck at about the same time.

January moved to one side of the quarterdeck where they would be out of the way of the rest of his team. De Napoli directed the Techs setting up the hardened computer system, laying out equipment for easy access, and dressing out Ash and Zeke to go "downrange." As he dressed, Ash paid some attention to his OIC coordinating their efforts.

"Gentlemen, let's start from the beginning." January said. "What happened on the flight?"

The young pilot was obviously distraught. Ash guessed he was not the Air Boss, the senior aviator normally in charge of the six pilots onboard the cruiser. That meant the Air Boss was one of the pilots on the flight. He could tell that it was difficult for the officer to gather his thoughts after having just watched three of his squadron-mates crash into the deck. One of which had already been pronounced dead.

"Well, everything was fine until the end. Something went wrong, I don't know what, and they dropped like a stone onto the VLS. They caught fire immediately."

"Did they attempt to fire the weapon on this flight?" asked January.

"No, it was just to test the systems."

"Are there any other weapons or ordnance on board the aircraft?"

"No."

"What side is the weapon on?"

"Port side."

"Have you been able to talk to them, ask what happened?"

"No."

January turned to the damage control assistant. He also looked very young, probably an ensign or lieutenant junior grade. He was sweating profusely, probably from the stress, but he had an air of confidence.

"Okay, DCA, tell me about the firefighting efforts."

"Right, I had my hot suit men extract the aircrew. We hit it with AFFF foam for about two hours and finally put the fire out. I think we basically controlled the burn until the fuel had all burned up."

"Did the missile ever appear to detonate? Or were there any smaller detonations?"

"I don't think so, what do you mean?"

"Well there are probably carts in the missile ejection rack, explosive cartridges that eject the missile from the bird on the pilot's command in case of failure or aircraft accident. I want to know if they or the missile cooked off."

"No, I thought of that, the weapon I mean. I specifically had a team on the port side send a high volume of water on it to try to keep it cool. That actually may have allowed the fire to burn longer because the water washed away some of the AFFF from the other team."

"Anything else I should know besides stuff in the VLS?"

"Not that I can think of."

"Okay. I think you did the right thing, DCA. You probably saved some lives by using the water. Good work."

The weapons officer was a department head, a lieutenant commander.

"Weaps, you know what I'm going to ask," said January.

"Status of the VLS. But first, let me give you a photo of the weapon as it now is."

He handed January a black and white photo.

"This was taken from the aft VLS camera mounted above the flight deck. We zoomed in on the weapon there. You can see that it is blackened but does not appear melted."

"Yeah, doesn't look like there are any explosives oozing from it either," replied January.

"Nah, it's medium rare, not well done."

January called to the XO still on the phone with the captain.

"XO, the DCA really saved the day here. This guy deserves a medal."

"I figured."

Hearing this, the DCA straightened a little, fully convinced now that he had done well.

"Okay, Weaps, so what happened in the VLS?"

"High temp alarms. Deluge system flooded it. Eductors drained the water overboard so we do not have a flooding problem."

"Are the temps high now?"

"No."

"Has anyone gone in there?"

"Not yet."

"Okay we'll get to that later. What is in there?"

"We have SM-2 surface to air missiles, Tomahawks, and four Vertical Launch ASROC torpedoes."

"Damn, loaded for bear, huh?"

"Yeah. We're deploying soon. We loaded out in Yorktown right before coming out here."

"Okay. Listen gentlemen, I need you or a trusted representative here so that I can be in communication with you during this evolution. How are we coming, Senior Chief?"

"Ready, sir," De Napoli answered.

Now Normandy's XO, weapons officer, DCA, and all of Detachment Norfolk stood in a semicircle around Lieutenant Commander January. Ash and Zeke were prepped to go downrange. Each resembled a medieval knight dressed in olive drab bib and pants with Kevlar lining. They would each complete the ensemble with spacesuit-like helmets before exposing themselves to the missile.

"Okay. Ash is the P-1, Zeke P-2. I suspect we already know what the procedure is based on what the TECHDIV gave us, but we need a good recon to ensure we know up close and personal the status of the missile. They have already secured all electronic emitters except for their commercial surface radar, and that doesn't pose any danger of setting this thing off with its e-mers."

"E-mers?" the DCA inquired.

"EMR. Electromagnetic Radiation. We don't know how this weapon is going to behave after the accident. It may receive a signal from EMR that may cause it to fire."

"Damn, I knew we used our EMCON bill when transferring some types of ammunition, but I didn't think an accident . . . ."

"Oh yeah, but more on that later, DCA. We gotta get going. We'll be using hardwire comms. Ash, Zeke, you guys ready?"

"Yes, sir," they said in unison.

"Well, let's get going."

Normally at night, ships at sea only illuminate their navigational lights. *Normandy* now had all of her deck lights on to draw attention to herself and to give the EOD Techs some additional light to work with. On the bridge they passed word on Marine Band channel 16 warning all other ships to stay clear.

With their helmets in place, Ash and Zeke shuffled like toddlers bundled up for a day in the snow. They stepped through the hatch on the quarterdeck, and headed down the port side aft, to the VLS. Ash carried the response pack and Zeke brought the Mark-36 tool kit, spooling out the hard wire from the communications set.

Zeke set the comms box next to the helo, placed the tool kit on the deck and opened it. "Anything else?"

"Nah, I'm good," Ash responded, his voice fogging the face shield. Zeke leaned over to the microphone and raised his voice.

"P2 coming back up range."

"*CP, copy.*"

Ash surveyed the scene. The whole aft VLS looked eerie. The deck lights cast long shadows over everything and reflected off water sloshing on the deck as the ship rolled. The helicopter hissed and dripped. The missile that had once been bright white and orange was now definitely black.

The flight deck photo that the weapons officer provided was accurate. No explosive residue or fuel steamed out of the round. The missile appeared to be held firm underneath the missile ejection rack which seemed firm on the pylon protruding from the helo's fuselage.

"*P1, CP.*"

"P1."

"*P2 is back in the CP*"

"P1."

Ash stepped up to the missile with a flashlight in one hand and a pen and notebook in the other. He aimed the beam right on the seam where the MER met the pylon and where the missile met the MER. The seams were tight. Ash could not see the cable that sent the signal to the missile when the pilot squeezed the trigger.

Ash stepped back again. He drew a quick diagram on his notebook of the general layout of the missile. Next he pulled out the digital camera from his tool kit. He took several photos of the missile from different angles and several photos of the general layout of the scene.

"CP, P1. Initial look is as expected. Looks cooked."

"CP, roger. Have you pinned it yet?"

"Damnit. Negative. Wait one."

Ash went over to the response pack and pulled out two toggle pins. Stepping back to the helo, he pressed a button on the end of each and slid them into two holes on the MER. After releasing the button, he gently tugged on each to ensure they would hold. Now the missile ejection rack would not accidentally release the missile or drop from the aircraft.

"CP, P1. Pins in."

"Good P1, Look for the battery box. See if that's an option."

"Roger."

Ash shined his light on the missile again. He found the first seam where the nosecone of the missile met the main body of the weapon. From there, he guestimated eight inches back. He put his hand to the deck, soaking it with water. Ash rubbed the missile body where he thought the battery panel was. It was still warm to the touch, but Ash was able to rub off enough burnt paint to find the edge of the panel.

"CP, P1. I found it. Anything else I need to do before I come back?"

"Negative. If you're ready, come on home."

EIGHT

HEAT, SHOCK, FRICTION

Back in the CP, Ash stripped off all of his protective gear. Sweat ran off him like he was a melting snowman. January noticed it right away.

"Get some water, Ash. Calm down some, then we'll talk about your recon."

"Okay, sir. Check out the photos in the camera."

January called to his team ten minutes later.

"Okay guys, circle up," said January. "Willy suggested a plan that I like. It's KISS—keep it simple, stupid. Everyone, lets' see if we can shoot holes in it. Step one, we go down and remove the carts, putting them into a CMC."

"What's a CMC?" asked the XO.

"Closed metal container, sir, like an ammo box. It keeps the emers out."

"Got it."

"I talked with the pilot and he says they have the missile's shipping crate in the helo hangar. We're going to put it back in.

"First we access the battery compartment, disconnect the battery and put it in the emer safe plug on the two open ends. The aircrew has the plugs also. We'll close the panel back up for good measure.

"Okay, next we set the missile crate right underneath it. To do this we'll need two A-frames and two chain falls. Essentially, we lift the crate up under and around the missile. Then we disconnect it from the MER. It will fall a fraction of an inch to the bottom of the crate. Once it is free we lower the falls enough to put the lid on, then lower it down to the deck."

The XO, weapons officer, DCA, and each member of the detachment quietly visualized each of the steps. The DCA spoke first.

"I have falls. I don't have A-frames. But, I could make them. Heck, we could make you a tripod."

"Actually better," said January.

"How high?"

"Six feet," Ash piped in. "Six feet will do plenty."

Bailey, silent until now, rubbed his chin as he thought.

"I have a question."

"Shoot, Bailey," Willy said defensively.

"What do we do if the MER won't release the missile? I mean, it has been through a crash and a fire. It may not let it go."

"I hadn't thought of that," Willy admitted.

"It's okay, it's okay," De Napoli chimed in "It is a good plan. Let's go with it and cross that bridge if we come to it."

Ash donned his protective gear again. Zeke joined him again as the P2. Ash fought back crankiness. It was now well into the evening. He was tired physically and emotionally. Still, he felt that he should return to the site at least one more time.

Each Tech carried a CMC with him. Zeke also had a wooden pallet that Ash would secure the CMCs to. If the seas got rough they would stay in one place. Ash heard of EOD teams saving the day only to have the ordnance they rendered safe roll off the deck of the ship and into the ocean.

They set the CMCs down next to the aircraft. Zeke placed the pallet fifty feet away on the other side of the ship.

"CP, P1 downrange. Opening CMCs."

"CP."

Ash and Zeke lifted the lids off the CMCs to make the transfer of the carts go faster. It would not be wise for the P1 to fumble with the lid with an explosive cart in his hand.

"Ready?" Zeke asked.

"Sure, Zeke, I got it."

"CP, P2 coming back up range."

"CP, roger."

Ash stepped up to the MER and located the two carts. Like everything else, they were covered with soot. It surprised Ash that none of the explosives associated with the weapon detonated. The DCA definitely saved the day by cooling the weapon with water. He wondered if the properties of the explosives remained the same. Perhaps they were more sensitive now.

"P1, CP. P2 is back in the CP."

"Hooya. Removing first cart."

The cylindrical cart was threaded on the end. Its size reminded Ash of a 35-millimeter film canister. The cart required a lot of force to break it free, but then Ash was able to unscrew it by hand. As it came out Ash carefully set the cart into the CMC and closed the lid.

"CP, P1. First cart in CMC."

"Heard it click shut. Hooya."

He repeated the procedure with the second cart.

"CP, P1. I'm gonna secure these CMCs to the pallet now. Then I'll come home."
"Roger."

An hour later Ash helped to dress out Zeke and Bailey. Zeke was to be the P1 now. The two tripods were constructed and all other equipment staged. Willy spoke as they dressed.

"Fellas, take the crate down first. Then you'll know about what distance to place the tripods. Then take the falls. Zeke, do you have the plugs?"

Zeke padded his bomb suit like a best man feeling for wedding rings. He pointed to a pouch on the front breastplate.

"Yep, in here."

"Okay, let's do it."

As soon as they left the quarterdeck, Ash curled up in a ball on the floor. He laid his head on his waterproof bag.

"Willy, LT, call me if you need me."

He was asleep before they answered.

"Ash, get up."

When he opened his eyes, De Napoli was standing over him.

"We got more work for you."

He rose and stumbled like a zombie over to where Willy and January were standing.

"What's up?"

"We think we got some cutting to do," Willy said.

Zeke's voice came over the comms box.

"CP, P1. We're coming back."

"CP," January answered.

"What's happening?"

"They can't separate the missile from the MER. Zeke thinks we can cut off at the pylon."

"How?"

"Blow torch. The DCA is having one brought up now."

"Damn, Willy, what's the first thing they teach you at EOD school? Heat, shock and friction don't mix well with explosives. Who the hell is gonna do this?"

"You."

"What! Forget it."

Now De Napoli spoke up. "Ash, we took some convincing, too. Listen to Willy. I think he has a good point. Willy, tell him what you told us."

"Ash, this thing has experienced a heck of a lotta heat, shock and friction already. It didn't detonate when the helo crunched into the VLS, it didn't cook off when it was on fire."

"The DCA hit it with water."

"You won't be cutting on the weapon, you'll just hit a bead along the pylon."

By now Zeke and Bailey had returned. The whole det was looking at Ash.

"So why me?"

De Napoli was quick with the answer. "You used to be a Hull Technician. You are the best of us at using a blow torch."

"Heat, shock, friction."

"Chicken," replied De Napoli.

"Fine, I'll do it. But after this thing comes from together and turns me into a big pink mist, you're the motherfucker that mows my lawn every Saturday."

"In more ways than one, baby."

De Napoli deflected Ash's punch with his forearm. The whole detachment laughed at the two friends.

"Okay. Well, if I am going down there to put fire on the damn thing, I am not wearing the bomb suit. I cannot work with that on."

Willy and January looked at each other a moment. Both felt a modicum of responsibility for Ash's safety; January as the OIC, Willy as the det member who derived the plan.

Finally January said, "Okay."

Zeke helped Ash move all the bottles and equipment to the site. Ash looked at the work accomplished while he slept. The tripods were in place, the chain falls hung from each, and the crate was hoisted up around the missile. Then he looked at the MER.

"Zeke."

"Yeah."

"Did you guys pull the pins out?"

"Huh?"

"If you don't pull the pins out the thing won't release the weapon. You pulled the pins out before you tried to release it right?"

"Uh, yeah, we just replaced them afterward to be safe."

Ash looked at Zeke sideways.

"I'm not fooling, Ash, we pulled them out."

"Fine, go ahead back."

Ash had not done any cutting with a blowtorch in a long time. He checked again to make sure he set up the equipment properly. Then he donned the protective visor, aron, and gloves. He reminded himself that his work did not have to be neat, just a quick cut along the pylon so that it would separate from the fuselage.

"Okay, P1, P2 is back in CP."

"Got it."

He lowered the shield over his eyes and brought the torch to life. The cut went very quickly. When he was three quarters of the way across the weight of the missile tore it free. It dropped into the crate, which then swung free in the chain falls.

Ash turned off the blowtorch and raised the shield.

"P1, CP. We heard something—are you done?" came January's voice over the comms box.

"Yeah. It's clear."

"Ash, this the first time you ever cut on a weapon like this?"

"Yeah. I'll never do it again."

"First time, you're buying a case a beer buddy."

"Fuck you guys. You owe me much beer for this one."

*   *   *

The shrill whistle of a boatwain's pipe sliced open the early morning slumber of the men aboard *Normandy*. It resonated throughout the ship emanating from the 1MC, the ship's public address system.

"Reveille! Reveille! All hands heave out and trice up! Breakfast for the crew!"

There was no doubt in Ash's mind why this tradition remained after hundreds of years at sea. Even a sailor filled with last night's rum could not doze through it.

He rose up hitting his head on the rack above his. Cursing, he slid out of it onto the floor. His flight suit hung on a hangar by the locker corresponding to his bunk number. The ship's laundry washed all of the detachment's clothes during the night, their third at sea.

The chow line was already too long. Many of the sailors in line had obviously been on watch, awake for the last four to six hours. Others were early risers, ensuring they got their fill before relieving their shipmates who kept them safe during the night.

Ash headed to the aft gun mount, one level below the VLS deck. The sun was just rising into view. He saw the silhouette of a few other sailors in front of the red light racing over the horizon.

The hatch closed with a heavy, "CLINK!"

Ash turned and went up the ladder. There were more sailors there, silently studying the helo. They spoke quietly, as if at a funeral, out of respect for their fallen shipmate. Most of them did not know Lieutenant Commander Lung well, but they knew who he was. They had sailed with him; that was enough.

A quick look revealed that the ordnance recovered from the wreck was still secured on the pallet. They fashioned a makeshift lid for the missile to encase the weapon with the MER attached.

Ash walked back over to the port side where he performed his render safe procedure thirty-some hours before. The tripods were still there, but the chain falls were gone. He noticed a fire hose laid out, but nobody was manning it. The crew had long ago secured from general quarters, but they were still ready to respond in the unlikely event that the helo should re-flash.

Normandy did not return to Norfolk. She sailed further, up the York River to the pier at Naval Weapon Station Yorktown, Virginia. Tied up outboard of her was the salvage ship USS *Grasp*. Lieutenant Commander January spoke with the OIC of EOD Mobile Unit Two Detachment Yorktown. They would store the missile in a magazine for demolition later. Undoubtedly some data would be collected on its survivability for the program office and defense contractor that developed the missile.

Ash watched as the crane lifted the crate to a flatbed waiting on the pier. After the weapon was swung clear, *Grasp* would lift the aircraft onto its deck. Like the missile, it would be thoroughly studied by the crash investigation team.

Chief Smalls of Det Yorktown drove his compatriots back to their facility at Norfolk. As they left the weapon station he spoke over his shoulder.

"Hey, Ashland, saw your orders on the message board today, brother."

"Really? What'd they say?"

"You're going to Ingleside."

NINE

GRADUATION

Melanie was in the auditorium already feeding the baby again. Jazz stood just outside the entrance of EOD School's main building with his two sons. He kept his eyes on the road, watching for his parents.

The boys were unusually quiet.

"I'm very excited to have you guys pin on my crab."

"Yeah, we practiced," said Nick.

"You guys are awfully quiet."

Nick spoke up again. "Mommy said if we're good we get ice cream!"

Jazz looked at his reflection in the glass door again. He still wore the gold Surface Warfare pin above his ribbons. He was proud of the destroyer's bow steaming through the sea superimposed over crossed swords. Jazz worked hard to earn this warfare qualification. It was recognition of his tenure as a mariner.

Today he would not be awarded a warfare designation but a qualification—Basic EOD Technician. In about an hour, Nicholas would pin the silver EOD crab commonly called the "slick bomb" on the pocket below Jazz's ribbons.

The Admiral's grey Volvo turned left into the parking lot and pulled up to the entrance where Jazz and his sons were waiting. Eleanor got out and the Admiral drove on, looking for a parking spot.

"He's just parking the car, dear."

"The Admiral's not in uniform today?"

"He didn't want to upstage you on your day. He didn't want the focus to be shifted from you by all the fanfare of having a flag officer present."

The thought surprised Jazz and he suspected that it came from his mother. Jazz did not like to advertise that he was an admiral's son. Officers in the Surface community plagued him constantly with the question, "Are you Admiral Jascinski's kid?" Jazz knew that an answer in the affirmative was usually accompanied by the unspoken notion that any success he experienced was due to his lineage rather than his own talent or hard work.

It was yet another reason to move to Special Operations. The community had no admirals. As a result its officer corps was less political. Culturally, EOD men were measured by performance, not by the rank worn by their parents.

Melanie emerged from the schoolhouse cradling the baby, now sleeping.

"I finished just in time. They've just marched in all the Navy students. They're all in formation in the back of the auditorium."

"Oh, dear," said Eleanor. "Can I take her?"

"Sure, Mom. We've got a seat for her inside."

"Mel, Mom, why don't you take the boys inside and get a seat?" said Jazz.

"Sure," Melanie smiled. "They're being so good aren't they?"

"Yes, they are."

Both lads looked up at their dad and smiled at his approval.

"You guys are doing great. Nicholas, do you have my pin?"

"Right in here, Daddy," said the five-year-old patting his pocket.

As the family disappeared into the building Jazz spied his sons holding hands. The eldest cupped his hand to his mouth and whispered something to Tyler, a reminder about ice cream.

The Admiral walked up and extended his hand. Jazz shook hands with him.

"This is a great day, son."

"Yes, sir. 'Couldn't ask for better weather."

"No, I mean I'm proud of you," the Admiral replied.

Jazz imagined his mother reminding him to utter these words sometime during the course of the day. The Admiral could relax now knowing that he met his obligation.

The Admiral and his son stepped past the formation of naval students to the front of the auditorium. Jazz noted that the hall was set up as if there were a full class graduating. He did not expect that. There were chairs for fifty people, a lot more than would be attending for the three students graduating. The stage was decorated with the Stars and Stripes and the flags of each of the four services. On the curtain at the rear of the stage was the seal of NAVSCOLEOD and the Basic, Senior, and Master EOD badges. The whole area was surrounded by ordnance from the mine museum that were disarmed and cut in half so students could study their innards.

Jazz took his place in the front row next to Fireman Hopkins and Hull Technician Second Class Huang. His extended family sat several rows behind him.

"Huang," Jazz whispered, "do I recognize those two women?"

"You mean my dates?"

"Uh, yeah. Who are they?"

Huang grinned. "Strippers."

"Oh shit, it's Mercedes and Jasmine."

"My favorites."

Jazz started to laugh. "You dumb sonofabitch. Keep that shit low key."

"Gonna celebrate later, LT."

Jazz shook his head in disbelief.

Lieutenant Commander Massie eyed Huang's guests as he stepped up on the stage. He removed his smile by the time he reached the podium.

"Ladies and gentlemen, please rise. Naval School Explosive Ordnance Disposal, attention."

York came to attention and bellowed, "NAVSCOLEOD, ATTEN-HUT!"

The students came to attention.

Massie spoke again, "Ladies and gentlemen, please welcome the Commanding Officer of Naval School Explosive Ordnance Disposal, Captain Thomas Grant, United States Navy."

Jazz did not know the school's commanding officer well. He saw him at the base gym periodically, but never had reason to speak with him.

Captain Grant stepped up to the podium and surveyed the audience. Jazz noticed him trying not to react to Huang's guests.

"Thank you, please take your seats."

The guests all settled back into their chairs.

"Ladies and gentlemen, students and soon-to-be graduates, welcome to this momentous occasion at NAVSCOLEOD. Because we have only three sailors graduating today, the pinning ceremony will be short. Therefore I specifically requested that the XO have all Navy students here so that I can use this venue as an opportunity to have a Captain's Call. I hope that you will permit me to provide a brief history and heritage of the beginning of Explosive Ordnance Disposal."

Grant paused and took a drink of water.

"E.O.D. If I had a nickel for every time someone asked me, 'What the heck is EOD?' . . . I'd be a rich man.

"I assume everyone in here realizes that it stands for Explosive Ordnance Disposal, the military's bomb squad. As I further answer the question for the uninformed I explain to them that to be in EOD you have to have the hands of a surgeon, the brains of an engineer, and the courage of a martyr. I tell them that in the United States Navy, planes don't launch until EOD is on deck and amphibious landings don't occur until EOD says the way is clear. When my brethren in the SEAL Teams suggest with sibling rivalry that we are lacking in comparison, I remind them with pride that when you want a man to swim underneath the hull of a ship to place a limpet mine you call a SEAL. When you need a man to disarm and remove that mine, you call EOD.

"I also like to point out how Hollywood views this small community. John Wayne was used to portray a Seabee. Tom Cruise was a fighter pilot in 'TOP GUN.' Charlie Sheen was a Navy SEAL . . . but for EOD it was . . . Elvis."

The crowd laughed.

"The film was 'Easy Come, Easy Go' staring Elvis Presley. I highly recommend it."

The chuckles continued a moment. Jazz even heard the Admiral guffawing. Now Grant waited until their quiet returned.

"Draper Kauffman is our father. In fact, he is the father of all disposaleers and demolitioneers. This group includes EOD, SEALs, and the former UDT, the toughest and fittest brood in the United States Navy. And yet ironically Kauffman graduated from the United States Naval Academy in 1933 with a medical record that said he was unfit for service due to poor eyesight.

"Kauffman joined the Royal Navy in 1940 and volunteered for mine and bomb disposal. In short order he proved to be their best disposaleer. In November 1941, Lieutenant Kauffman returned to the United States on leave. He was subsequently recalled to U.S. Naval Service because it was realized that his bomb disposal experience would be invaluable to our own anticipated war effort.

"Lieutenant Kauffman founded the Bomb Disposal School on December 9, 1941 at the Washington Navy Yard. The first students were midshipmen from Northwestern and Columbia Universities. Lieutenant Kauffman remained the first officer in charge for a year and a half. During that time the school expanded to additional locations at American University and to the other side of this facility at Stump Neck, Maryland.

"During World War II, graduates of the Bomb Disposal School, commonly called 'Disposaleers,' formed units called Mobile Explosive Investigation Units. These men served with distinction in every theater of operation rendering safe ordnance, performing emergent disposals, and training their comrades. Countless lives and material were saved by these few.

"The World War II disposaleers are the forefathers of today's EOD Technicians. The Mobile Explosive Investigation Units were the precursors of today's Mobile EOD Units."

The room was silent. Captain Grant had the genuine interest of everyone present.

"Since World War II, EOD Technicians have served in every conflict this nation has been in. We especially proved our worth in Desert Storm, when Saddam Hussein flooded the Arabian Gulf with mines. Long after the troops came home, Navy EOD Techs were diving through a thick layer of oil disposing of hundred of mines on the sea floor.

"Many of you undoubtedly know of these men's exploits. If not, don't allow this to interrupt your studies here, but you must read each of the books that chronicle their service. Read them and come to understand our roots."

Grant paused yet again, sipping his water. Jazz noticed that his sons were still very quiet.

"Following his tour as OIC of the Bomb Disposal School, Kauffman was asked to form units that could be used to destroy beach obstructions and mines prior to amphibious landings. He thus formed the first Combat Demolition Units at Ft Pierce Florida, which later became known as Underwater Demolition Teams or UDT. Kauffman himself eventually commanded UDT Five.

"In 1961, the need for a maritime component to Special Warfare was formed using UDT men. This new unit was called SEALs, which stood for sea, air, and land. The UDT were disbanded in the early eighties, so now only EOD and SEALs remain. You will work with our Special Warfare brethren from time to time. Remind them at every opportunity that we were here first."

Grant smiled to himself as everyone in the audience again chuckled at his remark.

"Again, our purpose here today is to graduate three of the original seventeen men from EOD class Twenty Bravo Ninety Eight. Eventually the others in the back there will matriculate, but only after repeating portions of the difficult curriculum. Right gentlemen?"

"HOOYA, sir!" someone yelled.

"Hooya. Today Lieutenant Jascinski, Hull Technician Second Class Huang and Fireman Hopkins have completed the difficult curriculum of diving and disposal. From this day forward they are counted among the Navy's underwater warriors.

"Ladies and gentlemen, men of NAVSCOLEOD, never lose sight of what you have and will accomplish. It is difficult. It is honorable. It is brave."

Captain Grant paused.

"Well, perhaps that is enough for now. Let's pin it on these guys so they can go celebrate."

Melanie had a huge grin on her face as she positioned herself to snap photos of Nicholas and Tyler. Nicholas stood on a chair in front of Jazz, pinning the crab on the flap on his pocket. Concentrating, he stuck his tongue out.

After Nick stepped down, his younger brother pulled himself up onto the chair. Tyler squared his shoulders with his father, reared his fist back and slammed it into the crab, "tacking it on" against naval regulations.

"Hooya, Daddy!" he said.

The onlookers laughed and Melanie blushed. She practiced with her boys every day for a week.

After the strippers pinned on Huang, and Fireman Hopkins was pinned by his father, the ceremony ended. Everyone shook hands, punched shoulders, and "Hooya-ed" the graduates. Melanie held the Jascinski clan back for more photos while everyone else filed out.

She directed photos of Jazz, she and Jazz, their whole family together, and of Jazz and his parents.

"Now, one just with you and your father," said Eleanor.

The Admiral and Jazz stood next to each other. The Admiral extended his hand again and Jazz took it. They shook once holding it for the flash.

How official, thought Jazz.

Huang and Hopkins left to give their guests a tour of the facilities. They planned to go to the training pool, and the buildings and practice areas for Ground and Air Ordnance Divisions. Jazz wanted to get back home. The boys behaved well and surely needed some ice cream.

Back at the house, Jazz stripped off his sons' church clothes and sent them downstairs wearing only gym shorts.

"Jazz!" Melanie yelled from downstairs.

"What, hon?"

"Shirts! We have company!"

Jazz selected two shirts from one of the boy's dressers and headed downstairs.

In the kitchen the Admiral handed him a beer.

"Let's go outside."

Jazz stood next to the picnic table on their back porch. He sipped his beer, waiting, feeling the Admiral had something important to say.

"It's a hell of a thing you did today."

Jazz could not tell by his father's voice if this was a compliment or an admonition.

"Uh, yes, sir."

"No, I mean it. You should be proud."

"Thank you, sir."

"I have two gifts for you. The first is a piece of advice. Don't worry as much about being a good EOD Tech because you'll never measure up. Be a good officer, a good 1140, a good OIC. The bomb tech stuff will come, but your success or failure will be based upon your performance as an officer."

"Thanks, sir. That is good advice."

Both men drank in silence a few minutes more until Eleanor opened the door, interrupting them. She smiled and handed her husband a gift.

"Here's the present dear."

"Thanks, Eleanor. Give us a moment will you?"

When she closed the door he handed the box to Jazz.

"Open it."

Jazz set his beer down on the picnic table. He took the parcel from his father's hands. It was wrapped in shiny gold paper and blue ribbon. Jazz noticed that it had some weight to it.

He slid the ribbon off and peeled back the paper. Then he opened the box. Inside was a knife. It was a dive knife. Jazz recognized the black plastic handle and the darkened blade. It was the Mark-III, the mission knife used by UDT, SEALs, EOD, and other specialized diving units.

"Holy cow, sir! Where did you get this?"

"In my cruise box."

"What?" Jazz was confused. "Uh, I didn't put it there . . ."

"It's mine. Was mine."

"What!"

Admiral James J. Jascinski sat down at the table and took another long drag from his beer draining it.

"Sit down."

Jazz sat.

"What I'm about to tell you is in confidence. Nobody in my family knows, probably nobody left on active duty. Only your mother, and now you, are aware of this."

Jazz noticed that his father was whispering.

"I tried out for UDT."

"What!" Jazz exclaimed.

"I washed out. I rang the bell. I quit."

Now Jazz was speechless.

"I volunteered during my first tour aboard USS *Spiegel Grove*. I had heard of UDT, and had seen the guys around the base at Little Creek. I went from *Spiegel Grove* right to UDT Replacement Training."

"Excuse my French, Admiral, but holy shit! I had no idea."

"Yes well, I did not want anyone to know. I rang the bell after four weeks into it. Before the day was out, I was thoroughly ashamed of myself. I had never failed in anything in my whole life.

"I tried to get back into training, but of course they wouldn't let me. It was too late. I was given orders to a new ship, and I never spoke of it to anyone again until now."

The Admiral paused, letting what he just said to sink in. Jazz unsheathed the knife and looked at it.

"When I left UDT training, I had to turn in my gear. Fins, mask, UDT vest. But I couldn't find the knife. I signed some paperwork for it and then discovered it in my sea bag weeks later. I almost threw it away, but I didn't. I couldn't. I decided to keep it as a memento of my failure, a symbol of my lack of fortitude. I put all my shame and weakness into that knife and locked it in my cruise box. I became determined to never again fail at anything.

"Not often, but periodically I would return to the knife. Sometimes by accident, sometimes on purpose, to remind myself of what it felt like to fail . . . so that I would never fail again."

"Damn."

"Yes, well. Perhaps you know a little more about me now. James, I genuinely thought you were making a mistake by doing this. I wanted a career for you, command at sea, admiral, everything. I wanted you to have a career like mine. No, I'd hoped you'd accomplish more than I did in my career. I even dared to hope you'd become Chief of Naval Operations. Leaving the mainstream Navy, going into this EOD thing, well all that was gone."

Jazz heard his father's voice cracking. He looked up at the Admiral. Jazz saw moisture in his eyes and his skin had crimsoned.

"Remember that night that you and Melanie came to the house?" asked the Admiral.

"When I told you we were gong to Ingleside? Yeah, I remember."

"Well, your mother and I had a knock-down-drag-out fight that night. She was angry with me for my behavior, said we'd never see you again. She gave me the full 'Come to Jesus' routine, a real hum-dinger. Of course I was having none of it. I swear it was the ugliest fight of our marriage.

"Afterward she banished me to my 'At—Sea Cabin.'"

"The basement?"

"Precisely. I sat down on the couch to watch TV and put my feet up on my coffee table down there."

"The cruise box."

"Right. So anyway, I opened it and found that damn thing. I looked at it and thought about things for a long damn time. Finally I realized that the knife had changed. I no longer felt like a failure for quitting UDT training and more importantly that it didn't matter that you were never going to be CNO."

Then the Admiral began to openly weep. He looked down and held his breath for a moment.

"I realized that you already have accomplished the one thing I never could."

A moment of silence passed before Jazz managed a, "Thanks, sir."

Jazz then smiled at his father and sheathed the knife. He stood and stepped past him to the door. He knew that James J. Jascinski Sr. needed time to himself.

"Son."

"Yes, Dad."

"Tell your mother I'm going for a walk. I'll be back."

"Yes, sir."

Jazz went inside and showed Melanie the knife his father found for him in an antique shop.

TEN

INGLESIDE

It was a short drive from Portland to Ingleside but the two places seemed a world apart. Jazz left the manicured lawns and franchised restaurants of Portland's suburbia and headed for Ingleside's Oncelerville of oil refineries and chemical plants dotting the Corpus Christi Bay. On his left were cotton fields, Jazz's proverbial grickle-grass. Their spots of white and brown reminded him of a spice cake. After a week Jazz was still amazed at how flat the land was. The miles upon miles of uninterrupted view reminded him of being at sea. You could see a pick-up truck, whipping up dust as it drove toward you from ten miles away.

Jazz guided the car down Ingleside's Main Street for the third time in the past week. He drove past the breakfast burrito shop, a myriad of drinking establishments, and on towards the naval base.

A sign at the main gate read:

Naval Station Ingleside
Mine Warfare Center of Excellence

Two days before he visited the base just to orient himself. He had driven along the waterfront passing the piers and the quay wall slowly so that he could take a good look at all of the ships in port. Twenty-two Mine Coastal Hunters and Mine Countermeasures ships were stationed in Ingleside. At any given time two or three were at sea and one or two were in the shipyard, but there was always a flock in port.

The larger Mine Countermeasure Ships or MCMs were christened with names that denoted bravery; *Avenger, Warrior, Chief*. The MHCs were named for birds; *Osprey, Black Hawk, Commorant*. Many of the MHCs had the same logo as their professional sport counterparts, *Oriole, Raven, Cardinal*.

Then there was the USS *Inchon*, towering over her charges. The Mine Warfare Command Ship was converted from an Amphibious Assault Ship six years before. A ship of the *Iwo Jima* class, she was the shape and size of a World War II aircraft carrier. *Inchon* looked very much like her older sister, USS *Lexington*, which now sat across the bay in the Corpus Christi Harbor, a museum and memorial of Admiral Marc Mitscher and the other men who served aboard her.

After Desert Storm, the Navy needed a ship to conduct command and control of mine warfare forces. *Inchon* became the answer to this problem. She was to command the MCM triad of EOD divers, surface ships, and helicopters.

Jazz drove in the main entrance and turned left, heading for the building that housed Explosive Ordnance Disposal Mobile Unit Six Detachment Ingleside. He smirked remembering that his new commanding officer disapproved of the title, "Detachment Ingleside."

Two weeks earlier, the Jascinski family stopped through Charleston, South Carolina, on their way to Texas. Charleston was home to Jazz's command, Explosive Ordnance Disposal Mobile Unit Six. Stationed here was the command element including the commanding officer and his staff, a training department, a diver locker, a detachment of minehunting sea lions, and five MCM detachments.

Jazz spent two days there in order to meet the commanding officer, the executive officer, the operations officer, and the men of the training department.

The captain, Commander Solarsky, was insistent that there was no such entity as "Det Ingleside."

"Don't ever let me hear or see anything with 'Det Ingleside' on it," he had said with a raspy voice.

"Aye, aye, sir."

"When that place was established there was some fool notion that the folks down there would not deploy, that it was a shore det. They decided on their own that they were to develop Mine Warfare Tactics. Horsepucky! I have seven MCM detachments, two of which just happen to be in Texas. Are we clear?"

"Yes, sir."

Solarsky and Jazz had a long philosophical discussion about being an EOD officer. As the commander explained it, there were two types of 1140, those who belonged to the SEALs, and those who belonged to the fleet. The pseudo-SEAL officers in his mind were "wanna-bes." They focused on fast-roping, parachuting, and small arms training. These men tended to be weak on demolition procedures and dangerous as divers and EOD Technicians.

"Most of those somabitches couldn't render safe a candle with a bucket of water," he said.

The other type according to Solarsky were pseudo-SWOs, they were ship-drivers, and divers. They focused on diving, demolition, and render safe procedures.

"Don't get me wrong, Mr. Jascinski, we are operators. All of the mobility skills are important. Just remember that they are not why you are here. You wanna cut throats and eat snakes, go with the frogs. You wanna swim into enemy waters and blow up mines, or render safe IEDs then this is for you."

Jazz actually found the discussion interesting. He sensed the division within EOD already, but Solarsky was the first to verbalize it.

"Which kind are you gonna be, Lieutenant?" he challenged.

"Uh, the second kind, sir."

"Damn right."

Solarsky's final remark was a reminder that Det Four was a mobile detachment and did not have the full responsibility of a shore detachment to respond to improvised explosive devices offbase.

"Warrant Officer Fontaine will explain in detail. In any case, if you have to respond to an IED always report to the command duty officer here so we know what you're doing. Got it?"

"Yes, sir."

As Jazz pulled into the parking lot he noticed that all three high bay doors were open. Inside he spied rubber boats of all sizes, pickup trucks, HUMMVEEs, and horse trailers. He saw dive gear hanging on drying racks and Mark-16s and scuba jugs laid out on a cart. Several EOD Techs were moving around the compound, shirtless in khaki UDT shorts and boots, the divers called "utes and boots." It was obvious that they just returned from an early morning dive.

I am gonna love this, he thought. *The captain was right, these guys are operators.*

The front of the building was all office space. The first offices were empty. Jazz guessed they must belong to Det Two. The second set then belonged to Det Four, his detachment.

A barrel-chested diver was sitting at one of the desks. Jazz noted immediately that he was wearing salt-stained shorts and a T-shirt.

Is this always the uniform here? he wondered.

"Good morning."

The man looked up from his paperwork.

"Good morning, sir. You must be the new OIC."

"I am."

The diver stood, came from behind the desk and extended his hand.

"Welcome aboard, sir. I'm Chief Keating."

"Lieutenant James Jascinski."

"Great. Well you actually came on a bad day, sir. Most of the det is gone right now. Warrant Officer Fontaine, Senior Chief Reed, Petty Officer Quinn, and Petty Officer Sinclair are on a Secret Service job. Petty Officer Ball, he's a new guy, is at Hazardous Materials Preparer's Course. So, SK1 Delgado and I are the only ones in house."

"What did you say Ball was doing?"

"Haz-Prep Course, sir. We have to have at least one person on the det certified to ship hazardous materials on aircraft. They learn how to properly package, store, and most important to prepare the paperwork required when we travel with explosives, diving gas, ammunition, fuel . . ."

"Got it. Fontaine and the others on the Secret Service op, where'd they go?"

"Houston, Texas, sir. The President comes in there about once a quarter."

"Hmm . . . good. We do much Secret Service support here?"

"Not really, sir. We pretty much eat, sleep, and breathe MCM."

"That is what I've heard, Chief. So, are you busy right now? I'd like to get the lay of the land."

"A tour? No problem, sir. We can do that."

Adjacent to the offices in the front of the building was a conference room. After the conference room was the passage to the rear of the building. There was a locker room with showers and a large vault shared by both detachments that housed all of the classified material.

The six inch steel door was open but an inner door that looked like a gate was closed. Inside was a skinny black man dressed in utes and boots. His blue t-shirt had bold yellow letters on the back that read:

BOMB SQUAD
TECHNICIAN

IF YOU SEE THIS MAN RUNNING
TRY TO KEEP UP!

Chief Keating knocked on the cage.

"Hey Dee, come meet the new OIC."

The Tech stood and opened the cage.

"Hi, sir. SK1 Delgado. Guys call me 'Dee.'"

"Nice to meet you, I'm Lieutenant James Jascinski."

"Welcome to Ingleside."

"Thanks."

Keating spoke up.

"Delgado's in charge of publications and manuals. He maintains all pubs classified and unclassified. He also controls all of the crypto gear, radios, encrypted GPS and the like."

"Good, I'm sure we'll be doing a turnover of secret material in the next few days. I look forward to getting to know you."

"Me too, sir."

"What are you doing now?"

"Downloading message traffic. We get it right here in the vault via that desktop computer over the base LAN."

"Great. We'll let you get back to it."

"Yes, sir."

The rear of the building had a dive locker for maintenance and storage of all the diving gear, an equipment office, an equipment storage room, and the highbay.

Detachment Two was still cleaning gear from their morning dive. Chief Keating introduced Jazz to each of the men, but he was not retaining any of their names.

Jazz and Keating stepped on the trailer and climbed into Det Four's twenty-four foot, rigid hull inflatable boat or RHIB. RHIBs became very popular for use by the U.S. Navy in the late 80's and early 90's especially for specialized units. The boat incorporates a strong fiberglass hull giving strength and allowing speed through the water. Just above the waterline inflatable rubber pontoons comprise the freeboard. The pontoons give the RHIB superior stability, especially in rough seas.

The RHIBs the Navy bought for MCM detachments had twin 150 horsepower engines with a hard mounted towing bar above them. They employed a single center console design so that there was plenty of deck space for an EOD team to travel great distances, up to 150 nautical miles, with all of their diving and support equipment. The whole boat was painted a camouflage scheme of light blue and gray. From a short distance the RHIB's outline would not catch even an observant eye.

"You're going to spend a lot of time in this boat," Keating remarked.

Det Four also had a fifteen-foot Mark-5 rubber boat for operating onboard the MCMs and MHCs and an F470 for casting out of aircraft. Keating explained that one crew cab pickup, one standard pickup, and one HUMMVEE belong to Det Four. They also had a container box about a third of the size of a tractor trailer. It housed the fly-away dive locker, or FADL, that was used to perform maintenance on all of the det's diving equipment.

After the tour Jazz and Keating headed back to the front of the building.

"Is there a place to stow my gear, Chief?"

"Uh, yes, sir. There is a locker in the officer's head for you to use for uniforms, civvies and PT gear. There is a bigger locker in the back for your dive gear, field equipment. All your hooya stuff."

"Great. I've got some gear to move in."

Some of the initial issue gear he obtained in Charleston. A pair of command sweats, t-shirt, and shorts went into the locker in the officer's head. A Protec helmet, mask, fins, snorkel, booties, and gloves went into the locker in the equipment room. He pulled out the mission knife that the Admiral had given him and hung it by its straps on a hook in the back of the locker.

Jazz looked at it for a moment. He wondered if his father was really free of his own notions of failure. Jazz felt that he was mostly free of his father's expectations. He thought that perhaps the knife was finally, just a knife.

Now it will get some good use, he thought.

Since it was a quiet day at the det, Jazz decided to obtain the service records of his new shipmates and review them. He went to the personnel office on base. As the relieving OIC he had the authority to draw and review his men's records at any time. It was a common practice when checking onboard a command, but he did not want to do it in front of Keating. Jazz drove home with the service records on the passenger seat.

Melanie was not home. Jazz figured she went to the pool with the kids. He surveyed the ranch house they were renting. They still had not unpacked all of the boxes. Melanie leaned pictures against the wall below the spot she thought they would go.

Jazz stripped to shorts and sunglasses, smeared sunscreen over his body and got a beer from the refrigerator.

I will never get used to this heat, he thought as he sat down at the picnic table.

Jazz skipped Reed's record and went right to Keating's. He wanted to find out more about the man he met today.

Keating spent his whole career in naval diving. He started as a fleet diver, working in the salvage Navy. All of his evaluations were glowing for the first ten years. Keating was on his way to reaching the pinnacle of the Navy's diving community as a Master Diver.

Then something odd happened, instead of continuing to pursue this path, Keating applied for EOD and was accepted. His first assignment in EOD was at EOD Mobile Unit Four in Key West, Florida working with mine-hunting mammals.

Damn, Jazz thought. *This guy has forgotten more about diving than I'll ever learn.*

Next Jazz perused SK1 Delgado's record. Delgado was not an EOD Tech very long; his two year anniversary would be in the fall. Jazz was surprised that 'Storekeeper' was a rate allowed into EOD. Most of the rates were ordnance related; Gunner's Mate, Aviation Ordnancemen, Torpedomen. Others were classic Navy rates with obvious advantages in the diving world; Boatswain's Mate, Enginemen, Hull Technician.

Jazz surmised that as a Storekeeper, Delgado was perfect for the pubs vault. He undoubtedly had the management skills required to maintain hundreds of volumes of ordnance related manuals.

The Texas sun worked Jazz into a good sweat. Sunblock started to run into his eyes. He went back into the house to clear his eyes and grab another beer.

Melanie came home while Jazz had his head in the fridge.

"Jazz, I'm home!" she called out.

He looked up.

"Daddy!" The boys squealed simultaneously, running toward him with outstretched arms. Jazz quickly set his beer down. He scooped up his sons in a bear hug. Growling, he ran around the room with them as they laughed with glee. Finally he set them down, collapsing in feigned exhaustion.

Melanie was laughing as she handed Jazz the baby.

"What is so funny?"

"I always wanted to say that, 'Hey hon, I'm home!' You're home early. Is this how the EOD thing goes? I like it."

"Yeah, we'll see."

Melanie picked up the beer from the counter and drank from it.

"Damn, it's hot."

"Yeah it is. So'd you go to the pool?"

"Yep, met one of the other wives."

"Oh. Who?"

"Jeannie Ball. She is married to Ted Ball."

"I haven't met him yet."

"She said he's at some school. Anyway she's very nice and I was very cool about the whole 'officer's wife' thing."

"Good."

The Navy has strict etiquette regarding relationships between officers and enlisted men. This often spilled over to the wives' support groups. Melanie had seen it in their previous wardroom functions. One memory that remained with her was from a luncheon she attended shortly after she gave birth to Nicholas. Children were not invited.

After two hours of tea and small talk she began excusing herself. The hostess cornered her.

"Melanie, honey you can't leave yet," she whispered.

"What?"

"The captain's wife is still here. Nobody can leave until after she does."

"I have a babysitter that needs to go to work and an infant that needs to be fed. I'm sorry, but I'm going."

Everyone else was pleasant but she knew that they were talking about her as she drove down the street.

"I would have pumped my breast milk and had the sitter feed my baby."

"She thinks she's special because her husband's an admiral's son."

Melanie never went to another officer wives' function. She went with Jazz for the group functions only because it was a political necessity.

The enlisted and officers' wives did not mingle. Oddly Melanie found the separation to be more driven by the enlisted wives that the other way around. She was often treated differently and even shunned by other women when they discovered she was married to an officer.

The Jascinski's heard and hoped that the EOD world was different. Because of the small number of officers, familiarity with the men was simply unavoidable. The more relaxed relationship of the men carried over to their families. Melanie decided that she would make an extra effort to fit in.

After she put the kids down for a nap, Melanie joined Jazz on the patio.

"Whatcha reading?"

"Service records."

"Isn't that a little creepy?"

"Nah, it is important to know who I'm working with. I've just been reading about Ball. What did you say his wife's name was?"

"Jeanine, but she goes by Jeannie."

"Yeah, anyway, he seems like a good guy. Hell, they are all good people. They wouldn't get into EOD if they weren't."

"Who else do you have in the det?"

"Well, apparently this is a period of personnel transfers. There's a Senior Chief Reed who is leaving soon. He came here from the shore det in Earle, New Jersey. I've got a Chief Keating who I met today. He is good to go, a very experienced diver. There's a guy named Quinn, a guy named Sinclair, and an SK who I met today named Delgado."

"A Storekeeper?"

"Yeah, I thought that strange too. I guess it is a source rating. Anyway all three of them came here right from EOD school, but not recently. Delgado is coming up on two years. The others have been here longer."

"Was the warrant in today?"

"No, most of them were on a Secret Service mission in Houston."

"Ooh, 007 stuff," Melanie said sarcastically, with a smile.

"You really don't care about this stuff do you?"

"Not impressed in the least. I told you before, I'm proud of you, but not impressed by what you do. What makes me happy is seeing you excited about this. That's what is sexy."

"Don't use that word around me right now."

"Sex?" she giggled.

"Please I can't take it."

Melanie stood up, leaned over and kissed Jazz softly.

"Care for a nooner, 007?"

"Hooya."

ELEVEN

NASIH

Nasih decided to check his email messages one more time before his meeting with Gabriel.

```
From: smit1941
To: bb6
Subject: toolbox
    I looked in my basement and my toolbox was not there.
The wife must have sold it at a yard sale or something.
```

The message angered him so much that, screaming with rage, he ripped the monitor from its cable and threw it across the room.

"Toolbox" was the codeword for the weapons that he was importing into the United States. By using "basement" in the email as well as the phrasing, the author was telling him that the shipment was lost. "Wife" meant that the American's captured it at sea.

The United States Navy boarded and searched *Green Leon*. Her cargo, weapons and explosives intended for his operatives in America, were confiscated along with the ship.

Nasih's mission was just postponed two years, but his dignity could not wait that long. Now he would be unable to supply his cells, he would have to move only with his insurgents. Suddenly, Gabriel and his friends grew in importance.

I will still be able to count on the Italians, he thought calming himself down.

Nasih descended the stairs from his apartment above the Army-Navy store in Aransas Pass. The manager was coming toward him from the front of the building.

"Is everything alright, hon?"

"Oh, yes, Mrs. Shields. I was moving my monitor and I dropped it. I'm fine really."

Nasih was adept at creating plausible lies. He smiled at his landlady as he got into his Land Cruiser.

Nasih had long ago decided that his intelligence was a curse. He resented the fact that his wealthy father had the ability to send him to the best schools. It indoctrinated him in the faith, but the analytical ability it provided also led to his removal from the battlefield.

He knew that something special was going to happen when he was summoned to the council from the position where he was fighting the Soviets. There were rumors that he was going to the Balkans to be a leader in the jihad planned there. He would never forget what his leader said that night in the dessert.

"I want to say before the whole council that taking you from the battlefield in this case is not an insult. It is an honor. In fact you have been chosen because of your ability for a different battlefield, one that is far more dangerous and that requires more courage and more cunning . . . ."

Nasih was still disappointed. For fifteen years now he trained cells of the faithful, in Libya, Afghanistan, the Sudan, and Yemen then inserted them in Europe, especially the Balkans, and finally the United States. In the last six years, he also trained and guided insurgents, members of the local populations whose means satisfied Nasih's ends. Only in the Balkans did he have any real effect. He needed something big to happen in the United States. Nobody thought of him as a warrior any more.

Nasih tried to re-focus his thoughts as he drove the quiet road slicing through the length of the barrier island named Mustang.

Soon there will be hotels here, he thought.

He was certain that the cancer of alcohol and debauchery that accompanies western beach resorts was spreading from South Padre Island even now. Unless something changed, it would only be a matter of time before these sand dunes would be soiled with western sin.

The notion reminded him of Dubai, where he was assigned to work in a shop that catered to the British ex-patriots and oil company employees so that he could learn English and begin a study of the great adversary. While he was there he watched miles of pristine oceanfront become scarred with skyscrapers, plush hotels and condominiums.

Nasih gripped the steering wheel of his Land Cruiser, recalling that the buildings themselves actually angered him. He was certain that western corporations, and really the Jews, were behind it all. It was clear in their design. Their height was a western symbol of power, with no attached practicality in the Middle East. Why build a seventy-story high-rise when there is plenty of open desert to spread into?

Ironically Dubai's behemoths lay mostly dormant. Their only real attraction was their own luxuriousness and they were priced for only the wealthiest of tourists. They did not even employ the local population; the staffs were imported from Pakistan and the Philippines.

Nasih wondered how many local businessmen put their life savings into the hotels after being assured by the aristocracy that their investment would return ten-fold. How many herders' sons were lured away from their father's house, only to be cheated out of their wages? To make matters worse, those footing the bill and watching the progress from the air conditioning of their luxury limos did not care if it all collapsed. The wealthy knew before it began that their cousins in government would subsidize them. If the elite did not make their money from the bending backs of the herders and merchants, they would make it from their taxes.

While he watched all of this happen, Nasih patiently did as he was directed; he learned English and bided his time.

He turned left, leaving the pavement and crossed through an access road cut through the dunes onto the beach. The wind was still today, a pleasant surprise. Once reaching the beach proper, Nasih turned left again and headed north with the sea on his right.

In a short time he saw the mile marker that he was looking for. Nasih stopped the truck and got out. He walked north a little more, surveying his surroundings. As far as he could see, there were only two other vehicles stopped on the beach. Both appeared to be older men fishing. There was some traffic, but it was light. Most people were still working on this early Wednesday afternoon. Nasih determined that there was only one vehicle passing on the beach before him every ten minutes.

He walked up one of the dunes for a better vantage and to ensure that there was nobody on the other side. It was clear.

After years of attempting to completely rid himself of the practice, he still had to remind himself not to squat in the manner of his childhood. He doubted that anyone would recognize it as the habit of an Arab, but they might think he was trying to take a shit. It would be poor form to attract the attention of a park ranger.

Looking out at the Gulf of Mexico, Nasih again focused on the memories of Dubai. He imagined, fantasized really, that maybe here his work, his patience, would finally come to fruition. Maybe his disappointment at being selected to leave the battlefield in Afghanistan would finally be wiped clean. Maybe his years of murderous restraint while smiling and being pleasant with the condescending British and the arrogant Americans, would be released. Maybe through this intrigue and manipulation the will of Allah would finally be done. Maybe it would be Allah's providence that he should save this beach.

The thought was interrupted by Gabriel's arrival. Nasih looked up as the American's truck came into view. He parked ten yards from the Land Cruiser, got out and walked up the dune.

Nasih expected that working with Gabriel's group would be another unpleasant necessity. He was surprised to find that he somewhat enjoyed teaching them. He had long since divorced himself from any notion of understanding their purpose, but he admired their passion. He recalled the ecstasy of jihad in Afghanistan, the joy of being able to direct his anger. Nasih watched his training evoke the same emotions in Gabriel and his friends. They would be ready soon.

"Good afternoon, Gabriel."

"Hello."

"How was your trip?"

"Successful. I brought my ID. Do you want to see it?"

"I don't see why not."

Gabriel already had it in his hand. Nasih took it and scrutinized it.

"Perfect. You did well. Any mishaps?"

"None."

Nasih knew already that he did not have to ask Gabriel twice.

"How is construction of the units coming?"

"Good. We have some more to do, but it is coming along. We are on schedule."

"I would not say that you are on schedule. It was important to be careful, but obtaining the identity cards took a little longer than I expected," Nasih lied. "Sadly there is no room for error now, Gabriel. We are running out of time."

"Don't worry. We'll be ready. I promise."

"I hope so. I do have other clients you know."

"I know."

Nasih looked up and down the beach again. There were still only the two fishermen. He sensed nervousness in Gabriel's posture.

Good, thought Nasih. *Just a little more and these men will be ready to explode*—literally.

"Walk with me to my car, Gabriel."

As Nasih got into the driver's seat he said, "Look on the passenger seat. Do you see that envelope?"

"Yes," replied Gabriel.

"Pick it up."

Gabriel picked up the manila envelope and opened it.

"Inside, you will find my contact information, a new cell phone number and email address. Contact me if there are any issues that will keep us from our schedule. Understand?"

"Yes."

Nasih turned the engine on. Gabriel backed away from the rumbling SUV and watched Nasih put in gear and drive away. Nasih looked out to the sea and frowned. He hoped that the units would be ready on time.

*   *   *

Jazz and Fontaine began turning over responsibility for EOD Mobile Unit Six Detachment Four after the warrant officer returned from the unexpected Secret Service gig. On Monday, inventory of the dive gear was scheduled for the morning and tours of the *Pioneer, Kingfisher,* and *Inchon* were slated for the afternoon.

T-Ball was the dive locker petty officer. He came in early and skipped morning PT to lay out all of the gear. As a result the inventory went smoothly. Jazz counted fourteen sets of scuba jugs, six Mark-16s, twelve lo-mu knives, ten masks, ten depth gauges, fourteen regulators, and a wide variety of test equipment and tools. As he counted each, checked the serial numbers, and signed the inventory sheet assuming responsibility for the gear, T-Ball neatly stowed the items in the appropriate drawer or shelf.

Fontaine wanted to give Jazz a familiarization tour of the *Inchon* and one ship from each class of minesweeper. So after the inventory, the two officers took the det HUMMVEE down to the waterfront. The doors and back window were never on it in the summertime, but the canvas roof never came off. Its diesel was very loud, but Jazz tried to ask Fontaine a few questions anyway.

"How often are you guys able to dive!" he yelled.

Fontaine kept his eyes forward, but turned his face toward Jazz yelling back.

"We try to get wet once a week, but sometimes it's difficult. What often happens is we'll get a ton of dives one month and less the next. For example, you have an exercise coming up with USS *Scout*. You will have long days of diving for about a week. You may not dive again until Readiness Training in Virginia."

Fontaine pulled the HUMMVEE into a spot adjacent to the pier and cut the engine.

"Captain Solarsky said I should ask about how you guys respond to IED calls in town."

"Yeah. It is actually a little complicated. Remind me to tell you about that later."

They started with a tour of *Pioneer*. The MCM's had an organic sonar and a sophisticated suite of computers to analyze the incoming data.

"These guys are good. It amazes me sometimes the stuff they find," Fontaine said.

Pioneer's fantail was covered with sweep gear designed to detonate influence mines and special cutters to part the cables of contact mines lying just below the ocean's surface. She also had a remotely piloted vehicle, or ROV, that could hunt for mines with its own sonar. *Kingfisher* was similar to *Pioneer*, only smaller. The MHCs did not have the exotic sweep gear, but as a result their fantails were wide open.

"We prefer to embark onboard these ships as a result," Fontaine explained from the open spot on *Kingfisher's* stern. "There is plenty of space for our Mark -5 inflatable and all of our gear."

Finally, the two boarded the Mine Warfare Command Ship. The hangar deck of the *Inchon* reminded Jazz of an aircraft carrier. It was probably fifty feet off the waterline, higher than the bridge on *Pioneer* or *Kingfisher*. It was about the size of four basketball gyms in length, width, and height. Fontaine explained that it housed the MH-53E Sea Dragon Helicopters, the Navy's mine-hunting variant of the Super Stallion.

"We call 'em 'Hurricanes.' And let me tell you they are big sombitches."

"How do they work?"

"What, you mean finding mines? Well, the helos drag a 'fish' behind 'em on a cable. It has sonar onboard that sends a signal to the operator in the back. The operator marks every contact and its position is recorded. The squadron has a CIC of sorts a few decks above us where all the data is downloaded, analyzed and disseminated. Sometimes we get info in a few hours. I've dove contacts in the late afternoon that a Hurricane found that morning. The helos also employ a sled that they can drag behind that sweeps for influence and contact mines. Just like the MCMs."

Behind the hangar deck laid an open space that belonged to EOD Mobile Unit Six.

"It is still called 'Aft V,'" Fontaine explained. "Used to be Marine Aft Vehicle Storage when they were aboard. We can fit three FADLs, a Fly-Away Recompression Chamber, and a support skid back here. It becomes EOD-land very quickly."

The rest of Fontaine's *Inchon* tour was unremarkable. He showed Jazz office space and berthing that was used by EOD. The most interesting part of the *Inchon* tour for Jazz was the boat davits. Modified with new cradles, winches, and cranes for raising and lowering EOD RHIBs, the Mine Warfare Command Ship could launch four at any time.

Back in the detachment's shop, Jazz asked again about responding to IEDs.

"You told me to remind you about IED incidents in town. I talked with Solarsky about it when I visited the command in Charleston. He said we only go out in a few circumstances."

"Not exactly true. Like I said, it is actually a little complicated. First, we do not have jurisdiction down here. Geographically it belongs an Army EOD unit in San Antonio, the 797th."

"Wow, that's two hours away."

"Right. Remember that we are a mobile det, not a shore detachment. So we have a memorandum of understanding to respond to calls out in town only when in extremis. If the stuff is stable, or once it is stable, you call the Seven-Niner-Seven."

"Then they come pick it up?"

"Yeah. We have transported stuff up there for them a few times when we have been free and they've been busy. As a result, they allow us to use their demolition range for training from time to time."

"Hmmm."

"Listen, you are not going to have to deal with this anyway. The ordnance that we find down here is usually either old World War II mines that get caught in commercial fishnets or hand grenades that grandpa brought back from the war. So, don't worry about it. You will never have to respond to an IED."

At the day's end Jazz went into the conference room and grabbed a beer from the refrigerator. He studied the plaques and photos around the room. Most were given as in appreciation for one of the EOD det's support during a Gulf or Squadron Exercise.

HOOYA TO DET TWO RONEX 95-1. FROM THE MEN OF OSPREY.

FROM GLADIATOR TO DET 4, RONEX 97-2.

CLEAN SWEEP! GOMEX 97-4

There were photos of Techs performing various EOD missions sprinkled in between the plaques.

A board in the middle of the room caught Jazz's eye. His name was on it, so was Delgado's, and two of the names he recognized from Det Two. The top of the board read, "SENIOR TECH," with a Senior EOD badge affixed below it. Each of the names had a Basic crab next to it. Jazz's was blue.

"Chief!"

"Sir?"

"What the heck is this?"

Chief Keating got up from the desk and came into the conference room.

"What's what, sir?"

"This chart or board or whatever . . . ."

"Ah, that's the progress report on all the slick bombs going for Senior Tech. As they progress by completing qualifications we move the Basic pin over to the right. Once they reach the end, they get to sit on the Senior Board.

"Why the fuck is mine blue?"

Keating smiled. "Inert."

"Huh?"

"See the two holes drilled in it? Inert ordnance is painted blue and has holes drilled in them. We figure you're inert till you do something."

"So, I'm worse than a slick bomb?"

"And an officer to boot . . ." the chief said with a twinkle in his eye.

"You dirty bastards."

"Welcome to EOD, sir. You realize that as an 1140, you will catch more shit from the team than anyone. I hope you can dish it out or at least you're thick skinned."

"Great."

"Oh and another thing, every first is a case of beer."

"What?"

"After your first dive you owe the det one case of beer. Same for first time underway, first cast operation, first fast-rope, and anything else we can get ya on."

Jazz smiled. "Wonderful." *I am gonna love this place.*

TWELVE

RONEX 99-6

The RHIB's radio crackled, waking Jazz.

"Tiburon Four, Tiburon Four, this is Pathfinder, over."

"LT, *Scout*'s callin' us," Delgado said from behind the helm. Jazz sat up at the sound of his new nickname, L-T, the initials for Lieutenant. He opened his eyes, squinting in the sun. The whole det sunned themselves while *Scout* hunted for mines in the exercise field.

"Maybe they finally found something," Quinn suggested.

Jazz grabbed the radio.

"Pathfinder, this is Tiburon Four, over."

"Four, this is Finder. Standby to copy lat and long of mine-like object."

Keating grabbed the Dive Supervisor's binder from the seat behind the console. He nodded at his OIC.

"Pathfinder, this is Tiburon Four. Send it."

"This is Pathfinder. November two seven decimal seven one tree tree six niner four, whiskey niner seven decimal one zero seven zero seven zero niner, how copy? Over."

"Got it, LT," Keating said.

"This is Tiburon Four, roger. Interrogative water depth, over."

"Four, this is Finder. Five nine feet, over."

"This is Four, roger out."

The boat immediately sprang to life as Keating began shouting orders.

"This is Chief Keating. I have the side! Delgado, enter those points in the GPS and call it waypoint ten. Ball and LT dress out. T-Ball, you're diving. LT is standby. Quinn, Sinclair, you guys are tenders."

"Dee, after you enter the waypoint, come up slow and head for it. We can close the distance, but I want these guys to be able to dress on the way there."

"I know, Chief, especially since the seas are picking up."

"Right. Okay, let's do it."

Jazz and Ball slipped on 'shorties,' one-piece wetsuits with long sleeves over the arms, but only shorts for the legs. They both stuck their heads into Mark-4 life vests that were shaped like a horse-collar yoke around their necks. Jazz thought of the Admiral as he strapped the knife on his left inner calf.

"Where in the heck did you get that dinosaur, LT?" asked Keating.

"Uh, my Dad got it for me at an antique shop."

"Damn, I haven't seen one of those bad boys in years."

"Yeah, you only see 'em in the schoolhouse these days," agreed Quinn.

Quinn and Sinclair helped the divers don the Mark-16 dive rigs, weight belts, and fins.

Keating staged the two-alpha sonar and then looked them both over quickly.

"Looks like you guys are basically ready. Okay get 'em sitting down low in the boat. Good. *Scout* is way the hell down on the other side of this minefield. I'm going to have Dee skirt the field, come back up in speed, and then turn back in. Everyone hold on."

"Comin' up!" Dee shouted.

Jazz felt like a fish out of water. He sat across from T-Ball who appeared to be dozing. The weight of the dive rig made the shoulder and waist straps cut into Jazz's shoulders and gut. Even though they were in the stern he could feel the RHIB pounding through the seas. Each bounce jarred his fillings. The hot Texas sun baked him, the thick neoprene of his wetsuit making it worse. He closed his eyes and tried to concentrate on the mission.

The seas were definitely getting rough, though it was a beautiful day otherwise. Not a cloud in the sky, just a light breeze, no portents of bad weather were there. It was just as Fontaine described.

An old familiar feeling crept into Jazz's mouth. He felt sweat beading on his forehead. His stomach began to churn like a washing machine.

I'm getting seasick.

He fought the urge to throw-up.

"There's *Scout*, Chief!" Delgado called out.

Jazz looked toward the bow. *Scout* was coming toward them on the starboard side.

"Should we call her?" Delgado asked.

"Nah, Dee. She is headed back north on one of her search legs, just don't get in her way. They know where we are."

"Well, we are almost there."

Delgado slowed the RHIB and turned it back into the minefield. Jazz opened his eyes and looked up. Keating turned back to his divers.

"Hold on, guys. We've slowed, but we're going to run with the seas on the beam for a short while."

Delgado turned the helm more to starboard. Everyone reached for handrails sewn into the pontoons and held on.

One moment Jazz was looking at nothing but blue sky, the next he watched green sea frothing next to the RHIB threatening to break and fill the boat with saltwater. He rolled over on all fours and pulled himself up onto the pontoon. The contents of his stomach spilled into the Gulf of Mexico. To make it worse, Jazz was very loud about it.

His men began to cheer and jeer him.

"Hooya, LT!"

"I'll get ya some medication, LT. Where's your purse?"

"Don't send an officer to do a man's job."

"At least he's got a pretty knife."

Only the chief was somewhat kind.

"You okay, sir?"

Jazz sat low in the RHIB again. He felt a little better, but his stomach muscles ached now. He looked at Keating. There was only one right answer to his question.

"I'm fine, Chief."

"Alright, fellas, we're almost there. Tenders, standby your divers. Dee, turn to keep the nose in the sea. I wanna be able to stand up again while we do this. What's our depth?"

"Five seven feet, Chief!"

Keating grabbed the binder and a grease pencil again.

"Okay, T-Ball, you will be on a sixty foot schedule for fifty seven minutes, but don't you dare use that much time. I'm gonna pull you in way before that. If you go to sixty-one feet you are on a seventy foot schedule for fifty one minutes max got it?"

"Hooya, Chief."

"Okay, divers and tenders, standby for checks."

T-Ball and Jazz were helped up onto the pontoon. Sinclair was Jazz's tender. He offered water from the Camelbak on his back. The officer took it.

Keating called out again, "Okay, here we go. Mark-4 life jacket on diver, carts installed, actuators up, red clips in!"

Both tenders pulled on the black inflatable life jacket hanging around each diver's neck. They verified it was secure and that the four CO_2 carts that could be used to inflate it were installed properly.

"Check, primary!" yelled Quinn.

"Check, standby!" yelled Sinclair.

"Mark-16 on diver, full facemask with primary attached, secondary installed.

"Check, primary!"

"Check, standby!"

"O_2 and diluent gas valves opened fully then backed a quarter turn. Divers do it, tenders verify."

Jazz and T-Ball leaned forward and reached back behind each buttock. The tenders watched as they opened each valve fully and turned it back a quarter turn to ensure it was not jammed open. Sometimes tenders would catch a diver, tired, seasick, in rough seas, at night, closing their gas bottles. Sometimes tenders missed it and the divers discovered the error within feet of leaving the surface.

"Check, primary!"

"Check, standby!"

"Weight belt on and outside all equipment!"

"Check, primary!"

"Check, standby!"

"Knife!"

"Check, primary!"

"Check, standby!"

"Fins!"

"Check, primary!"

"Check, standby!"

"Depth gauge and timer!"

A salt water activated, combination depth gage and timer was attached to the secondary display. The divers had to monitor their depth and time throughout the dive to ensure they did not exceed their prescribed table. To remain too deep for too long would mean decompression in the water, or a trip to a recompression chamber to treat or ward off the bends.

"Check, primary!"

"Check, standby!"

"Okay, one more thing before you on-gas—are both divers hooked up? T-Ball to the witness buoy, LT to the standby line?"

Both divers had a "tag line" tied around their waist with a carabineer affixed to the end that would be locked into a loop at the end of their respective lines. T-Ball's went to a float that would bob on the surface above him giving them an idea of his location, a witness buoy. Jazz was tied into a much longer line that would be tended by Sinclair if he had to deploy to aid T-Ball. Sinclair and Jazz could communicate via line pull signals if needed.

"Any questions? Okay, on-gas."

The men pulled the black facemask up and strapped it on. Only their eyes were visible now. Each bit down on the mouthpiece in the bottom of the mask assembly and opened the barrel valve there to allow gas to enter their lungs from the hose going over their right shoulder into the rig. When they exhaled the first time a hiss and a crinkle could be heard as the diaphragm on their back filled completely.

"Squeeze right hose, breathe in. Squeeze left hose breathe out. Give me a 'thumbs up' if you feel resistance in both."

There were two "thumbs up," indicating that the check valves in each rig were working.

"Give me 'thumbs up' when primary indicator is green and O_2 readings on the secondary are all point six to point nine. Dee!"

"Chief!"

"Get us there!"

"Aye, Chief, comin' around!"

Delgado turned the boat again. The RHIB rolled violently a few times. Jazz wondered if he would puke into his mouthpiece. The high O_2 he was breathing seemed to help a little.

"Okay, put on T-Ball's skull cap. Hand 'em the two-alpha."

"Forty feet!" Delgado called out.

"Alright, T-Ball, time to do some of that Navy Diver shit!" said Quinn.

"Get some, T-Ball!" exclaimed Sinclair.

"Twenty feet! Going to neutral!"

Keating looked to Jazz.

"LT, off-gas."

Jazz closed his barrel valve and removed the facemask. Keating gave him the binder. "Keep the logs."

"Ten feet!"

"Splash 'em!" Keating called out.

Quinn helped T-Ball splash over the side. He descended immediately.

"Diver left surface time one six one four!" yelled Keating.

Jazz wrote the time in the diving logbook. Quinn fed the tending line, paying attention to keep his teammate from becoming entangled as T-Ball dove deeper and deeper. At the end he set the buoy gently in the water.

Delgado looked over his shoulder, his hands still on the wheel and throttles.

"We good?"

"Yeah buoy's clear aft," said Sinclair.

"Coming up!"

Delgado goosed the throttles and opened their distance from T-Ball's float.

THIRTEEN

OPEN WATER

With the sonar gripped tightly in his right hand, T-Ball used his left to help pull himself toward the bottom. He made long wide strokes with his fins. Only once did he stop, pinch his nose, and blow air into his sinuses, equalizing the pressure in his ears. Within a minute he was on the bottom. T-Ball's primary display was green. He checked the O_2 sensor readings on his secondary gauge but could barely read the numbers, the silt in the water did not allow much sunlight to penetrate this deep. Finally, he was able to discern that they were all within specifications.

Next T-Ball looked at his depth gauge.

:02 60FT

He reminded himself that if he dropped to sixty-one feet he would be on a seventy-foot table.

He took a moment to square himself away. On his knees in the mud he tightened his shoulder straps and ensured his line was not fouled. He yanked on it hard, once, causing the float to visibly bob on the surface.

One. On the bottom.

He moved the switch on the back of the two-alpha, brining it to life. He closed his eyes and began searching with his ears.

The det got comfortable again while T-Ball hunted for *Scout*'s mine. Jazz shifted and sat low in the RHIB again. Quinn and Sinclair stripped to shorts and sunglasses. They lay on the deck next to him to resume sunning.

Keating and Delgado both watched T-Ball's witness float. Delgado put the RHIB into the seas, which were now even angrier. The waves grew in size and frequency. About every fifth one would slam into the RHIB jostling the men and all their gear.

Keating sat astride the pontoon, one foot on the deck, one in the water.

"Still okay, LT?"

"I'm still sick, Chief, but I got nothing more in me."

"Okay, then it's quiz time. What are our lost diver procedures?"

"Uh, we won't lose him, Chief, he's got a witness float."

"Come on, LT. We briefed this, this morning. It is obviously a harsh environment out there; it ain't the pool in Indian Head. Do you think the line could be cut?"

"I guess so."

"What is the lost diver procedure?"

"Um, we put the lost diver buoy in with a search line attached to the anchor. Standby diver follows the line down and performs a circle search."

"What do we do first?"

"First?"

"The line may part, but there are at least two other things we can do to locate him before we splash standby. Know what they are?"

Jazz thought for a moment. He had difficulty concentrating.

"No, Chief."

"Look it up and report back to me."

"Aye, aye, Chief."

"What's a caustic cocktail?"

"That's when excess water gets into the sodasorb canister. The diver will receive a chemical burning sensation in his mouth."

"What does the diver do?"

"Surface."

"Like a bat outta hell. Ever had one?"

"No."

"I have, burns like a motherfucker. Most guys shoot to the surface so you gotta watch 'em for AGE. What's the treatment?"

"Rinse the mouth with fresh water."

"Correct."

The return was getting louder in T-Ball's ears. He was close now. He opened his eyes so that he would not run into the mine. From four feet away he could make out a white shape. Now he turned the sonar off, he found the mine.

He quickly recognized the bottom mine. It was a Mark-52. This one was painted white with orange stripes identifying it as an exercise mine. Stenciled on the side was RONEX 99-6-15-EOD. The "EOD" meant this mine was designated for demolition or exploitation if found by an EOD team.

T-Ball reached into his vest pocket and removed a small battery operated noisemaker called a "pinger." It sent a metallic clicking sound into the water at a specific frequency. The chirping reminded T-Ball of a fathometer. He held it up to his jaw. "Click, click."

He felt the pinger's vibration indicating that it was working. T-Ball attached it to a lug nut on the top of the mine with two zip ties. Now the mine could be found again easily with the two-alpha in the passive mode. The diver who returned would dial in the frequency of the pinger. He would hear it when pointing the sonar in its direction.

T-Ball looked at his depth/timer again.

:10 60FT

"What if T-Ball goes tits up and I send you down after him? When you find him on the bottom, he's not moving."

"I'd check his primary and secondary."

"Primary is flashing red. Secondary readings aren't displayed."

"Okay, I'd have to go with the gauges I got. O_2 level probably dropped because of an electronics failure. I'd bump up his O_2 with the manual bypass valve, get him squared away and bring him to the surface."

"Okay, good. Gotta know that shit cold. You're going to supervisor school soon, right?"

"Yes, Chief."

"Study the dive manual. I'm gonna keep quizzing ya."

The tone in Keating's voice told Jazz that he was done for now. Jazz closed his eyes and leaned back. He tried to concentrate on not being ill. After a few moments the OIC actually began to doze.

He woke when the engines revved up.

"LT, get ready to splash!" shouted the chief.

Delgado was heading for the witness float. Quinn was on the bow now and Sinclair helped Jazz up onto the pontoon. The lieutenant was very confused, he sensed tension in the boat.

"What's happening!"

"Nothin.' Maybe nothing. But, there haven't been any signals from T-Ball on the witness float. It's been twelve minutes now."

"Think he forgot?" asked Sinclair.

"Maybe, he is a new MCM diver. Maybe he's sending us signals and they're not making it to the surface because he's fouled."

"Yeah, or maybe T-Ball's giving us limp-wristed line-pull signals."

Delgado slowed the RHIB as thy came alongside the float. Quinn reached in and grabbed it.

"Give 'em a one!" Keating yelled.

Quinn pulled on the line violently. The dive side stood in silence a moment.

"Sent a one! Nothing received!"

"Again!"

"One sent!"

Quinn looked at Keating and shook his head. Keating's voice changed.

"Okay, LT, you gotta bring T-Ball back. Follow his line down. He may be fouled, unsnag him. If he has an O_2 hit, turn off his O_2, don't bring him up if he is convulsing until it subsides. If his O_2 is low, bump it up like we just said. Push in on his diaphragm on the way up so he don't embolize, got it?"

"Hooya, Chief."

"GO!"

"SAVE HIS LIFE, LIEUTENANT!" Delgado yelled as Jazz rolled into the sea.

For the first few feet Jazz held onto T-Ball's line with both hands. He needed the line to find his shipmate, but he did not want to pull the diver off the bottom. T-Ball could embolize with only a two foot differential in pressure.

One second the line was taut, threatening to part under the force of the cresting waves, the next it was like spaghetti, threatening to entangle Jazz. He grabbed it hand over hand and kicked hard to get down.

As the depth increased Jazz had to equalize the pressure in his ears. He pinched his nose through his facemask and blew air into his sinuses. He could still hear the waves sloshing overhead, but it was calming with depth. At thirty feet he thought he began to see some of the bottom and the water temperature dropped significantly.

A thermocline, he thought.

A silt layer was in the last ten feet from the bottom. He was able to see T-Ball from only three feet away. The green light on his primary was flashing.

High O_2 registered in his adrenaline-filled brain.

Jazz grabbed his teammate by the shoulder and turned him over. His eyes were closed. Jazz reached for his secondary. He found it, but it was too dark to see the readout. He closed T-Ball's O_2 bottle valve.

He was not convulsing, so Jazz yanked on his tending line four times, hard then two more times, followed by four more.

Four—two, rig malfunction. Four, diver leaving bottom.

Jazz grabbed T-Ball by the vest and held him chest to chest. He kicked to the surface, harder than he ever had before. Jazz remembered from dive school, it was no joke pulling another man with you through sixty feet of water column. He kept kicking into T-Ball's legs, restricting his motion.

Now Jazz was aware that lines were in water, around him everywhere. He felt one snagging his left leg. Jazz stopped and looked down. It was not the line, it was the two-alpha sonar. He reached down with one hand to untangle it. As he did, both he and T-Ball sank deeper. Jazz knew time was running out.

Again Jazz kicked for the surface. When he broke free the situation seemed worse. One moment he and T-Ball were in the trough of a wave, rising up with it. The next they dipped under while it passed over them. He thought the two of them would be lost before they could ever be recovered onboard the RHIB. They were saved by the fact that their teammates had their lines.

"Grab the diver!" Keating yelled.

Jazz reached up with his right hand. Sinclair grabbed it with both arms.

Someone called out, "Dee, get those lines in!"

Delgado picked up where Quinn left off on T-Ball's line and began pulling in the slack.

"LT, off gas!" commanded the chief.

Jazz closed his barrel valve and ripped the mask from his face.

"Whatcha got?"

"O_2 hit. Primary flashing green . . . ."

Jazz got a mouth full of seawater as he and T-Ball disappeared in the rising sea. When they emerged he spit and continued.

"Couldn't read secondary. I closed O_2 valve and brought him up."

"Okay, okay, get 'em . . ."

Keating's next words were lost again in the ocean. Suddenly Jazz felt T-Ball being wrestled from his grip. A second after T-Ball was retrieved, Jazz felt Sinclair trying to pull him in. Jazz kicked hard helping his tender and struggled into the boat.

When he lay on the deck Jazz immediately felt ill again. He had swallowed a lot of salty water. The motion was compounded in the boat. Jazz saw his shipmate lying prone on the deck.

"Was he convulsing!" the chief asked.

"No."

"Damnit, T-Ball, I wanted you to convulse!"

Suddenly T-Ball was no longer limp.

"Off-gas."

The primary diver closed his barrel valve and removed his mask.

"Sorry, Chief. I didn't seem him coming in time. I was glad just to get my light flashing."

Jazz knew he had been had.

"SON OF A BITCH!"

"No, no, sir. You did well. Didn't he, T-Ball?"

"I'll dive with him as my standby any day."

"Me too. What was your depth and time?"

T-Ball grabbed his secondary and read the timer/depth gauge.

"Sixty feet for twenty minutes."

"Good. Find anything?"

"Mark-52 bottom mine."

"Did you put a pinger on it?"

"Yes."

"Okay gentlemen, time for a little boom-boom. LT, you are sick, sunburned, and tired. On top of it, the seas are definitely getting rough. You want to get unjocked? Or do you wanna blow shit up?"

"I wanna blow shit up, Chief."

"Right answer."

FOURTEEN

DEMOLITION MAN

Gabriel remembered that compartmentalization of information was one of Nasih's pillars for success. Nasih taught them to develop cells of four or five members, ten at the most. Liaison with other cells or with outside entities could only be conducted through a single member.

When the group needed explosives they considered breaking into a commercial magazine, perhaps at a mining operation or quarry. This blunt method, however, would likely draw some attention through subsequent police or ATF investigations. Therefore, the group decided to employ a more subtle means. Gabriel realized he knew a source of explosives that the ATF did not monitor. He recruited a supplier who seemed more motivated by ideology than cash. Nonetheless, Gabriel paid him well.

Gabriel chose the rear parking lot of a San Antonio hotel as the meeting point. He recognized The Supplier's vehicle and pulled into the spot next to it. The Supplier lifted two ice chests from his vehicle and put them into Gabriel's trunk.

"How much is there?" Gabriel asked.

"About two-hundred pounds," The Supplier answered.

Gabriel handed him a small backpack.

"When you get the chance, look inside the smallest pocket."

The Supplier slung the bag over his shoulder.

"This may be it for awhile," The Supplier said nodding toward Gabriel's car. "My situation has changed."

"I understand," replied Gabriel. He did not want to lose this asset. "Still, we will keep you on the payroll as before. This has been a mutually beneficial situation and I'm sure that your services will be required in the future."

"Yeah, thanks."

*   *   *

Keating leaned over and put a hand on Jazz's shoulder.

"Okay, LT, you are about to go under sixty feet of water with no visibility in a computerized diving rig built by the lowest bidder while carrying enough explosives to vaporize a skyscraper. And you're going alone. Are you scared?" he laughed.

Jazz shook his head in the affirmative.

"Good. Don't forget to follow the detonating cord to the surface to ensure it is not fouled and that you're not tangled in it. That would be a bad thing in about four different ways."

Jazz nodded his head up and down again. Keating turned back to the coxswain.

"Okay, Dee, talk to me."

"Forty feet!"

Keating turned back to Jazz.

"LT, try to find it with the sonar first. If you can't, go to passive and find it with the pinger T-Ball put on it."

"Ten feet!"

"Neutral!" Keating called. "Go, LT."

Jazz rolled backwards into the sea. He quickly surfaced again turned toward the boat. Keating handed him the demolition charge.

"Go!" the chief yelled again.

Jazz descended. Once on the bottom he sat on his knees. Grabbing the witness line, Jazz yanked on it like a bell ringer.

"One. Diver on bottom."

He looped his left arm through the bungee cord woven into the charge the det constructed on *Scout's* fantail the day before. With the demolition package resting on his arm, Jazz turned on the sonar.

The return from the mine was loud. Jazz kept the sonar pointing toward it as he swam through the water. He strained to see the mine through three feet of visibility and listened for the return to get louder.

Detonating cord trailed from the demo charge of C-4 on his arm to a float on the surface comprised of bubble wrap. The Techs called the float a "dogbone" because of its shape. Encased in the bubble wrap was the initiation train for the explosive system. Two igniters each with a spring-released firing pin were married to two lengths of time fuse, wrapped within the dogbone. The time fuse had blasting caps crimped on the opposite end, which were taped to the det cord.

When a Tech released each firing pin, the time fuze would begin to burn. Upon reaching the end, the heat from the time fuse would set off the blasting caps, which would subsequently initiate the detonating cord. When the det cord exploded, it would sympathetically detonate the charge. Initiating in this way would give Det Four time to move to a safe distance before the charge detonated.

As he swam through the water, the dogbone bobbed in the waves, straining the det cord and pulling on the demo charge on Jazz's arm.

The explosives began their journey ten days before. First, four men carefully removed a crate of composition four military plastic explosive, or "C-4," from a shelf in the magazine of Naval Station Ingleside. The forty-pound crate was transported slowly via forklift to a special vehicle configured to transport explosives.

An inspector certified the truck safe to transport explosives and ammunition prior to each trip. He verified that the driver was a qualified to drive explosive laden vehicles, possessed the proper documentation, and that the driver's medical record was up to date.

A police escort drove in front of the explosive vehicle to ensure it was not involved in an accident and that it got to the waterfront and USS *Scout* as quickly and safely as possible.

The pier was secured of all unnecessary personnel. A fire party dressed in full firefighting gear with a charged hose was staged onboard *Scout*. A crane lifted the forty-pound crate to the *Scout* where it was placed in an explosive magazine. A security watch vigilantly observed the magazine, recording its temperature every two hours.

Just the day before, with the same fire party standing by, Det Four drew the explosives from the magazine and built the demo charge on the fantail. Everyone wore safety glasses to protect their eyes from the initiators.

Now Jazz swam through rolling seas with the explosives tied to his left arm. The detonating cord alone could cut Jazz in half. If the charge detonated while he swam toward the mine he would vaporize faster than conscious thought. The standby diver and any recovery divers investigating the site would find a depression in the seafloor and bits of plastic from Jazz's Mark-16.

I've gotta be fucking crazy to do this, he thought to himself.

A white blur turned into the mine. As he got right next to it Jazz could make out the stencil T-Ball had reported; 'RONEX 99-6-15-EOD.'

Jazz turned off the sonar and again found the witness line, tugging on it five times. His buoy bobbed five times on the surface above.

"*Five. Found mine.*"

Jazz looked at his primary display; it was green. For good measure he looked at his secondary readings. They were barely visible, but all were within specifications.

Next he untied the bungee from his arm and tied it to the lug nut on the mine. Jazz pulled the Mark-III knife from its sheath and removed T-Ball's pinger. It went into his vest pocket.

Six minutes later the lieutenant was back in the boat. Keating told him to off gas.

"Diver on deck, diver okay," Jazz responded as his mask came off.

"LT, was that your first underwater demo charge?"

"You know it was, supe."

"Case a beer, buddy."

"Damnit!" Jazz said with a grin on his face.

"Okay guys, good job," Keating said. "We are running out of daylight so let's undress the divers and secure from diving for the day. Once they're clean we'll blow the charge. T-Ball, move to coxswain. Sinclair will be the demo supe. LT, it's your charge, you're gonna initiate."

"Hooya."

Jazz leaned over the boat and grabbed the dogbone.

"Come up more, T-Ball," Sinclair said from behind him.

Jazz pulled back the firing pin and released it. A spring snapped it forward. Smoke popped out through the time fuze.

"Smoke one!" he called.

He repeated this with the second initiator.

"Smoke two!"

"Fire in the hole!" yelled Sinclair. "Go, T-Ball."

T-Ball hit reverse and backed away from the floating initiation train. When they were a safe distance Quinn picked up the radio and keyed his mike.

"Pathfinder, this is Tiburon Four. Fire in the hole, fire in the hole, fire in the hole, over."

Smoke emanated from the burning time fuse for five minutes. Then a plume of water rose twenty feet in the air. The "boom" did not reach the divers until a second later when they saw the spray returning to the ocean. The pressure wave cracked and thundered, echoing across the waves as it made its way outward, toward Mustang Island and *Scout*.

"Hooya!" said Sinclair.

Jazz just smiled to himself. As he put the knife into his dive bag he wondered what the Admiral would think of this day.

Quinn called *Scout* again, "Pathfinder, this is Four. All clear."

The thirty-mile transit home was a beating the whole way. Det Two had already gone home by the time they arrived. Senior Chief Reed was still there. He helped his teammates unload and clean all the gear. The sun was below the horizon when Det Four assembled in the conference room for a quick debrief.

After they were finishing, Jazz looked to the board.

"Can we change the crab to silver now?"

"Hell no, LT," said Keating. "You still ain't done any real shit."

Jazz began the next day at the base pool. Swimming was always his favorite exercise. He often did not even count his laps. Jazz would just swim until he was tired. The

Naval Station Ingleside gym had one of the better weight rooms in the Navy and a pool second only to the one at dive school.

As a specialized command, Det Two and Four were authorized time for physical training, PT, each morning. Each member of the det had their own routine, some liked to run, some lifted weights; Quinn rode his bike into work each day. Although still in his fourth week, Jazz developed the habit of driving straight into the gym and using the weight room for forty-five minutes, followed by a thirty minute swim. Fridays were reserved for volleyball, an important tradition that Jazz saw no reason to interrupt.

By nine all Techs were in the building, beginning their workday. Back in the compound, Jazz showered and donned cammies. He walked around with a coffee cup in hand to visit everyone in the det each morning. It was a habit from Jazz's days in Surface Warfare. The lieutenant asked each sailor what their plans for the day were and what assistance they might need from him. As Jazz finished this routine he entered the office he shared with Chief Keating. Sitting in front of Keating's desk was a sailor dressed in summer whites. The sailor stood as Jazz entered.

"Good morning, sir. I'm Petty Officer Ashland."

"Nice to meet you, welcome aboard."

"Thank you, sir."

"Ash just came from Det Norfolk, LT," said Keating. "I told him to do whatever he needs to do to get checked in."

"Sure, no sweat."

"Sir, I told the other guys that today we are going to do post operation maintenance and stow everything. Next week we will begin preps for Readiness Training."

"Sounds good."

"One more thing, sir," Keating pulled a piece of paper from his cargo pocket. "Dee gave me this off the message board."

"What is it?"

"Orders for our last replacement, one Senior Chief Boatswain's Mate Grover Denke."

"Reed's relief."

"Yes, sir," Keating had an unrecognizable expression.

"Something wrong, Chief?"

Keating grinned widely and then started a belly-wrenching guffaw.

"Do you know him, Chief?" Jazz asked.

Keating held his breath a second, looked at Jazz and resumed laughing. Jazz noticed that Ashland had dropped his head and was hiding a grin. Just then T-Ball emerged from the hall.

"LT, what's so funny?" asked T-Ball.

"Our new senior chief, apparently."

"Who's that?"

"Senior Chief Denke."

Now T-Ball had a grin to match Ashland's.

"T-Ball, Ashland, you guys know him too?"

"Hell yeah," said T-Ball. "He was at Two with us."

"Alright, T, why are you guys grinning?"

"'Cause you ain't gonna get along, LT," said Ball. This made Keating laugh even harder.

Jazz looked at Keating. "Are you going to give me the gouge on this guy?"

Keating calmed down a little. "Hell no, LT. You are gonna have to find out for yourself."

As he left, Keating handed Jazz the message.

Thirty minutes later, Jazz walked past the vault back into the Det Four workshop. Quinn, Sinclair, and T-Ball were there conducting maintenance.

"All right, T-Ball, help me out. What's the deal with Denke?"

"He hates 1140s."

"Great, who doesn't? What else?"

"Denke is the exact opposite of Keating. Chief K is a diver with EOD skills. Denke is an operator first; totally high-speed, low-drag. Denke's all about fastroping, parachuting, IEDs, patrolling. Operating with Marines and SEALs is his thing."

Jazz remembered his conversation with Captain Solarsky about wannabe-SEALs in the EOD community.

"You said he's from Two?" Jazz asked.

"Well, he grew up there, and is officially stationed there, but recently he has been somewhere else."

"Yeah, Denke's with the boys who deploy to La Spezia," added Quinn.

"Yeah? I hear everyone talk of that place in hushed tones. What do they do there?" the OIC inquired.

"Black ops," Quinn responded. "Nobody knows until they goes. I guarantee they ain't sightseeing. Those boys are in the real shit. Point is, Denke is a bad motherfucker."

"So why is he coming to an MCM team if he's a pseudo-frog?"

"He needs an MCM tour to make Master Chief," said T-Ball. "I'll tell ya what, things are going to get interesting with Denke and Keating on the same team."

Jazz noted that comment with silence. Being a new OIC with Keating had been easy. He wondered how he would lead a man like Denke.

After his morning rounds, Jazz spent most of the day in Det Four's office. As the day was winding down, he drank cold coffee and typed away on his laptop completing the paperwork required post-exercise. Jazz felt administrative work was the bane of the officer's existence. He had to write an after—action report for the command and review the logs from all of the detachment's dives. He also had to write several messages. There was a message reporting use of explosives, a message reporting the training accomplished, sometimes he would even send a message changing the location for receiving messages.

Jazz looked up as Chief Keating threw his black backpack over his shoulder to leave for the day.

"Hey, LT."

"What's up, Chief?"

"You done good, sir."

"Huh?"

"You did well out there this week. You're not half bad for an 1140. 'Course I'll never admit that outside this door."

Jazz wondered if Keating's comment was genuine or if he was prepping Jazz for Denke's arrival.

"Thanks, Chief."

"You're still blue though."

FIFTEEN

INCIDENT

Jazz finished the last of his paperwork when T-Ball opened the door.

"Sir, we got a call. I think you should take it."

The "sir" in T-Ball's voice registered seriousness. Jazz was also surprised when the petty officer followed him into the office. Jazz sat at his desk and picked up the phone.

"Lieutenant Jascinski, can I help you?"

"Lieutenant, this is Sergeant Weaver, I'm the shift desk sergeant for San Patricio Police Department. We need your help. We have entered a residence that appears to have military explosives inside . . ."

"Whoa, hold on, Sergeant, let me get a pen."

When Jazz looked up, T-Ball handed him the IED binder and a pen.

"Okay, Sergeant, shoot."

"Well, sir, there's this old woman who owns a house north of town. She has been renting it to some guy; we're not sure who. Anyway he's been missing a few days and she stopped in to look on things. She went into the basement and found what she thought originally was drugs or something. Point is, she thought it was strange. She called us, so we sent a patrolman out . . . who went in with her. He saw in the basement what he believes to be military explosives."

"You're shitting me."

"No, sir. We think he might be right, so naturally we decided to call you."

"Okay. Wait one," Jazz put his hand over the phone and spoke to T-Ball. "We have military explosives in a civilian home out in town. San Patricio County is asking our assistance. Who else is in house?"

"Just you and me, sir. Everyone else has left for the day."

"Okay, get the MU Six command duty officer on the phone."

"Aye, aye, sir."

Jazz turned back to the phone. "Thanks for waiting, Sergeant. Now I need you to help me paint a more precise picture of what you got there. Can I assume you have this place secured and are watching for this guy to show up?"

"Yes, sir. We have a roadblock on both routes into this place. We have a photo of him and a description of his vehicle. The house itself is cordoned off and we have all kinds of uniforms around."

"I recommend that you pull back away from the house as far as reasonable. You never know if this guy may have placed a booby trap in there."

"We thought of that. Nobody has disturbed anything."

"Good. Okay, I need some more questions answered."

Jazz got as much information out of Sergeant Weaver as he could, including his phone number. When he hung up, T-Ball pointed to the phone on Chief Keating's desk.

"Lieutenant Harmon on button four, sir,"

Jazz met Harmon while they were at EOD school. Harmon was in the Navy class ahead of Jazz's.

"Thanks, Ball, start a recall—get everyone in here."

"Roger that, sir."

T-Ball sat back down at Keating's desk and began dialing. Jazz punched the button flashing on his phone.

"Harmon, Jazz here."

"Jazz, what's up man?"

"Did Ball tell you anything?"

"Yeah, explosives in some guy's house."

"Right. I've been told never to roll without calling you guys."

"Cool, got it. Well, I got the CO on the other line. T-Ball said they were military explosives."

"Suspected."

"Right, suspected military explosives. So the CO said go and advise. No RSPs, no blowing in place. No countering booby traps."

"Uh, okay."

"Take your cell phone and call us when you get things figured out."

"Got it."

"Hooya, brother."

T-Ball again pointed to the phone on Jazz's desk.

"Chief Keating, button two. I'm going in the back to load gear, sir."

"Chief?"

"Wassup, sir?"

"San Patricio PD asking for assistance in a house. They found what they believe to be military explosives. I know you guys just got home . . ."

"I'm not coming in, sir."

"What?"

"You and T-Ball can handle this. What did the mobile unit say?"

"We are to advise the San Pats on . . ."

"Advise, sir, advise. Take a radio, a cell phone, a pad of paper, and the digital camera. Call us if you need us."

"But, Chief . . ."

"Sir, you are going to a secure area where they suspect there may be military explosives that are undoubtedly in a storage configuration. Could there be booby traps . . . maybe . . . okay so take your flak gear. Be careful, that is what they pay you the big bucks for. If a render safe procedure needs to be done, wait and let the Seven-Niner-Seven do it. Got it?"

"Yes, Chief."

"Be safe, sir, I'll be by the phone."

The detachment's pickup truck was not obvious in South Texas. Fortunately the police on scene were briefed that some Navy bomb squad technicians would be arriving. A patrolman on the perimeter directed the Techs to the police command post. Jazz walked up to the first plainclothes officer he saw.

"Howdy, I'm Lieutenant Jascinski, Navy EOD from Ingleside."

"Great, I'm Detective Iglesias. We'll have someone escort you in, sir."

"That may not be necessary. Could we get a map?"

"Uh, sure."

By the time he got back to the dually, T-Ball had already put on a flak vest and a Kevlar helmet with a large face shield attached. Jazz noted that the sailor was affixing his IED thigh pouch, which hung from his rigger's belt. T-Ball snapped the leg strap holding it in place, then he helped Jazz to don his vest and helmet.

T-Ball wore the response pack. He handed Jazz two radios. As they walked back by the command post, Jazz gave one to Detective Iglesias.

"We're on channel two."

"We'll be standing by."

The hand-drawn map was inaccurate. T-Ball pointed to a door in the kitchen.

"I'll bet that's it, sir."

"Yeah or it's a pantry."

T-Ball took a flashlight from the IED thigh pouch and walked over to the door next to the refrigerator. It was slightly ajar. He pointed the light into it.

"Cereal and canned goods. That's gotta be it," he said pointing to the second door.

"Do we remote open it?"

"Nah, looks clean and someone has already been through it."

Jazz opened the door. The lights in the basement were already on, illuminating open stairs and part of a workbench. The two men slowly descended.

"Damn," T-Ball said. Jazz was speechless.

On the table in front of them were approximately one hundred blocks of C-4 plastic explosive. Some were wrapped in olive drab plastic with yellow-stenciled writing. Others had been opened, looking like long white bars of soap. Some were even molded like silly putty into indiscernible shapes.

T-Ball set down the response pack and removed the digital camera.

"Step back, LT."

The camera beeped as he took digital stills of the workbench.

"What's in the box, sir?"

Jazz stepped closer and peered into a cardboard box on the right side of the bench. Inside were smaller boxes the size and shape used for crayons. Jazz looked to the right and saw another longer workbench that ran the entire length of the far wall.

"There's more shit over there."

"Yeah, but what's in that box there?"

Jazz opened one of the crayon boxes.

"Holy shit."

"What's that, sir?"

"Electric blasting caps."

"Damn, these guys are not playing around. C-4 and military initiators. Tell ya what, sir, don't move anything else. This is like ATF and FBI stuff."

"Yeah, let's take some photos, conduct a good recon, draw a better map for these guys and get out."

"Okay, LT. What's on that other bench?"

Jazz looked closely at the components on the long workbench.

"I don't know, T-Ball. Internal components of some kind. What do you think?"

T-Ball stepped next to his lieutenant.

"Sir, those are proximity fuzes."

*　　*　　*

Something was wrong; Gabriel sensed it. First he noticed several police cars passed him within five miles of the house. One of them was an unmarked car. From a long distance away he could look over the fields and observe his house. This was one of the features that helped him in selecting this home.

At the intersection for his street he turned right instead of left. In his rear view mirror he noticed that his neighbor's driveway had more police vehicles in it. He was caught.

He cursed to himself, but tried to remain calm.

How the hell did they find me?

Gabriel grabbed a cell phone from the passenger seat in his pickup.

"Hello."

"Do you guys have a copy of 'When Harry Met Sally?'"

"Uh, wrong number buddy. This ain't a video store."

"Sorry."

Gabriel hung up. The verbal exchange was a secret code developed in case their phones were tapped. Dean's response told Gabriel that he was not compromised.

Twenty minutes later he drove by his friend's home. Gabriel noted that the garage door was open with the lights on. He drove around the block before pulling into the driveway. Dean was waiting for him there.

"I don't know what happened!" he said slamming the door of his truck.

"I do."

"Was it San Diego? I've been racking my brain and I cannot come up with anything there."

"No. We did San Diego by the book."

"It's our supplier then. He's breaking with us, called in an anonymous tip or something . . ."

"No, it's not that either. After all, he doesn't know where you live—or does he?"

"Uh, no he doesn't."

"Okay then. I am pretty sure that this is just a case of bad luck."

"How do you know?"

Dean surveyed the street.

"Let's go inside," he said putting his arm around Gabriel's shoulder. "Let's get you a beer, chill out, and I will tell you what happened."

Gabriel sat down on the couch in the basement. His friend remained standing.

"After you called, I did like we planned, like Nasih taught us. The missus was on the phone shaking her head at me with each call."

"Nobody else had been compromised."

"Exactly. Meanwhile I was listening to the scanner. It was the old woman."

"What? She knows?"

"No, they think it's her house."

"What!"

"She went over there today like she still owns the place . . ."

"I bought it from her a year ago!"

"I know, I know. Point is she's crazy. She went over there, poked around and then called them. First a patrolman goes in with her . . ."

"Thinking it's her place . . ."

"Right, thinking it's her place that she is renting to someone, because that's what she told 'em. He finds the shit in the basement."

"So they need a warrant right? It is illegal now. Illegal search and seizure."

"Idiot. We can beat them in court but it doesn't change the fact that you're compromised."

"Shit!"

"Ah yes, now it is really dawning on you."

"What do we do now?"

"Well, I've got a few of our closest friends coming over here. We'll figure something out."

"I have a better idea. Let's call Nasih."

*   *   *

An hour later Jazz was back in the command center while he waited for Harmon to pick up the line. Suddenly he realized that he had not called Melanie.

"Shit," he said under his breath.

"EOD Mobile Unit Six. Can I help you, sir?"

"Harmon."

"Jazz, what's up?"

"I'm in some heavy duty shit here."

"Really, whatcha got?"

"Military C-4, blasting caps, and a full up assembly line for building IEDs."

"You mean like a kitchen?"

"No, I'm talking Henry Ford stuff. We got several completed IEDs, obviously constructed the same. Each one has an opaque plastic housing."

"Proximity fuzing."

"Exactly."

"How many?"

"About twenty complete, but the material for many more."

"What's the net explosive weight?"

"Hundreds of pounds."

"Damn."

"We gotta get ATF, FBI, and NCIS involved now. Someone should send a message to the EOD Technology Division.

"TECHDIV . . . got it," replied Harmon

"I intend to get the Army EOD unit in San Antonio here. We do not have the storage or demo range to handle this stuff."

"Wow. I'm calling Captain Solarsky. He'll let me know what he wants to do."

"Right. I'll recommend to the local police here on scene to get ATF and FBI involved."

"Roger, call you later," said Harmon.

Jazz immediately dialed home. After one ring Mel picked up.

"Where the hell are you! I've been worried sick!"

"Sorry, hon, I . . ."

"Is T-Ball with you?"

"Yes."

"Damnit, Jazz, you always call! What's going on? Where are you?"

"I'm on a call in San Patricio County."

"What happened?"

"Some guy has got military explosives in his house."

"Oh, God . . ."

"Hon, I'm fine. This guy just has it stored in his basement. The police called us because they recognized it as military. We're just advising them."

"When will you be home?"

"I don't know."

"Fine. I'm going to bed."

"I love you."

"Yeah, I love you too," Melanie said as she hung up.

Jazz tossed the phone to T-Ball. "Call home."

He turned and walked over to Detective Iglesias.

"What do you recommend, Lieutenant?"

"Well, I think you guys need to get ATF and FBI involved. We'll also call the Army EOD unit in San Antonio and have them perform the recovery and disposal since the material is military."

T-Ball handed the cell phone back to Jazz. "LT, CO," he said.

Jazz paused a moment to gather his thoughts then held the phone to his ear.

"Good evening, sir."

"I've just talked with Harmon," Solarsky began, "but I want you to give me a run down of what has happened to now."

Jazz expected this. He provided his commanding officer with a lengthy narrative. Solarsky remained silent.

"Any questions, sir?"

There was a pause.

"No. Good job. Sounds like you and Petty Officer Ball have done everything correctly. Here's what we're going to do now. You call San Antonio. Let the cops there call FBI and ATF. Provide the on scene commander with your contact information so they can get a hold of you. At this point your recommendation should be for them to wait for higher authority."

"Roger that, sir."

"Do you have the phone number for the Army guys in San Antonio?"

"Yes, sir. It's in my IED response SOP."

"What is the name of their unit again?"

"The 797th Ordnance Company, sir."

It was 1:30 a.m. when Jazz pulled in the driveway. He told T-Ball not to come into work the next day; he also planned to skip.

Jazz tried to be silent as he entered the house. Melanie was in the living room, nursing the baby. She looked both exhausted and upset.

Jazz set his backpack on the ground and walked over to her.

"Hon, I'm sorry," he said leaning over to kiss her. "I should have known better . . . I know I should have called sooner. I guess I got excited."

"Yeah, well for you it's excitement, for me it's frightening," Melanie sobbed.

"Oh, Mel, don't . . . really it was not that big of a deal."

"I thought you were dead."

"What?"

"When you didn't come home I really thought that you had a diving illness. I was sure that after you called me you keeled over with an embolism or something."

"Hon, that could never be . . . it's been over twenty four hours since . . ."

"That doesn't matter to me!"

Melanie choked back some tears and held her breath a moment.

"I could not even gather the courage to call your cell phone. I had visions of you in a recompression chamber in Corpus Christi with people trying to bring you back to life."

"Hon, I'm sorry, I'm really sorry."

"Maybe the Admiral was right. Sometimes I wish you were still a SWO."

"We both hated that life."

"Yeah? Well, at least I knew you were coming home every night. If you were late I could call the ship and get a hold of you."

"Mel, you are right. But this whole thing would have been prevented if I called. You believe me when I said that this incident was no big deal right?"

"I do."

"Well, if I had called, you never would have had the worries that I was hurt or anything. I learned a lesson, okay."

Melanie stood.

"The baby is done, let me put her back to bed."

Dinner was still on the table. As he sat down to eat, Melanie came into the kitchen. She looked as if she were sleepwalking. She leaned over and kissed him on the forehead, then sat down across from him.

"Jazz, you are forgiven. But you need to know that I was really, really scared. Then after you called, I just got angry. I was pissed because it has been hard without you gone during that exercise, then I made this great dinner and you got called away before you could even come home."

"I know, I know. I'm sorry, hon."

Jazz ate in silence for a few moments. Finally Melanie spoke again.

"So, tell me what happened?"

"Just as I said on the phone, some nut had a basement full of military explosives."

"Was it dangerous?"

"Nah, T-Ball and I just identified what it was for them. Army guys are coming down to pick it up tomorrow . . . I mean today."

"Are you going in tomorrow?"

"Nope."

SIXTEEN

SILVER

Dean drove the Texas Highway Patrol cruiser that the group bought at a surplus auction. He and Gabriel even had on the proper uniform of the THP. Nasih sat in back, posing as a prisoner.

For Gabriel, everything changed now. He did not fully comprehend it when his comrade tried to point it out in the garage. It was not until Nasih directed him to kill the soldiers that he realized he was finally no longer a member of society.

Nasih knew this was the moment to push his American pupil over the edge.

"Gabriel, you do it," Nasih said from the back seat. "You have to go into hiding anyway."

Gabriel did not hesitate, using three rounds each to be sure, first on the armed one standing, then on the second one hunched over repairing the tire. They never even had the chance to call out or say, "Just a flat tire, officer."

"Now put them back in the vehicle, quickly," Nasih said.

The two men set about their task. Dean vomited when he saw the contents of the first soldier's head, as they dragged him toward the driver side door.

"It is truly in your heart, Gabriel. I always knew that you were the strong one, but you are more ready for this business than I thought. I expected you to hesitate," said Nasih.

"I knew there was no point," Gabriel replied. "I realized that we—that I, have come to a point. It was decision time."

He looked at the gun before putting it back in his holster. "And my decision was made for me when that senile old woman led the cops into my house."

"Do not fret, my friend. I have lived this life many years now. It is hard, but it is rewarding."

"Everything is in place," said Dean. "I think we are ready for the test."

"Let's hope it works," said Gabriel.

"If not, it is no matter," said Nasih. "Soon enough they will figure out who you are, but you will now disappear. If you followed my counsel, nobody else will be identified.

Making this appear as an accident really only makes it easier for the authorities. They will probably figure it out anyway. An accident removes political pressure for them to pursue it vigorously. Gabriel will simply be a . . . what's your word? A 'wacko' who slipped away. Is the demolition in place then?"

"Yes," confirmed Dean.

"Well then let's do it. I have a date at Riverwalk in an hour."

*   *   *

It was after noon the next day when Melanie woke her husband up.

"Jazz, wake up, honey."

"What?"

She handed him the portable phone. "Chief Keating. He said I should wake you."

Jazz sat up and took the phone.

"What's up, Chief?"

"Sir, you need to come in."

"Did we get another call?"

"Sort of, sir. It's the bubbas from San Antone, from the 797th . . . they're dead."

"What!"

"The truck blew up on their trip north. We're about to get a lot of questions. The base CDO called me, apparently there are a bunch of cops on their way over here to ask us questions we don't wanna answer."

"Fuck. Call the Mobile Unit CDO. I'll get T-Ball."

Twenty minutes later Jazz was in the shop. Chief Keating looked up as he entered the office.

"Here he is, Captain, I'm gonna put ya on hold a second."

Jazz sat at his desk.

"CO. He wants to know details on what went down at the ranch house, button two."

He hit the flashing light on his phone.

"Lieutenant Jascinski, sir."

"Jazz, what the fuck is going on?"

"Sir, I don't know."

"Well I need answers damnit! I got everyone from the CNO on down calling me asking 'What the fuck?'"

"Sir, I hate to sound like Pontius Pilate, but we did nothing to disturb the explosives. We turned everything over to CCPD and were gone before the Army guys were even there."

"What? You did not turn it over to the Army?"

"Uh, no, sir. I made the appropriate recommendations and departed."

"You dumb Polack, I told you to wait until the Army arrived to ensure a complete and thorough turnover!"

"Sir, that was not my understanding. Once we made our recommendations there was no value in remaining there. The material was in a stable condition."

"There were IEDs there correct?"

"Yes, sir."

"You call that 'stable?'"

"Should I have conducted a render safe procedure, sir? My understanding of our charter here is that anything above the high water mark I merely identify and advise. I only perform render safe procedures in extremis. This was not an extremis situation. The shit was just sitting there."

"You should have conducted a turnover with the 797th."

"Sir, if they can't . . ."

"The point, Lieutenant, is that they're dead. They are fucking charred black remains on the highway and you are the last remaining competent authority who was on scene!"

"Yes, sir."

"You're hosed, Lieutenant. You are about to be visited by the FBI. Answer their questions then call me back. I expect your crab in the mail by sundown."

Solarsky hung up. Jazz held onto the phone a moment then replaced it.

It was obvious that Keating knew the general tone of the discussion with the CO.

"Sir, don't worry. I'm sure this is going to work out."

"He has a point, Chief. Two men are dead and I'm the only supposedly competent guy left standing."

"Sir, it is common knowledge that how we respond in town is hosed up. You are going to be fine. Those Army guys, rest their souls whoever they were, made a mistake. They smoked in the vehicle, or didn't secure the stuff correctly. I mean, what were you gonna do, tell them how to pack their truck? They were EOD just like you and me. They knew what to do; they knew the risks."

Out of the corner of his eye, Jazz saw a San Patricio Police cruiser pull into the parking lot. Just then T-Ball arrived.

"Hey, sir. Hi, Chief. Did you see the cops behind me?"

"Yeah. We'll do this in the conference room," answered Jazz.

"Anything you want me to know before they step in the door?"

"Just tell it like it is, T-Ball."

"Sir, this is some scary shit."

"No kidding."

Jazz surveyed the police officers approaching the conference room. He recognized Detective Iglesias from the incident. Behind the detective was a San Patricio uniformed officer and two other plain-clothes officers. One was a relatively casually dressed man. The second was a very attractive Latino woman.

"Good morning, gentlemen, ma'am. Welcome to EOD Mobile Unit Six, Detachment Four. I'm Lieutenant Jascinski."

Iglesias extended his hand. "I'm sure you remember me, Lieutenant. I'm Detective Iglesias. You may recognize the other San Patricio officer with me, he is Sergeant Weaver. This is Agent Atkins of the ATF and Special Agent Elena Cruz of the Federal Bureau of Investigation."

Everyone exchanged handshakes and business cards. Jazz pointed them into the conference room and followed them.

Jazz was taken aback by the FBI agent. Special Agent Cruz looked more like a business woman than a federal agent. She was dressed in a dark pinstripe suit that complemented her figure. It was just on the edge between "attractive" and "sexy." She clearly had a long mane of black hair, but it was tied up.

Very elegant, Jazz thought.

She turned around just before walking into the conference room and smiled at him.

Keating and T-Ball were already sitting at one end of the conference room table. They both gave him a look as Cruz sat down. Jazz introduced them to the officers, saving Special Agent Cruz of the FBI for last.

More cards and pleasantries were exchanged as Jazz walked around the table and sat next to Chief Keating. Iglesias and Weaver sat to one side. Their body language told Jazz that they were here only to represent their department and make introductions. Iglesias did not pull out a notebook or paper as his federal counterparts did.

Atkins appeared as the three EOD Techs did, as if he had just woken up. It was obvious that he had not shaved or combed his hair in the last twenty-four hours. He rubbed his eyes as if trying to stay awake. On the belt holding his worn jeans up and rumpled polo shirt in was a badge that identified him as an Agent for the Bureau of Alcohol, Tobacco, and Firearms.

Cruz was another matter. Though she clasped a coffee cup, she appeared more together in dress and demeanor. She pulled out a pair of dark-rimmed glasses from a case and put them on with a hint of drama. Cruz picked up her coffee and blew on it through pursed lips as she considered her notebook. Jazz realized every man in the room was gawking at her. They all remained dazed as Cruz began sipping her coffee and flipping through her notebook. The fact that everyone was waiting for her told Jazz that Cruz was the one in charge of this meeting in more ways than one. He decided to get the ball rolling.

"Uh, how can we help you this morning?" Jazz said.

Cruz held up a manicured finger. She adjusted her glasses and flipped again through her notebook. Atkins made a show of looking through his notepad again and uncapping a pen, but Jazz decided that he was right, Cruz was the lead in the investigation. She finally spoke, turning to the men from San Patricio.

"Detective, Sergeant, would you leave us for a moment?"

Iglesias looked puzzled.

"Uh, yeah. Sure."

Cruz smiled sweetly at them as they left. Jazz did not know why, but beyond the sex appeal, something about the agent made him feel nervous. She waited until Iglesias and Weaver left the conference room before turning back to Jazz.

"Lieutenant Jascinski, we have some questions regarding the accident that occurred yesterday. Are you familiar with all the items in the explosive vehicle?"

Jazz almost melted at her husky voice. His brain froze a moment as he considered the possibilities. Cruz looked slightly over her glasses at him, her face holding just a hint of amusement. She knew what synapses were firing in his head . . . she was used to this reaction.

Jazz finally snapped out of it. "Yes, ma'am, in the sense that I knew it was C-4 and blasting caps. We work with those items commonly. In fact they were military. I believe they were stolen."

"You are correct. We'll get to that in a minute. What else was there?"

Now Atkins began writing furiously. Perhaps he was merely here to take notes for Cruz.

"Well, there were some IEDs there, or at least what Petty Officer Ball and I believed to be IEDs."

"How or why did you come to that conclusion?"

Her voice was almost condescending.

"Excuse me, ma'am, but can I ask a question?"

"By all means."

"Why are you asking me this? Wasn't there an FBI agent there on the scene?"

"Yes there was. In fact, it was me. I am a Special Agent but I have also been trained in post-blast investigations. I arrived from San Antonio a few hours after you left. I conducted an investigation of the site and decided that it was in fact best that the Army EOD team take the explosives to their facility for storage until we determined our next course of action."

Jazz sat back and breathed a sigh of relief. Cruz had agreed with the recommendation to have the Army move the explosives. In fact, she directed that exact course of action. He knew that Solarsky would be pleased to know this. He was tempted to ask to be excused immediately to phone his superior but decided against it.

"Again, ma'am, respectfully, then why are you asking me these questions? You were there? I'll be frank with you, we thought you were coming here to try to lay blame on us for the accident."

Cruz stared at Jazz a moment. He watched her blink several times as if she were considering something very carefully. Nobody moved.

Finally Cruz spoke, "Did you puncture the tire on the 797th's explosive vehicle, Lieutenant?"

"Of course not, I . . ."

"Did you set a demolition charge on the vehicle's gas tank? Did you shoot Sergeants West and Martin in the back of the head?"

Now Jazz had no response. The conference room became so silent that he could hear the lights humming.

"Lieutenant, I have just found out that there is a very organized group in southern Texas that would like to use military explosives to build IEDs and commit who knows what other sinister deeds. This group is so organized and intent on carrying out their agenda that they were able to discern, probably from intercepting emails, telephone conversations, and radio traffic, that Martin and West were picking up their explosives and transporting them to Fort Sam Houston in San Antonio. Somehow they punctured the 797th's explosives vehicle right front tire, probably during a fueling stop and, if the sergeants were following procedure, while the vehicle had at least one armed guard. They then approached the sergeants while they repaired the flat some ten miles away, probably to offer assistance, which came in the form of a nine millimeter round to the back of the head.

"They did all of this with only hours of notice, emphasizing their organizational skills and planning ability. Many highly trained military units would not have been able to carry out this same mission with more warning time.

"The only silver lining in this story is that this organization, ironically, is not very knowledgeable in the use of explosives. They tried to make it appear as if the vehicle was consumed in an explosive accident, which remains the official story. They did not place the explosives correctly, nor did they use enough. Undoubtedly, they wished to recover most of the cargo."

"Holy shit," murmured T-Ball.

"Gentlemen, we have failed being subtle," Cruz continued. "I hope you understand that my concern is to not let this leak. We have not even told the soldiers' families the true story, they may never know. More importantly, it is our intention to deceive the culprits into the notion that they are not under suspicion."

"So what do you need from us, ma'am?" asked T-Ball.

"I need any and all information you obtained during your investigation. You may have some insight or may have merely seen something that can enlighten us. Did you take pictures?"

"Dozens," Jazz answered.

"Could we have them?"

"Sure, T-Ball . . ."

"On it, sir."

T-Ball got up to go retrieve the photos. After Jazz saw Ball disappear down the hall, he felt Cruz staring at him. He turned and looked back at the Agent. Cruz's expression was indiscernible.

Is she looking at me or lost in thought? Jazz wondered.

After a moment, Cruz asked, "Lieutenant, please give me a verbal description of everything that happened. I will take notes and interject as you relay your story. Agent Atkins and I will both take notes. Okay?"

"Sure."

During his narrative, both Cruz and Atkins interrupted him several times. Atkins' questions seemed to be related more to the explosives and the proximity fuzes. Cruz's questions probed more into the specific the actions of Jazz, T-Ball, and the other law enforcement personnel at the scene. Jazz suspected that she might believe that someone at the scene was involved in the crime based on her line of questioning. He then realized why Iglesias was asked to leave the room.

Jazz gave as much information to Cruz as he could. When they were done, Keating offered to show all the law enforcement officers the way out. Jazz resisted seeing Special Agent Elena Cruz to the door.

Jazz sat and thought for a long time about the fact that it could have been he and T-Ball who transported the explosive materials to San Antonio. He could have been killed on the job the night before instead of West and Martin.

Then something in Jazz's brain clicked. He looked up to the PQS board. The EOD crab next to his name was silver.

Jazz debated how to tell Melanie about the 797th EOD men, though there was nothing to debate. It was clear that Cruz wanted to maintain the story that the vehicle had met with some type of accident. Jazz knew after the previous night that before he was finished telling his wife what happened, the conversation would turn into another argument.

"Damnit, Jazz, this is just what I'm talking about!"

"Mel, they fucked up! They packed the explosives improperly, or smoked in the vehicle, or used a cell phone. They were knuckleheads and that's all there is to it."

"Yeah, well I'm sure those EOD Techs have had this same discussion with their wives!"

"That is not fair."

"I'm leaving. Take care of the kids."

As Melanie drove off, Jazz wondered if this was going to happen regularly.

Elena Cruz drove two hours back to the San Antonio office. Almost nobody was there. She compiled her notes and transcribed them onto the computer. It was almost ten o'clock when she got home.

Frances, Elena's roommate, left a note stuck to a bottle of wine on the dining room table.

Thought you'd need this to end your day.

Elena consumed a few glasses of wine trying to forget about the case. The only thing that distracted her from the gruesome sight of the two victims was Lieutenant Jascinski. His blue eyes tugged at something within her. She fell asleep thinking of him.

SEVENTEEN

DENKE

An oiler of the *Supply* class caught Jazz's eye. She was entering the Thimble Shoals Channel at the mouth of the Chesapeake Bay. He could just make out men lined up on deck to act as linehandlers for entering port. A gathering, probably including the captain and the pilot, were on the port bridge wing.

Jazz continued without slowing. The sand on the beach reminded him of Panama City, Florida, because he was running in it. Despite being the junction of the nation's largest bay and the Atlantic Ocean, the seas were still. A light breeze blew over them and into Jazz's lungs. The cold air in his chest burned.

Up ahead Jazz could make out first Delgado, then Ball turning right off the beach. Somewhere behind Jazz were the other members of Det Four with Keating undoubtedly trailing.

Jazz turned right, crossing the street and entering the forest beyond.

Although an Army base, Fort Story was home to more sailors and Marines than soldiers. The Army had a transportation corps and its music school there. The Coast Guard maintained a small contingent to man the Cape Elizabeth Lighthouse.

The bulk of Fort Story, the forest, belonged to the Navy and Marine Corps' operators, though they sometimes could be seen on other parts of the base.

Dependants using the beach would sometimes see men in exotic diving gear suddenly emerging from the water. Base residents often witnessed high-speed watercraft disgorging a line of swimmers laden with weapons and tools of their trade into tepid waters. The base police force reminded its rookies not to be alarmed if they encountered soaking wet, heavily armed men working their way along the road.

Marines struggled through the last days of the Amphibious Recon Course here, patrolling for days across the base unobserved. SEALs practiced CQB, close quarters battle, inside a labyrinth of underground concrete bunkers that connected four shore gun emplacements. Now rendered defunct by radar and other technologies, the weapons were removed long ago.

114

The bunkers once housed Explosive Ordnance Disposal Mobile Unit Two and Training and Evaluation Unit Two. EODMU TWO moved to the Naval Amphibious Base at Little Creek, Virginia. EODTEU TWO obtained a more modern facility at Fort Story, but retained possession of the ancient bunkers.

Every two years each EOD detachment in the Navy rotated through TEU TWO on the East coast or TEU ONE on the West coast to complete six weeks of refresher training called Readiness Improvement Training or READIMPT. The training was in preparation for re-certifying the detachment as a deployable asset. Now it was Det Four's turn.

While in training the detachment would learn the newest information regarding each of their mission areas. The training routine was one or two days of classroom time followed by two or three days of drills imposed upon the det by the TEU TWO instructors. It was a great time for the det to hone their skills and to develop teamwork. It was also a great time for the junior EOD Techs, the Basic Techs, to work on their Personal Qualification System. Jazz intended to get his PQS book signed off in order to pursue Senior Technician.

When he told Melanie about READIMPT she was not happy. She could not fathom that he had to go to Virginia for six weeks while she was alone in Texas.

"This is feeling like the ship again," Melanie said as her shoulders slumped.

"How?" Jazz asked though he already knew.

"You're gone even when you're home."

Jazz could see that Melanie was defeated. He put his arms around her. "Maybe we'll fly you guys up while I am there. You could stay with Mom and Dad."

Jazz ran on an asphalt road now, he passed the demolition range and the helicopter landing zone. He continued on the access road winding through the forest until he arrived at the "Hill of Woe," a long steep incline of sand and turned ankles. He could see Dee and T-Ball already at the top gasping for breath.

As he ascended he felt the pain, mostly in his hips. Several times Jazz fell forward digging his hands in the sand in front of him as minor avalanches of sand slipped away from under his feet. He was nearly walking when he reached the top.

"Hooya," he croaked, trying to show spirit to his teammates.

"Bitch ain't it, LT?" remarked Delgado.

"Mmmhmm."

When the last det member, Keating, reached the top, they formed up and ran their last half-mile back to TEU TWO together.

In the parking lot T-Ball spoke up.

"Ash, recognize that truck?"

"Yep, looks like Denke's here."

Keating patted Jazz on the back.

Det Four was in the classroom phase of IEDs. Their instructor was a chief petty officer named Potter. Like all instructors at the training unit, Potter kept abreast of the latest intelligence and technology in his mission area by interfacing with the FBI, ATF, and the EOD Technology Division in Indian Head, Maryland. His first lecture covered bombings in the recent past carried out by known terrorists, followed by those that had no claimants. After that they took a coffee break and he gave a lesson on the newest techniques used by terrorists. The afternoon class was scheduled to be a review of tools and methods used in the IED mission area by U.S. forces and their allies given by Hull Technician First Class Yurwitz.

Through Potter's class, Jazz sat in the back of the room eyeing Denke sitting up front. Grover Denke was skinnier than Jazz imagined. He expected the senior chief to be built like a mythical superman, tall, blonde, and with an atlas-like figure. Instead, Denke was built like a triathlete. The senior chief was of average height, thin, and bald. Jazz surmised Denke would run like a gazelle and swim like a fish.

He approached him during a coffee break in the Potter's class.

"Hey, Senior Chief, welcome to the det."

"Why thank you, sir, and welcome to EOD. I look forward to working with you."

"How 'bout we get together over lunch and talk things out."

"Ah, the 'OIC-LCPO coffee klatch.'"

"Exactly."

"You got it, sir. I'll be here."

Denke and Jazz decided to meet in an empty classroom. Jazz poured himself a cup of black coffee and entered the room. Denke was already there.

"Senior Chief."

"Sir, how are you doing?"

"Fine, thanks. Again, welcome to Det Four. I look forward to working with you."

"Same here."

"Good. Let me tell you a little bit about myself," said Jazz. Jazz sat down across from the senior chief. "I started as a SWO, so I have a few years of fleet experience. I served two tours before lateral transferring to EOD. Obviously, this is my first assignment in Special Operations."

"Obviously. Well how do you like it so far, sir?"

"I like it a lot. Coming into EOD has been a goal of mine for a long time. How 'bout you? Have you always been an EOD Tech? I mean, since you entered the Navy."

"No, sir. I also came from the fleet," Denke took a sip of his coffee. "Look, LT, this is about the OIC-LCPO thing right?"

"Uh, correct. I think we need to get things straight before we can work together."

"Well, sir, you need to get this straight, I did come from the fleet and I do understand the 'lieutenant to senior chief relationship,'" Denke said curtly, "I want to make sure that you understand the 'Master Technician to Slick Bomb relationship.'"

"I think I understand, Senior."

"I would suspect that you don't. If you did you would not have gone on that IED call in Texas without a Master Technician with you . . ."

Jazz tensed. "Whoa . . . you are outta line, Senior . . . the command knew what I was doing, besides I had Ball with me . . ."

"Well, sir, Ball is as good as they come . . . but the end result was still two of our brethren are dead. If I was on that job, I would have rendered that shit safe before I turned it over."

"Senior Chief, you do not know what you are talking about."

"Oh, don't I?"

"No."

Jazz did not know what to say now. He was losing ground in the conversation already. He did not want to leave it this way. Denke spoke again.

"No offense, sir, but I've worked with a bunch of 1140s over the years. None of them figured it out on their own, some never got it . . ."

"Got what?"

"That you need to trust your senior enlisted people, your Master Technicians. You need to listen to them, to me. If ya follow my advice and do as I say, you will get through this tour fine and grow up to be Commodore someday. If not, we'll bump heads, the det will go to shit, and you'll be lucky to have my recommendation for a Senior Technician Board."

"I'll keep that in mind, Senior Chief. But I want you to remember this . . . I do not give a damn about being Commodore. What I do care about is this det and about growing into a Senior EOD Tech. I crawled and scratched my way into this community against the wishes and efforts of some pretty potent people in this Navy. I am not going to let anything get in my way of my responsibility to the det first and to my professional development second."

Denke frowned and rolled his eyes. "Okay, sir, whatever."

Jazz stood and left.

That did not go well, he thought.

As he walked back to the IED classroom Jazz realized that his initial reaction to the IED incident in San Patricio was just as Denke described. The new OIC called one of his Master Technicians, Chief Keating. Keating trusted him to react properly. Keating thought Jazz could perform on his own. Now Jazz wondered which of his chiefs was right.

Yurwitz asked the detachment to lay out all of their IED equipment in the front of the classroom before he began his lecture. Jazz surveyed their gear as Quinn and Sinclair laid it out. He recalled being taught how to use each of these tools in the IED division at Indian Head.

The det's response pack was the first item used by any Tech when downrange on an IED problem. The pack held all of the "Hollywood" tools. There were clamps, cutters, drills, and miniature sized screwdrivers and pliers. It had various rolls of tape, different sized magnets, and special metal containers for carrying blasting caps. Next to the pack, Sinclair had laid the det's portable x-ray and the remote operated dearmer. These were the bread and butter of IED work. Often, sophisticated devices could only be stabilized using the response pack. The P1 had to use his x-ray and dearmer to render the device safe.

The portable x-ray was invaluable to determine the layout and design of the improvised explosive device when fully enclosed within a container whether it was a cardboard box, a suitcase, or a pipe bomb. The Tech placed the x-ray on one side and a film cartridge on the other. After shooting the correct number of electromagnetic pulses through the device the P1 would return to the CP with the film cartridge. Each det possessed a portable developer to go along with their x-ray unit. In minutes the whole team could be studying the contents of the suspect package within the safety of their command post.

The remote operated dearmer was meant to destroy an IED's electronic components from the safety of the command post. The tool was in essence, a cannon, that spewed water at extremely high speeds into the suspect package. The energy imparted upon plastic, wood, and even metal by the first H_2O molecules cut a hole through which the more water could travel. As the water passed through, wires severed, timers imploded, and circuit boards became demolished.

The beauty of this technique was that high explosives may break apart under the force of a water jet, but the friction was usually not enough to cause detonation.

Jazz thought the dearmer was phallic-looking and apparently at least one other Tech agreed with him. Two cases housing the det's dearmers were labeled "HOLMES" and "JEREMY."

The classroom phase was complete at lunchtime the next day. Now Det Four would be given practical drills to demonstrate their proficiency. After returning from the base chow hall, the det waited in and around the classroom for their first drill to begin. Any minute they expected one of the instructors to come in and role-play a police officer, beginning their IED problem.

Quinn had his head on his desk, eyes closed. He slept soundly. T-Ball read a book. Ash was outside the IED classroom on his cell phone. Jazz noted he spent every free moment on the phone.

"Who's going to be the P1, LT?" Denke asked.

"I am."

"I advise against that, sir. It would be best if you were in the CP."

"I'll learn more as the P1, besides I need the signatures for my Senior Tech PQS. In fact there are four line items, so I need four signatures as the P1 on an IED to advance to Senior Tech."

"LT, you're the OIC and as such you belong in the CP. No offense, but I'll never let you go downrange on an IED problem. Chief K will back me up on this. Right, Chief?"

Keating was in an awkward position. Jazz knew he also had to develop a good relationship with his fellow chief.

"Well, Senior Chief, LT does have a point about his PQS. This is a great time and place to learn, he should take advantage of that."

"Hell, we can teach him, we'll coach him along in the CP," said Denke.

Jazz knew Denke was disguising an attempt to gain footing against him. The OIC clenched his jaw. Then he asked, "Will you sign my PQS for P1 on an IED problem if I do it in the CP?"

Jazz already knew what the answer was. It was clear when Denke provided no response.

"Then I guess I'll be the P1."

"Well, sir, just because you're the P1 does not guarantee you a signature. I'll only sign you off if you prove yourself to me."

Denke's tone was harsh, not quite disrespectful, but there was anger behind it. He stood and left the room. The rest of the team returned to silence.

Jazz wondered what his men thought of him right now. Keating seemed genuinely interested in training the OIC, almost paternal. Denke was obviously ready to embarrass him.

Don't fuck this up, Jazz, he thought to himself.

Ashland walked in the room carrying his cell phone with Grover Denke following behind him.

"So what did your broker say?" asked Quinn.

"Broker? I thought he was running a 1-900-horny diver phone service with that thing," said Sinclair.

Ashland ignored his teammates.

"LT, I just got a call on my cell phone. Sounds like an IED issue."

Jazz looked at Ashland puzzled.

Ash lowered his voice as if telling a secret. "I gave Potter my cell phone number the first day here so they could get a hold of us if needed . . . . they are obviously using it."

Jazz took the phone and opened his IED Standard Operating Procedure binder. The SOP was used as a guide for conducting the IED mission.

"Lieutenant Jascinski, here."

"Sir, this is Sergeant Squid of the Virginia Beach Police Department."

The OIC asked the standard questions and provided "Squid" with the Standard recommendations outlined in the SOP. After Jazz gathered all of the pertinent information he briefed his det.

"Okay guys, we just got a call from Virginia Beach PD. There is a local politician who has been getting threats, all of them documented with VBPD. This morning the politico comes out to his car to find a bomb in it. Specifically, he opened a gym bag he keeps on the passenger seat and saw a device inside."

"Is he sure that it wasn't an egg timer and a couple'a road flares?" Quinn quipped.

Everyone chuckled, including Jazz. "No, we're pretty sure it is a bomb. VBPD is faxing us a map to their location. Let's load up and head out."

As the other men moved toward the door, Denke approached Jazz.

"Lieutenant, if you are going downrange as the P1 at least give me the binder so I can act as OIC."

Jazz handed it over.

"Sure, Senior Chief."

He noted that Denke had relieved him subtly.

The fax directed Det Four to the demolition range a short distance behind the training unit. All of the response gear was loaded into Det Four's HUMMVEE, with the CP gear in the dually. Jazz drove up in the HUMMVEE with Delgado, the others followed behind.

The IED instructors were waiting in their HUMMVEE next to a gate that was closed to block the demo range from traffic. A red flag was displayed next to it identifying the range as "hot."

As Denke got out of the det's Dually he called out, "You guys from Virginia Beach Police Department?"

Chief Potter stepped forward.

"We sure are. I'm Sergeant Squid, the guy who called you."

"Is this a safe area to set up a CP?"

"Yes."

Denke pumped "Squid" for more information, using the SOP. Finally Denke turned to Jazz and frowned.

"Okay, sir, get dressed."

EIGHTEEN

MERCURY

Ten minutes later Jazz and Quinn, dressed in bomb suits, drove slowly toward the demolition range where the vehicle was supposed to be. Quinn was Jazz's P2. He sat on the tailgate of the HUMMVEE and payed out the hard-wire comm reel.

As they got closer, Jazz could make out a government sedan. Yurwitz was leaning on it. He figured that it must be the "vehicle." Yurwitz was there to grade his performance.

They stopped forty feet away and hopped out of the HUMMER.

"Walk the box down next to the vehicle while I get situated," said Jazz.

"Aye, aye, Lieutenant."

Quinn reeled the comm box out more and set it next to the vehicle as Jazz put on the response pack and grabbed the portable x-ray.

"Great, Quinn. Thanks. Now return to the CP. Let me know when you get there."

"Hooya, LT."

Quinn jogged stiffly back to the CP under the weight of the Kevlar.

Jazz studied the gym bag through the car window. He swept the opening with his penlight. The OIC spoke loudly so the comm box would pickup his voice.

"CP, P1. I can see in this bag pretty well. Inside is a box that is opened just a little bit. I can make out some dynamite, a timer, and a blasting cap into the dynamite.

Denke's voice came back at him. "Is it ticking?"

"No."

"Sure it ain't road flares and an alarm clock, LT?"

Jazz could hear his teammates laughing at the joke in the background.

"No, it is not, Senior."

"You are happy with everything you see?"

"Affirmative. It is in a cardboard box, but the box is partially opened. Did this guy open it?"

Knowing if the intended victim has opened the box could give the P1 some insight on the stability of the IED. If he opened it, it was disturbed at least once.

"We'll find out . . . so do we need to x-ray it?"

Everything was settling down in the CP. Ashland pulled out a paper copy of the sixty series publication on IEDs from the portable safe. He settled on the grass next to the dually and began to read.

Delgado sat on a camping stool in front of the computer set on the dually's tailgate and began to log everything that was happening, especially the conversations between the CP and the P1. Sinclair finished setting up the detachment's portable computer, also on the dually's tailgate, and called up the CD-rom version of the 60 series pub that Ashland was reading.

"T-Ball," Denke said. "Set up a second dearmer down the road a bit, closer downrange. Make sure you mark it with a bravo flag. We'll use it as backup."

"Roger that, Senior."

"Sinclair, I want you to set up the developer for the x-ray."

"No problem, Senior."

T-Ball donned a flak jacket and helmet. He hopped into the bed of the dually and found the case marked "JEREMY."

Thirty five feet in front of the CP he set it down and opened it. First he put on a set of protective glasses that were in the case, then he removed a red flag that signified the letter "B" or "BRAVO" in semaphore. This flag denoted explosives or flammable material present. He hung the flag from a tree branch. Next he extracted a stand of plywood and plastic pipe that the det used to store dearmers when they were primed with an explosive charge. T-Ball conducted the buildup of both tools as he had hundreds of times before.

Walking back to the CP he observed Denke and Keating talking together. It was obvious that they did not get along. T-Ball noted that he had great respect for both of them. He appreciated each of their leadership styles. Keating was a mentor, the kind of LCPO that coached you, let you make mistakes. Denke was a taskmaster of the old school, a disciplinarian, but men found they could accomplish much more under his scrutiny than they ever imagined.

T-Ball surmised that Keating was going to be the detachment's "mother" while Denke was the "father" personality. The OIC would determine if Det Four would be close-knit or dysfunctional.

Jazz slipped off the response pack and removed a tripod from a long thin pocket on the side. He set the tripod up close to the car door and fastened the x-ray on top of it. Next he quickly placed the film cartridge so that it would capture the x-rays emissions.

He noted that Yurwitz was still leaning on the car observing him. The petty officer said nothing.

Jazz flipped a switch on the back of the x-ray and ran behind the HUMMVEE. Once there he keyed his radio.

"CP, P1. I just initialized the x-ray. Give me a wait time."

Denke's voice came back at him. "Roger. Do not forget, tools in—tools out, LT. We want you to bring everything home . . . Okay . . . time. Take some photos with the digital camera, do what ya gotta do, and come back."

Jazz recovered the film cartridge and the x-ray. He grabbed the digital camera and took several quick photos of the scene, especially of the bag and its position in the car. He picked up the response pack and checked his digital photography on the display screen on the back of the camera. The IED came out clearly.

Fifteen minutes after arriving downrange, Jazz was driving back toward the CP.

When he arrived at the CP he noted that Quinn was still dressed out in a bomb suit bouncing on the balls of his feet. He appeared to be in the on deck circle. Jazz saw that Denke and Keating standing on the other side of the road from where the CP was set up. They seemed to be arguing. Potter and the other instructors were all leaning on their vehicle, arms crossed, silently observing.

Jazz took off his helmet and set it on the dually's open tailgate. Delgado was still at the hardened laptop stationed there. Jazz removed the disk from the digital camera and handed it to him.

"Here's the photos. Call'em up."

Jazz handed his X-ray film cartridge to Sinclair to develop. The lieutenant expected Denke to come over and pump him for information . . . but he and Keating were still in conference. Jazz decided to give them their space.

After the film was developed, everyone huddled around the computer including Potter.

Finally Keating spoke. "Definitely a mercury switch there. Good photos, LT."

"Thanks."

"I say we hit it with a dearmer. It will probably go, but nobody will get killed and we may get lucky and do only minor damage to the car."

"Negative," said Denke. "Quinn's gonna go down there and start cutting wires."

Denke's comment stung. He did not want Jazz to go back downrange again. Was this what the chiefs were fighting about?

"Senior Chief, Chief . . . come with me."

Jazz spun on his heel and walked away from the group to the spot across the road where the chiefs had just been standing.

T-Ball expressed concern to his teammates as their khakis walked away.

"I gotta tell ya fellas . . . this could get ugly real fast . . ."

"Nah," said Ash. "They'll work it out. Giv'em time, these guys will work it out."

"I dunno," said Delgado. "They all seem pretty bull-headed, especially the lieutenant."

"They may be bull-headed," Ash agreed. "The time to worry fellas is when they stop talking. If Keating stops giving input and sits in the CP with a scowl on his face and his arms crossed over his chest . . . that is when the det is in trouble."

Jazz heard the footsteps of his two senior enlisted behind him. When he was out of earshot of everyone else, he did another about face and faced them.

"First, Senior Chief, I am going back downrange. I need the training. Period."

"You are gonna kill yourself, sir, and I ain't gonna cut your grass when you're gone."

Keating piped in, "I agree with Senior Chief only if you think you are going to cut wires. Sir, you need to hit this thing with a dearmer. Worse case scenario the car gets peppered, but nobody gets killed. The guy's insurance will pay for it."

Jazz clenched his teeth and swallowed hard.

"Don't you trust my abilities, Chief?"

"Yes, sir, I do. But, I wouldn't cut wires on this thing. It has a mercury switch. Those bastards are very sensitive. If you fart upwind, it may go on you. Remember, sir, you never conduct a hand entry."

"I disagree wholeheartedly," interjected Denke.

Jazz could hear the impatient anger in Denke's voice again. The senior chief was clearly not used to being challenged.

"After all, why do you think we have wire cutters, LT? So you can wire your house on the weekend?"

Now Jazz saw Keating grit his teeth and drop his head.

"Listen, sir," Denke continued. "It is decision time. You wanna be one of the boys? You wanna be in the club? You wanna earn my respect, our respect. Then you gotta decide, are you a dog or a Tech?"

"Huh?" Jazz and Keating said together.

"I said 'Are you a dog or a Tech?' There are two types of guys in EOD, bomb dogs and bomb techs. The 'dogs' are guys that are no better than a real bomb dog. They can find a bomb but they can't render shit safe. 'There it is.,' they say. 'Yep, it's a bomb!' Their only answer is to blow in place or to function it. Well, any volunteer fireman can do that."

Keating was getting red. Denke challenged his legitimacy as a Master EOD Technician.

"The second kind is your true EOD Techs, real bomb surgeons who analyze the problem and render shit safe. So what's it gonna be, Lieutenant?"

"I'm a bomb tech."

"Fine. You got the balls, now prove ya got the brains and the hands to go with'em. Maybe we can train the 1140 outta ya."

Keating said nothing. He turned and headed back to the CP.

Denke stepped closer to Jazz and leaned toward him whispering, "I'm your LCPO now, Lieutenant. Stick with me and we'll be okay."

"I do trust your ability, Senior Chief, but let's not cut our guys down. If we are to be a team, everyone needs to contribute. This is not my det, it is not your det, it is our det," Jazz said motioning to the others standing next to the dually.

Denke briefed the plan to the rest of the team. Jazz could not tell if the senior chief's voice registered defeat or disdain when he reported that Jazz would remain the P1.

He finished unmercifully with, "LT is going back downrange, so, Quinn, standby. We may need you to recover his pieces parts."

As Jazz drove the short distance from the CP to the IED problem he kept hearing the two chiefs arguing in his head.

"*. . . you never conduct a hand entry.*"

"*Are you a bomb dog or a bomb tech?*"

They both had valid points. Jazz knew that this was one of the moments that OICs earn their money. In the end he had to make the best decision because he bore the responsibility.

It was not enough that Jazz needed to prove his mettle with Denke and the rest of the det, now he was at the center of conflict between two of his Master Techs. Whatever his decision, one of them would feel betrayed. Jazz wanted to earn Denke's approval, but he did not want to alienate Keating.

"*Go with the dearmer. Insurance will pay for any damage.*"

"*Why do you think we have wire cutters, LT?*"

Jazz stopped forty feet from the "politician's vehicle" and got out. Petty Officer Yurwitz was sill there. The instructor had rolled his sleeves up to tan his arms. As Jazz moved toward the vehicle Yurwitz moved to observe him.

"Whater ya gonna do, LT?"

"I'm going to conduct a wire attack."

Yurwitz looked surprised. Jazz wondered if Denke was wrong. *Should I have followed Keating's advice?* he thought. The chief had never steered him wrong yet. *Had he cowed to Denke in an effort to gain his respect? Right now in the CP were the others thinking the same thing? Was Denke doing this just to embarrass him?*

"What are you going to cut?" Yurwitz asked.

"I'm not sure yet."

Jazz was sweating now. He could feel Yurwitz staring at him. Jazz could not focus on the problem. He drank from his Camelbak, trying to gather his thoughts.

"Time on target, LT. Don't just stand here . . . do something."

Suddenly, Jazz remembered what the Admiral said after his graduation.

"*Don't worry as much about being a good EOD Tech because you'll never measure up. Be a good officer, a good 1140, a good OIC.*"

Then it hit him like a ton of bricks. He was going about this all wrong.

"CP, P1. I'm coming back."

"Uh, CP, roger. What is wrong?"

"I'll explain when I get there."

As he drove back Jazz got his thoughts together. He realized that he was so worried about impressing his chiefs that he lost sight of the problem at hand.

Solve the problem, not the conflict, he told himself, *Be a good OIC, and the bomb tech stuff will follow.*

When he pulled into the CP his two chiefs stepped up to the open door. They had confused looks on thief faces.

"Gents," Jazz said. "I have a suggestion."

NINETEEN

TEAMMATES

It did not take long for Jazz to convince his chiefs, though their reactions were different. Keating immediately expressed enthusiasm for the idea. Denke conceded with silence at first.

"What do you think, Senior Chief?" Keating said.

Denke rubbed the top of his head.

"Senior?"

"I think it is a good idea, let's try it."

Jazz thought he could convince them, but he was surprised at how impressed they both seemed with his idea.

Denke quickly briefed it to the team as Jazz drove back downrange to finally complete the task.

"Amazing," Ash asked with a grin.

"Yeah," said T-Ball. "Pretty smart really."

Yurwitz noted that on his third trip downrange, Jazz appeared to have it together. His work was very methodical.

The instructor watched as the young slick bomb made quick measurements of the package using the x-ray he had taken earlier. Then he extracted a very strong magnet and held it next to the device, affixing it with ordnance tape. Finally he tied a line to the bag, opened the car door, and ran the line to the center of the road.

Once there Jazz returned to the truck extracting a six foot metal stake and a sledge hammer. In a minute he drove the stake into the middle of the road. He attached a pulley to the top of the stake, and then he led the line through the pulley.

The instructor still had not figured out what the lieutenant was doing. He called Potter on the radio while he watched Jazz driving slowly toward the CP, spooling the line out behind him as he went.

Back in the CP, Jazz heard Chief Potter stopping the drill as he tied the line to the hitch on the back of the HUMMVEE.

"Okay numbskulls, explain to me what the fuck is going on."

Jazz felt everyone turn their heads toward him. He looked at his det for a second. Their looks did not make him feel like a culprit. He felt like their leader.

"Well, Chief, I had a talk over there earlier with Senior Chief and Chief K. We mulled over how to go about this. We thought of using a dearmer, accepting the risk of sympathetic detonation. Then we thought of a wire attack increasing the chance of success, but accepting the risk of an 1140 becoming a big pink mist."

"Okay."

"Well, now we are in the middle of the road. As you know the device had a mercury switch designed to detonate when the package is tilted. The mercury is very sensitive, but I felt I could work on it gently as long as I did not tilt the package."

"Understood . . . go on."

"Mercury can be held by a magnet. I used the x-ray picture to determine where the mercury switch was located. Then I taped a strong magnet next to it, and just under to hold the mercury in place. The idea being that it will not flow and make contact to complete the circuit as long as the magnet is there."

Now the other members of the det were grinning. They were impressed by the lieutenant's enthusiasm and there was a small bit of pride.

"Interesting, Lieutenant," Potter said rubbing his chin.

"Next I rigged for remote pull."

Now it was fully hitting Potter. "Holy shit."

"Yeah, Chief. Excuse my pun, but I'm trying to satisfy two Masters. I'm not gonna apply heat, shock or friction, but I'm also taking my action remotely. Worse case it detonates while I'm here in the CP."

"LT, this is a first. Well, go ahead and let'er rip."

Jazz got behind the driver's seat and nodded to Denke.

Denke keyed his radio. "All stations this is the CP. FIRE IN THE HOLE! FIRE IN THE HOLE! FIRE IN THE HOLE!"

He nodded back to Jazz who stepped on the gas.

It went as planned. Downrange, Yurwitz shook his head in disbelief and spoke to himself. "Hooya, Lieutenant."

Then he spoke into the comm box. "CP, downrange. This is Petty Officer Yurwitz. I want all hands to come down range and see this."

Jazz stripped off the bomb suit. He dumped it into the back of the HUMMVEE. Quinn jumped in beside him. They followed the dually and were followed by the instructors in the other HUMMVEE.

All the men hopped out and headed for Yurwitz standing in the middle of the road next to the bag. The "politician's" car was a few feet away with the passenger door opened. It was clear that they were successful.

Keating clapped Jazz on the back. He had a huge grin.

"Good work, LT."

"Holy shit!" exclaimed Sinclair. "I've never seen this done before. You ever seen anything like this, Dee?"

"Nah," responded Delgado. "LT, you must gotta ten-inch dick."

"No kidding . . ." chimed in Ash, "and a monster set of jimmies."

"Okay! Circle up here guys!" called Potter.

The men formed a circle around the bag.

Potter spoke again. "HT1, your assessment."

"I've never seen it done this way. This problem by the way gentlemen is designed to create exactly the conflict that Chief Potter told me on the radio that you had in the CP. Dearmer versus hand opening. One philosophy says never, never, never hand open, unless the device is ticking and is strapped to your grandma's girdle. This thought process leads one to try a remote dearmer. The downside is that detonation often occurs, and while nobody gets hurt . . . you have not really helped much have you?

"The other philosophy says, render fucking shit safe, right?" Yurwitz continued. "It is not ticking, we have all day . . . cut the blue wire. The problem naturally is, 'Who has the steady hands to defeat a merc switch?'

"Well . . . leave it to an 1140 . . . too dumb to know better or too arrogant to listen to anyone. LT, you outwitted a merc switch. Frankly, I'm impressed. The device did not function, it is out of the car. Now we can drive the vehicle away and blow in place. I call this day a success, one for the books. Hooya, LT. You have once again demonstrated the value of having a slick bomb on the team. Basic Techs gents, do not have bad habits, they think out of the box."

"Hooya, LT," said Keating. "Well done."

"Okay guys. Clean up, it is beer thirty," said Chief Potter.

Jazz started to help the others put equipment away until Denke called him.

"LT."

"Yes, Senior Chief."

"Bring your book here."

Jazz ran like an excited schoolboy to the dually and grabbed his PQS book. As he handed it to Denke he noticed him putting a wad of dip in his mouth. He worked it into his cheek as Jazz handed his book over. He sensed approval from Denke.

The senior chief sent fresh tobacco spittle into the sand. He looked at Jazz a moment studying him as if he were seeing something new. Then he handed the officer his book back.

"Lieutenant, I think you'll do," he said.

Jazz looked to his PQS book. Denke had signed all four line items.

Long after sundown Det Four was in a bar on Shore Drive frequented by EOD Techs. Most of the patrons had either a crab tattoo, an EOD hat cocked back on his head, or both. Many of the women were second wives. One even had a shirt that read "EOD, EveryOne Drinks, EveryOne's Divorced."

Det Four consumed pitchers of beer and platters of chicken wings. Throughout the evening they were approached by several old shipmates, classmates, and teammates. Ashland, T-Ball, and Denke were especially well received; Denke, because he was about to leave Mobile Unit Two for good, Ash and Ball since they had recently left. Some even complimented Jazz when introduced. Apparently, word of his performance a few hours before had traveled fast. Jazz even received accolades from Lieutenant Commander Massie, the executive officer while he was at NAVSCOLEOD.

"Good work, Jazz," he said. "Show 'em how 1140s do it."

Jazz noted as Det Four piled in the truck that nobody strayed. Once or twice someone in the group got up to talk to an old shipmate, but they always returned. He expected one of the guys to hook up with a chick or stay out drinking with an old dive buddy. None did. They came as a det, they drank as a det, they left as a det.

He listened to the banter of his teammates on the drive back to the base. They were definitely coming together. Still, Jazz knew that he needed to close ranks with Denke and Keating.

Jeannie decided to like Melanie Jascinski. They had a lot in common. They were the same age, had children of the same age, and their husbands both defused bombs underwater.

Their friendship was sealed with a simple act of kindness. Jeannie felt a little strange asking her husband's boss' wife to baby-sit, but Mel had offered several times. She even considered hanging up while Mel's phone was ringing.

"Mel, can I ask a favor?"

"Sure."

"Can you watch my kids for an hour or so while I get the brakes repaired on my mini-van?"

"I'll go one better, why don't I drive you there? We'll drop off your car, go to the pool, have lunch, and pick up the van later. This way you don't have to wait around watching a black and white television while your car is fixed."

Since then they spent a lot of time together. They got along with the other wives, but they all worked or had older children. Jeannie and Melanie became each other's support system while their husbands were gone. They formed a bond that would last through their husbands' deployment.

Jeannie and Melanie developed a daily routine. The day started dropping the eldest kids off at kindergarten. They alternated spending the day at the Jascinski or Ball residence. They spent their mornings sipping tea while the younger children played. After lunch the toddlers were put down for a nap. The "hostess" tended the children while the "guest" performed tasks easier accomplished without children, like negotiating the cereal aisle at the grocery store.

One morning Melanie said, "I think I'm going to fly up to see Jazz."

"Really? Are you going to surprise him?"

"No, we've already talked about it . . . after the new baby, the new assignment . . . we seem to be going in different directions. I think we both realized that we need some time together before the upcoming deployment."

"Sure, but with the training, will he have time to see you?"

"Well, in the evenings. I'll take the kids to visit friends during the day and we'll go to his parents over the weekend. Afterward he plans on staying and taking a week of leave."

"Oh, so how long are you going?"

"Two weeks total."

"Wow, I'm jealous. Do you need a ride to the airport?"

Melanie put down her tea and smiled. "That would be nice."

TWENTY

MASTER CHIEF

After the IED curriculum Det Four moved on to the surface division, followed by small unit tactics (SMUT). The SMUT instructors provided lessons on land navigation, patrolling, and small arms employment. They also trained on insertion techniques via small boat, fastrope, and rappel.

The det was told that the class would culminate in an exercise where the detachment was inserted onto Fort Story at night by boat. They would be expected to patrol across the base to their objective, a weapons cache found by "Marines" that was booby-trapped. To make the scenario more challenging, there was an opposing force composed of TEU TWO instructors acting as the enemy.

During the practical training, Jazz contemplated the chaos and confusion that would ensue during a firefight. He also came to realize the importance of being able to navigate unknown terrain, especially at night. The ability to shoot straight and true would be wasted if he was unable to get his detachment to the objective. It was another reminder that it was imperative that the det be a cohesive unit.

Keating and Denke were cordial but it was clear that they were not getting along. Keating was still smarting from Denke's attack on his abilities, plus Denke continually asserted himself as the only competent authority on the det especially regarding SMUT and IEDs.

While Jazz was considering what to do he even heard the other men of the det making comments. They struggled with their admiration for Denke and their loyalty to Keating.

Jazz knew that the key was Denke. He hoped that he had established a new rapport with his senior chief that would carry him through. Again, Jazz remembered his father's advice.

"Don't worry as much about being a good EOD Tech because you'll never measure up. Be a good officer, a good 1140, a good OIC."

He realized that the same rule applied to Denke. He was on this det not to be a Master Tech, but a senior chief.

Solve the problem, not the conflict.

Foregoing formality, Jazz approached him in the hallway during a lunch break.

131

"Senior Chief, do you have a minute?"

"Sure, LT. What's up?"

"I want to talk about how we are doing things in the det, specifically between you and Chief Keating."

Denke visibly stiffened.

"Hear me out, Senior Chief. Here's the deal. You guys are obviously of two minds and come from two different schools of thought."

"He's just a diver, sir," Denke said with condescension.

"Excuse me?"

"He's a diver, sir. There are two kinds of people in EOD, operators and divers. The divers never quite get the EOD thing. They don't know how to do the other stuff. Patrolling, shooting, moving, communicating, it's all foreign to 'em."

"Senior, I have heard this discussion before. I agree that we seem to have two flavors. But here's the thing—we are on an MCM det. Mine Countermeasures. We are all about diving, diving in minefields mind you, but diving. Now the other stuff is equally important. I would submit that while Chief K may be too close to the Fleet Divers on the EOD spectrum, you may be too close to the Frogs."

Denke tensed again and crossed his arms.

"I believe that we should be operators and divers, Senior Chief. I do not know where that happy medium is, but I do know that I can't get us there . . . only you and Chief K can do that. Do you get me?"

"I get you, sir."

"Why did you come here?"

Now Denke uncrossed his arms, he appeared a little defeated.

"I'm sure you heard, sir. The detailer and community manager have said that if I want to make master chief that it would help to have an MCM ride."

"Why is that if you already have your Master crab? Why is it important for a guy who is already a Master Blaster to go to an MCM team in order to make master chief? I'll tell you the answer . . . because they want you to *lead* an MCM det. Someday if you are going to be the Group Master Chief, they want you to have MCM leadership experience. Otherwise sailors under your purview will look to you and say, 'Master Chief Denke doesn't get it . . . he's just an operator, a Frog-wanna-be.'"

Denke was silent. Jazz realized that he turned Denke's own threat about making Commodore against him.

"Well?"

"I see your point, sir."

"Senior Chief, we have two choices before us. The three of us can fight and argue for the next two years. If we do that nobody will win and we will make the best job in the Navy a drag. Or, we can figure out how you, me, and Keating are going to get along and run this det. A Master Tech may not be able to figure out how to do that, but a master chief, a real leader, can.

"I want to become smart on the 'operator' skills, Senior Chief. And I am happy to have you on this det for that reason. But, I suspect that we will never use those skills.

I think we are going to spend most of our time in that Mark-5 and the RHIB. Keating is the det expert in those arenas."

Jazz noted that Denke was now rubbing his head. Maybe it was a sign that he was struggling with what Jazz was saying.

"Senior, this det was running fine before you arrived. I'd like you to make it better not worse."

Denke looked at Jazz a moment, then nodded his head silently.

Before class the next morning, Denke walked to the front of the room.

"Gents, I've got something to put out before we start today."

Denke looked directly at Jazz as the others quieted.

"One of the most important things to do while the detachment is going through READIMPT is to develop our SOPs. We have not really been doing that, have we Lieutenant?"

Jazz was not sure what Denke was saying but he sensed it had to do with their conversation the previous day.

"Uh, no, Senior."

"Well, we are behind the power curve then. You do have SOPs for each mission area, right?"

"Yes, they are Warrant Officer Fontaine's . . . I have not really changed anything."

"Well, we need to review them all and improve them where possible. Here is what I suggest we do."

Everyone noted Denke's use of the word, "suggest."

"I think we need to assign each man a mission area in which he is to become the subject matter expert. As such that man will be responsible to you, Lieutenant, for the applicable SOP. Additionally, while everyone needs to be proficient at all skills, I think we need to develop a notion that certain members are the P1 for a particular mission area."

"Interesting," said Keating.

"Here is my recommended breakdown. I think Sinclair should be in charge of surface ops, Quinn takes chem and bio, okay?"

"Sure, Senior," said Quinn.

"Delgado, as pubs and CMS handler, I want you to write an SOP for use of all our crypto and comms gear. I also want an SOP for small boat ops. I want specifics on how to load the boat, how to swing it over from a ship, how to perform basic troubleshooting for the engines."

"No kidding, Senior?" replied Delgado.

"No kidding."

"Got it, Senior Chief."

"All mobility skills will be under the purview of T-Ball. I want an SOP for fastrope, CAST, rappel, and even jump operations. T-Ball, you are going to become the det's premier HRST and CAST-master."

"I need the school, Senior."

"Already arranged. Ash, you are to take demolition. I do not want just basic range clearance stuff; I want a monster SOP that covers the demo required for all other mission areas. I'm talking underwater demo build up, special shape charge attacks on mines, and breaching."

"Wow, okay."

"I will take IEDs and Small Unit Tactics . . . and, Chief K."

"Yes?"

"You are obviously our diving and MCM expert, so I would like you to review our procedures there and spearhead all associated procedural changes. I recommend you include all emergency procedures for diving."

"Okay, Senior."

"Lieutenant Jascinski, I did not suggest a mission area for you because your job will be to review all mission areas, apply your common sense approach, suggest revisions, and of course exert veto power when needed."

Jazz just nodded.

"Two weeks gents, all SOP reviews need to be completed in two weeks. Then we'll each brief our area."

"Senior Chief," said Keating. "I think that this is a great idea."

Jazz was fined seven cases of beer during Det Four's time at TEU TWO. For him nearly all of the evolutions were firsts. First night patrol, first waterborne insertion, first rappel, first fastrope, first CAST, first CAST at night.

Navies the world over posses in their arsenals drifting mines, the jellyfish of naval warfare. These are the death orbs from World War II movies with multiple horns protruding from their top half. They float at or near the ocean's surface running with the ocean's current.

A drifting mine campaign is not precise. The minelayer merely hopes that the mine ends in the path of a ship, any ship. He does not know who, when, or where one of his mines will find its prey. It simply drifts, waiting for the force of an unsuspecting ship to impact the horns. Shortly after detonation, steel, oil, and flesh slip together into the sea. The victim's distress calls are as a stung tourist crying out in pain and disbelief. Like the jellyfish, the terror that ensues by only one mine is devastating enough that all ships flee at its report.

For the price of a used SUV a third world country can empty a small sea, prevent merchant fleets from using a strait, or close down a major sea-lane. Until of course, EOD arrives.

As EOD Technicians, part of Det Four's training to tread on land or in the water where others dared not included "pouncer" or CAST operations. Specifically, this is a technique of inserting two men via helicopter to countercharge the mine.

This quickly became Jazz's favorite of all the EOD mobility skills.

TWENTY-ONE

CAST

Jazz and Ashland donned wetsuits in the locker room prepping for Jazz's third CAST op. His wetsuit was still wet from his first CAST op the previous day.

Jazz called the house in Annapolis the night before just after Melanie arrived with the kids. He described to Melanie, Eleanor, and the Admiral how he and Ashland jumped from the open ramp on the stern of a CH-46 helicopter into the Atlantic Ocean. Jazz was disappointed that nobody was impressed, yet their varied reactions were amusing. Melanie was nervous about Jazz flying in the helo. Understandably, she thought it might crash. The Admiral was worried about him toting explosives through the water. He asked for a detailed description of their safety precautions. Eleanor wanted to make sure her son was dressing properly.

"Maybe you could wear long underwear, dear. I am sure the water is cold."

"Mom, I'm 27. I'm a parent," Jazz said with exasperation. "Not only am I a lieutenant in the world's greatest Navy, I'm a Special Operations Officer . . ."

"Lieutenant."

"Yes, ma'am."

"I'm still your mother and as such I outrank both you and the Admiral. You may be TACON to Melanie but you are still OPCON to me. Do you understand?"

"Yes, ma'am."

"You do as I say and dress warmly."

"Yes, ma'am."

Jazz thought of his Dad as he strapped the knife and a flare to his inner calf. Ashland offered some last minute advice.

"Remember, LT, don't swim at it like a bat outta hell. Make sure you stop and watch it in the seas. In three feet swells these things bob like a motherfucker. If you are not careful on your approach you could set it off. Got it?"

"Yeah."

"Hey, LT."

"Huh?"

"Get fired up man . . . EOD baby! It's a blast!"

Jazz smiled as he put on his UDT vest, then his dive booties. He thought to himself, *This is why I joined EOD.*

He noticed that his heart was pounding with excitement.

The lieutenant picked up his fins, mask and helmet and followed Ash to TEU TWO's back lot where Keating was waiting for them. Dressed in a flight suit with a helmet in his hand, he would be their CAST-master for the op.

"You guys ready?" the chief asked.

"Ready! I'm fired up! We gonna do some of that EOD shit!" screamed Ash.

"Fuckin-A right," said Keating.

The chief drove them down to the landing zone. Chief Potter was there leaning against a pickup. Jazz could see a box containing the explosives they would use in the bed of the truck. Potter had a backpack with a small radio in it, the handset dangled over his shoulder.

"Obviously, the first group is already out there," said Keating.

"Yeah, but we just got a call that they are on their way back. You guys will be flying in fifteen minutes," replied Potter. "They got Dee and Sinclair in the water, then Dee went again with Quinn. Denke said that T-Ball did real well on his U/I CAST-master. Denke said to make sure we remind him that he owes."

Something garbled came over Potter's handset. He grabbed it.

"This is LZ, go."

Jazz heard a static response.

"LZ, roger out."

Potter dropped the handset again. "Okay, they are five minutes out. Get ready to board the bird."

Jazz and Ashland donned their helmets and put their masks on over them. Keating grabbed two satchels from the box in the bed of the truck. He handed one each to Jazz and Ash. Jazz opened his to ensure the explosives were in it. Then he strapped it around his waist.

Before he saw it, Jazz heard the thumping of the blades of the CH-46 helicopter. Jazz had seen the—46, called a Sea Knight, throughout his life as a Navy brat growing up on bases around the world. He marveled at how the two counter-rotating blades, one on a pylon above the cockpit and the other on the higher tail kept the bird flying.

The three men closed their eyes and tucked their chins to their chests, hiding from sand and grass thrown at them by the helicopter's downwash. As it settled on the landing zone, Jazz could hear the RPMs decrease. He looked up just as the pilot surrendered to gravity and the aircraft settled, compressing the hydraulics on its landing gear.

The ramp came down from the rear of the—46. An aircrewman stepped out first, then Jazz saw the rest of his team emerge from the below the tail. They were all grinning as they cleared the prop wash. Jazz saw the aircrewman motioning at them. He followed Keating and Ashland through the brush up the ramp and into the helo.

In a moment they were strapped into the two canvas benches lining each side of the helicopter. Jazz sat across from Ash. Keating strapped on a long safety harness connected to the floor of the aircraft. He plugged his helmet into a comms box so he could talk on the intercom with the pilots.

From inside the whine of the engines was louder than the helo's blades. Jazz felt heavy for a moment as the helo's engines revved up and the aircraft began to climb.

Once airborne, Jazz noted Ashland visibly relaxed. The EOD Tech closed his eyes, leaned over and began to nod. Jazz looked out the window across from him. They had turned and were already over the Atlantic Ocean. He could see several boats in the mouth of the Chesapeake Bay.

When the boat traffic thinned Jazz surveyed the inside of the helicopter. It was nearly a relic. He noted the deck was covered with hydraulic fluid and there was a visible leak from the overhead. Keating warned him earlier to be careful not to slip off the ramp.

Jazz thought it a crime that most Americans drive a car no more than five years old while the Navy had to fly aircraft more than twenty. Not a single—46 pilot in the fleet was older than his aircraft. The most recent vertical lift aircraft expected to replace the Sea Knight was experiencing difficulty. Jazz surmised the Navy should simply buy new models of the—46 while waiting for the emerging technology.

As he pondered the ways that he would improve his Navy, the blades eventually lulled Jazz to sleep.

Once Chief Keating tapped Jazz, everything happened quickly.

The jumpers could barely hear the chief yell as he held up one finger, "ONE MINUTE!"

Jazz and Ash donned their masks again, then slipped their fins around each wrist. The aircraft was in a tight turn, pulling Jazz into his seat. He looked down to make sure the satchel around his waist containing the demolition charge was still fastened. He felt a rush of air as the aircrewman opened the ramp.

Keating moved aft to the ramp. When he got there Jazz saw him hold his hand up like a puppet screaming, "THIRTY SECONDS!"

Jazz and Ashland unbuckled their seatbelts. They could feel the aircraft nose come up some as it slowed forward airspeed and began to hover.

"STAND UP!"

At this command the pair stood and began walking toward the ramp. Jazz ducked his head as he stepped on the ramp. Keating slapped him in the ass.

"GO!"

Jazz jumped. He crossed his legs and pulled his right hand over his mask and his left arm over the satchel in one motion. The fall was just long enough for him to think about it.

He surveyed himself quickly after hitting the water; nothing was broken. He kicked hard to the surface and held an arm straight up over his head giving the "thumbs up" sign. He saw Ashland doing the same. Keating waved as the helo climbed again, leaving the EOD Techs to their work.

They both bobbed over on their stomachs, slipping the fins off their wrists and onto their feet. Jazz kicked, treading water as he looked for the mine. There was a two-foot swell with whitecaps from winds coming from the same direction.

Jazz first looked for the telltale smoke dropped by the aircraft to mark the mine. The winds were keeping the smoke low on the water and disbursing it quickly.

"Do you see it, LT!" Ash called out.

"No!"

"Ah, I got it . . . look to port!"

Jazz looked to his left side. He saw the swells breaking on it, each time a wave crashed over the mine it seemed to roll like a buoy.

"Go ahead, LT, I am right behind ya!"

Jazz began swimming for the mine. He concentrated on developing a rhythm of breathing that matched his stroke and the seas. Still, every now and then he got a mouth full of seawater when he tried to breathe as a wave came over him. Suddenly he realized that he had lost track of time.

Damn it! he cursed to himself. *Had he been swimming five minutes? Ten?*

Now he remembered Ashland's advice. *"Remember, LT, don't swim at it like a bat outta hell. Make sure you stop and watch it in the seas. In three feet swells these things bob like a motherfucker."*

Jazz stopped and looked up, he could not see the mine. He quickly became confused. The seas and winds were increasing still.

Did the mine sink? he wondered. *Have the seas dragged it under?*

He looked back from the direction he came from for Ashland. At first he did not see him, creating a moment of panic. He noticed the helo circling overhead passively. From Keating's perspective all was going well.

Jazz looked again and saw Ashland behind him near the mine. He had swum past it. By misjudging the current, not keeping his eye on the mine, and worst of all losing focus, he had gone past it by fifty yards. Immediately he realized his dilemma. *Now I gotta swim against the current and wind to get to it.*

He rolled over on his back and screamed, "FFFUUUUUUCK!"

He could not wait a moment more. Jazz began a hard swim into the current back toward the mine. He swallowed seawater with every breath. After what seemed an eternity he reached Ashland and the mine.

"What the fuck are you doing, LT!"

Jazz looked at Ashland sheepishly. The LPO could see the exhaustion in his eyes.

"Well, let's get it over with, sir. Put the charge on."

Jazz took a breath and rolled onto his stomach again. He opened the satchel and extracted the demolition charge. Then he swam up to the mine. Jazz timed the movement of the mine in the waves and being careful of its horns, attached the charge to it.

When he finished, Ashland was right behind him. "Good job, sir, now head for pick-up while I attach the dogbone."

Swimming with the current again was almost relaxing. Jazz noted that Keating was watching the evolution closely because the helo was in perfect position down-current, with the hoist already in the water.

He did not make the same mistake twice and repeatedly noted the position of the hoist to ensure that he did not swim past it. As he got close to the downwash of the—46 on the ocean surface he could feel the blade pushing air against him. It took the last bit of his strength to plow to the 'sweet spot,' the calm right under the helicopter.

Jazz slipped the hoist under his right arm, around his back and under his left arm. Then he clipped the free end to the lifting shackle and again gave the thumbs up signal. He looked up, watching the aircrewman guiding him as the helo got closer. At the top the aircrewman pulled him into the bird and got Jazz fully on the deck. He put slack in the cable and unshackled him.

Jazz gave Keating the "okay" signal and flopped back to his seat. Within seven minutes the process was repeated with Ashland.

The helo stood off at a safe distance and altitude. The two pilots, the aircrewmen, and all three EOD Technicians looked out the starboard side of the helo, watching for the mine to detonate. Ashland had the time running on his watch from when he lit the initiators. Jazz looked over and saw that it read:

00:00:05

He looked back to the mine. It erupted in a flash of fire and black smoke, followed by water spray and white smoke that lifted high into the air. All the sailors shouted simultaneously.

"WHOOOOHOOOO!"

Keating slapped Ashland on the back

Grinning, Ash mimed jerking off. "EOD, BABAY!" he yelled. "DAMN I LOVE THIS SHIT!"

Just as Ash and Keating sat down, Jazz bent over and threw up a stomach full of seawater all over his feet and the deck.

They both looked at him in disbelief as he sat up and screamed, "HOOYA!"

"ARE YOU ALRIGHT, LT?" yelled Keating.

"HELL YEAH! THIS IS MUCH BETTER THAN STANDING THE MIDWATCH!"

As Jazz laced up his boots in the locker room, Denke handed him a message to call Captain Solarsky. Jazz dialed the number on the det phone. Solarsky answered after one ring.

"EOD Mobile Unit Six, Commander Solarsky speaking, may I help you?"

"Sir, it's Lieutenant Jascinski."

"Jazz! How are you? I've heard you guys are doing very well up there."

"Yessir, we are learning a lot."

"Good. It seems you are wanted at the Explosive Ordnance Disposal Technical Division. It is related to your recent IED call in San Patricio. Ops is having orders cut for you and Petty Officer Ball. The rest of your detachment will return to Ingleside upon completion of training."

"Are we going now, sir, or after we finish here at TEU TWO?"

"You are going now. Your team has only a week left, correct?"

"Yessir."

"Fine, I see that you have done your IED, Surface, Small Unit Tactics, and the first part of MCM. You have done a few MCM-rides since you've been to Ingleside?"

"Well, sir, I have not embarked a minesweeper, but we did an exercise with *Scout*."

"You'll be fine then. You and T-Ball proceed to Stump Neck post-haste. Your orders will be waiting there for you."

"Roger, sir. How long will we be?"

"I don't know."

Jazz realized that his family vacation was about to go in the toilet. Melanie was not going to be happy when he told her the news. At least she would not have to drive to Norfolk.

TWENTY-TWO

INDIAN HEAD

The next day Jazz drove the rental car down Indian Head Highway to the main gate of Naval Surface Weapon Station Indian Head. As he passed through, a wave of old feelings returned. He wiped them, reminding himself that he was already a Tech.

He saw the base club, The Powder Keg, on the right hand side. Jazz turned into its lot and parked there.

The memorial was not far. Jazz always paused when he first saw the four obelisks of granite each with the seal of one of the four services on top. Under each seal were bronze plaques bearing the names of EOD Techs who died in the line of duty.

Jazz was first drawn to the list under the seal of the United States Navy. Its most recent addition was an instructor Jazz knew as a student.

GMC (EOD/PJ) Stephen J. Morris, USN

Morris died in a training accident the very day Jazz graduated. Jazz was on leave and did not hear the news until he reported in at Mobile Unit Six. As he looked at the name, Jazz recalled the cold November mornings less than two years before, his class standing in shorts on the pool deck. He remembered Morris, warm in a sweatsuit with coffee in hand, the class taskmaster.

"Get in the water!"

"Hooya!" the students would yell as they plunged into the cold water. Morris would wait a moment until a quorum of his charges was shivering.

"Anyone wanna quit?"

There would not be an answer.

"Ten thousand yards, crawl. Go!"

Upon finishing the swim, the students were required to exit the pool and get into the 'leaning rest,' the pushup position until the last of their classmates finished the swim. Jazz recalled looking at Morris' boots as he stood in front of him.

"Mister Jascinski, you had better square these people away. Two more failed room inspections yesterday. Come by after class today and we'll discuss."

"Aye, aye, Chief!"

Jazz looked to the Army column.

Timothy A. West, Sgt USA

Cameron P. Martin, Sgt USA

Jazz still struggled with his role in their deaths. He made the phone call that set their demise in motion.

There was a noise behind him. Jazz turned around to see a fossil of a man in a short-sleeved shirt with a bow tie. The man was stooped and wore thick glasses. He had long ago ceased combing the thin wiry hair on his head that matched the bush in his ears.

"Zero eight five eight," he said.

"Excuse me?" replied Jazz.

"Zero eight five eight."

"Uh, was that your class number, sir?"

"No. Ever heard of the Combined Federal Campaign?"

"Yes, sir."

"Get a pen and write it down. Zero eight five eight," the white Yoda growled as if Jazz was negligent to not have known and remembered this important number.

Jazz nervously pulled a pen from his shirt pocket. He then extracted an old receipt from his wallet.

"Zero eight five eight," the man repeated.

Jazz mimicked as he wrote it down. "*Zero eight five eight.*"

"What is it?" he asked.

"The number for the EOD Memorial Scholarship Fund in the Combined Federal Campaign. I assume you are a student?"

"I graduated a few months ago. I'm Lieutenant James Jascinski," he said extending his hand.

"Nice to meet you, sir. I'm Sergeant Horace Pickney, United States Army Retired. I'm one of the curators for the EOD Memorial and the scholarship fund. Army? Navy?"

"Navy."

"Are you here for someone in particular? That chief who was an instructor I guess."

Jazz studied the sergeant's face. He noticed that his eyes were glossy and that his teeth were stained from cigarettes and coffee. When he raised his bushy eyebrows in anticipation, Jazz snapped back.

"Uh, yes. The chief, and the two most recent Army Techs from Texas."

"Oh?"

"Yeah. I didn't know them directly, but we kinda worked together. How about you, do you know any of these men?"

The old man smiled at Jazz. "Well, Lieutenant, I've only met four of them, but I know all of 'em."

As soon as Jazz and T-Ball reported aboard at Stump Neck they were separated. Jazz knew that it was not by accident that they were met by a lieutenant commander and a first class petty officer, both Master EOD Techs and both senior to their counterparts. Jazz was invited to the wardroom for coffee, T-Ball to the enlisted mess. While the maneuvering was subtle, Jazz sensed it and Ball's look showed that he had too.

The wardroom looked much like that of a ship. The furniture was standard Navy issue. There was a combination dining room and conference table in the center and a small lounge area. A row of coffee pots, condiments, newspapers, and a bowl of fruit sat on a table along the wall adjacent to the entrance. Above them was a long mirror. The other walls had still photos of missiles, mines, and bombs. Jazz figured they were ordnance items tested by TECHDIV.

Lieutenant Commander Evans put a cup of black coffee in Jazz's hand. Jazz studied the ribbons between Evans' gold Special Operations pin and his silver Master EOD crab as he listened to his superior relay his six minute resume of where he was from, places he was stationed, and whom he knew in EOD. Jazz recognized some of the names but was too distracted to discuss any of Evans' sea stories.

Jazz sensed something odd about Evans. He thought this suspicion might not be about Evans specifically, but that he was still put off by being separated from his teammate.

"So where's Petty Officer Ball?"

"He is somewhere else in the building, the enlisted mess or a conference room I think. He will be interviewed separately."

"Interviewed or interrogated?"

"Relax, James. I heard that you were nervous about that. This is an interview. Nobody is out to find fault here. We are just trying to get some information."

Jazz thought about Evans' response for a moment.

"Then why have we been separated?"

"Because we want to compare what each of you says. If you are both sitting in a room together the tendency is for the junior man to agree with the senior's version of events. This is especially sticky in your case, since Ball may have better insight into the technical aspects of the devices that you encountered due to his broader EOD experience."

"Great," Jazz said sarcastically.

"No offense."

"What is this really about? You are not who you seem to be. You are wearing a Special Operations pin, but I'm not sure you are really an 1140."

"What?" said Evans almost choking on the words. "How the fuck do you know that!"

"I can just tell. You're polished but I can smell 'TED' all over you."

"'TED?'"

"'Typical Enlisted Dude,' no offense," Jazz said trying to mimic Evans' voice.

"Fuck you, Lieutenant."

"No, fuck you, Evans. Who are you and what is going on? Do you work for the FBI?"

"How did you guess that?"

"First, how did you know that I was nervous about being questioned? Special Agent Cruz had to tell you. Second, you know too much about EOD and too many people to be acting the part, so you are a crab-wearer, but I think you were enlisted. Eleven-forties do not suggest to one another that their experience is lacking so flippantly. I think your Master crab is real . . . but I think that you were enlisted."

Evans looked to one of the photos, frowning. Jazz watched him. Then he saw it, a camera lens was hidden in the corner. A microphone was probably behind the frame. This was an interrogation.

"Fine," he said turning back to Jazz. "I'm with the FBI. Damn . . . you want a job?"

Evans slumped with defeat. He sighed heavily before beginning again. "I'm surprised you got me this quick. Before you get your panties all in a bunch, hold on and hear me out. I was in EOD and I am an officer, though not an 1140 as you so astutely pointed out, in the reserves."

"What? Explain."

"The bio I gave you is mostly true. I served twelve years in the Navy in EOD when I decided to get out. We don't have the time or the beer required for me to tell you that story right now. I joined the FBI and became a Special Agent, but I stayed in the Naval Reserves. I was stationed at Mobile Unit Ten down there where you just were."

"Fort Story?"

"Yep. Anyway, after two years in the reserves I was offered a commission as a Reserve Intelligence Officer."

Suddenly the door opened and Special Agent Elena Cruz stepped in. Despite the circumstances, Jazz was still surprised.

"Lieutenant Jascinski, it is good to see you again," she said extending her hand. Cruz did not have a jacket on, which showed off her figure more than the first time they met. As Jazz shook her hand he noticed that her cream colored blouse was open at the neck.

One more button and I'd see cleavage.

Jazz reminded himself not to stare. He forced his eyes downward to Cruz's waist. On her belt, she was wearing a sidearm, a badge, and handcuffs.

Jazz engaged her green eyes again through her dark rimmed glasses.

Sophisticated yet sexy.

Cruz smiled at him almost devilishly and said, "Why don't we all sit down?"

Jazz and Evans sat at the conference table across from each other. Cruz topped off her coffee cup at the sidebar. While she took her time adding sugar and cream,

Jazz could not help watching her. He tried to calm down, then he remembered she performed this same maneuver in Ingleside. She took her time with the notebook, ensuring everyone in the EOD conference room was made to feel that they were waiting for her.

This woman uses her feminine wares to keep men off balance.

Finally Cruz stood at the head of the table. She took off her glasses and looked at the two men. Evans seemed just as captivated as Jazz.

"Lieutenant Jascinski, I am to blame for this," Cruz said in a conciliatory voice. "I thought this was the best way to retrieve accurate information from you and Petty Officer Ball. We were trying to create a low key, no pressure, 'Please, help us.' kind of environment. I have a murder investigation to run, one that certainly involves domestic terrorism. For understandable reasons, our first encounter was just not that helpful. You were clearly nervous, as we have said, and Chief Keating told me that your CO was pressuring you. I know how that is. My goal today was to remove that pressure and gain more insight to the deaths of your EOD brethren. Forgive me, but I am sure you can understand our motivation."

Jazz calibrated his brain before speaking.

"I understand your motivation," Jazz sat back in his chair, "but this isn't about Martin and West is it? What I mean is . . . they are not really your main concern anymore. This is not about the murder investigation, it is about the IEDs."

Cruz dropped her notebook to the table and looked at Jazz for a long moment.

"You are very perceptive, Lieutenant," she said through a sly smirk.

"That's what I said," Evans interjected with a guffaw.

"How did you reach this conclusion?" inquired Cruz as she sat at the head of the table.

Her voice and demeanor changed. Jazz felt like suddenly there was real respect, as if he had genuinely broken a barrier with her.

"Because you are certain that Martin and West were murdered, not killed by an explosive accident. Which therefore means that my knowledge of the IEDs has next to nothing to do with their deaths. So, you think or you know that the bad guys, these terrorists, are going to or have already built more of the IEDs that T-Ball and I encountered."

Cruz and Evans exchanged a knowing glance.

"You're right," she responded.

"Well, then let's get down to business. Turn on your tape or your camera, or whatever. I'll tell you everything I remember."

Cruz had Jazz and T-Ball sit for two to four hour sessions, reviewing what happened and what they remembered again. They each reviewed the incident four times separately on the first day. Cruz then decided she obtained as much uninfluenced information as possible. The second day she had them review the incident together on the chance that they would stir more information from each other's memory.

Emphasis was placed on the IEDs. The two EOD Techs described the devices and even drew what they remembered.

After two days, Cruz decided to take a break. Jazz and T-Ball were not, however, released to return to Ingleside.

"We may need you for a few more days. You must remain in the greater Washington DC area. We will contact you at your hotel when we need you again."

Jazz left immediately to visit his family in Annapolis.

Melanie turned off the baby monitor next to the infant sleeping in the portable crib. The sound of their sons playing in the pool twenty feet below came through the open window. The Admiral sounded uncomfortable being in charge. The man who once commanded a squadron of destroyers was still figuring out how to be a grandfather.

Jazz closed the window silently. When he turned, Melanie was waiting for him on the bed. He lay beside her and put his arm around her. She rolled toward him and kissed him softly, throwing her leg over him.

His mother's voice erupted from the kitchen.

"James!"

"Yes, Ma!" he yelled.

"Phone! A Mister Teebah for you!"

"Jazz! The baby!" Melanie hissed.

Jazz looked in the crib. Abigail stirred, but did not wake up. Melanie sighed heavily and sat up on the edge of the bed as he picked up the phone on the end table.

"T-Ball?" he said quietly.

He heard his mother hang up.

"Hey, sir. They want us back tomorrow morning."

"Damnit, Melanie just got here."

"Yeah, I was enjoying a mini-vacation myself. Oh well. At least we get to visit with Ms. Cruz again."

"Shut-up."

"I think she's into you, LT."

"I think you've been on the road too long," Jazz lied. *So maybe she is interested in me.*

"Whatever, LT. You want me to pick you up somewhere?"

"Nah, I'll see you there."

"Roger."

When he hung up the phone Melanie looked sick.

"Going back tomorrow?" she inquired to confirm.

"Yes."

"There is more to this than you're telling me, isn't there?" she asked.

"Melanie, come on . . . don't be a conspiracy nut."

"You are not a good liar, Jazz. What happened in Texas? What really happened to those men?"

"Nothing . . . it is just like I told you."

Melanie frowned at him, disbelievingly. She said nothing else as she put on her one-piece bathing suit, turned the baby monitor back on, grabbed a towel, and headed downstairs. Jazz realized that protecting Melanie from the dangers of his job was driving a wedge between them.

When Jazz walked into the interview room the next day, Cruz and T-Ball were leaning over the table, studying something.

"'Morning."

As they turned toward him, Jazz saw one of the IEDs from their incident in San Patricio on the table.

"Holy shit, where'd you get that? Have you guys captured another one?"

"No," replied Cruz proudly. "It's a replica."

"Pretty impressive, huh, LT?" said T-Ball.

"Yeah, it looks exactly like the damn thing."

Jazz studied the device closer. The mock-up appeared as if the builder was just about to finish the last stage of assembly. The lid was off, exposing the contents inside.

"Getting at this is going to be a sonofabitch," reported T-Ball. "Are you guys going to work on a render safe procedure?"

"Yes, we have drafted an initial memo for distribution to all municipal bomb squads. Additionally, we are constructing a second replica that is a cut-away so the initiation methods and the explosive train can be studied. We'll send a follow-up memo with a formal procedure if we are able."

"Shit, good luck. Let us know if you have any success."

"So what else do you need us for?" asked Jazz. *Maybe you just wanted to see me again.*

"We wanted you to look at our replica in order to verify its accuracy as you have already done. More importantly, I also wanted to inquire if you had any ideas."

"We've been working on it for sure," said Jazz. "I've actually started dreaming about it . . . but it is a tough one. My inclination right now is to clear folks out and let the thing function. Hardly an EOD solution is it?"

"No," said Cruz. "But I agree, it is going to be a bitch."

"Well, if we come up with something, we'll let ya know."

"Great, let me give you my card again."

"Fine," replied Jazz. "Here's another copy of mine."

T-Ball shot Jazz a look. Cruz sensed something. T-Ball's face changed just as she turned toward him.

"Agent Cruz, do you have a name for this thing yet?" he asked feigning innocence.

"Actually, yes. It is called the SANPAT Bomb since it was found in San Patricio County."

TWENTY-THREE

DEPLOYMENT

Airline flights were one of the few times that he was able to relax. It was as if time stopped. There was nothing he could do except wait patiently until he landed. Nasih ceased to be concerned about customs long ago. There were no more accurate photos of him in the Western World. And in this part of the world, travel for him was especially easy. His appearance and coloring allowed him to fit in easily. He was unremarkable in Italy, Greece, Turkey, the Middle East, and now the Balkans.

He smiled looking out at the beautiful Albanian countryside rising toward him. "The Balkans," directly translated to "A chain of wooded mountains."

How appropriate, he thought.

On his flight to Stockholm the in-flight entertainment was an American movie about the CIA manufacturing a war in Albania. As he looked out to Albania's mountains beyond the airliner's starboard wing he remembered laughing during the film.

Nasih's first visit was shortly after the coup in 1995. His superiors called it the new Lebanon, Tirane, the new Beirut. They could hide and thrive among the chaos, especially since their work was done in Afghanistan. Shortly after arriving the first time he realized the region's name was astutely named. Nasih and several of his brethren used it as a base of operations ever since.

The climate was much more comfortable than Texas this time of year. He stepped down the ladder and onto the tarmac. One of his brothers was waiting outside the main terminal.

"I have already taken care of everything . . . we do not have to go in."

"Well done. I hope that you did not pay too much."

"No, I did not have to."

"Good. It is not really necessary here, customs is merely an inconvenience."

"The car is this way."

They walked in silence in a moment, though they knew that nobody nearby understood their language.

"Everything is proceeding as we expected, except for the incident in Texas."

"That is none of your concern . . . and it amounted to nothing. In fact it may have been a suitable test of our friends there and they did well."

"Friends?" the shorter man said glancing sideways at Nasih.

"Well, infidel friends anyway."

Nasih reminded himself not to speak of the tragedy of *Green Leon*. It was also none of the junior man's concern.

*   *   *

There was no telling what a five year old would understand. Jazz and Melanie tried to prepare their sons for the six-month deployment. Tyler, the youngest, only knew that Daddy was going to leave for a long time. And he did not even comprehend what "long" was. His parents constantly reassured him that Daddy was not leaving the family, only that he was going away. At the end of these conversations he always asked one more time, "But you are coming back, right, Dad?"

"That's right, son," Jazz would respond with a lump in his throat.

Going onboard the ship with Tyler was difficult. The stairs were too steep for his little legs. The strange sounds often startled or scared him. But Nicholas, the eldest of Jazz's mancubs, at five, was old enough.

Father and son walked up the brow to *Inchon*'s quarterdeck. Jazz followed Nicholas, watching his feet carefully find each step.

God he's getting so big, Jazz thought to himself. *How much will he change while I'm gone?*

Nicholas grabbed his daddy's hand as they headed aft toward his stateroom.

When *Inchon* and her task group departed in March 1999, it was to be the first deployment of an MCM flotilla. *Inchon* was already fully loaded on this Sunday afternoon in preparation for deployment to the Mediterranean and Arabian Seas.

There were four EOD detachments onboard. Four, Six, and Eight from EODMU SIX and Det Eleven from EODMU THREE in San Diego, California. Mobile Unit Six also brought the FARC as Fontaine had described with a crew of Diving Medical Technicians to operate and maintain it.

The EOD force structure included support personnel from supply clerks and yeoman to boat mechanics and Seabees. The underwater portion of the MCM triad was commanded by CDR Solarsky and would be commonly referred to as EODMU SIX FORWARD.

The whole of HM-15 embarked with their minesweeping helicopters. They brought more boats than the EOD Techs did to control launch and recovery of their sleds and sonar fish. The hangar had just enough space to perform maintenance on two helos if they were folded and stuffed. The rest nested on the flight deck.

HM-15 also brought the largest complement of officers. There were at least four officers for every aircraft onboard. Jazz guessed that there were almost forty of them.

Four Mine Countermeasures ships were to follow *Inchon* to the Med as part of the flotilla. *Avenger, Pioneer, Gladiator,* and *Defender* were to remain within sight of *Inchon* during the trans-Atlantic crossing like ducklings following their mother.

As part of her conversion, *Inchon* was given the capability to refuel the sweeps via astern refueling. She could also transport food, mail, medical supplies, and people back and forth between each of the ships.

The mine warfare ships would separate while in the Med to participate in different MCM exercises with other NATO countries. Then all would rendezvous prior to going through the Suez Canal and on to the Arabian Gulf.

Jazz's stateroom looked much like all of the others aboard *Inchon.* All of the fixtures were made of gray sheet metal. There was a wall of lockers, drawers, and two built-in desks lining the left side. A sink with a mirror was on the right in the front of the room. One set of bunk beds was in the back right corner. Nicholas climbed into the bottom bunk.

"So this is where you will sleep, Daddy?"

"Yep, that's where I will sleep."

Nicholas surveyed the room. He had a look on his face of approval, but his father could also see that he felt the need to be inquisitive.

"And that's your sink over there?" he said pointing to the sink next to Jazz.

"Yes, this is my sink. I will share this room with one other diver guy. He has the top bunk."

"Are a lot of diver guys going on this trip?"

"Yes, there will be about twenty divers going."

Nicholas flipped on the reading light above Jazz's rack.

"Who is the other diver guy in here?"

"Uh, he's a man named Jake Duvall."

Duvall's detachment, Det Six was stationed in Charleston, so the two encountered each other only a few times before the deployment. Jazz met him when he passed through Charleston before reporting aboard. They got to know each other better during work-ups for the INCTASKGRU deployment. Duvall had been a SWO like Jazz. The Special Operations lateral transfer board picked him up the year before Jazz.

There were nine officers going on the deployment. There was one OIC per detachment. The other two lived next door to Jazz and Duvall. O'Malley and Thicke were both warrant officers. Chief Warrant Officers in Navy EOD are given the moniker "Gunner." As a result these two were affectionately known as "Gunner O" and "Gunner T."

Across the hall from Jazz and Duvall lived the Mobile Unit Six Operations Officer and the tactics officer. They would interface with the MCMRON and direct the employment of the detachments. Captain Solarsky had a stateroom forward of the superstructure, closer to the squadron spaces. All of the senior officers onboard had staterooms there.

Nicholas hopped off the bed. He stopped and looked around the room approvingly.

"This is cool."

"Yeah, I think so too. Do you want to see where they drive the ship from?"

"Yeah!"

The reaction of any visitor was the same. The five year-old could not even see over the helmsmen's console. He grabbed the helm and moved it back and forth. Jazz looked to the rudder angle indicator. It did not move, the rudders were in local control in aftersteering.

His son said, "Brooom, broooom," as he pretended to steer the ship. Jazz laughed.

"Is that what the ship sounds like?"

"Uh, huh."

"Okay."

Nicholas got the grand tour. Jazz could tell that it helped his son understand what his father was doing. Now Nick would have a visual picture when thinking of his father far away at sea. He knew where Daddy would eat, sleep, and work.

Some wives had to watch the ship pull away from the pier. It provided them with closure. Not until they saw the ship leave could they grasp that their husbands were truly gone. The Jascinskis knew of wives in Norfolk that would watch the ship leave the pier and then race to the Chesapeake Bay-Bridge Tunnel so they could see it once more as it passed to sea.

Melanie preferred the drop-off. She tried to pretend that it was as if one of their cars was in the shop and she had to drive Jazz into work. It helped her to deal with the sorrow.

Jazz's service dress blues were hot. His mind raced through all the things he wanted to tell Melanie before he left. He wanted to make sure she had all the information she needed to take care of herself and the family while he was gone.

"Hon, don't forget to . . ."

"I know, Jazz, whatever it is, I know. We've done this before. Now just be quiet so I can drive us without causing an accident."

The quiver in her voice registered with Jazz. He turned to see his children once more. They all stared blankly ahead, sleepy but not able to sleep. His thoughts turned again on the notion that they would change dramatically over the next six months, especially Abigail.

Closer to the pier, they could see a hundred teary goodbyes now. Men and women, children and parents, held onto one another for a final time trying to make it last. Melanie stopped on the side of the road across from the quay. Jazz got out and opened the sliding door of the mini-van. He reached in and gave each of his kids one more long hug and kiss.

"I love you, Tyler."

"I love you, Daddy."

"I love you, Nicholas."

"I love you, Daddy."

He leaned over to kiss his infant daughter. As he did he heard Melanie sobbing.

"I love you, Abby."

As he tried to close the door, Tyler reached his hands out.

"Daddy, kiss!"

He leaned over and gave each son one last quick kiss and hug. Now Nicholas was crying.

Jazz closed the door and walked around to the driver side window. Melanie rolled it down. Tears were streaming down her face.

He kissed her and wiped the tears from her cheeks.

"I love you," he said.

"I love you too. Go now before I really lose it."

Jazz turned on his heel and headed for the ship. He passed several women and children crying and clinging to each other. He saw the backs of many other sailors, walking slowly toward their ship.

Against his better judgment, the young husband and father turned to look at his family one more time. The van had not moved an inch. Melanie was looking at him. Her body shook as she sobbed uncontrollably. His two sons cried hysterically, not fully understanding why but sharing instinctively the sadness that their mother emanated.

Jazz turned again and walked toward the brow of USS *Inchon*. This time he did not look back.

TWENTY-FOUR

TASKING

"Echo One, this is Echo Two. We have your floor secure. We're beginning to clear those above and below you."

"Copy, Two," Jazz answered.

Jazz loosened his tie as he bent over to study the device. There was a small opening on the top. He turned on his flashlight and tried to see what was inside without touching it.

A noise in the other room startled him. He stood and walked toward the door. Jazz heard the noise again. He was shocked by what he saw as he entered the room.

"Special Agent Cruz."

"Hello, Jazz," she purred.

Elena looked stunning. She was wearing a fitting black dress, black silk stockings, and heels. Jazz's eyes wandered from her face, through her cleavage, to her shapely legs.

Elena smiled at him as she bent over, hiked up her dress, and removed a holstered pistol from her garter.

"Uh, Elena . . . you need to get out of here. There's a suspect package."

Now she pulled a pin from her hair, allowing shiny black tresses to cascade down. She bit her tongue, smirking at him playfully.

"Elena . . ."

She reached behind her back and pulled, untying her dress. She tugged on it slightly and it fell to the floor. Elena Cruz was now standing in front of him clad only in stilettos and thigh highs. That's when Jazz realized that she had placed the suspect package in the next room.

Elena saw the recognition in his face and strode toward him.

"Elena, wait, no . . . they'll catch us . . ."

A high-pitched whine startled Jazz, waking him from his dream. Instinctively he reached behind his pillow, grabbed his earmuffs and put them on to protect his hearing. It was the davit crane again; its machinery room was just next door.

The stateroom was pitch black. Not fully conscious, Jazz wondered what time it was. His right hand felt the lock knife clipped into his right pocket. Then his hands reached to his waist. They felt his rigger belt and cammie trousers. He wriggled his toes.

Yep, got boots on, he thought.

He remembered that it was just after lunch, he was napping. Even with the hearing protection on, he could not fall back to sleep through the noise of the pumps working the davit just outside. He heard Duvall's muffled voice from the bunk above him sending expletives toward the overhead. The Detachment Six OIC was irritated at having his JORP, his Junior Officer Rest Period, interrupted.

Suddenly the door opened, the light from the passageway blinded him. More expletives came from his stateroom-mate. As Jazz's eyes adjusted he saw Quinn in the doorway.

Jazz stood and walked to the door, Quinn was trying to say something but Jazz could not hear him. The noise from the davit's electric motor plus the knocking of the winch's hydraulic fluid was loud enough to destroy thought. Jazz shook his head and pointed to his ears, then he pointed down the hall. The two walked ten feet. Distance and steel now muffled the davit machinery. Jazz took off his 'ears.'

"What's up?"

"I bumped into Captain Solarsky a few minutes ago in Aft V. He wants you and Senior Chief Denke to come see him."

"Okay. Have you found Senior Chief yet?"

"Yeah, he is on his way up here."

A few minutes later Jazz knocked on Solarsky's door. He heard the captain shuffle and chairs sliding on the deck. Then the door opened.

"Jazz, Grover, come in, sit down."

The captain's cabin was small. It was intended to be the stateroom for a junior department head. The room was suitable for its occupant and one visitor, but with two extra chairs and two extra bodies and it became cramped. Jazz sat, his shoulder brushing against the sink.

"I've got a special tasking for your det. You are going to Sigonella and Mobile Unit Eight for awhile."

"Really? What for?"

"Mostly Secret Service Support. Fiona Koss, the Secretary of State, is doing an Eastern European tour to include the Balkans. You'll be with her in Italy, maybe Greece, and probably not Bosnia-Hertzogovina. We want you to take field gear anyway in case you're called upon to go there."

"Why not B-H?"

"There are two Navy teams and a variety of Army and Air Force teams there already. They'll probably take care of it."

"Why us? Why not a det from Eight?"

"Damn, Lieutenant! Don't you wanna get off the ship and go operate?" Denke said incredulously.

"Well, yeah . . ."

Solarsky smiled. "Our young OIC is just gathering intel, Senior Chief. The problem, Jazz, is that everyone at Mobile Unit Eight is gone. You know EOD is stretched thin all over. They have a det in La Spezia, two dets in B-H, a det at TEU TWO, and a detachment in stand-down. The stand-down det is apparently short about six guys. They are waiting for guys to transfer in."

"Wow."

"Yeah, it is busy out here. Anyway, Group Two decided that a team from MU SIX had to take up the slack. It makes sense, right? We're out here anyway."

"Okay, sir, when do we go?"

"In about two days. We'll helo you into Sig with all your gear. Get packed for every mission except extensive MCM. Eight will provide any boats you may need and you never know when you may have to get wet. Take your dive gear."

"Aye, aye, sir."

*   *   *

The streets of Brindisi felt more like Greece than Italy to Nasih. It was as if the city were not Mediterranean, but Adriatic.

Near the waterfront the nightlife began to boil. He walked slowly looking at the multitude of olive-skinned teenage girls. They were more like women. Every one was voluptuous and had beautiful long black hair and grasping brown eyes. He knew it was blasphemy to praise Allah while examining the fashion of the day. The light summer dresses that showed much leg made it difficult for him to fight impure thoughts. These women were like snowflakes, all the same yet each magnificently different and more beautiful than the one before.

He stepped into a disco. The young men stood against the wall, drinking and smoking. The women danced with each other and made a big show of ignoring any would-be suitors.

As he made his way to the restroom he looked in the mirror on the disco's back wall. Nobody appeared to be observing him or following him. Nasih paused in the middle stall for ten minutes.

After working his way through the crowd he stopped just outside the door and carefully surveyed the entire scene. To a citizen he appeared merely as a tourist looking for his friends. He did not recognize anyone. Nasih concluded that he was either not being followed or was being tailed by an organization that was professional enough to avoid detection.

The crowd thinned as he moved further away from the small resort area and closer to the marina. He walked down the quay wall unobserved since the lights died long ago with no replacement.

He stopped and conducted another survey of the area. There were about twenty boats secured to the quay at their stern with their bow pointed to the harbor center in a "Med-moor." Few of them had lights on. He looked back toward the foot of the quay wall where it met the shore. Nobody eclipsed the lights of Brindisi behind him. His eyes adjusted as he scanned the area for lovers or late-night fishermen. There were none.

Nasih looked at the stern of a boat in the third slip. The main deck was dark, but the deck below had lights emanating from the windows. The aft-most of three windows had no curtain over it. Thus the occupants signaled to him that it was safe to board.

Quickly he stepped up the brow to the hatch. He opened the sliding door with his elbow and proceeded directly below as if he were the owner.

The men he met with were not as sober, literally and figuratively, as the Americans. He appreciated their passion but it also meant they were often careless. Still, they were his most promising asset in Europe.

They were gathered around a table in the galley. He could tell they were imbibing heavily as they waited for him.

The woman was there too. Nasih thought of her often. She was absolutely beautiful, an older version of the throng of women he just traversed. She was wearing a tight blouse that showed her firm cleavage.

Renata was the name that she used, but he was sure it was an alias. She caught him staring at her, then met his stare with a devilish smile as she lit a cigarette.

While he often entertained the thought of having her, Nasih was certain that she was Guido's.

He looked to the leader.

"Buongiorno, Guido."

"Hello, welcome," said their leader. "Would you care for a drink?"

"Grazie, no. I have a schedule to meet. Please reach into my shirt pocket."

Guido reached into Nasih's shirt pocket and pulled out an envelope folded in half. He smiled.

"You don't trust us, eh? Afraid we'll get caught with evidence that will trace us to you?"

"Believe me, my friend, it is for your protection that I take such precautions. I am unconcerned with being traced to you. It is you who should worry about being linked to me."

He looked to the men around the table again. One of them took a drag on a cigarette. Their silence and demeanor suddenly registered seriousness.

Good, he thought. *Perhaps this will work after all.*

Nasih spoke again as Guido opened the envelope. "The information you require is in there. I trust that you already have the proper tools?"

"Yes. Are you sure this will work? Their security is very good."

"It will work. When you read that, all will become clear. And now I must go. Ciao."

"Ciao."

*   *   *

Jazz rose from his cot and followed an enticing smell. In the back of his mind he knew that he was still partially asleep. He found himself in an open doorway at the back of the building. He saw Ashland standing in front of a contact mine with a large metal spatula in his hand. Smoke was rising from the middle of it. Ash smiled at him.

I'm dreaming, he told himself.

Then Jazz watched as Ashland grabbed one of the horns with a gloved hand and lifted the top half of the mine. Someone had emptied its guts and transformed it into a grill. Ash was cooking steaks and potatoes.

"Howdy, LT. I put one on for you already."

Jazz rubbed his eyes.

"Thanks, smells good. Where's everyone else?"

"Should be back soon, I hope. T-Ball's in the shower, Denke's on a run. Keating's on the computer. Dee, Quinn, and Sinclair are buying more groceries at the exchange."

They were on a deck built on the back of Building 519 of Naval Air Station Sigonella, home to the EODMU EIGHT detachment spaces. The purpose of the deck was purely recreational. There was a bar, a refrigerator, even an outdoor sink. The center of the porch had a homemade table that could easily seat twelve. Jazz noticed Ash was drinking a beer and that there were several empties about.

"Beer in the fridge?"

"Yessir."

"Damn, that smells good."

"Better than the ship for sure."

Jazz reached into the fridge, grabbed a beer and headed inside. As he stepped in the office Keating stood up from the computer.

"Finished, LT. You're up."

Jazz sat down, logged on, and read an email from Melanie.

```
From: jazzmnj
To: jascinski

Jazz,
    I love you. We are doing okay here. The boys are
slowly getting used to you not being around. Tyler still
has his temper fits. He asks, "Is Daddy there?" every
time we pass the LEXINGTON and then has a fit when I tell
him that you are not. I'm learning to distract him as
we go past it.
    Abby is doing well. She is sleeping through the night
now . . . a real blessing. I even thought she may have
cooed, "Daa" when I showed her your picture at bedtime
the other night.
    Jeannie and I have a workout routine going . . . that
helps me stay distracted a little, otherwise I'd miss
you a bit more. ☺ I'm also thinking of taking a class
at the Junior College to keep myself occupied.
    I was able to put an extra $100 in your account. Spend
it irresponsibly.
    I love you and miss you. The bed feels empty.

                                        XOXOXOX.

                                            Mel
```

Jazz felt a pain going from his throat, down his esophagus to his stomach. He began typing a response to his wife.

"LT, you done yet?"

Jazz turned around to see Sinclair in the door. He couldn't speak. His teammate saw the pain in his eyes.

"Sorry, sir . . . I, uh, I'll come back later."

Jazz took a deep breath and continued typing.

```
From: jascinski
To: jazzmnj

Mel,
    I miss you terribly. I cannot wait to come home. It
feels so much longer than a month and a half.
    Hearing about Tyler breaks my heart. Sometimes I
wonder how we do this. I am thankful that you are his
mother.
    If you have not heard from Jeannie or the other wives
yet, we are in Sigonella Sicily now. We'll be here for
a few days of Secret Service work. Thank God we brought
our suits! It is nice to be off the ship.
    I hope that you and the boys are doing well. Tell each
of them that their Daddy loves them bunches. Especially
Tyler.


                                                     —Jazz
```

"LT, catch."

T-Ball tossed a beer can and almost hit his OIC in the face. Jazz popped the top and watched the top quarter of it fizz and foam over his hand. He held it up in a salute to his teammate. They drank together.

"Come have a steak, Jazz. You need it."

"Yeah, no kidding," he noticed that he was addressed by his first name.

The steaks were fantastic. The men ate wordlessly. Before Jazz finished his beer, T-Ball set another one in front of him. He drained it quicker than the first.

"LT's setting the pace, boys. Let's go," T-Ball said.

"What are we doing, T?" asked Delgado.

"Drinking."

"Okay, where?"

"Pizza Village."

The next morning Keating found Jazz asleep standing in the shower.

"C'mon, LT. We meet the ops boss in fifteen minutes."

Jazz rubbed his eyes and turned around slowly.

"Meat gazer."

"I'm not joking, LT. Let's go."

"My head hurts."

"Damn broke-dick 1140! Get dressed, sir!"

Jazz stepped out of the shower. He had a headache and was feeling dizzy. Someone, probably Keating, had laid a uniform out for him. He struggled to get his pants and boots on.

Keating returned to find Jazz throwing up.

"Sir, we gotta go now."

Jazz grabbed his uniform blouse and his cover and followed Keating out the back door. Cans and square bottles lay like leaves around the porch. The ground seemed to move like a ship in heavy seas.

"Where's everyone else?"

"Still in bed."

Jazz rolled into the passenger seat of a MU EIGHT pickup truck. Keating handed him a bottle of Gatorade and four aspirin.

"Breakfast of champions."

"Oh fuck me, I feel terrible."

"Sir, I warned you last night . . . but you wouldn't listen."

Jazz remembered playing pool with T-Ball. They did not speak for two hours. They simply pushed the balls around the table and drank beer followed by shots of an unknown clear liquid.

At sea the work distracted them long enough. After a day of diving they would collapse in their racks, asleep before their eyes closed. Now with time off, time to relax, their separation crept too easily into their minds. The two young men commiserated, chasing their families from memory with felt, ivory, and alcohol. They tried desperately to fool themselves, tried desperately to forget they were gone.

They were not successful.

The main building of EODMU EIGHT was a five-minute drive across the base. It was the backside of a building attached to a hangar on the flightline. Jazz and Keating went up to the second floor where the staff worked.

"Rough night last night, Lieutenant?" the operations officer inquired as he sat down at the conference room table.

"Yessir."

"Call me 'Lou.' And don't worry about it. Happens every time a visiting det comes in, especially off a ship. If you're worth your salt and been underway awhile, you gotta steam."

"So what's the job, sir?" asked Keating.

"Secret Service support in Rome. Secretary of State Koss is coming for a visit. Admin has your orders already. You'll meet with the Technical Support Division Agent in two days. He'll direct you from there. The Rome part of the trip is a boondoggle, but then she is going to see the troops in Bosnia. Whether or not you go is up to TSD."

"What if we don't go?" said Keating.

"Report back here for further tasking or release."

"What do you need us to do in the meantime?" asked Jazz.

"Keep howling at the moon for all I care, just don't get caught. You got forty eight hours to get your shit together and get to Rome."

"Roger."

Keating looked across the table at his OIC. Jazz's head was down on the conference room table. He was snoring.

TWENTY-FIVE

USSS

Det Four sat in a hotel suite waiting for their brief. They were dressed casually now, but would wear business suits when working with the agents of the Department of the Treasury. There were also three Air Force dog handlers from a unit in Germany.

The Technical Support Division handles special aspects of Secret Service Protection including response to explosive devices. They do not have their own bomb squad; military EOD and bomb dog teams fill the void.

Finally the TSD agent came in.

"Gentlemen, how do you do? I'm Special Agent Allen of the Technical Support Division. Do we have everyone? Uh, who is in charge?"

"I'm OIC of the EOD det," said Jazz.

"Okay, all of your guys here?"

"Yes."

"What about the dogs?"

One of the handlers identified himself as the senior man.

"I'm sure that you all heard that we are supporting a SECSTATE visit. Here is the op. Secretary Koss comes in tomorrow. She's going to meet with U.S. ambassador for breakfast. Then she is going to the European Technology Symposium with John De Luca."

"The computer guy?" asked Quinn.

"The very rich and god-awful smart computer guy who donates money to her party," replied Allen.

"What's he got, like fifty patents?" said T-Ball.

"Yep," said Allen. "He is one of the guest speakers and his company, Texas Silicon and Software is co-sponsor of the symposium. They were working on increasing their market here. The two of them together are going to raise a bunch of media attention. This leads to our biggest challenge. They are going to walk the conference room floor for about twenty minutes for a photo op."

"You mean like where companies set up their displays and information booths?" asked Keating.

162

"Exactly."

"You don't expect us to search it do you?" Ashland said incredulously.

"No. It is too difficult. We cannot search everything in that room, nor control traffic in and out. I briefed SECSTATE's people and they are comfortable. Remember guys this is SECSTATE, not POTUS."

"You tell her that?" Denke said with a guffaw.

"I'm just being matter-of-fact with you. She knows where she is in the food chain."

*   *   *

They actually knew a lot about the equipment that they were setting up. Guido insisted that Vin and Renata study the literature and practice installing the three different internet cameras. They had to be able to speak intelligently about the features of each and relate tales for problem solving for inept clients to the other twidgets at the conference.

The device was placed on a specially constructed stand underneath the cloth-covered display table. Only the front side of the metal table was open.

"I'm going to move into my position . . . ah, to get a cappuccino now," Renata said to Vin.

He nodded. Then he watched her as she headed across the conference room floor and through the doors that led to the hotel's entrance.

*   *   *

The hotel lobby café provided some fantastic eyeball liberty. Jazz, Ashland, and Airman Jamal Ita sipped cappuccinos as they eyed a plethora of voluptuous spokeswomen for the various dot-coms come in and out for coffee.

Jazz wondered if the black backpacks instead of briefcases on the floor next to the three men in suits would make them look conspicuous. He then smiled and realized that the dog was their give-away.

A black Belgian Malinois lay on the floor next to Jazz. The canine's head was up and alert. He surveyed the room as purposefully as the men he was working with. His handler, Airman Ita, stroked his head every now and again.

"Good boy, good boy."

"Look at that one, boys," Ash said nodding toward a leggy vixen in a short brown skirt and blazer over a light blue blouse.

"Simply marvelous," agreed Ita. "Must be a dancer."

Suddenly a voice came through the earpiece in Jazz's right ear.

"Innkeeper, this is Motorcade. Two minutes out with Ms. Moneypenny."

"Roger 'cade. Innkeeper ready. We have Q in place."

Together the three men looked out the glass window separating the coffee shop from the lobby. They could see De Luca, three television crews, and several agents standing around.

The team's job at this point was simple. They had to stand by for an incident. Since they were overseas Jazz, Ashland and the others were not restricted by *posse comitatus,* which prevented EOD Techs from performing render safe procedures within the United States when assisting law enforcement officials. When on U.S. soil they could only advise the local government bomb squads. This law did not apply when in a host country.

"One minute out."

The dancer was gone. Jazz swiveled his head, looking for her. Then he noticed a cup of cappuccino on the counter. The woman at the register was also looking around confused.

He looked back toward the lobby and saw her stepping out just as SECSTATE came in.

"Moneypenny is in the building."

The three men sat silently now and listened to the radio traffic as Koss and De Luca moved about the conference center.

In the café the sound and pressure of the explosion was muted. Ashland had a furled brow. The dog became agitated.

"Easy, boy," said Ita soothingly.

"Was that an AC system kicking on?" asked Ash.

"I don't know," replied Jazz. "Didn't sound good"

Then they witnessed the panic. People began pouring out of the convention center and out of the hotel. The fire alarm went off. Several women screamed, many were crying.

"EOD. Conference center!"

"Fuck!" yelled Jazz as he got up. The three men slipped their black packs over their shoulders. Ashland led as they forced their way through the throng of people evacuating like rats from a sinking ship. By the time they reached the conference center nearly everyone was gone.

Jazz saw some dust and smoke in one corner. Two agents were standing there with guns drawn. Two more were trying to save Fiona Koss. He put his hand to his nose and mouth as a horrific smell reached him. He knew immediately that it was burnt flesh.

The three men stood there in shock for a moment. Jazz focused again on the men trying to save SECSTATE. She was obviously burned and bleeding but appeared to be holding on to life. Jazz could see that she was still moving. Her legs were writhing as if she wanted to run. She was already covered in bloody bandages probably covering multiple cuts. Jazz wondered where the agents working to stop blood flow obtained a medical kit.

De Luca on the other hand was gone. His body was a mass of black and burned meat from the waist up. Jazz first identified him by circumstantial evidence; he was wearing his signature cowboy boots.

Additionally, two of the media were still there lying on the floor. The reporter was cut and bleeding in several places. Blood ran from his ears. He was saying something loudly, repeating the same words over and over, but Jazz did not understand. The cameraman had a similar blank look and was shaking.

"Hey!"

Jazz looked at the agent who grabbed his arm.

"Snap out of it! You need to look for secondary devices. We have more agents and medical people on the way! Make sure there is not another bomb placed to take them out!"

Jazz tried to focus as he looked for another device. It was difficult to do when computers, coffee cups, pens, briefcases, were everywhere. In the immediate vicinity of the blast there were thousands of large pieces of material that were now unidentifiable.

The men continued to search as emergency personnel arrived. They looked under tables, behind chairs, in boxes and briefcases. Ashland pointed out that any computer could have a device inside. Jazz extracted a wrench from inside his bag. He walked through the conference center searching for a secondary device, smashing each monitor he passed to peer inside. Ashland did the same.

Ita and his canine also searched the room for explosives. The airman focused as much as possible on items whose innards the Techs could not easily search, such as the computer towers, locked briefcases, and sealed boxes of give-aways. Jazz was considering moving these items to one place out of the way of the emergency medical workers when an FBI agent approached him.

"Lieutenant, you and your men are done for now. Go back to your hotel and sit tight."

"Uh, okay. The whole place is not necessarily secure. We don't know about all these computers. We looked in the monitors that are smashed."

"Understood. At this point I don't think there is a secondary device. These guys hit their target. The Caribineri bomb squad will continue the search. TSD and FBI need you guys to go back to your hotel room. We are going to seal this place off. We will be by later to ask some questions."

"Roger."

Jazz sat in the same room where they had their initial meeting. The television was on to the BBC. They were covering the events at the symposium. As he watched it for the third time Jazz realized that he was still in shock.

The FBI agent from the Rome office identified himself as Pucharelli. Jazz wondered if he was assigned here because of his Italian heritage. Maybe he spoke the language.

Jazz noted that the agent looked exhausted. *Hell, I probably look the same,* the lieutenant thought.

There was a moment of déjà vu as the officer began his questioning.

"Okay, LT. Let's start with your name unit, address, et cetera. Stuff for the record."

"Sure. I'm Lieutenant James J. Jascinski, Untied States Navy. I am Officer in Charge of Explosive Ordnance Disposal Mobile Unit Six Detachment Four, stationed in Ingleside, Texas. Currently we are deployed aboard USS *Inchon*."

"Where do you live?"

"Um, my home right now is 2524 Beechwood Street, Portland, Texas."

Jazz answered all of Pucharelli's questions, but he was not sure that the agent was really getting all of the info. Maybe he and Ashland were not that important to the investigation.

"LT, did you secure the conference room prior to the visit?"

"No. We discussed it with the TSD agent and agreed that it was too big, and had too many people. It was not possible to secure it with the manpower and the time constraints. The TSD guy said that SECSTATE was briefed."

Jazz waited while Pucharelli wrote some notes.

When he finished he looked up again. "Are there any insights you can give me regarding the device?"

"Not really, nothing your post-blast guys won't be able to figure out. We did not really see anything, no remnants."

"Roger."

"How is she?"

"You didn't hear?"

"No, she's alright isn't she?" Jazz said remembering her moving on the floor.

"Nah, she didn't make it, LT," the agent said solemnly.

After the interview concluded, Pucharelli told Jazz that he could go, then wasted no time in getting out the door himself.

The phone in Jazz's room was ringing as he walked in the door. It was Denke.

"LT?"

"Yes, Senior."

"Pack up. We're rolling in thirty minutes."

"Why?"

"Sir, while you were being interviewed we were given permission to scram back to Sigonella. I suggest we take it while we can. We may be in a dangerous environment for Americans. Do you concur?"

"Sure."

As Jazz packed a depression came over him. It was the same sense he had after West and Martin perished. He was responsible for SECSTATE. He was her bomb squad, assigned to keep her safe from explosive devices. He failed and now Fiona Koss was dead.

*   *   *

Melanie was enjoying naptime. She enjoyed more than an hour without interruption from baby Abigail or one of the boys. She decided to relax. There would be time in the evening for her to devote to the house.

The lemonade was heavenly. She flipped through a copy of Cosmo.

Damn, what I wouldn't do for the life of some of these women.

She imagined putting on her make-up being the most taxing part of her day, or deciding what outfit to wear for the evening.

The phone interrupted her reading; it was Jeannie.

"Mel, have you seen the TV?"

"No. What is it?"

"I think the guys are on television."

"What?"

"Fiona Koss and John De Luca were just killed in Italy."

"Oh no, oh my God are they alright?"

"No, they're dead."

"No, I mean Jazz and T-Ball."

"I don't know. Oh my God, I hope they are all right. I'm sure they must be, right? I mean, they didn't mention anyone else on the news."

Frantically, Melanie ran to the bedroom with the portable phone still in her hand. She flipped on the TV and cycled through the channels. The breaking news was coming over many stations, but she flipped until she reached an all news channel.

Jazz, if you die, I'm gonna kill you.

"Mel? My other line is beeping. I'll bet it's Ted."

"Call me back if you hear anything."

"I will."

As soon as she hung up, the phone rang again. It was Eleanor.

"Melanie, dear, have you seen the news?"

"Yes, someone called a moment before."

"I'm sure Jazz is alright dear. I didn't get any funny feelings . . . I seem to always be able to tell when he is in danger."

"Me too," said Melanie through tears. "I'm sure he is alright."

Her call waiting started to beep. She was sure that it was Jeannie or Jazz.

"Mom, someone is calling on the other line it might be Jazz . . ."

"We love you dear."

"Jazz?"

"Sorry, Mel, it's Jeannie again. I just talked with Ted. He said that he has not talked to Jazz, but he knows that he is okay. Koss and De Luca were killed and two reporters were injured."

Melanie sat on the bed and started crying. She tried to hold it in so that Jeannie could not hear her.

"Mel, did you hear me?"

"Uh huh."

"Damnit, Mel, are you alright?"

"Uh, huh."

"I'm coming over there. Don't move."

Tyler and Abby were awake now. Melanie put Tyler in front of a cartoon while she nursed. Ten minutes later Jeannie came in without knocking.

"Mel!" she called out.

"Back here. I'm nursing."

"Are you okay?"

"I suppose so."

Melanie held back tears as Jeannie came into the bedroom.

"Oh, I wanna hug you," Jeannie said.

"I'm fine, really."

"No, you're not. I've called Judy. She is coming over. You need some sisterhood right now."

TWENTY-SIX

REMORSE

Mobile Unit Eight was still empty when the detachment returned. Jazz was quiet during the trip back. He let Denke give the men direction.

"Okay guys, stow gear. One day stand-down and then we'll get ready for our next op . . . whatever that may be."

Jazz moved to the OIC office and called home. As the phone rang he looked at his watch; it was still early afternoon in Portland.

"Hello?"

"Hey, Mel, it's me."

"Oh, thank God," Melanie said as she began crying. "Damn it, Jazz! Why didn't you call earlier?" she said through tears and anger. "All of the other wives got phone calls. I thought something happened to you and they weren't telling me. I've been waiting for the base chaplain to drive up all day."

"I'm sorry, hon."

"Answer my question! Why! We have been over this before! Why didn't you call!"

"I'm the OIC, Mel. The others were able to call when I was talking to the FBI. Afterward I had no time. I had to practically run from my hotel room to the plane."

"So where are you now?"

"I'm back in Sigonella."

"Oh, thank God."

Jazz listened to his wife sob for a moment. He understood why she was upset, but his own frame of reference was different. This was now the second time in a few months that he was close to death. Slowly, Melanie regained some of her composure.

"James J. Jascinski, next time you call."

"Mel, I couldn't . . ."

"Call. I do not care if you miss your plane. I do not ever want to feel this way again. Do you understand me?"

"Yes."

"I thought you were dead, Jazz."

"I'm sorry, really. Next time I'll call."

"I'm serious, Jazz. I'm not going through this again."

"I love you, hon."

"I love you too, but I can't talk right now. I'm just too upset. I just needed to hear your voice . . . I need to try to calm down. I'll send you an email later, okay?"

"Um, okay."

Jazz held the phone for a moment after his wife hung up. He realized that the life he has chosen was slowly killing their marriage. He wondered how long Melanie could take the stress of being a bomb-tech's wife.

Within one hour of returning, Det Four was on the porch drinking and barbecuing again. Denke noticed that Johnny Ashland was very sullen and that Jazz had disappeared. He went in search of his young OIC.

The senior chief found the lieutenant lying on his cot in their makeshift bunkroom.

"Hey, LT. What's up?"

"Senior."

Denke walked over to his cot and sat down on it.

"Lieutenant, I've got something to say to you and I'm only going to say this once, so listen. I know how you feel about this whole thing. I know because I've been there, I've lost lives on my watch."

Jazz swung his feet over and sat up on his cot. He looked Denke in the eye, ready to take in every word.

"You don't need to know all the details. Basically I had a dive buddy die on me. We were diving Mark-16 and he suffered an electronics system failure. The rig stopped giving him O_2. I didn't notice he had a problem until it was too late. To make matters worse, I did the pre-dive maintenance on his rig."

"Wow, Senior Chief, I'm sorry."

"Yeah, well so was I. I was his dive buddy; I set up his rig. For a long time I figured no two ways about it, I'd killed him. But the JAGMAN investigation determined that it was not my fault and deep in my heart I knew that I hadn't fucked up. My setup of the rig was sound and my emergency procedures to get him to the surface were correct.

"Still, I felt guilty. It ate at me for a long time, but eventually I got past it. In the meantime I developed a drinking problem and got a divorce.

"Lieutenant, this was not on you. And if it were, I would be the first to tell you. Despite the fact that you are an 1140, nobody has any doubt in your ability. SECSTATE knew the risks and she took them. You performed your duties as the Secret Service asked you to, and in the same manner that any other EOD Tech would have."

"Sure, Senior Chief . . ."

"I'm not done . . . you still have a responsibility to this team. If you are going to continue to lead these men you need to put this shit behind you and move on. I'm not saying forget it, just learn from it and move on. I can see the funk you are in already. If you don't come out of it right now, you will not be able to lead these men . . . if you cannot do it quickly then you need to turn in that crab and go home. Period. End of lecture."

Denke stood up.

"Don't disappoint us, LT. Don't disappoint me."

With that, Denke set a can of beer at Jazz's feet and headed back to the porch.

The OIC sat for a long time staring at it. He realized now why Denke was such a relentless taskmaster.

The ops boss required Jazz to check in with him each morning. Lou set up a guest account in MU EIGHT's vault so that he could read message traffic. The COMSHIFT message that he sent before leaving *Inchon* ensured each of the communications centers throughout the world knew all messages for EODMU SIX DET FOUR went to Sigonella. He read in the daily traffic that the other detachments were participating in an exercise with the Spanish Navy. Jazz now wished he was with them. It was not enough that the fun of being off the ship, beers, steaks, and cappuccinos disappeared after the attack on SECSTATE. Now he knew his brethren were having more fun than the men from Ingleside. He tried to erase visions of his fellow EOD Techs diving in warm clear waters, laughing together in the boats at the end of a long day.

As he emerged from the unit's compound he ran into the Command Master Diver.

"Hey, LT, your boys are over at the Bee Bar. They said for you to meet them over there."

"Where?"

"The Bee Bar, the coffee shop over by the gym."

"Oh, thanks, Master Diver."

Jazz found Denke and Keating sitting at the Bee Bar having cappuccinos.

"Senior Chief, are we ready for training?"

"Yes, sir. I put Ashland and Sinclair in charge. They have already set up the minefield on the far side of the runway where there is a training area. We're ready when you are, sir."

"Let's go then."

Ashland began with a training lecture about how to operate in a minefield. He reviewed all the proper safety lectures and use of the Mark-29 Ordnance Locator. The—29 was an effective version of a civilian metal detector. It could be used to find ferrous material on land or in shallow water.

Sinclair then gave a lecture on the various mines that were common in the Med, especially in the Balkans. The Italians produced and exported a wide variety of anti-personnel and anti-tank mines. They incorporated non-ferrous materials like plastic to make them near impossible to detect. Sinclair also had mines from Russia and the former Yugoslavia in his repertoire.

After the lecture each man was given a problem. They exercised as individuals rather than as a full detachment. The Techs were each assigned an area to search with the others watching. Ashland and Sinclair cleverly designed learning points into each man's "game."

Jazz was determined to do well. He knew that Denke was right; he needed to regain confidence in himself and his teammates.

Jazz listened intently to the—29. Each time he got an audible return he set it behind him and squatted. Then, pulling out the Admiral's knife, he would gently probe the earth, feeling for a solid object with the blade. When the tip hit something, he then sifted through the hot, loose soil with his hands. If his fingers found a mine, he would prosecute it, rendering it safe.

After countless attempts that uncovered rocks or old soda cans, Jazz sensed that he finally found an ordnance item. He stopped and sipped from his Camelbak considering the situation.

Don't rush, he told himself. *Calm down. Remember this thing does not have a timer.*

Gently slipping the knife in again, he felt and heard a soft, "click."

Yep, definitely man-made.

Jazz dug with his fingertips lightly, rubbing sand away from the object. Finally the sand he moved away revealed a dark brown land mine. From the size he guessed it was an anti-tank mine. He had to balance safety with speed.

Move quickly, but don't kill yourself.

His procedure had to be correct, but he also could not dawdle on the problem and take all day. His fingers dug down and found the bottom of the land mine. Seven minutes after finding it he fully uncovered an eighth pie-section of the mine.

Jazz paused and drank again water from his Camelbak as he looked at it a moment to determine what type it was. He was unsure of the exact nomenclature, but knew it was an Italian mine. Next, he would remove the fuze.

As he leaned over to remove more sand from the top of the mine there was a loud, "Pop!"

Smoke rose from under the mine.

"What the fuck?"

He looked up at the sound of laughter. Sinclair was forty feet in front of him behind a dune with a detonator in his hand.

"BOOM! You're dead, LT!" the petty officer said gleefully.

It was then that Jazz saw it. Emerging from the ground ten feet in front of him was a small black cable. It ran toward the dune where Sinclair was hiding.

Ashland came up behind him.

"Command detonated, LT."

Jazz registered somberness in Ashland's voice.

Maybe he is still upset too.

"What?"

"See the wire?" Ash said. "A lot of ordnance in B-H is command detonated. They suck a team of engineers or EOD guys into a minefield and wait for them to focus on what they are doing. After you tunnel vision into your mine, boom . . . big pink mist. Always, always, always take the time to recon the whole area."

"Fuck," Jazz muttered to himself.

"No sweat, LT," said Ash. "Next time you'll get it. That's why we're here, that's why we did this problem."

Jazz shook his head and Ashland chuckled.

"I'm sorry, LT, but that is my favorite training point. If I was a 'bad guy,' this is how I'd do it."

Maybe they haven't given up on me yet.

At the end of the day, Denke had won the contest. Ashland has set up a complicated minefield and booby trap trail that Denke easily defeated. Everyone agreed that he was clearly the victor.

A HUMMVEE was driving toward the men of Det Four as they cleaned up the land mine training area. Jazz watched it as he handed tools to Sinclair in the back of a MU EIGHT pickup truck. He had a feeling the HUMMER was bringing them news.

As it got closer he thought he saw Lou driving. His fellow officer got out and walked up to him.

"Just got an 'Immediate' off the wire for you."

Jazz read the entire message quickly. He had never heard of Kosovo.

"Why are Albanians living in Kosovo?"

"I dunno man, but you guys got twelve hours to get to Aviano, then back to your ship."

"Okay."

"What's up, LT?" inquired Denke.

"Noble Anvil."

TWENTY-SEVEN

EVIDENCE

Elena stared at the bulletin boards around the room. There was something important about this case that eluded her. She wondered if it was on one of these boards staring at her, yelling at her, taunting her.

An executive assistant knocked on her office door with a folder in his hand.

"Here you are, Elena. I was asked to give you a copy of the report from Rome. It just came in."

"Thanks, Mark."

Elena sat down and shuffled through the file. Maybe something could be found from the recent incident in Rome.

Elena first flipped through the report casually to refresh her memory of the event. Then she sat down to read it in earnest, studying it for clues or patterns that could help her with the SANPAT case. When she saw the clue that she was looking for, she knew it immediately.

"You bastard," she murmured to herself.

Forty eight hours later Special Agent Cruz stood silently in front of the desk of Special Agent in Charge Cameron Thompson, her boss. She waited patiently while Thompson sipped his burning hot coffee. Elena noticed him squinting as the Colombian roast passed through his lips. It was a sign that he was thinking.

While he focused, Elena surveyed her boss's office. Books and papers were strewn everywhere. Half filled cups of coffee and several ashtrays made an aroma that permeated Thompson's clothes.

Elena smiled to herself.

This place is a mess.

Thompson appeared tired and unkempt. He wore a different suit every day, but it was always rumpled. He would leave the office for only a few hours at a time in the late evening, returning before the sun was up. Most agents in the office believed that Cameron lived on coffee and tobacco. He was a mad scientist of criminology, more like a mystery novel detective than anyone else in the bureau.

It's no wonder the guy's not married, Elena thought.

Thompson's cluttered personality was accompanied by an air of wisdom. The man was not arrogant; he just often solved the case before the lead agent did.

Elena enjoyed working for the guy despite his quirks. She realized that he was teaching her to analyze in new ways. As a result, her investigation skills were improving. Thompson, known as Cam even by his subordinates, did not seem to think much of Elena however. In fact, he was the only man that Elena Cruz never caught looking at her. The fact that she could not impress him in any way was a sore point with her, one she was working hard to fix.

Special Agent Cameron Thompson looked at Cruz quizzically.

"Elena, you've been working hard on this, I appreciate that. But I think you haven't had enough sleep. Go home."

"No, Cam, listen to me . . ."

"I think it's just a coincidence."

"Sit down and listen to me again."

The agent in charge threw his hands in the air in mock surrender and sat down at his desk again.

"Okay, here are the elements missing from my investigation. One, how did this group gather the information or intelligence to research, plan, and execute the take-down of the explosive vehicle? Two, who provided or where did they obtain demolition training so sophisticated that no explosive residue was at the site? Three, why were the explosives so important to them that they carried out this operation, including murdering two armed soldiers?"

"Okay, I'm with you."

"Obviously the supposed owner of the house is involved."

"Obviously."

"Okay, so he's on the run. But there has to be more people involved in order to pull this thing off."

"I'm still with you. Have you had any mention of the caliber of the weapon?"

"No, but I knew it was fishing anyway. I am surprised at that. I really thought that I would get some reaction from either the police or the EOD det when I told them it was a nine-millimeter round. I figured somebody would come up with a supposition that either police or military were involved since they both use nine-millimeter weapons. Nobody even asked about checking forensics on weapons held by officers on the scene."

"Yeah, good try though."

"Okay, so who else? We'll start with the associates of the guy who owned the house. Maybe that will lead to something. But, I'll bet we don't find any.

"Then there is the takedown of the explosive vehicle. Intercepting radio traffic regarding the arrival of Martin and West is impressive, but I'm not sure that can lead us anywhere. So here's what is really interesting, one of my suspects had to know about the nuances of the movement of the explosives. Specifically, the security and re-fueling procedures that Martin and West would follow. That actually removes a lot of people. Of those living that I can connect to this incident, it leaves Jascinski and Ball. Right now they are the only guys I know of who answer all of these questions. My instinct tells me Jascinski."

"Why?"

"Jascinski was there at the scene. He made the calls to 797th EOD and undoubtedly could easily find out or would already know their route and timetable."

"Right."

"He's also had military demolition training, the best in the world."

"Obviously."

"One of the things they taught us in post-blast analysis is that when the job is perfect, when there is no explosive residue as evidence . . ."

"You've got a military trained guy."

"Exactly. And he's gotta be a Green Beret, or a SEAL, or most likely an EOD Tech since they work with explosives all the time."

"Those guys are very particular about that stuff."

"Precisely."

"Did you get any reaction from that ruse, about the job being shoddy?"

"No."

"Hmmm."

Elena continued, "Finally, Jascinski's motivation is that he is involved with this group. He probably has been siphoning off explosives to these guys and may even be assisting in the construction of the IEDs. I believe there was something about these explosives . . . maybe something as simple as a fingerprint that would point us to Jascinski. He'd have to destroy them so we couldn't trace them to him."

Thompson sipped his coffee, squinting again. The two sat in silence for another moment.

Finally Cameron said, "Okay . . . now you've got my attention. Continue."

Elena felt like she just won a small moral victory.

"Okay, again, the only two people at my scene that fit the description as far as I know are Jascinski and Ball. Now we got Jascinski at the scene of an attack on Secretary Koss."

"Okay, good point. Convince me it simply is not a coincidence."

Now it was becoming as a chess match.

"Let me walk you through a scenario. Jascinski is providing explosives to these bad guys. We already know that the stuff was military. He arrives on scene and realizes that the game is up; he is going to get caught. So he needs to get rid of the demo. How does he do that? Jascinski has an accomplice damage the vehicle tire somehow. He comes to the rescue, certainly in uniform, maybe even with another EOD truck. Three rounds to the back of the head, blow the truck up and make off with the rest of the stuff. I've begun with a cursory look into his background. Guess who else has had some demo training?"

"Who?"

"Dear old Dad. Jascinski's father is a retired admiral who started training for UDT back in the sixties. He washed out after receiving demolition training."

"You're shitting me? Okay, I'm beginning to see. You think this is like the kid who went through EOD school a few years ago? Remember they caught him right as he was in the demo phase."

"Exactly . . . so maybe we got us a family of white supremacists or something. So I've called around about this guy . . . the admiral. Fits the profile depending on whom you talk to. Some refer to him as old school Navy, a very tough, stern son of a bitch. Others say he is on the far right."

"'Old school' or 'on the far right,' huh? To many they are the same thing."

"I'm sure."

Thompson leaned back in his chair and put his feet up on his desk. He stained his teeth with more Bureau coffee.

"Okay, Elena, now I play devil's advocate. Your argument is weak. First, if Jascinski were smart enough to pull this off without a hitch, he'd be smart enough to hand over the C-4 without it being linked to him. Second if he is just worried about the evidence why not destroy all the C-4? Make it really look like an accident. Why did he save some?

"The father? Phooey. So what, Dad tried to be UDT. His son follows in his footsteps and does him one better. Take all that away and realize that young Jascinski's response will be that he was assigned to escort SECSTATE. It is not as if he walked up to the Secret Service and said, 'Hey guys. Can I help?'"

"And therein lays the beauty of it," Elena responded. "Look at it from the other angle. As an EOD Tech he knew that he'd eventually get detailed on a job with a dignitary. It doesn't matter which one. His goal was not to take out SECSTATE, his goal was to get a high ranking government official."

"In which case, he'll never do this again. A second time would be too much of a coincidence to not consider him a suspect."

"Or he'll do it one more time and skedaddle in the ensuing mayhem."

"Elena, you are either brilliant or a complete conspiracy nut."

"I'll be honest, Cam, I'm desperate for something on this one."

"Okay, write up a formal report to propose how we proceed. I'll consider it. I still need some convincing that this is not circumstantial."

"I've already started it. You'll have it on your desk tomorrow."

"Fine, Elena. Before you go, I want to make one thing clear."

"What?"

Thompson sat back up and placed his cup on the desk. His voice became more serious.

"If you fucking screw this up, I'll kill you. Got it?"

"I got it."

"I'm serious. I've got ten acres, a shotgun, and a shovel."

"Boss, you know what you get when you add up three coincidences?"

"What?"

"Evidence."

TWENTY-EIGHT

CRYSTAL CITY, VIRGINIA

The parade of secretaries and receptionists down 23rd Street on their way to and from lunch distracted Sergeant Thomas Donohue. Most wore conservative blouses and suit jackets, but the legs were all bare. He loved the legs.

From the back seat came a growl. Donohue looked in the rearview mirror. His Dutch Shepard was also eyeing the ladies.

"Easy, Guinness. Steady, boy."

Donohue turned his cruiser left onto Jefferson Davis Highway, heading back into the jurisdiction of the Defensive Protective Service.

Donohue worked at the Pentagon first as an Air Force Security Police Officer. DPS recruited him while he was there and he joined them a year after leaving the military. Donohue completed the perfunctory rookie year as a patrolman followed by two years on the elite Emergency Response Team. Since that time Thomas Donohue was a K-9 handler. His dog, Guinness, was a triple threat. The animal was an attack dog as well as a bomb and drug sniffer.

*   *   *

The speed limit was fifty-five miles per hour. Gabriel ensured that he was not a mile over the limit. He had a video camera propped on a camera bag in the passenger seat of his sedan. It was aimed out the window, the power was on, and it was recording.

It was his first reconnaissance of the area. Gabriel thought the camera would appear innocent enough.

After all, he thought, *it's not like owning a video camera is illegal.*

He noticed an apartment building on a hill to his left.

I could get a room in there and set up a nice observation post.

Gabriel decided to look into that.

*   *   *

It happened about four times a year. Donohue was visited by his police sense. The hair stood up on the back of his neck. It was the silver sedan; something was not right about it. Donohue pulled in behind it and began to observe it more closely.

"Come on, bud, drive into my parking lot," Donohue said out loud.

In the rear view mirror he saw Guinness through the screen between the front and back seats. The pooch was now looking over his shoulder at the grey sedan. He had the same instincts as his handler. He growled again.

"Come on, baby, turn right, turn right."

Saint Michael, patron saint of policemen, was working with Donohue and Guinness. Their prayers were answered and the sedan turned right into the parking lot.

Donohue flipped a button on the console between the two front seats. From the grill of his unmarked cruiser, blue lights flashed and a siren began to wail. Guinness began barking. Donohue followed the suspect vehicle as it turned down one of the hundred rows of cars and stopped. He kept his eyes on the vehicle as he made a call on his radio.

"Base, this is Kilo Five. Pulled over a silver Pontiac Grand Am for routine safety inspection. Vehicle tag is Virginia Mike Hotel Charlie One One Five. Requesting back-up."

In his mind's eye, Donohue could see Marsha's eyebrows rise.

"Roger, Kilo Five. Say again regarding back-up?"

"That's right, base. I am requesting courtesy back-up."

"Roger."

*   *   *

This was a confusing turn of events. Gabriel wondered if he was seen filming.

Impossible.

He turned the camera off.

Did he do something wrong? Were the feds onto him?

Gabriel went through his wallet and pulled out the military ID he placed there an hour before when he was in the hotel. He grabbed the Virginia driver's license that matched it. There was a tapping on the window.

"Yes, officer?" he said, rolling down the window.

"Good afternoon, sir," the patrolman responded. "I'm Officer Donohue of the Defensive Protective Service. May I see some ID, sir?"

Gabriel handed him the military ID card and driver's license. He noticed the K-9 next to the cop.

Holy shit he's got a dog?

After studying his credentials a moment the officer said, "Thank you, Lieutenant Smith. I am just doing a cursory safety inspection of your vehicle. I am sorry for the delay in your day. I also need your registration, sir. Wait one moment, sir."

*   *   *

Donohue put the IDs and registration in his pocket.

"Guinness, seek." Donohue kept his eye on the driver while following Guinness around the car. Near the trunk the dog gave him the sign.

"Good boy," Donohue said giving the dog a treat.

Okay, wait for the back-up, he thought.

Donohue returned to his cruiser. Guinness hopped into the back seat. Donohue got in front and called dispatch.

"Base, this is Kilo Five. I needed back-up like, yesterday. Guinness gave me a positive on this guy's trunk, probably drugs. I'm going to run his info, but I'll bet it is clean. He's a Navy lieutenant."

"Roger, Kilo Five. We have one unit on the way, we'll send a second."

"Thanks, base. Let's run this guy's vitals. Standby to copy."

*   *   *

Gabriel noted another police cruiser arriving. This one came from the other direction and parked in front of him. The officer did not get out. He just stared over his dash at Gabriel through his cop sunglasses.

There was no moving. Gabriel knew the game was up. The dog probably sensed the explosives in the trunk. He wondered about the right to search his car. *Was the dog probable cause?* He decided to calmly try to fight them at every turn.

You idiot, he thought to himself. *You should have remembered what Nasih taught you.* He remembered the man's voice as he lectured them.

"Never mix two missions. If you are going to conduct surveillance, only bring surveillance equipment. If you are going to carry out an assassination, only bring weapons."

Now what could have been explained away as simply forgetting to turn off a video camera was going to become possession of explosives on federal property.

I'm fucked.

To make matters worse, he gave the police officer his military ID. He now realized that that would be his last, fatal mistake. The ID was never made to undergo scrutiny. Now this guy was running a check. He would soon find out that Gabriel was not Lieutenant James P. Smith. Had he handed over just a driver's license he could have acted lost. The military sticker could have been on the vehicle because he bought it used, just as he had done in San Diego.

Now there was a third police vehicle. He could see a perimeter was being set up. Twenty yards away there was a dark Suburban. That would be the Emergency Response Team. Gabriel knew that inside were a couple of mean boys with MP-5 machine guns.

Yep, I'm fucked.

He saw the first officer approaching the window again. The dog was with him.

"Lieutenant Smith?"

"Yes?"

"Will you step out of the car, sir?"

"What's wrong, officer?"

"I need you to step out of the car now, sir."

"Calm down, officer . . ."

"Sir, step out of the car."

*   *   *

Donohue stepped back. Guinness was ready to do the dirty work if needed. There were three other officers within ten yards ready to react.

The man got out of the car and looked at him. He was sweating. Donohue thanked Saint Michael again for his police instinct.

"Turn around slowly and place your hands on the front of the vehicle."

The man did as instructed.

"Officer Perelli!" Donohue shouted.

Perelli came up. Donohue put one hand on his service weapon.

"Put your right hand behind your back," commanded Perelli.

He clipped a handcuff on the suspect.

"Now, the other one . . . okay, turn around."

"Step away from the car," said Donohue. "Smoot, let those good people get to their cars so they can leave now."

*   *   *

Gabriel could not see Donohue's eyes through his sunglasses.

Calm down. You are not in control of the situation. Don't give him anything.

"Lieutenant Smith, as I stated before, I stopped you for a routine safety inspection. While on federal land, the Defensive Protective Service, of which I am an officer, has the right to conduct such inspections as a matter of routine. In fact by driving your vehicle on federal land you tacitly agree to have your vehicle searched at any time. Do you understand?"

"Yes. But . . . no, I don't understand. Why the handcuffs?"

"Well, sir, my dog is trained to detect explosives and illicit drugs. He detected a substance in one of those two categories in your vehicle. Can you explain that?"

"No, I . . . I don't do drugs or anything."

"What about explosives, sir? Do you have any firearms in your vehicle or fireworks . . . something like that?"

"No . . . none."

"Okay. Here is our second problem. We have no record of a 'Lieutenant James P. Smith.' What is your social security number, sir?"

"Five one two, three three, six six seven nine."

This was the first thing he had done correctly, memorizing his false social security number. Gabriel swore that he would never forget or ignore another lesson that Nasih taught him if he got through this.

"Okay, LT. Here's what we're going to do. I am going to ask you to wait in the back of Officer Perelli's squad car. We're gonna figure out what to do about all this."

Gabriel remained silent. Perelli walked him to his car and put him in the back. The door closed behind him. There was steel mesh separating the front from the back. Perelli opened the front door, leaned in, and turned off the radio.

"The air conditioning is on, Lieutenant. You should be comfortable. If you become ill or if you need medical attention . . . anything like that . . . call out. I'll roll your window down a skosh."

He watched the officer walk back toward his car.

*   *   *

Donohue put Guinness back in his vehicle. He opened Smith's car and found the trunk latch below the dash, left of the steering wheel. Donohue pulled it and heard a click. He walked back to the tail of the Grand Am.

"Perelli."

"Yeah?"

"Better get the bomb squad down here."

*   *   *

Elena sipped a cappuccino in the Starbucks across from the federal courthouse in San Antonio. The clientele this Wednesday morning were either clerks or lawyers who would spend their day across the street or tourists on their way to and from the shops and cookie cutter restaurants.

She looked into the swirls of white and brown foam on the top of the paper cup bearing the café's logo and considered one last time what she was about to do. Elena was almost surprised that her boss accepted her theory. Perhaps it was the desperation of the case. There were rumors that even the Governor of Texas was calling the FBI weekly now, wanting to know how the hell someone could kill two soldiers and steal explosives within the border of his great state and not leave a trace of evidence. The criminal investigative services of both the Army the Navy were maneuvering carefully to get more involved in the investigation, but Cameron was keeping them at bay.

Elena wrestled with her uncertainty, and yet Jazz seemed the only lead. She remembered the sounds of Cam's voice passing through coffee and tobacco stained teeth.

"If you fucking screw this up . . ."

Was she just grasping at straws? Had she missed something? Or was there nothing to be found?

Deep down she believed that there had to be something else, some evidence buried somewhere within the case files in his office that still eluded her. The FBI Academy taught her one certainty—there is always at least one remote clue that leads to the perpetrator. The key was to find it and exploit it before the criminals were able to separate themselves from it. But it had to be the right clue.

Was it the blue-eyed naval officer?

One more time Elena went over it in her mind. It was the best thing she could do right now to keep the case moving. She remembered what Frances said to her just hours before.

"Listen, I think you should go to the judge and get the ball rolling. I mean worse case you don't find anything, right? Then you guys pack your stuff and go home. Nobody gets hurt, right?"

"Yeah, I guess, except it would mean that we devote a lot of time and energy to nothing."

She watched Frances take a drag on her cigarette.

"Does that ever happen?"

"Yes, but not often."

"What is it about this case?" Frances asked. "This one seems different somehow."

It's different because I want to bed my suspect.

Elena's thoughts returned to Jascinski. She finished her drink and looked at the form requesting surveillance on Jascinski one more time. *Maybe this will lead to something,* she tried to tell herself.

She got up and threw her paper cup in the nearest trash can. Then she walked across the street, up the steps, and into the chambers of Judge William Normal.

*   *   *

Thomas Donahue was exhausted after a long shift. He entered the department's locker room at dawn, and considered napping on a couch in the squad lounge before driving home. He couldn't stop thinking of the incident the day before. Perelli came in the locker room just behind Donohue.

"Donny, that was good stop," he said slapping Donohue on the back.

"Then why the hell is he walking?"

"The man posted bail," Perelli replied.

"He was going to blow up the fucking Pentagon! He had a false ID card!"

"Illegal possession of explosives of firearms and impersonating an officer."

"So why isn't he behind bars?"

"The man has got himself a lawyer," Perelli said with resignation.

Perelli took the nine-millimeter Sig-Sauer out of its holster and released the clip. He pulled the slide back and ejected a round from the chamber. Out of habit, he sited the bore in the light above his locker to make positively sure there was not a round in the barrel. Then he released the slide and set the weapon in his locker. He looked at Donohue sitting on the bench in front of his locker, hunched over with his head in his hands.

"Listen, Donny. I have seen a lot of things in my day. Believe me this is not the first time some James Bond, Dick Marcinko wanna-be drove around the parking lot with an arsenal in his trunk."

"You're kidding me."

"No. You should know by now that there are a lot of nuts out there. Heck, we even had a guy a few years back who posed as a DPS officer."

"No way."

"I shit you not. The guy studied us closely. Bought uniforms from the same supplier. He got a patch from somebody at a recruiting fair."

"How did you catch him?"

"Bud Coffey caught him doing a traffic stop."

"In what? Did he get a car?"

"Yep, bought a surplus cruiser from Prince George's County. He had it painted white and acted as if it were an unmarked car."

"No shit."

"Donny, you done good. Now put it behind you. Let the lawyers do the rest of that stuff."

*   *   *

Fortunately, Gabriel still had the contact number Nasih provided him in case he was ever in legal trouble. He noticed that the attorney that took care of him, like Nasih, spoke flawless English but seemed to be Middle-Eastern. Gabriel cursed himself again for his foolishness. He knew that his mentor would be angry with him. In the last few hours, much of Nasih's teachings were coming back to him.

Damn, why didn't I pay more attention?

He now realized that there was more to be learned from the man's rhetoric than he originally thought. Gabriel endured Nasih's ramblings just to get to the good part.

Come on, man. Teach us how to make bombs, he recalled thinking once during a particularly long session, *besides we're missing Monday night football.*

It was becoming clear just how brilliant the man was. As he descended the stairs of the Navy Annex, Gabriel looked down the hill toward the Pentagon. He recalled something else Nasih said that same night.

"The Justice System of the United States of America will be your greatest ally."

It would be a busy night. Gabriel would have to ditch the car, the "James P. Smith" Virginia license and accompanying social security card, and then the credit cards. He decided to make some purchases at a surplus store first. It was time to slip into the mountains. He was pretty sure that the Appalachian Trail was only a few hours away.

TWENTY-NINE

NOBLE ANVIL

"So, what the hell is Noble Anvil?" Jazz asked Duvall as he sat across from him in *Inchon's* wardroom.

"It's the operation going on in Kosovo and Albania. Seems Milosovich and his boys are doing some ethnic cleansing on the Ethnic Albanians. They are fleeing over the border into Albania."

"Whoa, I'm confused already. Ethnic what, to ethnic who? Albanians fleeing to Albania?"

"Yep. You missed our intel brief the other day. Way back when, and I mean like in the 800's, the Serbs revolted against the Turks and got their asses kicked. As a punishment the Turks forced them out of Kosovo and moved in Albanians who were also under their control."

"You're shitting me."

"No joke. Milosovich in his mind is trying to correct a two thousand year old wrong."

"So, what are we going to do?"

"Security for the helos. Apparently there are few good roads in Albania. The Air Force is flying humanitarian rations into Tirane, the capitol. Our MCM helos are now going to become heavy lift cargo birds. They're going to take rations, blankets, and other humanitarian stuff to the displaced Albanians."

"In Albania?"

"Right. There are no Marines in theater, so Mobile Unit Six Forward has been directed to send EOD Techs along for force protection."

"Wow."

"Yeah, we are about to morph from MCM to Mobile detachments. It is not like we are welcome in the Balkans. The intel guys said that the government in Albania supports us being there, but they are not in real control. Apparently, Albania is like Beirut in the 1980's; every village is controlled by a separate faction. Heck, in ninety-five they had a coup and weapons were stolen all over the country. So now every farmer has a

Kalishnikov or an SKS. One major news station even has footage of a farmer towing a MIG with his tractor."

"Unbelievable. So what are we going to do?"

"Like I said, 'Security. Force Protection.' We are going to ride shotgun on the helos and keep the refugees and the minor warring factions from stealing the chow and humanitarian stuff."

"Fuck, this sounds a lot like Mogadishu, not Beirut."

"Oh, I hope not."

Jazz though for a moment before asking Duvall about Italy. Nobody else was at their table. He lowered his voice a bit.

"Hey, Duke?"

"Mmmm?" Duvall mumbled through a forkful of peas.

"Anybody say anything about Italy?"

"You mean your Secret Service job?"

"Yeah."

"Wow, sure. I dunno if you realize it man, but you got the thousand yard stare going on."

"Do I?"

"Yeah. Are you okay?"

"I guess. I'm mostly wondering if people think I fucked up."

"Well, we talked about it at first, but the conclusion was that we'd all have done the same thing. I mean it was a conference center for God's sake and it was only SECSTATE. If it was POTUS you definitely screen everyone, but SECSTATE."

"So, nobody blamed us?"

"Nah, never. Heck, I already forgot about that. We're on the *Inch-long*, man, we've focused on planning for Noble Anvil."

Jazz did not completely believe Duvall's answer. He wondered if some of his brethren thought he was culpable. Despite Denke's words back in Sigonella, he knew that he was still wrestling with it.

*   *   *

Portland became more comfortable as the temperature dropped with the sun. Melanie felt like a shepherd herding her two boys through the neighborhood. They laughed and giggled, pushing and shoving each other. Abigail cooed, observing everything from her stroller.

Melanie called out, "Stay on the sidewalk, boys!"

Melanie could sense the weekend beginning as she passed by each house. Teenagers were heading out on dates, families were packing their cars for San Antonio or Mexico, and shirtless men were cutting their grass or working in their garages.

She slowed her pace to watch a particularly handsome and muscled man mowing his front lawn. As Melanie got closer she saw his wife on the porch sipping tea and keeping eye on two little girls playing on the steps.

The fact that he was a family man only made him sexier.

As she passed, Melanie kept facing forward. A lump rose in her throat. She was jealous of the woman.

She can't appreciate how lucky she is just to have him home, Melanie thought to herself. *What a luxury to sit on the porch while her husband does yard work, to have someone to help her with the children, to have a man to share her bed. I'll bet she even has a career.* She focused on her kids again. *Meanwhile, I'm basically a single mother.*

Eleanor advised her a long time ago that developing a routine was key to surviving a deployment. The routine gave the kids comfort and helped all of them cope with the time that Jazz was gone. Melanie followed this advice on each of his first two deployments and found out that Eleanor was right. Now Jazz was on his third deployment. Before he left, Melanie expected this third deployment to be the easiest—she was seasoned, she knew all the pitfalls. Sadly, she was mistaken. Nicholas and Tyler were older, in a stage where they definitively needed a father's influence. By the day's end, they wore her out physically and emotionally. Whenever all three kids vied for her attention at the same time she was reminded of the adage, "Three is not one more than two."

While Melanie believed that her children were gifts from God, she maintained her sanity during the moments when she had time to herself, like when they were asleep. Jeannie was also heaven-sent. If naptime secured her sanity, Jeannie repelled her sadness. Their friendship was carrying Melanie through the separation. Jeannie often fulfilled the role of husband in all but one way.

When they invented "Margarita Night" it solidified their sisterhood. This auspicious occasion was held every Friday night. After only a few weeks, Judy Ashland and the other wives frequently joined them. They all started using it as a way of marking the time until their husbands returned. Thus the ladies who were married to the men of Det Four commiserated and endured together.

The Ball residence became the most popular meeting place. The ranch house on Sycamore Street was central and within equal walking distance, albeit a long walking distance, from all the others.

"Slow down, boys!" Melanie called to Nicholas and Tyler.

They both stopped and turned to face their mother. Each had a look of disdain as their mother strained to catch up to them from behind the weight of the stroller.

"Okay, go ahead now."

They raced ahead again, playing some nondescript game with a secret language that only lads under seven understand.

"Boys!"

* * *

Two days after Judge Normal signed Elena's warrant, a surveillance team from the San Antonio office headed by Special Agent Kilkenney arrived in Portland. They spent two days studying the physical layout of the Jascinski residence and the surrounding area. Kilkenney and the men of his surveillance team then observed Melanie Jascinski and her neighbors' routines for three weeks. They determined that a Friday night between 6:00 and 8:00 p.m. was optimum for entry. By that time Melanie should be at the Ball residence with the other Detachment Four wives and things in the neighborhood normally quieted down. Only one neighbor, the insurance salesman across the street and two doors down, seemed to spend a lot of Friday nights in his garage and driveway, tinkering on his car or woodworking.

A camera placed in the grill of an FBI car parked across from the Ball home transmitted its feed to room 514 of the Portland Inn. On his video screen, Kilkenney saw Melanie Jascinski and her sons follow Judy Ashland into the Ball house.

"Subject and children have reached destination," Kilkenney said into his radio. "Recommend a 'Go.'"

"Corner One recommends a go," said Steffensen from the park bench on one end of the block where the Jascinski's lived.

"Corner Two, go," agreed Agent Magee from his car on the far corner, almost ten doors down.

"Roger. Entry Team, go," Kilkenney ordered.

"Entry."

Kilkenney's team used this bugging method five times before. It worked like a charm. He kept his eyes on the screen displaying the Ball house, but was visualizing what was happening at the Jascinski's. First, a van with a false air conditioning company name on the side pulled up. Two men got out and quickly approached the house. The first picked the lock to the front door easily. They were inside before the insurance salesman even looked up. Then they methodically placed the bugs into the air ducts in each room.

The air conditioning van was Kilkenney's touch and he was proud of it. If anyone came in unexpected, the team would feign ignorance and claim they were asked to inspect the ducts while the family was gone. They even used paperwork with a similar, yet different address to aid in the ruse.

The bugging team was back in the van in fifteen minutes.

"Entry, clear."

"Roger, all units stand down. We'll rendezvous in one hour," said Kilkenney.

*   *   *

"Well, I needed that," Melanie said pointing to the last of the slushy green margarita as she entered the kitchen.

"Yeah, I keep forgetting to get Judy's recipe, she should be a bartender."

The company and alcohol put Melanie in good spirits, but the buzz was wearing off now. Only she and Jeannie remained, cleaning the kitchen and sipping sodas.

"I suppose the baby will sleep good tonight," giggled Jeannie.

"I know, and so will the boys," replied Melanie. "That is the second best thing about 'Margarita Night' . . . the boys sleep in on Saturday mornings."

"How is Tyler doing?"

"He is still taking it hard, they both are, but it is still hardest with Tyler . . . he just doesn't understand."

Jeannie looked over the breakfast bar to their children playing in the living room. She kept her eyes on them as she said, "Makes ya want to get out sometimes doesn't it?"

"That, and being in South Texas."

"You don't like it here?"

"Not at all. The only redeeming thing for me is the schools."

"Mel, I can hear acid in your voice. You're serious."

"I am serious. I have finally realized that I can't take this life anymore. I'm going to tell Jazz to get out."

"Holy shit, girlfriend! Really?"

"Yep, I've had it."

"Wow. Well . . . when?"

"I'll wait until he gets back. There isn't anything we can do about it now."

THIRTY

ALBANIA

The door on the starboard side and the stern ramp of the MH-53 Sea Dragon, "Hurricane 224" were open. Jazz's seat across from the door provided him a good view of the Albanian countryside. At a high altitude the countryside looked sparsely populated. They only passed one or two villages. Luscious green farmland stretched from the Adriatic to the mountains, which dramatically rose from the plain.

The—53 really was a behemoth, the largest helicopter in the U.S. inventory. It sported eight blades, three engines and a cargo hold big enough for an old style military jeep. Now the hold was empty except for four aircrewmen and four EOD Techs. Jazz's security team included himself, Keating, Ashland, and T-Ball. Ashland lay prone, sleeping as usual. Two members of the aircrew sat on the open tail with their feet dangling over the side. Through the opening Jazz could see another—53 trailing them, Hurricane 218. Inside were Grover Denke, Dee, Sinclair, and Quinn.

The green dive bag on the deck at Jazz's feet was open. He peered inside, checking that he had all the proper equipment.

Flak vest, load bearing vest, 210 rounds of 5.56, 45 rounds of 9mm, butt pack. Kevlar helmet. MRE, first aid kit, GPS, toilet paper in butt pack. Three day pack. Camelbak. AN/PRC-112 for emergency comms, rain poncho in three-day pack.

Jazz leaned back into his M-16A3 placed behind the canvas seat. He had collapsed the stock and pointed the barrel toward the deck for their transit into Albania. On his left hip was his nine-millimeter pistol, the M-9.

Hopefully, I have everything I need, he thought.

Airframe vibration increased as they descended. Jazz could see that they were going to land at an airport near what appeared to be a small town.

Tirane, the capitol of Albania had the only airfield that could accommodate large military fixed wing aircraft. Two Air Force C-17s sat on the flightline. Like ants, men swarmed around the aircraft offloading cargo from their innards. The line stretched to a small tent city next to the terminal.

The—53 stopped descending at about fifty feet off the deck. Now it moved slowly forward toward the end of the airfield. Jazz stood and headed toward the cockpit. He looked between the two front seats. One of the pilots looked back at him and smiled. There was a parking lot of helicopters ahead. Jazz recognized most of the helos as French in design.

A man on the ground motioned at the—53 with a pair on wands. The pilot followed his direction and set the bird down in the field between two concrete airstrips.

The blades stopped, but the engines kept running. One of the aircrew shouted in Jazz's ear.

"You guys need to go with the pilot for a brief at one of the tents."

Jazz nodded.

The Techs removed their UDT vests and Protec helmets, replacing them with flak vests and Kevlar. Each man had already positioned his load-bearing vest over his flak. Jazz slipped the sling on his rifle through a carabineer affixed to a D-ring on the shoulder of his load-bearing vest.

"Do we need to put on our three-day packs?" he asked.

The aircraft was too loud, nobody heard him. He saw T-Ball and Ashland stepping off the ramp. They had left their packs behind.

I guess we'll be near the bird most of the time.

Keating, Ashland, and T-Ball were waiting for their lieutenant. They looked like they were ready for war. Jazz hoped they did not have to be.

"Come on, LT. We gotta get to this brief," said Keating.

Grover Denke and his "squad" came out of the second helo. Denke walked next to Jazz as the group moved toward the American compound.

"This reminds me of Bosnia," said Denke, slinging his rifle over his shoulder.

"How so, Senior?"

"The land looks the same. The tent city up ahead there. A little bit of military chaos. And the cold."

Jazz surveyed the scene. The French-made helicopters he saw from the air were in fact French military, and Swiss, and Dutch, and three were even from the United Arab Emirates. Trucks with aircraft pallets on them drove past, heading for their helicopters followed by slower moving forklifts.

"What was on those pallets?" asked T-Ball.

"Looked like HDRs," answered Quinn.

"What are HDRs?"

"Humanitarian Daily Rations. They are basically MREs in yellow packaging. Written on the side of the packages in several languages it says, 'Given to you by the people of the United States.' I suppose that is our cargo today."

"How do you know about HDRs?"

"I did one of these things in Liberia once."

There were men and women from many different foreign military forces around. Jazz studied each of their weapons and uniforms. He was only able to distinguish a few. They followed the pilots through a sandbag gate in the corner of the tent city. There a soldier checked their identifications while a second sat at the ready next to an M-60 machine gun.

A civilian toting an M-4, a version of the M-16 even more compact than the CAR-15 was waiting for them just inside the checkpoint.

"You guys off the *Inchon?*"

"Yes, sir," replied the senior pilot.

"I'm Thomas Henderson. I'll be giving you your mission brief today. Please follow me to the briefing tent."

Within a few steps the men were slipping on the muddy ground. They followed Henderson through a maze of tents and camouflage netting.

"LT, look there," said T-Ball pointing to a large tent with a sign out front. The sign had an EOD crab on it and read:

617 CES/EOD Ramstein AFB GE

"Cool. Maybe we'll get some work with those guys."

"Maybe."

The men all took their seats inside the briefing tent. Henderson was a thin man with long blonde hair. He wore a khaki vest that had pockets all over it, a blue sweatshirt, and blue jeans. His boots were caked with mud. Jazz noticed in addition to the M-4 Henderson had a pistol in a holster underneath his belt. Without the weapons the man looked like a journalist, and a hippie one at that.

In the tent were the senior pilots from both aircraft, the men of Det Four, and also Army and Air Force aircrews and Air Force security personnel.

"Gents, again I am Thomas Henderson. I am an Air Force civilian. Today you will be flying to Kukesh to deliver humanitarian rations, blankets, and tents. Kukesh is in the northern part of Albania, just over the border from Kosovo.

"Right now the threat level is high. We have intelligence assessments that there are terrorist elements throughout Albania. We know that the population is heavily armed. Most of the country is controlled by local mafia and there are black-marketers throughout.

"Any one of these elements may try to test the United States' presence here. We just do not know how they will react. Plus, you never know when you will be shot at by an annoyed farmer as you fly overhead."

Henderson surveyed the men in front of him. They were silent.

"The good news is; nobody has had any problems yet. The trip up there is about two hours by helo. Any questions?"

One after another, half the men in the tent asked questions. Jazz sensed that everyone wanted to be recognized. Realizing he didn't have any intelligent questions to ask and he kept his mouth shut.

Twenty minutes later he was back in the—53, lifting off the grass in Tirane. The hold of the helo was packed to the gills while they had their meeting with Henderson. There were several aircraft pallets with cardboard boxes on them. Some were labeled "WORLD FOOD BANK," others said "U.S. GOVT HDRs," with a greeting on them just as Quinn described. One of the pallets in the back appeared to have blankets on it. Each pallet was covered with a cargo net and chained to the deck.

There was no longer any room to move fore and aft in the helo. Jazz positioned himself in the small space in front of the cargo near the forward door. Keating sat across from him and they were joined by one aircrewman. The others, including Ashland and T-Ball, all stepped up the ramp and found a spot in the back behind the cargo.

The countryside grew even more mountainous as they headed inland. The pilots used a chart and a road map to navigate their way to Kukesh. They followed one of the valleys that stretched liked splayed fingers connecting the highlands to the coast.

Through the window Jazz could see a treacherous road hugging the side of the mountains, winding its way through the valley. It was definitely a difficult passage in the best of weather.

Sometimes the pilots decided the best course was to dodge over a mountain peak. Then flight became as unpleasant as an amusement park ride. Both Jazz and Keating would look up as the nose of the Sea Dragon rose. Wind pushing on and around the peak would buffet the airframe violently as they crested over the summit or ridgeline. Then the helo would drop again quickly leaving Jazz's stomach at a higher altitude. On the worst occasions the pilots would circle and bank steeply, searching for the road again.

When they got to Kukesh the aircrewman tapped Jazz on the knee. He leaned over and yelled in the officer's ear.

"WE'RE ALMOST THERE, SIR! YOU MAY WANNA GET UP AND TAKE A LOOK AROUND!"

Jazz nodded, unclipped his seatbelt and stood. He slipped off his Protec helmet and traded it again for the Kevlar. Affixed to the helmet was a set of flight deck goggles. The helo buffeted up and down. Jazz held his M-16 in one hand while bracing himself with the other as he looked out the window.

The village appeared as any Mediterranean village except that to the north between the town proper and the mountains was a field filled with color and movement. Jazz suspected that he was seeing a bird's eye view of the Albanian refugees.

Suddenly the helo banked, dropping in altitude and heading toward this field. As they got close, Jazz saw that it his supposition was correct. Many of the displaced Albanian worked to set up shelters. Some were still streaming from over the mountain.

Though it was now late March, the peak towering over the town of Kukesh was covered with snow. Clearly winter was going to be present until mid-April at least.

They circled the camp three times, just high enough to get a good look but not so low as to disturb the Ethnic Albanian farmers with the downwash from the blades. Now Hurricane 224 and 218 headed for the eastern part of the town.

There was another field, but this one was open. To the north of the field was an orchard. As they descended further Jazz could see that the field had a barbwire fence surrounding it. There were a few buildings and military-looking trucks.

Nobody said there was a military facility here . . . strange . . . , he thought.

Suddenly the aircraft dropped dramatically. The aircrewman grabbed Jazz by the shoulder this time and yelled in his ear.

"WE'RE GOING TO LAND HERE, SIR! DO YOU CONCUR IT IS SAFE?"

It was a requirement that the senior EOD Technician determine that the landing zone was not hot and that the aircraft could take off. Jazz looked around; there appeared to be no threat.

"YES! IT IS SAFE!"

The aircrewman gave him a "thumbs up" as he spoke into his lip mike. The—53 descended faster. At about twenty feet off the ground they began to move forward again. The pilot was taxing away from the buildings. Finally they hovered for a moment and the helo set down on the field.

It felt like he was in a movie from the moment he stepped through the door. All Jazz could hear was the thump of the blades. He got outside the arc of the blade where it was somewhat quieter.

Jazz moved to the two o'clock position on the right side of the—53. Keating moved around to the eleven o'clock. A quick three sixty revealed that the field in front and to the right of the helo was clear. Then Jazz looked toward Ashland at the five o'clock position. Ash was gesturing toward the building beyond.

Soldiers.

There were soldiers running from the building armed with Kalishnikov AK-47's.

Oh, fuck. This could be bad, thought Jazz.

THIRTY-ONE

CONTACT

Jazz jabbed a finger toward the soldiers. Ashland's head swiveled toward them. Jazz could see his shipmate's body tense from forty feet away.

Are they coming to greet us, or do they think we are invaders? he wondered.

From his vantage point Jazz could tell that the aircrew were oblivious. He could see the first of the pallets now on the grass under the tail. A crewman in the door waved at him and motioned that the helo was moving forward. The—53 lifted slightly and taxied forward.

There was an officer with the soldiers. Jazz noted the man forming his troops in a line along the field. Each man had his weapon slung at the hip, pointing right at the men from *Inchon* disgorging aid. Either they wanted to be threatening, or they had very poor weapon's discipline.

Fuck, this is not good. Hopefully this guy knows the deal.

Suddenly Jazz saw a flash of light come from the Albanian line, or had he imagined it?

He looked again at the Albanian officer who was shouting and pointing at Denke's aircraft. Several flashes now erupted from the weapons the soldiers were holding.

They're shooting at us!

Jazz was surprised by his own reactions as he carried them out. His movements reminded him of wrestling moves he developed in high school—he didn't have to think, it just happened.

As Jazz stepped over to where Ash was standing he pulled back on the charging handle of his M-16, chambering a round. By the time he was abreast of his teammate, Ash was already shooting.

Jazz raised his weapon, flipping the fire selection switch from "SAFE" to "SEMI." He put it in his shoulder, sighted it at the officer and pulled the trigger. The sound of the helicopter turning and his earplugs prevented him from hearing the rounds going downrange. Jazz did feel a slight kick and he smelled the familiar gunpowder residue of the 5.56 ammunition as he swept the rifle down the line of soldiers.

The wash from one of the Hurricanes lifting off pushed against him. The Albanians now broke into a run back toward the building they emerged from. Jazz could not tell if they hit any of them.

Time to skedaddle, he thought.

Quickly, Jazz surveyed the scene. It was Hurricane 218, Denke's helicopter, that took off. Denke, Dee, Sinclair, and Quinn, however, were still on the ground.

Keeping their weapons pointed at the main building, the men of Det Four moved toward Jazz. He motioned toward Hurricane 224.

"GET ON THE BIRD! LET'S GET OUTTA HERE!"

Jazz and Keating went through the starboard door while the others climbed up the ramp in the rear. Jazz noted that one pallet remained. As the helo lifted off, Jazz counted heads twice. All of Det Four was onboard.

"Anybody hit!" he called out.

Keating patted himself down and shook his head, "No."

"Hey back there! Senior Chief! Anybody hit!"

Denke also shook his head, "No."

Jazz was surprised.

He sat down in the seat next to Keating and put on his safety belt, just in time.

Suddenly the aircraft started to shudder. The aircrewman up front with Keating and Jazz fell over as the helo banked violently to the left and began to descend. Jazz's stomach went up into his throat. He tried to reach for something but found his hands flailing. The aircraft righted itself, but then nosed forward. Now hydraulic fluid began to pour from the overhead just behind the cockpit. Through the window, Jazz could now see treetops sprinkled with snow. Just when he thought they were going to hit, the nose came up again violently. He felt the aircraft's descent slow slightly and the blades thwopped louder as it seemed they were trying to grip the air.

Then they hit.

Jazz did not remember getting out of the aircraft. It was as if he woke up sitting under the tree just outside the starboard door. His whole body ached.

"Uh."

As the helo in front of him came into focus and his ears stopped ringing he heard several moans.

"Who's up!" came Denke's voice from his left.

Jazz looked toward the aircraft's tail and saw Denke standing there.

"LT, are you okay?"

"Uh, yeah. I think so. What happened?"

"We crashed."

"Huh?"

"I think those soldiers were shooting at the aircraft. That's probably why 218 left without us. We were certainly next, though."

Jazz scratched his head trying to understand. Then he noticed that the side of the aircraft was peppered with bullet holes.

They were shooting right over our heads.

Keating emerged from the cabin.

"Oh, fuck. That fucking hurt like a motherfucker."

"Is everyone up there okay!" Denke called out again.

Keating turned and stepped back into the aircraft. He emerged with an ashen face.

"Aircrewman looks dead. Pilots are out but I think they are alive."

Jazz remembered that the aircrewman who was up front with them was tethered to the aircraft on a running line, but he was not strapped into a seat.

"Lieutenant, where is your weapon?" Denke asked.

"What?"

"Your weapon. Where is your long-gun?"

Jazz realized that he was more out of it than he thought. He got up and stepped into the cabin.

The aircrewman was on his back, feet together, arms folded neatly over his chest. Jazz figured that Keating must have done that. His helmet was cracked and his face looked swollen. Jazz had a morbid thought.

He just looks broken.

Jazz realized that he did not even know the name of this man he flew with, cruised with, served with. He pulled off the Velcro nametag on his flight suit.

SAM MARTON
AD2(AC) USN

Jazz saw his weapon on the deck. It was still on "SEMI." As he clicked it back to "SAFE," Jazz cursed himself.

Damn that was careless.

He stopped for a moment and tried to gather his thoughts. *How had the weapon come unslung from his carabineer?* Jazz looked down and noticed that the 'beener was still on the sling of the M-16. The force of the impact had ripped it off of his load-bearing vest.

Jazz stepped up to the cockpit to check out the pilots. They were starting to stir. When he turned around, he paused again. Something felt wrong. He slung his rifle over his shoulder. He looked at his hands as he tried to catch his breath. They were shaking.

With his right hand, Jazz reached down and pulled his knife out. He gripped it, held it up, and tried to concentrate on it.

Do this. This is why you are here.

"LT, are you okay?" said Ashland from the doorway.

"Yes," he replied firmly and replacing the knife. "How is everyone else?"

"Banged and bruised, sir," he heard Delgado say from outside.

Jazz stepped back into the light.

"Quinn, Sinclair, rig up a body bag somehow for Sam here. Ash, you and T-Ball get the pilots out. See if they need any first aid. Are the other aircrewmen okay?"

"Yes, sir," said Denke. "They are doing a once-over on the bird for fuel leaks and such. I think we are alright though. So what's your plan, Lieutenant?"

"Well, first we gotta salvage the wreck and call the *Inchon*. Second we should set up a security perimeter and prepare for extraction. That may entail moving out of these trees to a more suitable landing zone."

Fortunately the pilots did a good job of crashing the airplane. As a result the det was able to get most of the gear out including the ammunition. Each man stuffed essentials into his vest and his three-day pack, leaving their kit bags behind.

"Well, their radio isn't working," said Ash.

"Do you have the E and E radio, LT?" asked Quinn.

"Yes."

"Well, let's get the '*chon* up on that."

Jazz got the radio, the PRC-112, out of his bag. He leaned against the helo as he turned it on. The pilots were now out of the bird sitting under the tree where Jazz had been. They still looked groggy.

He looked over to the sleeping bag that now held Marton.

"Bright Star, Bright Star, this is Tiburon Four, over."

Denke was directing the members of the det to form a perimeter around the aircraft. They appeared to be in a relatively level spot, but it was in the bottom of a valley.

"Bright Star, Bright Star, this is Tiburon Four, over."

After ten tries, Denke came over next to Jazz. He spoke in a hushed tone.

"You turn the on-off switch, sir?"

"I did, Senior."

"Well, we're too far, too low, or nobody's listening."

"Maybe 218 saw us go down."

"I'm sure of it, sir. The pilots were probably talking the whole time."

Denke turned to one of the aviators. "Lieutenant, does 218 know that we are here, that we went down?"

"Uh, I don't know. They got hit in the field, had a mechanical issue and decided to split."

"Yes, I'd noticed that."

"Anyway, I don't know if they heard us."

"Well, at the very least, Tirane will notice when we don't return," remarked the co-pilot.

Quinn came over with a handheld GPS.

"We're up now, Senior."

Denke turned to Jazz.

"LT, I think we need to separate ourselves from this aircraft a little; do a little escape and evasion while it is still light."

"Okay."

"I think we should mark the helo's position on the GPS, pick up our fallen shipmate, and patrol to higher ground. We can make a call then about digging in and waiting or continuing to move. Who knows? . . . maybe we can reach the '*chon* from up there," he said nodding toward the ridge.

"Escape and evasion?" said the pilot incredulously. "I'm staying with the bird. Someone will come and get us."

Just then the sound of metal piercing metal, "dink, dink, dink," was immediately followed by gunfire from the slope in the direction of Kukesh.

"Shit, they followed us!" yelled Denke.

Now Jazz saw the pilot holding his leg. Blood poured from between his fingers.

"CONTACT RIGHT, CONTACT RIGHT!" someone yelled from the nose of the aircraft.

Jazz ran to the nose and flipped his weapon back to "SEMI." He could see movement but no distinct man or men coming down the hill.

T-Ball was prone on the ground ten feet in front of him. He saw his teammate open fire, and did the same.

As he was changing his clip, Denke grabbed Jazz by the shoulder.

"LT, you gotta lead us outta here. Head up that hill, the airmen will follow. Me and the boys will cover the back door."

Jazz turned around and saw the co-pilot carrying the wounded pilot in a fireman's carry. The two aircrewman held either end of the sleeping bag that secured the body of Sam Marton.

A large volume of fire erupted behind them. Jazz kept turning around, tempted to run back. He knew he could not, not yet.

Jazz caught up with the men carrying their dead shipmate, slung his weapon and grabbed Marton around the middle.

"Go! Let's go!"

The co-pilot in front kept stumbling. He even ran the pilot's head into a tree, knocking snow off the branches. As they climbed higher and higher, the brush and the patches of snow thinned. The land became a little rockier, with boulders beginning to dot the landscape.

They had not quite reached the peak when Jazz thought he saw a good position. There were several boulders close together. They hooked around to the left, away from Kukesh. The ground sloped away from them on all sides.

Jazz could still hear shooting and when he looked back he occasionally saw muzzle flashes.

"Here, stop behind these rocks. I'll be back," the lieutenant commanded.

Now he ran down the hill toward his teammates. Quinn was the first one he saw.

"Quinn! Over here!"

T-Ball came running from somewhere. Quinn pointed toward Jazz. T-Ball ran toward his OIC.

"We're going up that way, T-Ball."

"Got it."

The firing had stopped now.

After T-Ball came Ash, then Denke, Dee, Keating, Sinclair, and Quinn. As Quinn passed Jazz he tapped him on the shoulder.

"Last man!"

Jazz flipped his selector switch from "SEMI" to "AUTO." He scanned the forest in front of him for the enemy. There was no sign of movement.

He gave Quinn about two minutes to leap frog up the hill then he followed. First he passed T-Ball and tapped him on the shoulder.

"Last man," he whispered.

The det had to be quiet now to hide their escape. When Jazz got to Denke he pointed up the hill to where the Hurricane crew was.

"We're going up there."

Denke nodded.

Then he got in position further up the hill from Quinn. Jazz held up a fist. Quinn saw it and repeated the signal.

Hold.

He waited for the signal to get passed back from T-Ball. Then he motioned by waving his arm.

Follow me.

Quietly the det patrolled the last twenty yards to the aviators. There, behind the cover of the rocks, they huddled.

"Sinclair, rear-guard down that hill. T-Ball, watch to the right in case they try to flank us. Everyone else, smoke 'em if you got 'em," said Denke.

Canteens, MREs, and energy bars came out of vests and cargo pockets. Keating tended to the wounded pilot. Jazz tried again to reach the *Inchon*.

"Bright Star, Bright Star, this is Tiburon Four, over."

He drank from his Camelbak while he waited for a response.

"Bright Star, Bright Star, this is Tiburon Four, over."

Denke looked at him and shrugged.

"How's he doing, Chief?" Jazz inquired of Keating.

"It's just a flesh wound. I've 'ad worse," responded the pilot through gritted teeth.

Suddenly everyone was laughing.

THIRTY-TWO

NOTHING

Dee and Ash took the next watch. All the men sat quietly and tried to stay loose. Periodically Jazz made a call on the radio to *Inchon*. There was no answer.

"I haven't seen a thing," Dee said keeping his eyes down the hill from his observation point. "Do you think we scared 'em off?"

"Ha!" Denke chuckled. "Who scared who off? They are pouring through that helo right now, gathering intel and probably having a late lunch of HDRs. The first chance they get, they'll be back."

"It's been almost two hours," said Sinclair. "Search and Rescue should be up here soon."

"Count on another four, Sinc," responded Keating. "It was a two hour flight from Tirane to Kukesh. That means two hours for 218 to get back or for us all to be noticed missing. Then they'll need two hours of prep to get their poop in one sock followed by a two-hour flight back."

Jazz felt the eyes on him again.

What are we going to do, Lieutenant?

"LT, Senior . . . come look at this," said Ash.

Jazz got up, hunched over to reduce his profile, and scooted over to Ash. Denke was right beside him.

"Look between those trees. See that dirt patch?"

"Yeah," said Denke.

"I think it's a road."

"Huh?" said Jazz.

"Watch, every now and then I think I see something . . . maybe a vehicle."

Jazz saw something moving across the spot that Ash was pointing toward.

"See it?"

"I do, I do, Ash."

"Well maybe we can Shanghai a truck or something . . . find our own way back."

Jazz looked at Denke.

"I think that's a good idea, sir. We should at least have a look-see. The pilot is stable now, but for how long? Four hours from now we could be south-a here, on radio comms to a bird *coming here*."

Jazz gripped his rifle and thought a moment.

"Okay, Senior. I'll take Ash's position here. You two go recon the road first and see if it is even feasible. We'll hold here."

"Got it, LT."

Several scenarios began to dance in Jazz's head as he watched Ash and Denke descend the hill further to the left, almost ninety degrees from where they came.

Thirty minutes later the det moved to a position along the road. Jazz could see first-hand now why they had to get rations to the Ethnic Albanians via helo. It looked like it would take days for a convoy to get up here even with four-wheel drive. The road was washed out in several places and was pitted with holes. Jazz wondered if they were from ice or from mortar rounds.

He reviewed the plan in his head once more. Denke was on the road, closest to Kukesh. He would check each vehicle as it passed. If one looked like a real option, they would commandeer it. On his signal, they would rush the vehicle with weapons drawn, hoping that the occupants would surrender quickly.

Another thirty minutes passed before they heard what sounded like a truck coming toward them from Kukesh. As it drew near, Jazz could make out what appeared to be a Russian-made quarter-ton truck with a canvas covered flatbed.

Perfect.

The vehicle sputtered and stopped right in front of them. Jazz watched incredulously as the driver, an Albanian soldier, got out and walked around to the back of the truck. He saw Denke moving down toward the road. Had he missed the signal?

Jazz looked at Ash who gave him the "hold" sign.

The driver emerged from the flatbed with a jerry can.

Holy cow, he ran out of gas.

On any other day Jazz would have been shocked what he saw next. Denke emerged from the forest with a knife in hand. He ran up behind the driver, grabbed his jaw and lifted it up and to his left. Then with his right hand he plunged the knife into the soldier's neck.

Denke got blood on himself as he dragged the solider to the road's edge and rolled him into a ditch.

As the rest of the Hurricane 224 survivors stepped onto the road, one of the aircrew exclaimed, "Holy shit!" Everyone else was silent.

Denke snapped them out of it.

"Dee, gas 'er up. Everyone else get in back. Lay our shipmate in the bag on the deck. I want two Techs on the tailgate ready to shoot anyone who causes us a problem. LT, you are riding shotgun with me. Let's move!"

After Dee poured the contents of the jerry can into the gas tank. He hopped in back. Someone banged on the cab. Denke turned a switch on the dash, put the vehicle in gear, and started driving.

"Don't know where we're going, LT, so I am going to follow standard liberty procedure for the Med."

"What's that?"

"Head downhill."

"Ha!"

"Seriously, get the GPS outta my bag. I did a 'mark mark' in Tirane. We can at least make sure that we are closing distance with it."

"Senior Chief."

"Yeah."

"I want you to teach me how to do that."

Denke looked at his lieutenant. "No you don't."

"Yeah, I do."

After six hours of no word on Hurricane 224, Solarsky decided that he needed to at least call the next of kin for everyone in Det Four. He thought it necessary to at least inform them that an incident had occurred. Using a satellite phone on the *Inchon*, he called Melanie first.

"Melanie?"

"Yes."

"This is Commander Solarsky, the commanding officer of EOD Mobile Unit Six."

"Uh, yes, sir?"

"I'm calling to inform you that there has been an incident."

"Another one! Oh, oh my God . . . Is Jazz alright?"

"Well, we don't know. The helicopter that he was in departed this morning for Kukesh, Albania. The aircraft has not returned. Most of the other detachment members are with him."

"So, do you think they crashed?"

"Well, we are not sure. They may have set down for mechanical trouble and are unable to contact us," Solarsky lied.

He already decided to give the families one piece of news at a time. In fact, while they knew from the return of Hurricane 218 that the flight was shot at, they may in fact have landed somewhere due to mechanical failure.

"What are you doing to solve this?"

An astute question, he thought.

"We are sending out search and rescue teams to find them right now."

This was another lie. The weather precluded anyone from taking off from *Inchon* or departing from Tirane.

"The executive officer is still in Charleston. He and the ombudsman will do anything you need to get through this. Please stay in contact with them, and they will be in contact with you. Okay?"

"Okay. Thank you, sir."

"I'm going to call the other wives next. Uh, can you give me some time before you speak to them? I think this information needs to come from me."

"I understand."

"Okay, thank you."

Melanie hung up the phone. Just then Abigail began to cry. Melanie extracted her from the crib took her to her own bed and lay down, crying with her.

Nine and a half hours later the co-pilot, Denke, and Jazz were standing in the briefing tent. Though it was now early morning, they were rested. The drive was long but uneventful. Jazz even slept in between attempting to reach someone on the radio.

Henderson came into the tent with an Air Force captain in tow. The captain had a sidearm slung under his armpit in a shiny black patent leather holster as if he were a police officer.

"Where the fuck have you guys been?" said Henderson. "And what the fuck happened up there?"

"I dunno. You tell me," said the co-pilot.

"You guys landed in a damn Albanian military compound for chrissakes!"

"Well, now I realize that it was a mistake. They were obviously not happy about it."

"You're damn right they weren't . . ."

"Hey!" shouted Jazz. "Hold on a second . . ."

"Fuck you, Lieutenant. You're the clown who said it was safe to land there in the first place."

"Yeah, and you are the clown that sent us up there with fucked up intel. Why didn't you tell us there was a military base? Why did you not tell the military we were coming? Why did you not have someone there waiting for us to get the stuff? It was safe to land . . . and if it is not safe to land in the host nation's military base, you, sir are the one who should be telling us."

"Now calm down, LT . . . ."

"'LT!' It's 'LT' now! Bullshit! I am an officer in the United States Navy. You will address me as 'Lieutenant,' Mr. Henderson! All of the men on that flight got shot at, got shot down, and had a shipmate killed because of your shoddy preparation. You didn't know there was a military base there did you, you dumb motherfucker? How many times have you been up there?"

Henderson was silent.

"How many!"

"None."

"None! Any of your men?" Jazz already knew the answer. "I guess not. So you walk around here with your spec ops weapons and your leather shoulder holster like you're the shit. Then you send us up there to get shot at. Don't get indignant with us, you are damn lucky I don't put you in a fucking body bag with Samuel Marton!"

"Who?"

"Samuel Marton! That's who you killed today! Don't you ever forget his name!"

Silence again filled the tent briefly.

"Well, here's the deal. I am writing a report that will say that on your recommendation, you guys flew into a hostile environment . . ."

"No you're not," said a man in civilian clothes at the entrance to the tent.

"Excuse me?" said Henderson.

"You are not going to write anything of the sort."

"And who the fuck are you?"

"I'm Tracy."

Henderson got white.

"Here's what you are going to write."

Tracy threw some bound papers at Henderson.

"It says that these guys went to the facility at Kukesh with poor intel. When they arrived, the local militia, which by the way is really a black market operation with ties to a local terrorist organization, opened fire because they thought the Americans were coming to clean them out and take their territory. As a result, these men crashed, commandeered an unattended vehicle, and drove their asses back here, period. Got me?"

"Yes, sir."

"Additionally you will note that there is no mention of one Senior Chief Grover Denke in that report. Senior Chief was never here. Were you, Grover?"

"No, sir, I've never been to the Balkans."

Denke and Tracy had a chuckle at that comment.

"We are gathering up the other men involved. I want everyone here for a debrief of this story. We need it straight before you leave. Another front is coming in and we are expecting torrential rain. The weather is going to keep you guys here awhile—maybe another twenty-four hours. After that you are not to come back, understand, Grover?"

"Yes, sir."

"We'll work it out with your CO, Grover, don't sweat it. Now for Pete's sake, make master chief so we can get you back."

"I'm trying, sir."

Tracy looked at Jazz a moment. Even in the dim light of the tent, he thought he saw him wink just before he turned and left.

*   *   *

There were at least three other cases that Elena worked with Kilkenney and his surveillance team. She knew them to be very good at their specialty. The last of her bagel lunch was swallowed quickly as she saw Kilkenney walking toward her desk.

"Hey, Elena, how are things?"

"Oh fine, George, you?"

"Great," said Kilkenney taking a seat on the desk across from Elena's. "My report is short. We did all the normal stuff; mail, internet, phones, cameras, and finally the house internal."

"The vents again?"

"For sure, it is becoming my signature."

"I see," Elena said sarcastically.

"Anyway after the setup we were at it for one week. We've got nothing so far. I can continue to watch the house, but I recommend that we back off. I can use tape on the cameras and bugs to be picked up weekly and continue to get weekly reports on mail and internet. For my money, you're not going to get anything, not until the husband comes home."

"You are probably right, I'll take that under advisement."

Kilkenney handed Elena a manila envelope.

"Here is the first report. I'll standby for your decision."

"I've already made up my mind."

"Oh?"

"Let's go with your instinct. Continue to monitor, but back the team out. We'll get in place when Jascinski gets home."

"You got it, and reports?"

"Give me your weeklies regardless of what is in them."

"Done."

THIRTY-THREE

TIRANE INTERNATIONAL AIRPORT

The tent sagged, heavy with water. In a few spots the rain began to drip in on them. Still, they were warm and dry.

Tirane was the perfect place to hide. The International Red Cross provided everything and even paid for their way. They had warm clothes, rain ponchos, and the best tents and sleeping bags money could buy to keep them cozy at night.

Guido smiled to himself. He was sure there must be steam lifting from the abode he shared with Renata. It was more than cozy, Renata had been a vixen since they arrived. She was always passionate after they took violent action, but this time was different. Perhaps she liked the fact that their neighbors could hear her yelp with delight while they . . . made love?

No, he thought. *We're fucking. Morning, noon, and night.*

The volunteers in the tents next to theirs would grow silent as he and Renata began to move together. He imagined them smiling and pointing to their tent while he and his woman copulated.

Later the two would emerge, acting as if they had no idea the others could hear them. After two weeks of living in tents, Guido and Renata were not the only ones who were having loud sex. He thought it was interesting how quickly shame disappeared and base instinct took over when the higher needs like privacy and bath water were not available.

The aid work was not unsatisfying. Guido had no love, but no hate for the people they were helping. They certainly were not enemies of his cause.

Each morning after breakfast he and Renata helped the others load helicopters, then trucks with humanitarian aid. Some days they would fly in the helos to Kukesh or some other remote town to hand out the foodstuffs and materials donated by the Red Cross and the European Community. Most days they would ride in the back of a military truck and hand out items to those who made it to a village on the coast.

Just as Nasih predicted, it was a perfect retreat for them. They escaped, all their needs were taken care of, and he was enjoying his woman. Guido's only real task was to provide information through Nasih's henchman, Ayman. Ayman told him that that a prime objective for them was to get back into Nasih's magazine and destroy its contents, whatever they were.

He varied the time of day that he would take his trip to the base of the mountain. Guido was trained to both change his routine and to watch the routine of others. The Americans were predictable. They changed the guard at the same time each day, they never altered the number of personnel watching the magazines, and they rarely questioned foreigners. Guido thought that it was fortunate that he was not the only aid worker who liked to stroll through these woods and up to the mountains.

Renata threw her leg over him. She put her hand on his chest and kissed him softly on the ear.

"Again," she whispered.

"I must go have another look."

She reached down and rubbed him gently a moment. He continued to look at the ceiling. His lover gave up and rolled over pulling the covers off him.

Guido disappeared in plain sight yet again. Nobody noticed the civilian with a camera bag walking along the runway in the rain. The guards on the airfield were all huddled in and under the aircraft to keep as dry as possible.

Poor bastards, he thought.

He crossed into the woods by the fuel farm and headed toward the mountains. As Guido stepped into the first clearing he crouched down and looked back toward the field. The low brush was thin enough here that he could observe the flight line opposite the tent city and the international airport.

The Apache attack helicopters looked frightening even on the ground. He counted them twice and wrote the number down in the notebook he kept in his pocket. The number did not change for four days. He noticed them flying in pairs from time to time, but they always returned.

"Probably training missions," Ayman had surmised.

"Why does Nasih want to know these things?" Guido asked.

"I do not think he cares," said Ayman shrugging his shoulders. "I think he is selling the information."

Guido and Ayman met sporadically. Guido would give him information and film. Ayman provided him with light supplies that were not readily available in the aid camp. Guido sold as many cigarettes as he smoked.

He worked his way through the woods to a spot at the base of the mountains north of the magazines. The road running along the base of the mountain and the last magazine were visible from here. Guido climbed the mountains, circling above and around the last two magazines. He sat in the mud at his observation position and waited. Within two minutes he was soaking wet and cold.

Who's the poor bastard now? he thought. *And to think I could be shagging right now.*

*   *   *

The tail section of the Sea Dragon provided pretty good protection from the torrential rain for Jazz and Ashland as they ate their MREs. They were the only men in or near the two helos parked on the grass at the far end of the airfield. Everyone else had made their way to the mess hall or one of the other tents of Camp Tirane.

One of the concrete airstrips stretched out from their left toward the tent city and the international airport. They could just barely see the lights of the tower through the curtain of water. The tents disappeared into the landscape. Every now and again they would see the lights of a military vehicle driving toward them, dropping off watch-standers or aircraft maintenance personnel.

The weather grounded all the NOBLE ANVIL aircraft for hours now. The man who identified himself as "Tracy" was right, there was even talk of staying overnight. Jazz had not thought to pack a sleeping bag.

He looked at his knife, the blade that his father gave him, stuck in the mud just beyond the ramp. He had used it to pierce the top of his plastic MRE cooking pouch. Its contents leaned against the knife emanating steam with a distinctive chemical smell as it cooked his chili macaroni. Jazz sucked some more water from his Camelbak, washing down the thick crackers and peanut butter.

The rain on the runway popped like applause, the drops hitting the fuselage above his head thunked like a thousand base drums beating out of rhythm.

At least I'm dry, he thought. *Dry and alive.*

"What do you think of all this shit, LT?" asked Ashland.

"What do you mean?" Jazz tensed.

"I am sick of this shit. Fucking Haiti, sir. Fucking Somalia. Fucking Bosnia, Kosovo, and Albania. The mother-fucking Balkans! What the fuck are we doing here?"

"I don't know."

"Think it is worth getting killed over?"

"No."

Jazz sensed that Ash strained to hold this in for some time; that he needed to vent.

Should I bring up Rome?

"You know I gotta buddy who's a gunner at Mobile Unit Two," Ash continued. "He took a det to Bosnia. While he was there one of his interpreters told him, 'Whether you leave in five or fifty years, the second you're gone we are going back to war.' Can you believe that shit?"

"Sadly, yes. I just keep remembering a cold morning in 1992, driving to SWOS in Newport, Rhode Island with some classmates. We listened to the President's speech from the night before on the radio when he said we'd definitely only be there one year. Now its nineteen fucking ninety-nine and I know guys who've been there three times. Personally, I do not know what we are doing there. What is our strategy?"

"Exactly, LT. Now we are doing this shit. I'm an EOD Tech for God's sake, not a ground-pounder. This mission is for the Marines. Excuse me for saying so, sir, but sometimes I think we oughta leave and let all these motherfuckers kill each other."

"I agree."

"The purpose of the military in my view is to drain the lifeblood of our nation's enemies until they either submit or succumb to our will. Anything that detracts from that is pure unmitigated bullshit."

"Like this op?"

"You're damn right like this op. You wanna get killed handing out chow to refugees? Is it worth your life?"

"No."

"Sir, this is a European problem yet we're footing the largest chunk of the bill in money, materiel, and people. And watch, two months from now, the French and the Germans will be back to criticizing us. Fuck, let those motherfuckers come down here."

"There are some Frogs here."

"Fuck those guys. They got a company of paratroopers and four helicopters."

"Damn shipmate, you sound pissed."

"You don't know the half of it, LT."

"Huh?"

Ash looked at Jazz a moment, then he looked away.

"Forget it, sir. Forget I said anything. I'm just amped up from that mission. Plus, I'm just tired of being deployed I guess . . . and like I said this shit does not seem worth dying for."

Jazz stepped down the ramp, leaned over and pulled on the knife, removing it from the bag. He poured the hot water onto the grass as he replaced the blade into the sheath on his rigger's belt. Jazz then picked up the bottom of the bag and slipped out the pouch containing his lunch. He sliced it open long ways with the blade on his multi-tool.

Three spoonfuls into his chili mac, he heard T-Ball calling out to them.

"LT! Ash! Come here!"

T-Ball was standing on the flightline next to a HUMMVEE.

"It's raining, man!" shouted Ash.

"Come here, Ash! You are not going to believe this! I have something I want you to see!"

The first class petty officer and the lieutenant looked at each other. Ash shrugged his shoulders, grabbed his M-16 and stepped off the ramp. Jazz sighed, picked up his weapon and followed Ash toward the HUMMVEE.

Ash got in the back seat behind T-Ball, so Jazz walked around and got in behind the driver. He noticed when he shut the door that it was heavier than the other HUMMERS that he had been in. The inside of this HUMMER was very comfortable.

"What kinda HUMMER is this?" asked Ash.

"Bulletproof and air-conditioned" answered the driver. He was a black Air Force sergeant. Something about him was familiar to Jazz.

"Guys, this is Benny Ironhorse," said T-Ball. "Benny, this is Ash and LT Jascinski."

"No way!" said Jazz as Ironhorse turned around exclaiming. "Holy shit, Lieutenant, what's up! Damn, T-Ball, why didn't you tell me Jazz was your LT?"

"Benjamin Ironhorse. EOD's only Native African American, or is it African Native American, Ben?"

"Shit, sir, you know I ain't politically correct. Whenever they have me fill out them forms I check 'other.'"

"You guys have met?" said Ashland.

"Benny and I were in EOD school together. I almost convinced him to transfer over to the Navy."

"Believe me, I am still thinking on it, Lieutenant. Say, you were in that helo thing too then, huh?"

"Uh, yeah. It really wasn't as big a thing as people are saying, Benny."

"Okay, okay. So what's this about, T-Ball?" asked Ash.

Jazz looked at his LPO.

Good transition, Ash, he thought.

"Well, I bumped into Benny here over the way getting chow. Fellow crab-wearer, we start shooting the shit, right?"

"Right."

Jazz noticed now that Benny and T-Ball both had shit-eating grins.

"As you guessed he is with the 617, the sign we saw the other day. So he tells me that the Albanians used this airport for military aircraft as well as civilian. They have a bunch of magazines across the way in the hills. When these guys rolled in here they said we could use them to store explosives and such as long as we cleaned them up. Apparently they were ransacked and booby-trapped during the siege in '95. Benny and his boys went in to clean up."

"That's right, man," added Benny. "We rendered a lotta shit safe and did a bunch of disposal shots. There were booby traps, and a lotta land mines, bombs and shit."

"But then they come to the last magazine."

T-Ball looked at Benny. They were both smiling again.

"What!" said Ash and Jazz together.

"Let's just show 'em," said T-Ball.

Ironhorse put the HUMMER in gear and stepped on the gas.

THIRTY-FOUR

MAGAZINES

They passed the tent city compound that belonged to the non-governmental organizations (NGOs). It was smaller than the U.S. facility and had no security perimeter. Here the homes were all commercially bought at camping outfitters. Geodesic domes of yellow, blue, and red sat precariously in the mud, protected only by moats that drained the downpour toward the forest beyond. Doctors, priests and philanthropists sat and smoked under homemade porches of plastic tarp that once covered humanitarian pallets. The standards of Switzerland, France, Austria, America, the Red Cross, and the Red Crescent drooped in the rain on makeshift flagpoles.

Jazz noted that the rain chased even the media into shelter.

Ironhorse drove off the runway and down a dirt path cutting through the woods that was now nearly a canal. As they rounded a bend Jazz made out a gate similar to the one at the airport proper. The—60 gunner looked asleep. His compatriot reluctantly came out from the sandbagged fighting position only to open the barbed wire gate and let the HUMMER through.

They were now heading closer to the mountains whose presence began to overpower the narrow view through the HUMMVEE's low windshield and the rain in front of the EOD Techs. The inside of the vehicle became darker as the peaks loomed over them.

The HUMMER circled left back toward the international airport. The tower and the top edges of the largest of the aircraft on the field could be seen. The last remnants of the sun were blocked by dark clouds; the late afternoon was now completely illuminated by headlights, campfires, navigation aids, and chemical sticks.

The diesel grumbled and stopped as Ironhorse flipped a switch on the dash. Rain sounded louder on the roof of the HUMMVEE than the—53.

Ironhorse pointed to the mountains on their right.

"You guys see that?"

"What?" said Ash.

"See those doors?"

In the side of the mountain were several metal doors set in concrete that appeared to be painted brown and green camouflage.

"Yea, I see 'em now," said Ash. "Those things are all over the Med. So what?"

Ironhorse turned around and faced Jazz and Ash. "Those are the magazines that the Albanians gave to us," he said in a hushed tone as if telling a ghost story at camp. His eyes shifted back and forth nervously.

"There are ten of 'em along this ridgeline. We think the government gave them to us because they lost control of them. They figured that we'd move out the local junta and turn 'em back over to the federales when we leave.

"The current government tried to get into them after the coup. The ones that they tried to open were booby-trapped. One guy got killed, came from together as he opened the door. A couple of others got injured, fragged.

"Most of them had trip wires fixed to a hook on the door. Pull it open so far and it tugged a nonconductive barrier from between two metal contacts in a homemade firing circuit wired to an APERS mine facing the door. The mine was plussed up with metal fragments. Nails and shit like that.

"Open the door, pull out the barrier. Bang. Big pink mist."

"Damn," said Ash.

"Yeah. If you knew that the device was there it was a simple op. You only had to open the door slowly, a few inches and then you could slip the pull line off the hook on the door.

"When we went in them, as I said, some were empty, some had shit in them, and two of them even had training aids."

"Training aids?" said Jazz.

"Yes, sir. Full out cut-aways of landmines, grenades, anti-tank rounds, just like EOD school except for one thing."

"What?" said Jazz and Ash together.

"We ain't never seen a one of 'em."

"You're shitting me," said Ash.

"Naw, and remember this is our backyard. The 617 is out of Germany. We have guys in my unit that are on their fourth stint in Bosnia."

"LT and I were just talking about that," said Ash.

"Are they Albanian?" asked Jazz.

"We are not sure. Some say they are Russian weapons that the Albanians modified. A lot of them do look like former Soviet stuff, but the dimensions are all wrong. We even think that they may have had technical drawings with no sizes on them."

"That's weird."

"Yeah, so we took photos of all of them and sent them to the Technical Division at Indian Head."

"Can we see them?"

Ironhorse turned to T-Ball. They smiled again.

"Okay, Lieutentant."

The Air Force EOD Tech pointed and commented with each one as they drove by as if he was a tour guide on a safari.

"Number one, a general purpose magazine. This one had anti-tank mines, APERS mines, hand grenades, and small arms. It was booby-trapped. Number two, general purpose. This one had tank mines, APERS mines, rockets, RPGs. It was booby-trapped. Number three, tank rounds and arty. This place had boxes and boxes of 76mm to 155 mm. Booby-trapped."

They passed seven of the magazines. From the outside they all looked non-descript to Jazz. Brown metal doors, probably steel, concrete frames.

They stopped at the eighth bunker. Ironhorse turned the engine off. He and T-Ball got out, followed by Jazz and Ash. Per regulations governing operations in Albania, all of them still had their sidearms strapped on and rifles slung over their shoulders. Only back in the tent compound could they secure weapons.

Jazz mimicked T-Ball and Ash, collapsing the stock on his weapon so that it was less obtrusive.

The men sank in the mud while standing still waiting for Ironhorse to open a two-inch thick lock used by the U.S. military for securing magazines.

He opened the door and they all moved in quickly to avoid more of the rain. Jazz heard a click as Ironhorse turned on a light. In the back of the room was a pile of ordnance "cut-aways" that showed the innards of each; half mines, half rockets, and half artillery shells. It reminded Jazz of the replica of the SANPAT Bomb.

"Holy cow," said Ash. "It's a Bosnian EOD school."

"Yep," said Ironhorse proudly. "We found a lotta good shit. I can't wait to hear back from TECHDIV."

"Was this one booby-trapped?" Jazz inquired.

"Nah," Ironhorse answered. "All training aids. Who cares?" he chuckled.

Ash walked to the stockpile of faux ordnance. He picked one up.

"These are right off the line, metal not plastic. Manufacturers must have demilled a couple and cut them in half, or built some from the ground up as training aids."

"Smart really," allowed T-Ball. "That way there are no mistakes. I know that we've had training ordnance at Two, stuff that we used for years, that we later found out was nowhere close to what the stuff really looks like. Limpets especially."

"What are you going to do with these?" asked Jazz.

"Most will be shipped to TECHDIV, sir. After that, who knows? I will tell you this, some of them will end up as mantelpieces at the 617 and will become ashtrays in the homes of a few Airmen."

Jazz could see that Ashland was studying the devices closely. Ash looked at Ironhorse.

"Could we see the pictures of these, or better yet obtain copies?"

"Sure," said Ironhorse. "You guys ready to see the next one?"

*   *   *

Quickly, he opened the camera bag and pulled out the body with a telephoto lens on it. Ayman even provided false press credentials in case Guido was questioned about his sophisticated camera gear.

The rain was still heavy. He fumbled for the rubber covering that would protect the front of the lens from rain.

Shit, why wasn't I ready? he cursed to himself.

He took two photos before the last man disappeared into the magazine. He snapped another one of the vehicle in case it revealed anything.

It was only the second time he observed anyone moving into the magazines. Usually they just drove back and forth on the road in a security patrol. Perhaps he could discover what was stored in the magazines now. Nasih suspected it was ammunition for further action in Kosovo. Guido wondered if this was an advance party that was about to draw ordnance in time for an attack.

He waited until the men emerged. There were four of them. The camera whirred as Guido snapped photos. He was sure that he only got one face.

Just as he thought he observed nothing of significance, a cursory inspection revealed that they were moving toward the ninth magazine. His magazine.

This time he was ready when they emerged from the vehicle. Fortunately the rain muffled the constant click of the camera as he held the button down, moving it from man to man like a sniper rifle. He got a good still shot on each of them as they lined up and entered the magazine.

*   *   *

Another two-inch lock was fumbled and pulled open. T-Ball squirmed as if he were a child on Christmas day. Jazz wondered what was so exciting about this magazine. It was obviously the center of Theodore's excitement.

"How was this one booby-trapped?" Ash inquired.

"Hmmm. This one was the toughest. There was a sensor on the door. We had a brand new Basic Tech in the unit who actually noticed it."

"Wow, what did you do?"

"We removed the sensor from the door and taped it to its mate. We still remote opened the door a few inches at a time in case there was a tripwire device like on some of the others. There was."

Ironhorse clicked on the light. The magazine was filled front to back with cylindrical objects sitting on racks about waist high. When Jazz realized what he was looking at he actually stepped back.

"HOLY SHIT!" said Ashland.

There were bombs, torpedoes, missiles, and rockets. All fuzed.

Ironhorse and T-Ball were laughing now.

"What?" said Jazz taking a step closer to the door. He was confused. There was a ringing in his ears. "What the fuck!"

"Calm down, LT," said T-Ball. "Look again."

It took him a moment.

"They're all training aids," said Ash.

"Damn. I thought they were real," said Jazz. "I thought we were looking at live ordnance waiting to go."

The other men were all giggling at the 1140.

"I'm serious. I thought, 'Who are the dumb motherfuckers that stored this shit ready to go?'"

"They have not yet been fired, LT," said T-Ball. "They'd be safe."

Ash walked to the first bomb closest to the door. It was Russian in design. He pulled on a niche on the side and opened a door that revealed the connection between the nose fuze and the high explosives in the body.

"Do they all have cut-aways?"

"Yeah," said Ironhorse. "Mostly Russian and Chinese, variants thereof. There are a few Egyptian, Italian, and even a few U.S. bombs in the back."

"I'm surprised," said Ash. "Since when did the Albanians have a legit EOD force? And if they did, why couldn't they render safe the booby traps and get back into these mags after the government got a handle on things?"

"Because they were not here for the Albanians," said Jazz. "This 'school' was not for the Albanians, was it Ironhorse?"

"I told you he was smart," said T-Ball.

"I knew it," said Ironhorse. "I predict it will take another five seconds . . ."

"Until I realize that there is more to this magazine than cutaways."

"Damn, LT. Are you psychic? Cruz is right. You oughta be a G-man," said T-Ball. "How did you guess?"

"Simple. The last magazine had training aids and was not booby-trapped. This one had the most sophisticated trap among them all. True it had some high speed training devices . . . but it doesn't add up. Something far more important had to be in here."

"Lieutentant. I've got something to show you," said Ironhorse with his now trademark grin.

They all followed Ironhorse as he threaded his way through racks of training ordnance to the back of the magazine. As they moved further from the door the sound of the storm outside grew quieter and the light around them grew dimmer.

"We were in here four days before we found it. We kept feeling a little breeze back here and hearing a strange sound as the door up front was closed. Then one time when we were goofing around, we turned the light out and closed the door on one of the other Airman in the unit. He felt the breeze, heard the sound, then he saw the light."

"Huh?" said Ashland.

Ironhorse reached up and pushed on the back wall. A section of it opened. It was a false door with a room beyond.

Now Jazz and Ashland were too shocked to speak. Suddenly Jazz knew what T-Ball was excited about.

T-Ball's voice became very serious. "Sir, I wanted you to see this the same way I did. It has been hard for me to contain myself."

"What? What is it?"

"Follow the rabbit down the hole."

Jazz looked at the door. A concrete slab was affixed to a steel door behind. He stepped through. It was a lab. A lab for making IEDs, laid out exactly like the one in San Patricio County.

Jazz felt faint. The implications hit him immediately. He needed a moment to consume what he was seeing.

"Holy shit," Ash said again. "So the sound you heard . . ."

"Some small pressure difference between the two rooms. As you closed the front door this one moved a little on its hinges making the sound. Just a small amount of light was coming through the bottom of the false door. It was not enough to be noticed when the light up front was on."

"None of this is full up or fuzed is it?" asked Ash.

"No," Ironhorse replied. "Funny isn't it? What are we going to do? Recover it and store it in a magazine?"

"Benny, tell me that you have gone to the FBI with this," said Jazz.

"Well, yes and no. We told the OSI guy."

"Henderson?"

"That's the one. He and a couple of other guys came in and looked at this stuff. They took photos, asked us not to move anything, and said they'd be back. We took more photos and sent them to TECHDIV."

"Were the other guys Air Force?"

"I think they were from the company."

"Benny, T-Ball and I saw this same lab in Texas."

"He told me, sir. I think these wackos got their info from the same website."

"Maybe. Or maybe these wackos are working together."

THIRTY-FIVE

MEETINGS

Ayman answered the phone on the first ring.

"Yes?"

"It's me. We need to meet now."

"Okay. I'll come to the road behind your camp. I'll be there in fifteen minutes."

"Good."

The rain had let up somewhat. Guido ducked as he felt the downdraft of one of the big U.S. Navy helicopters as it flew overhead. He looked up as it passed and noted that two of them were headed for the coast.

Ayman was on a moped, smoking casually as if he stopped here all the time.

"Buongiorno."

"Greetings. What do you have for me?"

"Photos. There was activity in the magazine today. I think something is about to happen there."

"As long as it is not soon we will be okay. It is time for you and the girl to leave. Nasih is going to take action soon. If you are here you may be implicated."

"Such a shame, I wanted to help."

"You have. Your role here is not of action. That will be carried out by someone who has direct interest and greater flexibility than you here."

"I understand."

"This may be our last meeting. I wish you success in your cause."

"And you."

Ayman slipped the film into his pocket, started his moped and drove off. Guido wondered if Renata was still randy.

*   *   *

Melanie almost dropped Abigail running for the phone. She waited for Jazz to call for two days since the executive officer of EOD Mobile Unit Six reported to the Det Four wives that their husbands were okay. She even watched the news constantly, hoping to see Jazz in the coverage.

"Hello."

"Hey, hon, it's me."

"Oh, thank God," Melanie exclaimed.

"How are you doing?"

Jazz heard Melanie crying.

"Mel, are you alright?"

"I'm just glad to hear your voice," she said. "I'm glad that you're safe."

"Hon, it was no big deal, really."

Jazz looked down at his feet. He wondered how many times he was going to have to lie to his wife for the sake of operational security.

"Malarky. You almost died on me again."

"Mel, you are being overly dramatic . . . how are the kids?"

Melanie allowed him to change the subject. She filled him in on how the family was doing and made sure he got to talk to both of the boys. Neither one of them wanted to hang up.

"Mel, I gotta go. I don't want to, but I have to go."

"Be careful you big lug. I want you back in one piece."

"I will. I love you."

"I love you too, Jazz."

After hanging up, Melanie realized that she did not really tell him how angry she was. She wondered how long she could handle this new life.

*   *   *

Plowing through email messages was the bane of Elena's Monday morning existence. One message forwarded from Thompson caught her attention. The subject line read:

```
FWD: Improvised Explosive Device (IED) "Factory"
      discovered in Tirane, Albania.
```

She opened the message.

From: Thompson
To: Cruz
Subject: FWD: Improvised Explosive Device (IED) "Factory" discovered in Tirane, Albania.

Elena,

   Read attached message. See me regarding our suspect.

   R/ Cam

   p.s. If you screw this up this, I'll kill you.

From: pucharelli
To: tanagier
Subject: Improvised Explosive Device (IED) "Factory" discovered in Tirane, Albania.

Boss,

   An IED factory was discovered in Tirane, Albania by an Air Force EOD Team deployed there as part of the military response to the Kosovo crisis. The factory was hidden in the back of a former Albanian Army magazine.
   AF EOD reported their findings to the local OSI contingent. OSI conducted an initial investigation and drafted a report. EOD sent photos to TECHDIV. OSI and EOD determined that the explosives were stable and could remain in place until its investigators were dispatched to gather forensic evidence.
   OSI's report came across my desk yesterday.
   OSI man called in, as I was knee deep into his report. A second EOD team observed the factory and said that it mirrored a factory they saw INCONUS. I pulled up FBI Bulletin on San Patricio incident handled by San Antonio office.
   Second team consisted of Lieutenant James J. Jascinski, BM1 John Ashland, and BM2 Theodore Ball.
   Rome office worked with this group only weeks ago on SECSTATE debacle. Odd coincidence.
   Draft of formal report attached.

                                          V/R

                                          Pooch

Attach: iedtiralbinirpt.doc

The clock on the wall with "Rome" written under it could be seen from her desk. The hands told her that it was 3:00pm there. She clicked on Pucharelli's name and a box opened up with all of his amplifying information down to his badge number. Elena dialed the number.

"Pooch"

"Agent Pucharelli?"

"Hell-o, and who may I ask who this is?" Pucharelli said flirtatiously.

"This is Special Agent Cruz from San Antonio."

"Doh! Sorry, I uh . . ."

Elena possessed an advantage already.

"I saw your email about the IED factory in Albania. I did the job in San Patricio. Do you mind if I ask some questions?"

"Sure. What ya got?"

"It is about Jascinski."

"Who?"

"The Navy lieutenant."

"The EOD officer?"

"Yes."

"Why?"

Elena imagined Pucharelli furrowing his brow over the phone.

"He may be our man."

"Are you kidding me? Just because he was at the scene of an IED incident? Then a bomb factory? To be honest, one probably led to the other. We are in Europe remember, there are not that many EOD Techs to go around in the first place. The fact that a guy shows up on two incidents that may or may not be related does not make him a suspect."

"May be related?"

"We do not know for sure. I've not put eyes on in Tirane yet. I'll have more information after we get forensics back."

"What do you think?"

"Without seeing the place my gut tells me the bomb that got SECSTATE and De Luca were made in this factory. At the very least the guys that made the device in Rome are connected to the guys in Albania. And by the way, the only way we connected them so quickly was *because* of Jascinski. Until he saw the factory, OSI thought it belonged to a local Albanian Mafia group."

Pucharelli paused to let that sink in.

Elena kicked her heels off and sat back in her chair. She tapped her pen on her lips thinking.

"Still think he is your man?"

"Maybe not, but I'm still curious. How did he find out about the factory? Did he ask questions, or was it shown to him?"

A heavy sigh was audible through the receiver.

"I see what you are driving at. Did he inquire about it? To be honest, I don't know. I will ask the OSI guy, Henderson. Listen, Cruz, I know you want to look at everything, but I think you're grasping at straws."

"Noted. Ask OSI and get back to me please," she said.

"You got it."

The last of her emails were now deleted. Elena sipped her coffee again and looked at the second report from the Kilkenney's surveillance team. It was sealed in an envelope. Elena did not have to open it; she already knew that it said nothing of importance. Melanie Jascinski and her children were not among her suspects. The wife would undoubtedly know if her husband was involved in something sinister, but she would likely never tell.

Still, it was possible that a phone call, an email, or a visitor related to the events surrounding his investigation would show up.

The important thing was that now she felt better, she felt like she was doing something and was able to focus. More importantly she no longer struggled with any guilt around the fact that there was a monitoring post tracking the Jascinskis. In fact she was sleeping better at night.

Just as Frances said, she told herself. *If it reveals nothing, nobody gets hurt.*

So Lieutenant James J. Jascinski no longer distracted Special Agent Elena Cruz and she was able to think about other aspects of the case. From this morning her new tactic was reviewing as much information as possible from Pucharelli's case in Rome and the incident in Albania. She would start by looking at the photos and the report of OSI on the magazines in Tirane.

* * *

Out of habit and without speaking, the two men sat on the floor. This brought them an old familiar feeling. It was solidified by a pot of hot tea.

Nasih looked at his friend and wondered if he aged as much. They certainly came a long way in twenty years.

They moved around the world, struggling for their beliefs. They were no less passionate now than a decade before, but their speed was measured. There were few of their era left. Many had died in Libya, Lebanon, Sudan, Somalia, Afghanistan, and now the Balkans.

"Here are the photos," said Ayman laying them out on the floor.

Two mugs of hot tea were consumed before another word was spoken.

"Who are these men?"

"The soldiers are engineers or disposaleers. The civilian in the vest is CIA, FBI, or maybe OSI. We are not sure. He seemed to be in charge of their inquiry."

"Ah, and the men in the second set of photographs?"

"Soldiers, the same ones from before I think."

"Look closely my friend. These men are outfitted differently. The weapons have collapsible stocks. That is a telltale sign of U.S. Special Forces. Look at their hats; those men are Marines or U.S. Navy. Many of the helicopters we have seen are U.S. Navy. Guido even had a few flights in one of them."

"Well then they must be sailors, but I do not see the significance."

"I do. In fact, I see much significance."

How ironic, he thought.

Ayman gave his friend a look. Nasih was much wiser than he and he admired that.

"Meet me here in two days. Then we will talk of this again."

Two days later they met in the same room and again shared a meal. Nasih provided his plan to Ayman. It was carried out that night.

The whole attack was over before any anyone was able to react. Upon hearing the report of what happened, Nasih was extremely pleased. It was clear by the performance of the man who was both his subordinate and friend that he had not lost his touch.

As expected, a little plastic explosive on the lock and the door opened easily. Most of the soldiers at the airport did not hear the report of the lock coming apart. Those that did looked in the direction of the sound. When another did not follow it immediately, they assumed it was a car backfiring or an accidental weapons discharge.

Only the guards at the entrance to the magazine road reacted. The senior of the two, a corporal, saved both their lives by taking a moment to radio the compound for assistance. In the time it took to wake up someone with the authority to send out EOD and reinforcements to investigate, the door was opened and quickly the contents of three satchels of explosives were delicately and precisely placed in the factory.

Everyone at Tirane International Airport, civilians and military alike, woke at the second detonation.

Ayman walked back toward the camp. By the time he reached the flightline, hundreds of people were awake and looking toward the magazines. His greatest concern was that some young soldier, still half asleep would accidentally snap a round off at him.

Nobody noticed as he stepped over his moped, turned it over, and drove away.

THIRTY-SIX

SUSPECTS

Ironhorse was among the first to arrive. He parked the HUMMER, pointing the headlights at the front of the magazine to illuminate the scene.

"Fuck. Johnny, get on the horn and tell the bubbas back at the compound we gotta do this one by the numbers."

"How come, Benny?"

"Look at the door. If this were an accident, it would be bent or blown off its hinges. It was opened. See where the lock was? It is charred black. Somebody busted in there. The place could be booby trapped again."

Four hours later Benny, fully dressed in a bomb suit, emerged from the magazine. Henderson and his OIC were waiting down the road behind Benny's vehicle. As he walked toward them he took off the helmet and started slipping off the Kevlar bib.

"Anything left?" asked Henderson.

"Nothing, sir," replied Benny.

"Nothing at all?" repeated his captain incredulously. "Not even some snotted plastic explosive?"

"No, sir. They knew exactly what they were doing. It's all gone."

"Well, I'll send my forensics team in now to collect evidence."

"You don't understand," said Benny. "There ain't no evidence to be had in there."

A forensics team arrived twelve hours later from Rome. They brought twelve men, all in blue coveralls, boots, and dark blue jackets that read "FBI AGENT" in bright yellow on the back.

Pucharelli directed them through the task. Ironhorse's notion was correct, so their work was short and simple. They took a lot of photos and tried to find traces of chemical residue or fingerprints. While his team cleaned and stowed their equipment, Pucharelli stood outside the magazine and dialed a number on his satellite phone.

"Federal Bureau of Investigation, San Antonio Office, Agent Cruz speaking, may I help you?"

"Very formal. I like that."

"Pooch?"

"Yep. Is this a secure line?"

"Yes it is."

"Well, then guess where I am, Elena."

"Uh, Albania?"

"Yes. I'm actually here ahead of schedule. Do you know why?"

"No."

"We had a detonation here last night. Everything is destroyed."

It took a moment for the full implication of what he said to sink in with Elena.

"Everything?"

"I'm here with a forensics team. We are looking for fingerprints and chemical residue."

"Damn it!"

"I talked with the OSI guy. Guess what he said? Jascinski was a troublemaker. He remembered him well. The guy said that Jascinski fucked up on a couple of missions. Seems he was in charge of security and allowed the birds to land in some hostile situations."

"Holy shit, I cannot believe this is really happening. Do you realize where we are going with this?"

"I know precisely where we are going. We gotta bring him in, Elena, but I don't know how to get him away from the Navy."

"I do. In fact this will be perfect. He reported this stuff to OSI. Now it is gone. He is the only reliable material witness. We utilized him before on the San Patricio job; we'll use him on this one. We must formally request that Lieutenant Jascinski and Petty Officer Ball be flown to TECHDIV to help us with our investigation. They will be questioned in an effort to link these three cases; San Pat, SECSTATE, and Albania."

"I like it."

"It will be like music. If he is involved, eventually this guy will screw up and reveal something to us. Then he becomes a true suspect. If this is just a coincidence, he will be an expert witness."

"Brilliant."

"I'll send out the request for them today. I suggest you pack your bags for DC. I'll see you there in . . ."

"Two days. I can be there in two days."

"Fine. See you then."

Elena felt flushed as she put the phone down.

*   *   *

The birds woke him. He lay with his eyes closed and listened. Gabriel imagined that they were talking to each other about him.

He opened his eyes and looked at his watch. It was just 6:00 am, yet he felt completely rested. In his childhood he always had the most restful nights of sleep while camping. Gabriel believed that it came from a primal sense of home.

A quick zip and he was out of his sleeping bag. He moved to the front of the tent and opened the small screen door. Outside were his boots. He put one foot, then the other out of the tent opening and covered each with a boot. Then he slid out and pulled his backpack out with him.

The burner and coffee were in the outer pouch on the left. While the water was heating he struck down his tent and folded it up.

It was his third day on the trail. If all went well, he would be sleeping in a no-tell motel by sundown.

The feds did not know where he was, Gabriel was now sure of that. Periodically as he walked, Gabriel would stop and move ten yards off the trail and hide. There he would sit for an hour or two to see if someone was following him. He listened for helicopters that may be trailing him. From time to time he observed other campers and hikers on the trail, but he never saw anyone twice.

Since he detected nothing Gabriel determined that if someone was following him now, they were military trained and he would never see them.

The next step was to move into a nondescript hotel, continue to grow out his beard, and wait some more. Hopefully his friends in Texas would be able to help him.

There would be time to think.

Each morning as he sipped his coffee he thought of Nasih. It was almost becoming his personal version of daily prayer. Moving to the woods was Nasih's idea.

"*Move to the land. Disappear in the desert or the forest. Following you then becomes a significant problem. Most governments of the world cannot mobilize the sophisticated means to follow you in such a short time.*

"*In the city everyone is potentially government, every camera is used against you. While on the land their logistics become difficult. You can physically hide while observing them as they follow you. Vehicles and aircraft are easily identified.*

"*The United States is a perfect environment for this. Slip between rural areas and the forest. If you are clean-shaven, grow a beard. If you have long hair, shave your scalp. It is easy to move in and out of society.*"

The last sip of coffee was cold and filled with grounds. He poured it in the soil at his feet, and stuffed the mug into the top of his pack. Gabriel hefted it onto his back and started on the trail. He predicted to himself that he would not see anyone on the trail today.

All he needed now was a room with cable television, a place to hide out for a few days. If he were really lucky he would find one near a truck stop with an internet café.

*   *   *

Men at sea develop rituals. Some evolve from tradition like the zaniness of the Shellback initiation that occurs when crossing the line of the equator. Some men even develop rituals or a routine so that they can remember what time of day it is.

Jazz developed a ritual while onboard *Anzio*. Before each watch he would head aft in the passageway in officer's country. He would emerge onto the aft missile deck and take in the seas, the horizon, and the sky.

The habit developed after two weeks of standing watch as an Anti-Air Warfare Coordinator in *Anzio*'s Combat Information Center. After he was relieved from watch, Jazz went to the wardroom. He was looking forward to a good breakfast. When he joined the mess, he realized that it was dinner. Lack of sleep, sunshine, and living watch to watch destroyed his sense of time. From that day forth he took a look outside on his way to CIC.

Denke and Jazz developed a Sunday evening ritual. They met on *Inchon*'s flight deck after dinner to discuss their plans for the rest of the week.

Every evening, several members of the crew jogged about the deck. Tonight, sailors from HM-15 were busy washing the last of the helos removing salt and grime from the sea and the dirt of Albania. Jazz watched rainbows of fuel oil in the pools of water on deck slosh back and forth as *Inchon* gently rocked to and fro in the swells of the Adriatic.

Denke emerged from the island superstructure on the starboard side of MCS-12.

"Evening, LT. What do we have planned for this week?"

"I've got some news, Senior Chief . . . news that I suspect will overjoy you."

"What's that?"

"T-Ball and I are leaving."

Denke looked at Jazz quizzically.

"Apparently Cruz wants us back at TECHDIV. They want us to give them info on the magazines in Albania."

"So why you? Why not Ironhorse and his boys?"

"Benny or one of the others may be coming too, but the Feds seem to think that the guys in Albania are related to the guys in Italy also."

"You're shitting me."

"No, if you think about it, this all makes sense. Now we got a group in Texas, a group in Italy, and one here in Albania that all are in cahoots. Frankly, it scares the shit outta me."

"Damn it."

"What?"

"I should have stayed in La Spezia."

Now it was Jazz's turn to look silently at Denke.

"Don't ask, LT. So this means that I have the det short two guys. No problem, we are almost on the backside of the float anyway. You're gonna miss Palma."

"No kidding. I hope I am back by then."

"When do you leave?"

"Tomorrow. Will you send T-Ball up to see me? I'd like to tell him."

"Sure, I'll have him in your stateroom by nineteen thirty. And you know you're right, LT."

"About what?"

"I am overjoyed."

Jazz couldn't discern if Denke's grin was portraying sarcasm or true happiness.

THIRTY-SEVEN

TECHDIV

Jazz and T-Ball flew on a CH-46 from *Inchon* to Sigonella. From there they flew commercial to Rome, Atlanta, and Baltimore. They both rented compact cars and headed south on Route 3/301 to Waldorf, Maryland.

As soon as he got to his hotel room, Jazz called Melanie.

"Hello."

"Hey, hon. I made it in to Waldorf okay."

"Oh thank God," Melanie said with a quivering voice. "I feel better knowing that you are back on U.S. soil."

The kids were in bed, so the couple talked for twenty minutes, planning their time off when Jazz returned. They decided that the best thing to do would be to take a road trip to see family and friends.

Finally Melanie said, "Jazz, I need to talk about something serious."

"What, hon?"

He could hear trepidation in her voice.

"I'm thinking we need to get out."

"Wow, really?"

"Yes."

"Hon, are you alright?"

"I am alright, we are okay . . . but we have three kids now, Jazz. I don't know if I can do this again."

"Uh, I don't know what to say."

"Don't say anything and don't worry. I will be here when you finally get back. I just want you to think about it and be prepared to talk about it when you get back for good."

"Uh, okay, hon."

"I love you, Jazz."

"I love you too."

Jazz lay back on the bed after he hung up the phone and looked at the ceiling. He thought for a moment and realized that he was not surprised.

*   *   *

Four days after leaving *Inchon* Jazz sat at the same EODTECHDIV conference table from months before.

"Well, Lieutenant, this time your visit is tacitly different," said Elena Cruz.

The veil in her words was not lost on her. She sat down on the corner of the table, crossed her legs and looked at Jazz and T-Ball. Each of them had a folder set in front of them. She realized that she had to proceed very cautiously. Elena purposely left her glasses on.

"Last time we needed information on the IEDs only. We still want that, and it will be part of our discussion. The focus this time is different. As you suggested, we now believe that there is a real possibility that the group in San Patricio, the terrorists in Rome, and the magazine in Albania are related."

The pair was holding on to her every word. Elena reminded herself to keep Jascinski off balance, but not to flirt too much.

"Naturally, you two gentlemen are our best source of information because you are linked to all three incidents."

Elena tried not to wince at her faux pas.

Be careful damnit! she thought to herself.

"I need you to review the evidence compiled here, be ready to answer more questions, and hopefully provide more information for this investigation. The difference is that now we are well beyond trying to learn anything about the SANPAT bomb. Now we hope that you may actually help us to crack this terrorist ring."

Elena paused to gather her thoughts. She looked at the faces of the two EOD Techs before her and decided that she was still doing well.

"Take the morning to review the reports. Write notes down on any thoughts that you have regarding their content, however insignificant it may seem to you. I'll be back this afternoon to discuss with Special Agent Pucharelli from the office in Rome. Okay?"

"We got it, ma'am," replied Jazz.

"Lieutenant, please, call me 'Elena.'" *There, now flash the smile.*

"Okay, Elena. Please call me 'Jazz,' all of my friends do. We look forward to helping in any way we can."

*   *   *

Despite the fact that rush hour should have passed, there was traffic across the Woodrow Wilson Bridge.

Thank God I don't have to drive in this everyday, Elena thought. She could see stress in the shoulders of the man in the driver's seat and was glad that she was not the one driving in it now. She leaned back and closed her eyes, trying to concentrate and rest at the same time.

Her mind wandered back to Jazz. She liked it that she would now be able to call him by his nickname. She pictured the two of them in the back of a limousine returning from a night at the opera.

Oh, Jazz, that was a great evening, thank you.

She imagined Jazz leaning over to kiss her, stoking her breast through her dress as their lips touched.

Then her phone rang.

Damnit, she thought. *Don't forget he's your suspect!*

Elena extracted her phone from he briefcase, "Cruz."

"You're going to screw it up aren't you?"

"Good morning, Cam."

"Explain to me again how you are going to get this guy. He is a suspect, any decent lawyer will rip you apart on Mirandizing him alone."

"You know, I have thought some more on that one, Cameron. I'm not going to get him within our justice system. I'm going to get him in his."

"I don't follow you."

"UCMJ, the Uniform Code of Military Justice. We'll start with treason."

"Oh?"

"We are still conducting an investigation and are not yet ready to charge anyone. If we find something we'll say that I'm not questioning a suspect, I'm conducting a sting. The fact that I am acting as an FBI agent is immaterial."

"Oh, Elena, I do like it. You may be in my good graces after all."

"I'll call ya later, Cam."

At FBI headquarters in Washington, DC Special Agents Cruz and Pucharelli were having a working lunch in the cafeteria. Pooch read over a copy of the case file given to Jazz and Ball. What the two EOD Techs did not realize is that the file contained subtle misinformation throughout. They hoped that Jazz would make a statement outside the investigation or contrary to the case file that was in fact true. Then they would know that he was on the inside of the IED factory connection.

"Elena, this is brilliant, really."

"Thank you."

"So if this guy is guilty . . . if he is connected, how do we think this whole thing proceeded?"

Elena reached into her bag and pulled out a wallet-sized notebook. She flipped the pages, finally stopping and reading a moment.

"Okay, here it goes. First, Jascinski for some reason is a member of a domestic terrorist organization. Part of his role in this organization is to attend a military school where he can learn advanced demolition and subsequently move into a position where he can obtain, to wit, steal military explosives. Likewise he can provide training to his fellow members. Jascinski gets into EOD school, after three tries mind you.

The coup de gras is that he will be able to get close to someone while on a Secret Service op."

Pucharelli was nodding his head. "I'm with you, go on."

"Okay, Jascinski gets in with the local bad guys in Texas. I don't think this is a small organization; it is nationwide. He could have been posted anywhere, he merely got in with the local chapter."

"Right."

"So they get found out by the dumb luck of some confused older woman who thinks she still owns the house. Sometime en route to the scene, Jascinski is called by his cronies.

"'Fuck,' they say, 'We've been found out. What can we do?' These guys are pretty well organized, so they mobilize."

"When do you think the call was made?"

"I think before . . ."

"'Cause the second guy . . . Ball . . . is not involved."

"Right. He has been around Navy EOD for a while. Nothing to date points to him being involved in anything like this. Also, he was not there for SECSTATE."

"I thought I remember the name 'Ball' from that op. Wasn't he there?"

"He was on the job, but at a different location. Jascinski was posted at the hotel with a guy named Ashland."

"That's right, I remember now. So what about Ashland?"

"Like Ball, good record. He came to Texas from Detachment Norfolk. And he was very new to Ingleside when the incident happened."

"Okay, continue."

"So he either places the device for SECSTATE's visit, or better yet, ensures that it is not located. It could be as simple as searching the location of the device and declaring it safe. Or, as the OIC he probably has influence on how the search proceeds. He probably even has the ability to decide that the team will not search an area."

"That is correct. They chose to not search the conference hall."

"See?"

"Got it."

"Now our two incidents are not merely linked, they are part of the same campaign. In fact they are perpetrated by at least the same group and possibly the same man."

"So now we get to Albania."

"Albania, correct. I do believe that Jascinski's presence there is a coincidence. Obviously he had no part in Kosovo and the *Inchon*'s subsequent involvement. I also believe however that there is some connection between Albania and Jascinski's group. Maybe their training is provided by the same source. While he is there, he contacts or is contacted by this group. They ask for his assistance.

"'Go see what they have on us. Is the stuff still there? What are the defenses like?'

"Jascinski provides them with the intel. How long had we been in those magazines?"

"Couple of weeks I think."

"And how long after our friend was in there did they get hit?"

"Days . . . damn, I am starting to believe this more and more."

"Good. So am I," Elena glanced at her watch. "Well, it is that time. Let's take a drive back over the Potomac."

The two agents sat in the back of the same car that drove Cruz that morning. The traffic was no better at one than it was at ten.

"We need to pursue other avenues on this guy," said Pucharelli.

"I've have already covered it. We have looked at phone records, emails and the like. I've started watching the house, but we have not come up with anything yet."

"He's been gone though."

"Exactly, the surveillance will be stepped up when Jascinski returns."

"Still, I recommend that you go back and look again at records during the time surrounding each incident. We need to begin with the night of the incident in San Patricio County, the days surrounding the incident in Rome, and the days around the magazine hit."

"That is probably a good recommendation. I can have my guy, Kilkenney, and his men look into it again. I think it may have been an unknown cell phone contact or it was a face to face meeting which may be impossible to trace."

"When was he absent from the command? Oh, damn."

"What?"

"Elena, he had all the time in the world to meet with someone in Albania. There are hundreds of cats and dogs there. It really was madness. Jascinski would have hours to talk with a foreigner there in plain sight and it would not have drawn any attention."

"Interesting. Well, we cannot do anything about that right now. We'll go with your recommendation and start again on emails and phone records."

*   *   *

Jazz noticed in the material Elena gave him that the FBI had in fact started calling the device the "SANPAT bomb." What the feds gave them was somewhat confusing. Jazz understood that they were the only living link to all three episodes, but he struggled to imagine exactly how he and T-Ball could provide insight based on the information provided. Much of the case file had nothing to do with the explosives.

Finally, he closed his eyes and thought of West, Martin, De Luca, and Koss. Jazz decided to look at the case not as an EOD Tech, but as an investigator.

He opened his eyes and started with the evidence gathered at the residence in San Patricio. First there was a list of all the explosive and electronic components. Then they had miscellaneous damning material that in the absence of the explosives would seem less incriminating. There were maps of several cities in the Southwest; detailed maps of the downtown areas that tourists use when walking. There were also satellite photos and base maps of the major installations in the state of Texas, including Ingleside.

Who are these guys going after? he wondered.

Next he looked at the evidence from the Technology Symposium hosted by De Luca and his company Texas Silicon and Software. The photos of De Luca, the media crew, and Fiona Koss brought back his feelings of guilt. He wondered if this was a similar feeling doctors had when they lost a patient.

The conclusion of the report was that an anti-American group known as "Anarchy" did the job. Jazz had heard of this group. They had a more peaceful arm that conducted protests outside the gates in Naples and Sigonella.

So how are these two related?

It hit him at once.

"Holy shit!"

"What?" said T-Ball.

"These guys aren't anti-government, they're anti-technology!"

"Huh?"

THIRTY-EIGHT

INSIGHT

Just then the door opened and Special Agents Cruz and Pucharelli stepped in.

Jazz called out as they entered, "Elena! I got an idea!"

The two g-men looked at each other quizzically. They could sense genuine discovery in Jazz's voice.

"What?"

Jazz recognized Pucharelli from Rome.

"Hi, Agent Pucharelli. How are you?"

"Fine, thanks, Lieutenant."

"Listen, did Anarchy claim responsibility for the attack on SECSTATE?"

"No they didn't," said Pucharelli. "But terrorist groups don't always . . ."

"Does Anarchy *usually* claim responsibility?"

"Well, yes but . . ."

"Then I would suggest to you that Fiona Koss was not your target, De Luca was."

"What?" Elena said incredulously.

"These guys are not anti-government, they're anti-technology. You don't have a McVeigh on your hands, you've got a Kaczynski."

"Slow down, We needed some insight, not an Encyclopedia Brown secret decoder ring solution," Elena said acidly.

Pucharelli put on hand on Elena's shoulder. "Hold on, Elena, let's hear what the man has to say."

"Don't you guys see it? This is how the cases are linked. The guys in Texas are going after De Luca and Texas Silicon and Software. Same thing with the group in Italy. They may be linked closely, or loosely . . . but he was the target."

"Then explain all the maps and satellite photos of government installations."

"I'd say to you, 'Explain all the maps of the major cities in the Southwest.' To explain maps of all the military installations is easy, that is where the explosives came from, whether bought or stolen. I'll wager that every map in San Patricio was of a city that had a tech conference or symposium that De Luca attended."

236

Now Elena was turning red.

"I'm sure. The guy has been in every city with a population over 100,000 in the U.S. selling his product," she said with sarcasm and disdain.

Jazz turned toward Pucharelli, ignoring Elena's rebuke.

"Well, that is your start. I know it will be a heady task, but you should identify who attended all of the conferences in those cities. That will begin to narrow it down. My guess is that they are or were conducting reconnaissance on how this guy moves, what his modus operandi is. Then they plan or take the right opportunity and bang . . . big pink mist."

Now Elena stepped in front of Pucharelli. She could tell that Jazz was winning her fellow agent over quickly. It made her angry, yet attracted to him at the same time. She leaned over and placed her hands on the table, shooting an angry look at Jazz.

"Okay wise guy, why not just mail a bomb to this guy, why not put one at his house or on his car?"

"Simple. These folks do not want to miss. They had to get him the first time. And they know that De Luca probably does not open his own mail, business or otherwise. Similarly, he probably has security on his house and vehicles. No, they had to get him in public . . . remember they have already proved to be very sophisticated and calculating."

Elena was furious. She stood tall again and pointed an accusing finger at Jazz.

"You're a bastard you know that? I've been working on this for months now! Months!"

"Elena!" Pucharelli yelled. "Sit down. Calm down." He waited until his counterpart had in fact sat down.

Though she was no longer crimson, Elena gave Pucharelli a look that said, *"Idiot! He is trying to throw us off the trail!"*

He answered the look.

"Elena, the fact is that the lieutenant here has a good point. Sometimes it takes someone from the outside to see all the pieces in a different way."

Now Jazz stood. He spoke with a softer tone.

"Agent Cruz, . . . Elena, . . . I'm just trying to help. Believe me my excitement in seeing an answer to this case has nothing to do with a desire to embarrass you or the FBI. And I don't fancy myself as an 'Encyclopedia Brown,' as you put it.

"The fact is, ma'am, that I have been an EOD Technician for less than a year. In that time I have indirectly or directly been involved in the deaths of four people and the maiming of two more. Quite simply, I feel responsible for those people.

"My exuberance revolves around bringing those responsible to justice. I'll sleep better when that happens."

He could see Elena getting red again. Standing next to her, Pucharelli put a hand out toward Elena, motioning her to remain silent.

Jazz realized that he was cutting deep, but he continued anyway.

"I suggest that you get past who is going to get the credit or the blame in this investigation and find the answer. I am not an agent, I may be completely wrong. But the fact that your colleague is willing to listen to me indicates that there is at least one possibility that you have not considered.

"My shipmate and I are going to my parents' home in Annapolis now. We have seen and done a lot of shit in the past six months particularly and we need a break. You guys decide if you need or want our help, and give us a call."

Jazz looked to T-Ball who sat dumbfounded during the whole exchange.

"T-Ball, you feel like crabcakes?"

"Yes, sir."

"I know a good place to get cakes and malteds."

"I'm there."

The agents said nothing as the two sailors walked out.

Pucharelli waited a few seconds and followed them out. He watched as Jazz and T-Ball got into their car and drove away.

When he returned, Elena was still sitting quietly in the same seat.

"I don't think he's our man."

"Hmmph."

"Take it easy, Elena. We can keep all of this in this room."

"I don't know how I'm gonna get outta this one, the surveillance I mean."

"Well at least you can do it on your terms. Suggest that it end, new evidence reveals that he is no longer a suspect. You had to look right? I'll back you up on that. I was with you on this one not two hours ago."

"How did this happen?"

"I'll tell ya what, that guy should be an agent."

"I wish people would stop saying that."

"Elena, really, take it easy."

"No, don't you get it? I feel the same way he does. I feel like Koss and De Luca are on me. If I had done a better job . . ."

"You're wrong . . . dead wrong, Elena, so don't go there. It is just time to regroup."

Elena stared into space, angry with herself. She wondered if she had allowed Jazz to distract her on this case for all of the wrong reasons.

*   *   *

Jazz was nervous entering the house with T-Ball. He was concerned that the Admiral would view their familiar relationship as fraternization. He spoke to his mother about it on the phone from his hotel room before they left Waldorf.

"Mom, just make sure he understands."

"I will dear. The Admiral really has grown to understand this EOD thing, you know."

"I know, Mom, but there is still part of him that is old school."

"James, your father and I are not so cavalier, in fact quite the opposite. When the Admiral was a lieutenant . . ."

"Mom, I am just saying that you need to prep him or he'll make an ass of himself."

"James J. Jascinski Junior, that is enough!"

"Promise me, Eleanor."

There was a pause at the other end of the line.

"I promise."

* * *

Eleanor greeted the men at the door.

"James, it is so good to have you home," she said hugging him.

"I've missed you, Mom."

"And you must be the infamous 'T-Ball.'"

"Yes, ma'am. Thanks for having me."

"Oh don't be ridiculous, we are glad to have a friend of James' here. And please call me 'Eleanor.'"

"Thank you, Eleanor. This is for you," he said handing her a bottle of wine.

"How sweet. Thank you."

"James! Welcome home!" the Admiral called out as he walked down the steps. He seemed a little animated. Jazz suspected that his Mother had in fact prepared him.

"Thanks, sir," Jazz said taking his father's hand. "It is good to be back."

"And welcome, uh, 'T-Ball' is it?"

"Yessir. Theodore Ball, but 'T-Ball' to my friends."

"Well, 'T-Ball' it is . . . how about a beer?"

"That would be outstanding, sir."

"Eleanor, could you bring three beers and some sandwiches out on the back deck for these men of the sea?"

"Of course, Admiral."

"This is a fantastic view," T-Ball said as they sat down.

"Yes, we love it especially in the summer time," the Admiral said.

Jazz looked out over the Chesapeake Bay.

"Wow, it is good to be back, sir," he said.

"Well, son, tell us again why you're back early."

Jazz sat down and took a sip of his beer.

"It has to do with the bombs we found in San Patricio County and the one in Rome."

T-Ball silently ate his sandwiches and drank beer from a frosted mug as Jazz relayed their adventures to the Admiral. Just as Jazz was finishing the story Eleanor returned from one of her trips between the men and the kitchen.

"Admiral, we have heard enough from James. Now don't you have something to tell him?"

Jazz's father rolled his eyes.

"Admiral," Eleanor said with a stern voice.

"What, Dad?" said Jazz, sensing something was wrong.

"I had a minor heart attack."

"Sir, you're kidding me, why didn't you tell me!"

"It was no big deal."

"It is so a big deal, you grumpy old man!" Eleanor yelled.

"It was a minor heart attack. I called the ambulance myself."

T-Ball silently began to extricate himself from the table, wanting to let this remain a family matter.

"Sit down, T-Ball," the Admiral barked. "I am not hiding this from anyone, nor am I worried. James, we just didn't want to bother you on your deployment; I did not even want Melanie to know. It was not serious."

"But, sir, I don't understand, you look fit as a fiddle."

"Yes, well that is what the doctor said," agreed Eleanor. "They cannot figure it out."

"Fact is, son, I've been decommissioned, I've been in mothballs for years, but I expect it will be that way for some time. And then, someday it will be time to tow me out to sea and sink me . . . just the way life goes."

Jazz did not know what to say.

"So, now you know," the Admiral said with finality.

The next morning, Elena had a Bloody Mary on a 7:00 am flight back to San Antonio. She was not sure how she was going to tell Cam that Jascinski might no longer be a suspect. The case was now back to square one.

How could I have been so wrong?

Pucharelli's advice was sound. She would lead the case down another path and let Jascinski fade away. If Cam confronted her she would remind him, "*Cam, not every suspect is guilty . . . you don't want me to 'screw this up' do you? I looked into it, Jascinski's not our man.*"

Elena felt that she could not see Jazz again. Her objectivity eroded each time she saw him. Before the close of business the day before, she arranged for another agent to meet with Jascinski and T-Ball this morning. She told the agent to ask the two sailors some cursory questions and add their answers to the file. She stressed that he should sing their praises for their participation and ensure that a letter of thanks went to their command from the Director.

So now she would start with the naval officer's idea and look into Texas Silicon. She drained her drink and motioned for another to a stewardess who was already giving her dirty looks.

THIRTY-NINE

REUNIONS

As Jazz entered the Powder Keg, he noticed that the EOD memorial was gone. He remembered that it was scheduled to be moved to the new location for EOD School at Eglin Air Force Base in Fort Walton Beach, Florida. He reminded himself to send Horace Pickney and the memorial foundation a donation to assist with the costs of the move.

After lunch, Jazz called Solarsky on the *Inchon*. A sailor on watch in combat picked up the phone.

"EOD Mobile Unit Six Forward, SK2 Themopolis speaking. May I help you sir or ma'am?"

"Theo, it's LT Jascinski. Can you get the CO on the phone?"

"Hey, sir! One moment, he's in his stateroom. I'll get him for you."

Jazz waited only two minutes for the captain to pick up the line.

"Jazz! How are things?"

"Good, sir. We are done here so I was calling to ask for guidance in regards to T-Ball, I mean Petty Officer Ball and me."

"Get down to Andrews right away and wait for a space-available flight out to Rota, Spain. We'll meet you there."

"Aye, aye, sir."

"Jazz, Jazz, Jazz, chill out!" the captain laughed now. "There is no point to you guys coming out here. We'll be back in nineteen days. At this point you'd probably miss us and have to fly back. Go home. Senior Chief Denke has the det well in hand for now."

"Yes, sir."

"How did it go?"

"Uh, fine, sir."

"Anything new?"

"We gave them some new ideas, sir, but we'll see if it amounts to anything."

"Fine, fine. We'll see you in nineteen days then. Have beer on the pier for us."

"Aye, aye, sir."

*   *   *

The beard was not yet comfortable. Gabriel found himself stroking it often.

Stop it, he would think to himself. *You'll look obsessive compulsive and that will draw attention.*

The town he settled in had a small coffee shop with an internet connection in its loft. He gave himself a few days to observe his surroundings so that he could ensure that he had not been followed.

Finally, Gabriel went in early to the coffee shop and sent a message out on the small email provider that the group was using. Now it was evening, dinnertime. Only the staff was in the shop below him. He logged on and found the response that he was waiting for from his friends in Texas.

```
From: cookie
To: ringo
Subject: Mail

Ring,

    It was good to hear from you. It sounds like your
trip is going well. Don't worry, your fish are fine and I
have collected all of your mail.
    Bye the way, a couple of the guys at the shop have
quit. When you are back in town I'd like you to come
work with me again, even if it is only part time.

                                              —Cookie
```

It was a good sign. The DPS did not connect him with the folks in Texas and they were still operating. It was clear that they had tasking for him.

Gabriel looked out the dormer at the truck stop across the way. It was full of eighteen-wheelers stopped for a bite to eat. He was sure one was headed for Texas.

*   *   *

Jazz and T-Ball stepped off the plane. Their children charged toward them, as valkrie armed with balloons. Nicholas and Tyler nearly knocked Jazz to the ground. He bent over and scooped them up in his arms.

"Look at my mancubs! You boys have gotten so big! I have missed you so much!"

"We missed you, Daddy!" said Tyler.

Jazz kissed and hugged both of his sons.

"Okay, boys, gosh you have gotten heavy! Let me put you down."

He looked to his bride. She was holding baby Abigail. Though it was a Wednesday, his wife was dressed for Sunday. He wondered if that theme changed underneath.

Jazz felt his sons still tugging and pulling on him as he walked up to Melanie. He took Abigail from her arms and kissed his daughter on the forehead.

"She's gotten big, Mel."

"I know . . . they all have. You have missed too much."

"I know."

Melanie stood on her tiptoes and kissed her husband as he held their daughter. "Welcome home."

Ten feet away, the Ball family was enjoying a similar scene.

Cameron Thompson wanted another progress report. Ironically, writing the progress report halted Elena's progress. It took her two days; she would have to make up ground on his investigation over the weekend. She had never billed so much overtime.

The case was driving her insane. Despite the meeting in Indian Head, by the time her plane landed, Elena was back to suspecting Jascinski. She looked into De Luca as a target, but it was not bearing fruit.

She checked on her superior several times throughout the morning.

"Any questions, Cam?"

"No, not yet, Elena. I'll call if I have a question."

She called Kilkenney confirming that his team was in position and ready for Jascinski's arrival. Then Elena tried to sort through the various incident reports again, San Patricio, Rome, and Tirane. She was not able to concentrate and could not see anything new.

Finally, one of the secretaries approached Elena while she nibbled on a muffin in the snack bar.

"Cameron wants to see you as soon as possible, Elena. He said it was about your report."

A wave of smoke hit her when she opened the door. In violation of government regulations, Cameron was enjoying a lunch of cigarettes and coffee. Elena could not tell if her report was buried in the landfill of papers on and around Cam's desk.

"Elena, come in and have a seat."

The chair across from Cam's desk was comfortable. He did not want anything to distract his audience when he chose to pontificate.

"Elena, I have read the report. It was fine. I want to talk about it though. Shoot holes in it once again."

"Okay."

"Begin with your basic premise."

"San Patricio, Rome, and Tirane are joined not just by a common IED. They are joined by a common IED factory. This leads me to believe that they are linked by an organization. It may be loose, but it is linked. The nuances involved in the factory layout and the weapon's design are too precise and too similar for this to be merely three guys who bought the same set of plans from the internet."

"Okay. Who are your suspects?"

"I'm still looking at the list of people who attended all of De Luca's conferences. None pans out yet as a suspect, so officially I only have Jascinski."

"So why Jascinski?"

"He was at all three sites."

"Being there should not incriminate him. Why not Ball?"

"Ball was only at two of the incident sites. He has a long, perfect record in EOD. Nothing leads us to suspect him to date."

"Ashland?"

"He's further out there. He just barely arrived in Texas from Det Norfolk when the San Patricio issue occurred. Again, another perfect record."

"Okay then, give me more than he was just at all three sites."

"I'd like to parry with a set of return questions."

"Fine," Cam leaned back in his chair and puffed the end of his cigarette. He was thoroughly enjoying this.

"One, why did Jascinski leave Surface Warfare? He was a shoo-in for admiral. He had some protection from his father's reputation. Two, why come into EOD when he'd have one, maybe two operational tours before he is behind a desk? My answer is that it was not about the career, it was about the schooling. This guy wanted to learn how to blow shit up."

"Okay, continue," Cam said, lighting another cigarette.

"There are very few people who had both the capability and the know-how to locate and stop the explosive vehicle with Martin and West. Jascinski is one of them."

"That is one of your better points, Elena. That is convincing."

"Thank you," said Elena.

Selling the case to Cam became as important to Elena as solving it.

"Now listen, Cam, my carousel of evidence is coming full circle. Let's look at why Jascinski is my prime suspect again.

"The other two cases are connected to each other and San Patricio in two ways. First, it is the same weapon in all cases, the factories and the attack. The second way they are connected is that Jascinski was at all three locations."

"Okay. Again, Elena, I say his presence at the second two can be argued to be circumstantial. After all he was assigned to be there."

"If Jascinski happened to be at all three incidents and they were linked in no other way, it would be circumstantial. When you add the specificity of the devices used, it is no longer a coincidence. Look at it this way . . . have there been any other uses of the SANPAT bomb?"

"No."

"So at every SANPAT incident, Lieutenant James J. Jascinski has been there."

"Good damn point. Now you got me again."

Elena waited as Cam sat back in his chair and puffed on his cigarette silently, thinking.

Finally he sat up and spoke, "Okay, keep after Jascinski. Keep on the De Luca angle also, but Jascinski is still your prime suspect."

*   *   *

It was the same feeling he experienced whenever he disappointed his mother. Gabriel lifted his head from its droop of shame and looked at Nasih sitting in the chair on the other side of the hotel room. The tone of voice Nasih used, even his look, made Gabriel feel like a child again.

"I'm sorry," he said.

"Well, it could have been worse. Fortunately, I do not think that they know who you are. If they did your friends here would already be in jail."

"I am sorry."

"You are fortunate. I actually like you," Nasih lied. "I have killed men for lesser mistakes. The initial detention by the police officer was just as he said, I'm sure . . . a routine inspection. It is for this reason that I have told you never to mix two missions."

"I know. I should have followed your advice."

Nasih was silent again for a long time. Gabriel patiently watched the minute hand slide past two numbers. He knew better than to speak.

"You seem to attract bad luck. First, the old woman finding your house, now this. I am sympathetic only because I too have faced bad luck recently. The details are inconsequential, but it affects both of us. If we do not act soon, we may be discovered. I have made moves to erase the evidence leading to us . . . but more action is needed."

"Fine, whatever you need."

"Your supplier will now play a pivotal role. Unwittingly, he has already provided us invaluable assistance since you have gone underground. He is positioned to give us valuable information. I would say that he is now more than a supplier; he is a mole. I need to ensure that he is clean during this task, separate from the others in every way. That means that you need to be the one to communicate with him."

"Okay."

"You'll have to go back to South Texas."

"I understand."

"This is going to involve more violent action, something that we have never required of him. But if he does it correctly he will never be under suspicion."

Gabriel realized that he was to blackmail the supplier.

"Now, let me tell you what he must do."

FORTY

STANDDOWN

They were in a semi-normal routine. After returning home, Det Four was supposed to be in a thirty-day stand down. Denke and Keating came up with a leave plan that would ensure that at least a full dive team, four men, was available at all times. When not on leave Det Four shortened their business days to half days.

Their mornings were filled with physical training and light maintenance. The afternoons were spent at home, devoted to getting back in touch with their families.

As always, Jazz began his workday by heading to the equipment room, coffee cup in hand, to see what the guys were up to.

When he stepped in, Denke was on the phone. He looked concerned.

"Yes, sir. Yes, sir, I understand."

Jazz looked at him quizzically.

"Ah, that is correct, sir. Yes, I will take care of it and report back to you, yessir. Thank you."

Denke hung up the phone.

"Who was that, Senior?"

The man appeared to be at a loss for words.

"LT, let me explain it later."

One of the traits of a successful naval officer is to be able to understand clearly when your chief is subtly saying, *"Don't ask me that question."*

"Roger that, Senior."

Denke got up and left the room. Jazz thought it was odd, but knew that if he needed to know he would be told, and often the junior officer really did not want to know.

Twenty minutes later the OIC looked up from his computer to see Denke and an officer stepping into the office. Denke moved to the window and closed the shade.

On closer inspection, Jazz noticed a cross on the officer's collar.

A chaplain?

The chaplain closed the door behind him.

"Welcome, Chaplain," said Jazz. "Is something wrong?"

"Yes, sir," said Denke. "It is about the call I got earlier."

"What is it, Senior Chief?"

"It's the admiral, sir, your father. He passed away this morning."

*   *   *

True to form, the events surround the Admiral's wake and funeral went flawlessly. James J. Jascinski Senior made arrangements with both a classmate and a lawyer, years before.

Eleanor was composed throughout. Showing overt emotion in public would have insulted her husband's memory. She kept herself busy by directing the whole evolution as if it were a "Hail and Farewell" or CO's garden party.

Jazz was only vaguely aware that his wife was present. The children all disappeared, undoubtedly holed up with a neighbor's au pair.

In the last moments that anyone would gaze upon him, the Admiral appeared just as he did in life, stoic and cold. Jazz knelt next to the form of his father and tried unsuccessfully to pray silently.

Emotionally, the moment was confusing. The ten-year-old boy still within James J. Jascinski Junior was relieved that he would no longer have the sick nervous feeling in his stomach each time he went home. The young man and father in him was truly sad. In his prayers, he was able to muster a "thanks" that he and his father at least began to reach an understanding of each other.

Jazz laughed to himself nervously as he thought of his father not in Heaven, but in Purgatory. Deep down he knew that the Admiral was in "Boat School" Purgatory. First he pictured him in full uniform, rifle at 'Right shoulder arms,' marching off restriction points back and forth on Red Beach under the watchful eye of Saint Peter and John Paul Jones.

In Jazz's mind the Admiral would be allowed some leisure. Certainly in the evenings his father would retire to the basement of the Alumni House in the sky, sitting quietly in the corner sipping a gin and tonic. Jazz imagined his father trading sea stories with other classmates who had passed, all of them waiting for the next Army-Navy game to come on television.

Jazz composed himself, took one last look at his father, stood and turned on his heel.

The funeral director was waiting in the back of the viewing room. Down to his manner of dress, the guy reminded Jazz of comedian Richard Belzer.

Guy probably does funeral jokes at Chuckles on Tuesday nights.

The man bowed slightly as he whispered respectfully.

"If you will wait a mere moment outside, sir . . ."

Though the arrangements were made ahead of time, Eleanor was adamant that Jazz remind the director.

"Just the ring," he said.

"Excuse me, sir?"

"The family wants the class ring. The medals, the watch, everything else stays. We just want the class ring."

"Yes, sir."

The lobby outside the viewing room was empty now; everyone had gone. Jazz looked at his leather case next to the couch where the grieved often sat to reflect.

"What is in the case?" Eleanor had asked him.

"Just some things, Mom."

There was still a chance to slip it into the Admiral's box. The funeral director was being paid handsomely. He would practically get in the box himself if Jazz asked him to.

But Jazz knew that by bringing the knife he was really just grasping for a way to say his goodbye in a special way. He realized after long reflection and a bottle of port in the Admiral's study the night before that the man would not want to be buried with it.

So there would be no last gesture and no last public words from this son on the occasion of his father's death. The Admiral arranged for a eulogy from two of his classmates long before his son was commissioned.

James J. Jascinski merely helped his mother grieve and paid his last respects.

*   *   *

The stand-down period gave T-Ball time to work uninterrupted on the detachment's Mark-16 dive rigs. Each day he came in, completed a rigorous workout, showered and began the required annual maintenance checks.

There were no other Techs in the building. Detachment Two was at Ft. Story attending their READIMPT before a deployment to Bahrain. Ash was at medical. Denke and Keating were at a planning conference for an MCM exercise across the bay in Corpus Christi.

There was only time to complete one rig per day by lunch. The annual checks required that he work in the O_2 clean room following strict re-entry control procedures. This was because T-Ball would be opening the lines that provided passage for the oxygen to the diver's breathing loop. O-rings lay on the work table next to tools that would be used to inspect and test the Schrader valve.

Somewhere in the shop, a phone began ringing. He ran to the front and picked up the phone on the OIC's desk.

"EOD Mobile Unit Six Det Four, Petty Officer Ball speaking, may I help you?"

"Uh, is this EOD?"

"Yes, sir. Can I help you?"

"Yeah, this is base security dispatch. We have a report of a suspect package in the courtyard between buildings one and two."

"Okay, one moment."

T-Ball sat in the OIC's chair and pulled the IED response binder from the bookshelf behind his desk.

"Okay, dispatch, I have several questions for you, but I want to begin with some recommendations."

"We have a copy of the standard recommendations."

"Okay, good. What have you done so far?"

"Both buildings are in the process of evacuation using doors not facing the device. Security is setting up a perimeter and is searching for secondary devices."

"Okay. Could you send someone over to medical and send BM1 Ashland over?"

"I'm here!" came Ash's voice from the hallway.

"Thanks, dispatch, he is here already. Ash, we gotta IED at building one!"

Ash stepped into the office. "I know. I heard when I was at medical and came right back. I'm senior man, T, plus a Master Tech. Give me the phone and begin load out."

"Roger. Security dispatch on the line."

T-Ball handed Ash the phone and ran to the back of the shop to begin the equipment load out.

Ten minutes later Ash drove the detachment dually toward the medical building parking lot. T-Ball was dressed already to be the P-1. Ash briefed as they drove.

"Okay, listen up. Step one, go down and listen with the Marty Kaiser. If it is ticking, place the tool and we'll shoot it.

"If it is not ticking, place the Mark-32, your film cassette, back out and take a picture. If it is too big, use two X-ray film carts. Place the dearmer, come to the CP, and we'll look at what we got. It is probably a box some knuckle-head officer left sitting there by accident."

"Probably."

"If we got something, we'll shoot and go from there. Questions?"

"None."

Ash pulled in front of medical and parked the truck. Both men got out walked to the back and opened the tailgate.

Ash keyed a radio in his hand. "Test, one, two . . ."

A radio tucked into T-Ball's vest answered. He keyed the mike clipped on a D-ring in the shoulder of the vest.

"One, two, three . . ."

His voice emanated from Ash's radio. Ash helped T-Ball put the response pack on.

"Ready?"

"Yes."

"Go do it."

T-Ball headed toward the headquarters building. Ash surveyed the surrounding area. It was clear. From training exercises with the base, Security knew to create a large perimeter to protect personnel and to ensure nobody could photograph or film an EOD procedure.

Ash set up the X-ray developer. Just as it was ready for use, T-Ball's voice came over the radio.

"CP, P1, I see it. This is my last transmission for awhile, I'm approaching the device."

Ash keyed the radio twice.

Thirty five seconds later there was a detonation. The blast wave echoed between the two sides of the building breaking glass and lifting dust as it went. Car alarms in the main parking lot wailed and a small fire started on the clothing and flesh of what once was Theodore Ball.

*   *   *

Elena Cruz sat in her car, doubled over. She rubbed her temples. She had actually seen them take T-Ball away. For four hours she coordinated ATF, Naval Investigative Service, and FBI forensics and tackled the scene.

It was definitely another SANPAT bomb.

Now her investigation was crumbling before her. It was an anti-government hit, not anti-tech. This time James J. Jascinski was not there.

She recalled the conversation with a stunned Johnny Ashland.

"Petty Officer Ashland, where's the lieutenant?"

"He's, uh . . . gone."

"What do you mean 'gone?'"

"He is on emergency leave, his father died."

Cam called to say that he wanted to visit the scene. Elena expected him any minute. She had precious time to decide what, if any, new theory she had.

Certainly another member of Jascinski's organization could have pulled this off. The fact that he was gone did not mean he was not involved. Was targeting Ingleside while he was gone a way to divert attention from himself?

Elena sat back in the driver's seat and looked at the orchestrated mayhem between the two buildings.

"What the hell was he targeting? Didn't he realize that one of his men could be killed?"

She became so agitated that she could not wait for Cam's arrival. She picked up her cell phone and dialed her boss's number.

"Cam here."

"Cam, it is Elena. I think Jascinski just murdered Theodore Ball."

"My God."

"I've been told that he is at his father's funeral in Maryland. We need to confirm that."

"You think that someone could have acted for him?" inquired Cameron.

"Yes. We do think there is an organization here. I also think this one was command detonated."

"Why?"

"Ashland said that Ball never began his procedure; it detonated just as he arrived."

"Could be a clock that just ticked down as he came on it."

"Statistically, what do you suppose the chances are that a device detonates just as the EOD Tech stands next to it?"

"Hmmm."

Elena looked again at the scene before her. The forensics guys would be wrapped up soon.

"We do have some good news."

"What?"

"The device did not work exactly right. We have components and explosives."

"Tell the lab guys overtime is authorized."

"I will."

"Elena, I will be there in thirty minutes. Hold all the EOD guys there for me, will you?"

"Yes, sir, I will hold them. At the rate we are going, my scene may be cold by then."

"I understand. I am coming more for the governor than for myself, Elena," Cam paused for a moment. "Elena, hang tough kid, you are doing a good job."

"Thanks, Cam."

FORTY-ONE

KNIVES

Jazz walked around in a haze, first from his father's death, and now T-Ball's. Denke was waiting for him in the driveway when they returned from Annapolis. He told his lieutenant the news after Melanie and the kids were inside. As he did, Mel emerged from the house with tears streaming down her face.

"Jazz."

"I know, hon, Senior just told me. How did you know?"

"We got a phone message."

In the days following Theodore Ball's funeral, Melanie could not stop crying. Jazz's natural reaction each time was to put his arms around her and hold her. He found her sobbing in the kitchen over a pot of spaghetti. As he raised his arms she blocked him and moved away.

"No, Jazz, stop."

"Hon, I want to help."

"I don't want your help?"

"What?"

"You're the problem."

"Mel, that is not fair. Look we have had a tough year okay? We've both been under a lot of stress. We had school, then the baby, then the deployment."

"You don't get it do you!" Melanie yelled. "You think this is going to get better? Wake up, James! Everyone around you is dying! Those Army Techs are dead! De Luca is dead! Koss is dead! And now Ted! You yourself have come near to death at least twice that I know about and probably more times that you haven't told me of! On top of all this, something is going on that you are not telling me about. Those Army Techs did not die in an accident did they, Jazz? Did they?"

Jazz looked at her, unable to answer.

"Someone is coming after you guys," Melanie continued. "T-Ball was murdered wasn't he? Well, I've had it, Jazz. I've had it with this life, I've had it with the danger, and I'm not going to live with it anymore. I'm afraid, Jazz. I'm afraid for you, for the safety of our children."

She went into a full sob. Jazz stood quietly and watched his wife hold her breath to try to gain control of her emotions. Melanie turned on her heel and began stirring the spaghetti. He looked at Mel's back, not knowing what to say.

Keeping her back to him, Melanie said, "I'm leaving, Jazz. I'm going to take the kids and go with Jeannie to New Jersey."

Jazz paused considering his wife's statement.

"What for?"

"She needs my help. Jeannie's brother is going to come down and help her move. I'm going to put all the kids in the van and drive them up there. I'll even visit your Mom on the way. I'll stay with Jeannie and watch the kids during the day and help her get settled each night."

"Well, I'll take leave and come with you."

"No, Jazz. She does not want another daddy around right now. And besides . . . we need time apart. In fact, I may not be coming back."

Jazz stared at his wife. He heard a ringing sound in his ears. He did not expect this response from her.

"You're leaving me?"

"I don't know. I don't know what is going to happen. I just know we need some space for awhile. I do know this, I'm not living this life anymore."

For the men of Det Four, the funeral was not enough. For three days after the service, the men of Detachment Four rarely spoke. Jazz wondered how long it would be before they got out of their funk.

He emerged from the locker room after shifting into civilian clothes. Denke and Ashland were in the hallway already.

"Hey, LT. What are you doing tonight?" asked Denke.

"Nothing. I was just going home."

"Your wife is gone, right? With Jeannie?"

"Yes."

"Do you mind if we come over for a few beers?"

"Sure. You guys are welcome anytime."

"I mean all of us, sir. I think the guys need to, ah . . . tie one on."

"Uh, yeah, come over."

Jazz did not feel like drinking. When Keating arrived Jazz's first beer was only half empty and warm. Keating was followed by Quinn, Sinclair, and Delgado. Then Ashland came bearing a large jug of clear liquid and several mason jars.

"What's that, Ash?" asked Quinn.

"Porch wine, my brother."

"Ah you mean like, 'Made under the porch, drank upon it.'"

"You got it," said Ash.

He handed a jar to Jazz. "Drink up, LT."

"Damn this is harsh shit, Ash," said Delgado.

Ashland was aggressive filling and re-filling their jars. Jazz nursed his. After almost an hour of watching his det work themselves into becoming furniture he noticed that Denke was not there yet.

"Hey, where is Senior Chief?"

"I dunno," slurred Delgado, "but I saw him on the way over and he said that he'd be late."

They were all in the backyard smoking cigars and drinking Ash's porch wine when Denke finally arrived. He peeked his head through the sliding glass door.

"Hey fellas, come in here a second."

As they all filed into the Jascinski living room they looked at two green kit bags in the middle of the floor. Immediately they knew what was in the bags.

"That's T-Ball's gear, ain't it?" said Quinn.

"Yeah, it is," said Denke. "Jeannie didn't want it. I gave the wetsuit and other dive stuff to the Texas State Aquarium. This is all of his field gear. I didn't want to throw it out."

"Well, I don't want any of it," said Keating.

"I do," responded Jazz.

He reached into the bag and pulled out a K-bar knife that Ball wore in the field and on the demo range. It had a leather pouch with his crimpers attached.

"I'll keep this to remember him by."

Jazz walked into his room and tossed the knife into his kit bag in the bottom of his closet. By the time he returned to the living room, the rest of T-Ball's kit was divvied up and the drinking resumed. Jazz continued to play host. He kept himself busy lighting cigars, throwing away empties, and microwaving appetizers.

Ash kept forcing the white lightning on Jazz. Finally when Ash tried to pour another Jazz said, "I'm fine, Johnny. I've gotta beer."

Ash grinned at him in an odd way.

"You hammered yet, LT?"

"Yeah, Ash, I'm toast," he lied.

As his teammates slipped further and further into a stupor, the evening became surreal for Jazz. He noted that unlike him, the alcohol seemed to wash away the pain of losing a teammate for the other men of Det Four. Watching them become a little free of T-Ball made Jazz realize even more that he needed to remove the heavy weight created by Martin and West, De Luca and Koss, and now T-Ball. To make matters worse, Melanie was certainly going to leave him if he did not get out of the Navy.

Jazz was not sure what the cure was. He wished that he could talk to the Admiral one more time and get a last morsel of advice. If only he had a knife like his father, an albatross that he could bring back to life so that it could fly away bearing his shame and failure.

After seeing the last of his teammates to the door Jazz found himself sitting on his bed, holding his father's knife . . . or was it his knife? It sang as he drew it from its sheath.

*   *   *

Elena and her roommate had a delightful dinner. Frances took her to a fantastic French restaurant to help her forget about work. Elena could not remember the last time she felt so relaxed. She sipped the last of the second bottle of wine they consumed. Since ordering dessert, they said nothing, just enjoyed the evening. She smiled to herself thinking of the chocolate mousse about to emerge from the kitchen.

I've almost forgotten about Jazz.

Then Elena heard a "beep" coming from her bag. Frances immediately recognized the look on her face.

"Oh babe, no, don't. Don't answer it."

"Relax. It's probably the guys at the Jascinski place checking in."

She pulled the phone from her purse.

"Cruz, here."

"Elena, it's Cam."

"Good evening, Cameron. How are you?"

"Elena, listen to me. We just got the labs back on the Ingleside case."

"Yes, and . . ."

"The explosives came from a naval magazine at Norfolk."

"Cam, we always knew they were military."

"Norfolk, Elena, Norfolk!"

*   *   *

In the Portland hotel, only Special Agent Kilkenney was awake. He sat at the window, peering at the Jascinski dwelling. Through the earphones on his head he could hear Jascinski snoring. He flipped a switch to the monitor in the kitchen.

From his peripheral vision he caught some movement. He looked at his watch; a midnight walker?

There was something about the man that he recognized. He flipped through the binder on the table next to him. That was it; it looked like one of the det members.

One of the boys coming back for another drink?

*   *   *

Elena hung up on Cam. She stood and pulled her wallet from her pocketbook.
"Elena, for God's sakes sit down! What's wrong?" Frances said.

She ignored her roommate's lamentations and spilled the contents of her wallet onto the table. Money, receipts, scraps of paper, and business cards mixed like straw before her. Violently, she shuffled through them.

"Come on, come on. Where is it!"

In tune with Elena's panic, Frances was visibly embarrassed. Elena ignored the stares that she did not see, but felt from the other patrons as she looked for Jascinski's business card.

"Elena, I don't understand. Let me help you."

Though she found it in thirty seconds, it felt too late. She dialed the number on her cell phone.

*   *   *

Something interrupted Jazz's sleep. He did not truly wake up, but he became conscious and opened his eyes. There was a ringing in his ears. Was it from the everclear? No . . . he did not have that much to drink.

He struggled to return to full consciousness. When he did he realized the phone was ringing. The hands on his watch told him that it was either Mel or a wrong number. It was better to have her talk to the answering machine right now.

Jazz sat up to get some water. His father's knife was in his hand. He stared at it in the dark. He vaguely remembered holding it as he went to sleep, hoping it could give him some solace of the past year.

When the phone stopped, he heard a sound in the living room. Someone was there. He slipped into the closet behind the door. Just as he did, the door opened.

A large dark figure stepped into the bedroom.

Jazz lunged, turning sideways and jamming his hip into the intruder's, knocking him slightly off balance. His left hand went around his head and pulled it back while his right hand plunged the knife into the neck on the left side. He pulled and tried to slide it to the right.

The knife did not want to move. He could feel blood spurting onto his hands and forearms. A gurgling scream came from his victim. Jazz pulled him backwards now toward the floor. He tried to move the knife in a sawing motion. There was some movement but not enough.

Now he dropped his opponent on the floor, let go of the knife and sprang for the bed. He reached underneath and pulled out a baseball bat. Clutching it with both hands, he prepared to crack the skull next.

The man lay still, arms at his side. There was little air moving through him.

"Uk, uk, uk," were the last sounds that emanated from the body.

Jazz turned on the bedside light. He first looked to his hand, which was sticky with blood. He then looked at the man on the floor of his bedroom.

It was Johnny Ashland. Johnny Ashland lay on his bedroom floor, blood draining slower now since his heart stopped pumping, a gun on the floor beside him.

Jazz stared at him for a long time. His teammate did not look real with a Mark III mission knife sticking out of his neck and a pool of blood on the floor.

Then, in true form, Jazz ran to the bathroom and threw up.

When he looked in the mirror, James J. Jascinski gained clarity of thought that he would never again have in his life. In an instant he realized that Ashland was one of the SANPAT terrorists and was involved in killing Martin, West, and T-Ball. He surmised that Ash was connected to the De Luca murder and the detonation of the magazine in Tirane.

Before the moment of clarity washed through him, Jazz took one more action with Ashland's carcass. He returned to the body and placed his knee on Ash's chest. With both hands he pulled and removed the knife. The blood did not come off easily under hot water, so he wrapped it in a towel.

Jazz went to the closet and found his kit bag with extra gear stored in the floor of his closet. He put the Mark III knife there and extracted T-Ball's K-bar.

It was a struggle to get the knife back into Ashland's neck, but it worked. There was no way he would allow his father's knife to end up in an evidence cage. Perhaps there was justice that T-Ball's knife would be recorded as the blade that killed Johnny Ashland.

He picked up the portable phone and dialed 9-1-1. Just as the operator answered there was a knock at the door.

"Portland Emergency Services. Can I help you?"

"Uh, yeah one moment."

He went to the door. Three men in suits were outside.

"Who's there?"

"FBI, Mr. Jascinski. We know what happened. Please open up."

FORTY-TWO

ASHLAND

The conference room and the coffee gave Jazz a sense of déjà vu. He sipped the bitter liquid from a mug emblazoned with the EOD Mobile Unit Six logo, waiting for Elena Cruz to return and finish their debrief. He recalled his telling conversation with Ash on the flightline in Albania.

"I am sick of this shit. Fucking Haiti, sir. Fucking Somalia. Fucking Bosnia, Kosovo, and Albania. The mother-fucking Balkans! What the fuck are we doing here?"

Jazz understood Ash's frustration; he shared some of his notions. Plus, the det endured a firefight and a narrow escape only hours before. They were all still decompressing.

Jazz would never forget Ash saying, *"The purpose of the military in my view is to drain the lifeblood of our nation's enemies until they either submit or succumb to our will. Anything that detracts from that is pure unmitigated bullshit."*

But it was the tone in his voice that even then set an alarm off in Jazz's mind.

"Damn shipmate, you sound very angry," Jazz had said.

"You don't know the half of it, LT."

So Jazz's theory was wrong and Elena's was right on. Ash was not a Kaczynski, he was a McVeigh.

Elena walked back into the conference room. She set her notebook and a stack of files on the table and sat down. Jazz waited for her to speak.

A moment passed. Finally Elena spoke.

"Well, Jazz, we seem to have it all laid out now."

"Did you receive confirmation about the explosives from Norfolk?"

"Yes. I was just told over the phone that Ash was Det Norfolk's Ammunition and Explosive Manager. In that position he was able to draw explosives from the magazine and report them as expended. In reality he was saving them for his organization."

"Well how are we able to prove that now if not before?"

"We contacted Norfolk and had them compare logs at the demolition range against the det's internal monthly operation reports, and the monthly inventory sent to the

Navy's explosive managers in Crane, Indiana. Apparently an inspection was scheduled right before Ash transferred here from Norfolk, but the det was away responding to an incident at sea."

"The helo crash, the one with the test missile. I remember hearing about it and Ash telling us about it later."

"Yes, well as a result the explosive safety inspection was cut short. They merely checked what was in the magazine versus what Crane said that they should have."

"And they matched?"

"Yes. We are going to have to look into Ashland's history, but he may have obtained hundreds of pounds of explosives for his organization."

"Fuck, well who are they?"

"We don't know yet. But undoubtedly they are connected by this fundamentalist terrorist cell that we know about in Albania and in Italy. Pucharelli and I are hoping that the cell in Albania is the head."

"So, Ash was a member of an anti-government organization?"

"Yes, or a white supremacist group. We suspect that up until recently Ashland was not an active agent, but a merely a supplier of explosives. Who knows, maybe he was not even a full-fledged member, maybe he was only sympathetic to their ideals, or he supplied them only for personal gain."

"But he obviously joined them recently, otherwise why did he kill T-Ball, why did he try to kill me?"

"That answer brings us back to San Patricio."

"How?"

Elena pulled out a file and slid it over to Jazz. He opened it. On the top of the file was a mug shot of a man.

"The name there says Marcus Levitt. It is a false identity. First he tried to pass as a Navy lieutenant named James Smith. The Levitt identity passed scrutiny. His real name is Gabriel Miller. Sound familiar?"

"Yeah," said Jazz flipping through the file.

"He was the owner of the house in San Patricio where the explosives were discovered."

"Is he in custody?"

"No. Notice that the mug shot says DPS on the ID plate. That stands for Defensive Protective Service. He was caught in the Pentagon parking lot with a trunk full of explosives. Guess where they are from?"

"Norfolk."

". . . also just recently confirmed. Gabriel Miller was released by DPS shortly after taking that photo. Eventually we would have connected him to San Patricio. So it seems that we were closing in on them, albeit from their own clumsiness and our good fortune. First we lucked upon Miller's factory, then the incident in Italy, followed by the factory in Albania. Add to it that Miller was detained . . . they figured it was only a matter of time that we put all the pieces together. So in order to cover their trail as best as possible . . ."

"They decided to take out T-Ball and me," Jazz paused. "Well, then Ash had to be an active member."

"How's that?"

"How else would the group have known that T-Ball and I were helping the investigation?"

"Mmmm. I had not considered that."

Jazz and Elena exchanged pleasantries before she left. She tried to hold onto his hand a little longer than normal.

He has no idea, she thought.

Jazz tried to burn her image in his mind as she walked out the door to Det Ingleside.

Elena held her breath until she drove out the gate of the naval station. Then she wept.

*   *   *

Guido's photos of Detachment Four and Benny Ironhorse curled, melting in the fire warming Nasih's feet. It was the last of the physical evidence connecting him to his pupils in Texas. He knew that their fear of him far outweighed any threats or promises the FBI could inflict upon them. Nasih felt fortunate. Once again, Allah demonstrated that there was still work for him to do.

Soon enough the United States would be looking for him in Albania. But it was no matter; he would be back in Afghanistan.

FORTY-THREE

EGLIN

He almost took it to the hill in Annapolis where the Admiral was buried. The ground above his father was still fresh. It would have been easy to perform a small midnight excavation and return the knife to its original owner.

After considering it for a long time he realized his instincts in the funeral parlor were correct, that such an action would have violated his father's intentions. The man was finally free of the damn thing; he needed to let the Admiral rest in peace.

But now Jazz also needed to be free of it. He wasn't going to pass it to his sons.

The consolidation of the whole of NAVSCOLEOD at Eglin Air Force Base made sense to Jazz. The facility at Indian Head simply could not be modernized any more. It was time to rebuild.

Hundreds of NAVSCOLEOD graduates recently received a letter from Horace Pickney that included an artist's conception of the new memorial. The pillars from Indian Head, Maryland were moved to Eglin Air Force Base in Florida. A walkway and pavilion of red brick would be added. Charitable donations would be recognized by adding an engraved brick into the walkway.

The memorial was now in place. They were almost finished with the landscaping and the brick walkway. Jazz wondered if the workers understood what they were erecting.

Fortunately he was not too late. Several of the bricks in front of the memorial were not in place yet and the crew was not working on a Sunday.

Many of those already laid had names etched in them.

In Memory of
Pvt 1/C Charles McCann, USMC
By his family

BM2 Thomas Sharpe, USN
Jun 1945-Apr 1970

Capt. Aidan Case, USA
From his loving wife, Maria

Jazz looked at the four obelisks, though not closely. He did not want to see the names on them. Not now.

He drew out the Mark-III dive knife one last time. With it he quickly scraped a shallow grave for it, just deep enough to not be noticed. He cleaned the blade and placed it in the sheath. He laid it to rest and covered it back up with his hands and then stamped on it with his feet.

He stood a moment in silence and thought of T-Ball.

Then he said out loud, "In memory of Boatswain's Mate Second Class Theodore Ball, United States Navy. From his friend and shipmate, Lieutenant James J. Jascinski, United States Navy."

Jazz turned as hc heard someone approaching from behind him. A kid of about eighteen walked toward him and the memorial.

"I'm sorry, sir, do you need a moment?"

"Zero eight five eight."

"Uh, excuse me, sir?"

"Zero eight five eight."

"Are you alright, sir?"

"Zero eight five eight. You are a student right?"

"Yes, sir. I'm Private Schaffer. I'm going to graduate soon. You're a grad I take it."

"Yes. Ten Bravo Ninety Eight."

"A Navy guy."

"Zero eight five eight, Private. Write it down. It is the number in the Combined Federal Campaign for the EOD Memorial Scholarship fund."

Jazz stared at the kid hard while he stood there a little confused.

"You need a pen?"

"Uh, no, sir."

"Get out a pen and write it down."

The private fumbled in his shirt pocket and extracted a pen. He pulled out his wallet and took out a receipt.

"Sorry, sir. Say it one more time."

"Zero eight five eight."

". . . five eight. Got it, sir."

"Give what you can. The families of our brothers on that wall need our help."

"Do you know any of these men, sir?"

"Well Private, I've only met two of them, but I know all of them."

Jazz got in the car with a singular purpose; to find Melanie and his family. As he left the memorial and the schoolhouse behind Jazz realized he had changed. With each mile, the car seemed faster and Jazz felt lighter. His guilt for the deaths of Martin, West, and T-Ball left him. The weight of the Admiral and his expectations was gone. Jazz had buried it all.

ACRONYMS AND ABBREVIATIONS

1140—("eleven-forty") Special Operations Officer

AFFF—Aqueous Film Forming Foam

AGE—Arterial Gas Embolism

ATF—Bureau of Alcohol, Tobacco, and Firearms

CDO—Command Duty Officer

CDR—Commander

CIC—Combat Information Center

CMC—Closed Metal Container

CNO—Chief of Naval Operations

CO—Commanding Officer

CP—Command Post

CQB—Close Quarters Combat

CSO—Chief Staff Officer

DCA—Damage Control Assistant

DESRON—Destroyer Squadron

DPS—Defensive Protective Service

EMR—Electromagnetic Radiation

EOD—Explosive Ordnance Disposal

EODMU—Explosive Ordnance Disposal Mobile Unit

EODTECHDIV—EOD Technical Division

FADL—Fly Away Dive Locker

FARC—Fly Away Recompression Chamber

FBI—Federal Bureau of Investigation

GOMEX—Gulf of Mexico Exercise

GPS—Global Positioning System

GW—*George Washington,* as in USS *George Washington*

HDR—Humanitarian Daily Ration

HRST—Helo Rope Suspension Team

IED—Improvised Explosive Device

INCTASKGRU—*Inchon* Task Group

LCDR—Lieutenant Commander

LCPO—Leading Chief Petty Officer

LPO—Leading Petty Officer

LT—Lieutenant

LZ—Landing Zone

MCM—Mine Countermeasures, also used to denote Mine Countermeasure ship

MCMRON—MCM Squadron

MCS—Mine Warfare Command Ship

MER—Missile Ejection Rack

MHC—Mine Hunter, Coastal

MNV—Mine Neutralization Vehicle

MRE—Meal Ready to Eat

MU—Mobile Unit

NAS—Naval Air Station

NAVSCOLEOD—Naval School Explosive Ordnance Disposal

NCIS—Naval Criminal Investigative Service

NGO—Non-Governmental Organization

OOD—Officer of the Deck

OIC—Officer in Charge

OPCON—Operational Control

P1—The primary Tech working on a problem

P2—The secondary Tech working on a problem, assists the P1

PD—Police Department

PERSTEMPO—Personnel operational Tempo

POTUS—President of the Unite States

PQS—Personal Qualification Standards

PT—Physical Training

READIMPT—Readiness Improvement Training

RHIB—Rigid Hull Inflatable Boat

RONEX—Squadron Exercise

ROV—Remote Operated Vehicle

RSP—Render Safe Procedure

SEAL—Sea, Air, Land commandos of Naval Special Warfare

SCI—Secret Compartmentalized Information

SMUT—Small Unit Tactics

SOP—Standard Operating Procedures

SWO—Surface Warfare Officer

SWOS—Surface Warfare Officer School

TACON—Tactical Control

TECHDIV—Technical Division

TEU TWO—Training and Evaluation Unit TWO

TSD—Technical Support Division

UCMJ—Uniform Code of Military Justice

UDT—Underwater Demolition Team

U/I—Under Instruction

USA—United States Army

USMC—United States Marine Corps

USNS—United States Naval Ship

USS—United States Ship

USSS—United States Secret Service

VLS—Vertical Launch System

XO—Executive Officer, the second in command

ABOUT THE AUTHOR

Stephen Phillips served in the United States Navy as a Special Operations Officer and Explosive Ordnance Disposal Technician at EOD Mobile Units Six, Ten, and Eight. During his naval career he deployed to Haiti, Somalia, the Arabian Gulf, the Balkans, and the Global War on Terrorism. He currently lives in the Washington DC metro area with his wife and two sons.

Made in the USA
San Bernardino, CA
25 February 2014